Family Ties

Family Ties

WENDY ROBERTSON

headline

The June Tabor poem referred to on page 121 from her album
Against the Stream is a version of 'Beauty and the Beast: An Anniversary'
from *The Faery Flag. Stories and Poems of Fantasy and the Supernatural*
by Jane Yolen. Quoted with the permission of Curtis Brown, inc

First published in 2006
by HEADLINE PUBLISHING GROUP

1

Cataloguing in Publication Data is available from the British Library

0 7553 0946 4 (ISBN-10)
978 07553 30946 7 (ISBN-13)

Typeset in Bembo by Avon DataSet Ltd, Bidford on Avon, Warwickshire

Printed and bound in Great Britain by
Mackays of Chatham plc, Chatham, Kent

Headline's policy is to use papers that are natural, renewable and
recyclable products and made from wood grown in sustainable forests.
The logging and manufacturing processes are expected to conform
to the environmental regulations of the country of origin.

HEADLINE PUBLISHING GROUP
A division of Hodder Headline
338 Euston Road
London NW1 3BH

www.headline.co.uk
www.hodderheadline.com

For
Barbara, Billy, Tom and Angus –
an inspiration before and after

With their secret skills
in their secret places
women spin the binding ties
and weave the tangled web
of family life

Acknowledgements

Although it is not autobiographical, my main source of enquiry for this novel has been my memory of the twentieth century, homing in on my own experience of family life and its compelling ties. In that sense, for the way they resonate in my memory, I have to thank Susan Bloomfield, Ian Wetherill, Bryan Robertson, Debora Robertson, Sean Donnellan, and Grahame, Theresa and Angus Robertson, for being the (albeit unwitting) mainspring inspirations for this story.

I would also thank Dr Judith Gates for drawing my attention to the poem about parting (on p 41), which she always thought was written by her mother but was, as it turns out, a much loved Edwardian parlour song. Thank you as always to Gillian Wales for her strong creative support. Thank you to my editor Harriet Evans for encouraging me to write the story I really wanted to write, and Yvonne Holland for endorsing my judgement that the words here are the best words in the best order. And thank you to my agent, my good friend Juliet Burton. Yet again you kept me from panicking.

My heartfelt thanks to the distinguished American writer Jane Yolen for permission to quote from her wonderful poem 'Beauty and the Beast': An Anniversary.

Wendy Robertson
Bishop Auckland, April 2006

Part One

Borderland

Bronwen Carmichael's Durham Day

January 1991

This half-lit river path is very quiet. I change my heavy book-bag to my right shoulder and begin to kick at the drying leaves as I walk. The only sound I can hear is behind me: the splash-swish of oars, as a small rowing boat makes its way through water still black with night. The rower is cutting neatly along, leaving a turbulent trail behind him. I put down my bag and lean against a tree. The crusty bark nudges me through my cape and I feel the damp.

This is such a Durham day. The dense morning light throws out sparks of gunmetal as the cool sun eases through the grey cloud into the dark of the morning. The shadowy bulk of the cathedral and castle looms above me in the loop of the river, presiding over the tangle of steep streets no longer littered with the workshops of medieval silversmiths and saddlers.

Those shops are gone now, but the elegant eighteenth-century houses of lawyers, academics and bustling clergy have survived. Sadly these days they have to endure the indignity of sitting alongside the hippy dress shops (never out of fashion in this university town), the public houses, the cafés and bookshops that seem to have such quaint appeal for twentieth-century travellers.

The rower still cuts his way through the water. It's quite common for someone to be on the river at this peaceful early hour, before the city becomes its bustling student- and tourist-ridden self. For me, with my obsession for the old city, this modern Durham can be jarring, like hot pants on an otherwise graceful old woman.

Long ago I used to walk these streets hand in hand with my mother, Rosa. I grew up with that soft murmuring voice in my ear. *Just look at the size of those stones, Bron. Those workmen who built the cathedral didn't have lorries and steel scaffolding, you know! They had donkey carts, wooden scaffolding, and straw baskets. And just look at the carving! Think how many years it took those masons to get that right. And just imagine the monks in their hoods walking round and round here in the chilly cloister. And just think of this great nave without the rows of seats but with dozens of mean campfires keeping those poor Scottish prisoners warm. Just think, Bron!*

Always the teacher, my mother.

When I was much older, one afternoon during the Winter of Discontent, I was alone in the cathedral at four o'clock one afternoon when the electricity went off. The nave was plunged into a chill, medieval darkness that made me see the monks standing in the shadows, masked by their hoods, their arms clasped in their sleeves to ward off the cold. I stood there in the dark silence, grateful to all those strikers and short-time workers for delivering me that eerie vision.

The rowing boat is drawing level. Now a stray glint of light catches the rower's thick fair hair, caught back in a red bandanna; his brown, wiry arms pull at the oars with the regularity of a pendulum. His head dips on to his chest in concentration, his eyes shaded by his broad brow. My senses prickle to life and I can smell the bitter mallow and the rotting vegetation on the riverbank; in my ears the morning song of each individual bird is clear as a crystal bell.

Now, in the dark, decorated quiet of the morning, the rower feels my concentrated attention, lets his oars trail and sits back. For a single, stretched second he glances across at me, his eyes sweeping me from head to toe. And for a millionth of that second his gaze meets mine. How is it possible that such a brief glance can express such amusement, such contained irony?

Of course, now I am blushing to the roots of my hair, cursing my wired-in sense that one should not look directly at strangers, even at eight o'clock in the morning. I lean down to pick up my book-bag and when I stand up the boat and its rower have vanished.

As I walk on again, I begin to smile at my own fancy. The bright sharpness of the rower's glance was a mere trick of the horizontal morning light. Filled with energy, I stride on, kicking the leaves so high that they come falling down again like rustling brown rain. Above me the trees, some still clinging stubbornly to old leaves as the new buds swell, scrape and scratch at the dove-grey morning sky.

I live five miles from here but I've always known and loved this city. Even so, it's only recently that I discovered that parking close to the university is just a wild dream. Just last September I was humiliatingly late for my very first lecture because I couldn't find a parking spot for my battered Riley. So the next day I came in early and found a regular place on South Street, a smart row of old houses on the high ridge across the river from the mass of cathedral and castle. (I once saw a house on South Street advertised for sale as set in 'possibly the best location in Europe . . .')

Anyway, nowadays my mornings begin with the walk down from South Street through the trees, to the river crossing at Prebends Bridge. After that there are two choices: another steep climb upwards to the cathedral, or the shallower path that follows the curling meander of the river and means a climb up stone steps on to Elvet Bridge in the centre of the town. On wet days I usually tackle the steep climb and take shelter in the quiet of the cathedral until it's time to go to lectures. On finer mornings I like to stroll round the peninsula, climb Elvet steps and take my early morning tea in the Royal County Hotel among the tourists 'doing' the medieval city of Durham on their way up to Edinburgh or down to York.

The Royal County Hotel is an old haunt of my mother, Rosa's. *Just see, Bron! It might be slick and modern now but in the old times it was a coaching inn. An English king stayed here, d'you know? Feel it, Bron! And even in these modern times it's more than an hotel. Do you remember the Miners' Big Meeting? All those prime ministers, union people – usually men, I fear – standing on the balcony here, watching the marching bands and the banners of the miners.*

This morning the waitress, a small, neat girl with the face of an eager squirrel and bitten-down fingernails, remembers me from last term and doesn't bother to ask me if I'm resident at the hotel. She merely gives me a confiding wink and delivers the usual large silver pot of tea and plate of toast, with the bill on a small metal dish. The Buttery is full of visitors having their breakfasts. At one table a family – father, mother, son and daughter – sit reading books in silence, eating their food automatically, without relish. The woman is reading a battered, paperback edition of *The Magus* by John Fowles, a favourite of mine.

I dip into my bag for my own book, my small notebook and my fountain pen: it's old, this pen, quite a collector's item. It was my mother's but when I graduated the first time, she gave it to me. The nib is soft and forgiving. It writes like a dream. I lay these things on the table, making sure the tea and toast are within reach, and begin to read and make notes.

A phrase catches my eye: 'To survive borderlands you must live on the frontier.' I copy this phrase into my notebook, hoarding the words like gold. Then I write my own thoughts: 'Even this city is a borderland, between the past and the present, between town and gown, between the miners who dig the ground and the priests who save the souls. I am a borderland between my past and my present, between my mother and my daughter . . .'

I've eaten a slice of toast and completed one page of notes when suddenly I feel someone staring at me. The desire to look up is almost irresistible but I resist it through one more page of notes and one more slice of toast. Then I do look up and meet the gaze of a man two tables away. He's perhaps in his early forties, wearing a casual leather jacket formalised by a pale green shirt and toning tie. No bandanna. His curly gold hair stands out like a narrow halo. In front of him sits a Full English Breakfast with all the trimmings. (My friend Cali, who, before she ran away from school, did a course in Nutrition, calls this Heart-Attack-on-a-Plate.)

The man has fine, long-fingered hands. The formality of his shirt and tie is contradicted by the anarchy of the wild golden hair. A red handkerchief drips carelessly from his top pocket. The long, deep-set eyes now looking straight into mine are a bright sea grey.

A shiver ripples through me. Of course, it's the man from the river. The rower. He lifts his fork towards me as if he's proposing a toast. His fair brows are raised, inviting me to respond, to smile, to say something. Anything. But I drop my gaze and begin to read with great concentration. When I look up again, the rower has gone.

So now I feel guilty, about being rude, stand-offish. People often think this of me. My unwillingness to engage with people bites deep but sometimes it's the only way I can cope. People who don't know me think this shyness is a pose. They say how can I be shy if I can teach a class of thirty leather-clad monsters who have more than a passing acquaintance with drugs and air rifles? How could I even be known to be good at it? So good that I get a paid sabbatical to do this course?

I sometimes wonder this myself.

I'm dragged away from my thoughts by a body crashing through the double doors, all bags and capes, scarves and books, bringing with it a gust of chill morning air and the faint scent of patchouli. The murmuring hotel guests look up from their croissants, then down again.

'Early bird, Bron!' My friend Cali's voice is loud but always tuneful. It never hurts your ears. 'Thought I'd cop you here, hon. Always the early bird.' She collapses on to the banquette and peers at my book. 'You read the queerest books, hon.' With her dyed black, scraped-back hair and her distinctive eyes, Cali looks a decade less than her thirty-two years. She hates being called a mature student. 'Mature? Me? That'll be the day.' She peers across at my notes. 'You sweet old swot! First day of term and here you are, down to it. You want to get a life, my darling.'

She makes me laugh, this woman. I'm always invigorated by the sheer life that fizzes and bubbles right through her and spills over on to me.

'I have a life, Cali. Anyone who has a seventeen-year-old daughter is forced to embrace life. Anyway, there's plenty of life for me in books. We can't all do three gigs a week and survive on three hours' sleep a night. In any case, I need to be genned up for this research. We've got this supervision seminar today, remember?'

Cali is giving me that quizzical look I first met when, early in our acquaintance, I tried to explain my own set-up at home: that my daughter and I have always lived with my mother although I'm not tied to my mother's apron strings (not that she ever wore an apron); that even though both my mother and I have been married, we are all still called Carmichael (something to do with sixties idealism); that no one but me – not even my laid-back mother, Rosa – knows who is my daughter's father.

Now Cali chortles. '*Genned* up? You sweet old-fashioned thing.' She leans over and scavenges the last bit of toast. 'Whenever will you learn to busk it?'

California Vax – born Marjorie Rawlinson but reinvented and renamed by herself – is a world expert at busking. In the seventies she ran away from a frozen home and literally busked for a year in London, playing the penny whistle on the underground to support herself and her boyfriend in their squat in Camden Town. She survived the pressure to do drugs by busking *the effect* of being stoned. She was the world expert in not inhaling. By the eighties, bored with squat life and dismayed at the death of her boyfriend, then the girlfriend who succeeded him, she rechristened herself with a memorable outlandish name, bought a suit at Oxfam and metaphorically *busked* her way into a job at the fringes of the booming City, temporarily conceding that Greed Might Be Good. 'Had to start some way up the ladder, Bron; couldn't type.' Once established in her City office she *busked* her way up that ladder, where her finely honed intuition and aggressive charm secured amazing bonuses that, in turn, bought her a nice apartment and a sleek car. She tells me doing drugs was as *de rigueur* in the City as it had been at the squat, so once more she played the game of being stoned, and hung on to her wits. By the late eighties, driven to distraction by the high-flying, humdrum nature of this life, she kept boredom at bay by performing poetry-and-penny-whistle gigs in chichi bars and gaining an Open University BA on the side.

8

Cali's a life force, a modern girl. She likes her learning in bite-size chunks. Knowledge Lite. Her boast to me when we met in the first week of our MA course was that she'd never read a whole book. I did pay her the compliment of saying you'd never have known that. The art of *busking* has got Cali Vax a long way in life. I envy her that skill.

Rosa Carmichael's 1954 Ledger

Rosa Carmichael
11 Butler Street
Spennymoor
County Durham
Great Britain
The World
The Universe

1 June 1954

My name is Rosa Carmichael. I'm five foot one inch tall and what my mam calls gangly. I'm fourteen years old but am flat as a board and still waiting to start my periods. I do know all about periods, though, from Moira Cash at school, who not only has her periods but also Has Been With Boys. I've just been given this ledger by Mrs McAllan who has the corner shop. She's always used ledgers like these for food and things people get on tick (they call them tick books), but now Mrs Mc says she's been Let Down so often that she won't give tick any more. She says, 'But I've got this spare tick book, never used. I thought mebbe you'd like it. Go to the grammar school, don't you? You must be a good scholar.' She's small, with black permed hair and a wide smile that's the same for everybody, so it doesn't mean much. But her giving me this tick book's just great, seeing as my own mother is one of those who have Let Her Down. I've seen our page – 'Mrs Kate Carmichael' at the top and between the red lines '12 pounds, 3 shillings and 9 pence *owing*'. The 'owing' is in red too.

The book's tall and narrow but nice and thick. And the red lines down the page don't matter. I am writing straight through them.

I've got time to write because this term I've been bunking off school quite a bit, as I can't stand the racket and the way the teachers nip your ears and bawl at you, and the other kids laugh and sneer at the state of your uniform and your grey-white socks, and call you Medusa because your hair is rough and wild. And anyway, you are so tired when you get in from school that you can't manage to get down to the homework. This makes you stay off school in craven fear of those nipping, shouting teachers and jeering lads. You have to tell lies to your mother about the marks you get. Your brother Charlie comes in at quarter-past four, throws down his cap and says, 'Have you nicked off again, lass?' But Charlie still keeps your secret. He's all right, is Charlie. And your little brother, Brock, comes in later, buzzing from his long walk from his junior school. All he wants to do is to get back out into the street to play kick-the-can. He has no idea that when he left for school this morning you just took off your blazer, turned up the gas fire, lay on the couch and read your pirate's hoard of library books, sleeping now and then when your eyes were tired.

I do go to school on some days, to keep teachers off the scent, clutching a note about my recurrent illness. 'Recurring debility.' I looked that up. I need an illness that can come and go.

I can read four or five books on the couch. Last week I read *Anna Karenina, Tarzan of the Apes, The Way of an Eagle, The Thirty-Nine Steps*, and *The Chalet School*. But it took me nearly the whole of another week to read *War and Peace*. I read, read all the time. My brother Charlie says I talk like a book.

When it gets to a quarter to five I lay the table for tea, so it's ready when Mam comes in looking white, tired. She has walked from the factory where she makes circuit breakers for cookers. There are small sharp bits of metal and sometimes her fingers bleed. She gives me money to buy fish and chips and I pull my blazer over my gymslip and go to the fish shop. She never suspects. She's always very tired. She'd really be a hospital nurse but she works at the factory because she can't manage the hospital shifts, having us to care for. She makes so many sacrifices for us. She tells us this quite often.

When I get back with my paper parcel – fish for her, chips for us – she lays it carefully out on four plates. She always gives Brock, my younger brother, a bit of her fish. Once, Charlie risked a black look to ask her why we couldn't have fish like her. Like her and Brock. She told Charlie she wasn't made of money and anyway we'd had proper dinners at school and our dinners were free. And Brock was a growing child, wasn't he? Of course I couldn't tell her that mostly I wasn't at school so had not eaten any dinner. Just toast.

My mother did get worried once about how thin I was when we were examined at school and I was sent for an X-ray. She frowned a lot that day, and I was more scared of her even than the machine. I heard her say to the nurse she was concerned about TB. Having been a nurse herself she knew about TB. But no, there was no TB. The nurse had a squeaky voice that I could hear from the corridor. 'Though I can see why you might think that, Mrs Carmichael. The lass's so skinny. Not a picking on her.'

They muttered away.

I wasn't bothered. I just thought how much nicer my mother's voice was than the nurse's. Nobody round here talks like her. She's clever. That makes up for being hungry and sometimes cold, even her bad temper. When she's in a good mood she gives us spelling tests or we do a Brains Trust. There's never any prizes. She has no money for them and anyway, she always says, 'The Honour Should Be Sufficient Reward'.

Yesterday as she put down her work-bag she just said, 'How was school?' I said, 'It was all right.' And that was that.

Anyway, now I have this ledger and will write in it and make my own book. But not like a diary. Not I-got-up-and-cleaned-my-teeth. What I want to write about are things in my life. In the past, in the present, in the future. Who knows?

I've decided to write first about our Brock, who is a proper puzzle in our family. He's only ten but is nearly as tall as me and has this soft fair hair with a quiff and eyes like shining grey water.

He is 'an enigma'. Enigma. I looked that up.

A Convenient Narrative
for Bronwen

January 1991

I settle down in my seat at the back of the empty lecture room and put my book-bag on the seat beside me to save it for Cali, who raced off at lunchtime to catch up with a man she met at registration, a bodhrán player who – she thinks – might just fit in with her small poetry-to-music crew blessed with the name Ceolas Monkey.

Just as I like to read up and prepare for lectures, I like to arrive early, first in, to settle my mind for any important lecture. Cali teases me about being a swot but that falls on deaf ears. Coming back to college after ten years has been a treat but a challenge as well – quite a challenge. Forewarned is forearmed, as my mother Rosa would say. Anyway, after ten years in schools where the kids are a masochist's delight and the teachers stressed and bitter, I've relished the sheer pleasure of sitting listening to some of the cleverest minds in the country communicate their obsession.

As Cali says, I'm a simple soul.

The room is filling up. Most of the students here are young, progressing on automatic pilot from a good first degree to this good second degree. They're demure, delightful, laconic and laid-back, the geeks and the gorgeous alike radiating the graceful low-key confidence that is the marker of privilege. One boy in this group is older, having fitted in a spell in the army – peace-keeping in Northern Ireland – between his first and second degree. He's quieter and more watchful than the others. And there is a handful of more mature students, ranging from myself and Cali in our thirties, to a retired chief inspector of police and an educational psychologist changing careers midstream.

The small groups and the intimate nature of teaching and learning here at Durham have been a revelation. My first degree was at Sunderland Polytechnic: studying there was a cheerful, brisk, efficient, densely monitored process, which involved large-scale lectures, a crowded timetable and little close contact with our tutors. The key to *my* achievements there was my ability to mine the booklists and the journals, then stockpile information and ideas in my notebooks, from which my first-class degree seemed to emerge without human intervention. This independent, isolated approach suited me very well then. As a nineteen-year-old with a three-year-old daughter to rush home to, I couldn't join in with the drinking at the Union or the trips away to rockfests. I barely had time to regret that then, though I did later.

Now the heavy door at the front of the seminar room crashes open and in sweeps Cali. The small room is crowded now and Cali has to squeeze her way along the row to get to her seat by me, sprinkling her particular brand of fairy-dust all around, kissing and being kissed all the way along the row. She hands me her book-bag, gives me a smacking kiss and takes her seat.

The door opens again, and in glides the pristine Dr Mary Devine. Her lipstick is immaculate, her dark bob gleaming, even the stack of files she carries under her arm seems colour-co-ordinated. Everyone in the room knows that Dr Devine's sweet femininity cloaks a mind like a razor that can cut and slash at will, leaving her victim smiling at the privilege of being thus injured. But I do like her. What you see is what you get with Dr Devine. She plays no games.

Then the chatter in the room fades altogether as we move our gaze to the man who follows her in, a fair-haired man in a leather jacket. He sits down in the front row facing Dr Devine.

Dr Devine puts down the files, leans on the table and casts her eye round. The room falls into complete silence. I sometimes wonder if inducing this absolutely pure silence, engaging this concentrated attention, is the key to all teaching. Alongside this, curriculum, fancy methods, are very secondary.

She welcomes us all back for the new term and ploughs on with business. 'This year, as you are all aware, your focus will be your dissertation.' She taps the pile. 'I have your proposals here and each file carries the name of a possible supervisor. Collect these at the end of the session, sign up to see your assigned tutor this week and discuss your proposal with them. Any further problems with this, please get back to me. There is some leeway for reassignment if strong difficulties occur.'

'If you can't stand the sight of your bloke,' mutters Cali beside me.

Dr Devine shoots her a cold look. 'Was there something, Miss Vax?'

Cali grins. 'I was thinking it would be like a marriage, Dr Devine. Issues of compatibility . . .'

Some people smile at this but Dr Devine's glance remains frosty. 'Just so,' she said. 'Now!' She turns to the man sitting at the table. 'I should introduce you to Dr Richard Stephens who is here on sabbatical from Harvard and will be giving three seminars on phenomenological research methods starting today. Dr Stephens has signed up to supervise some of the more – esoteric – dissertations.' She makes it sound as though the man's specialism is a disease. 'Dr Stephens,' she says, 'welcome to the faculty.' She sits down with her knees and ankles neatly together.

Dr Stephens stands up, grins and lounges against the table. He looks around the room, his gaze glancing over me without recognition. 'I have to tell you these phenomenological approaches are not always popular with more . . . er . . . traditional scholars, who worry a great deal about problems of verification and objectivity. I respect their views. But to me history itself is a kind of fictive truth, a convenient narrative, which can, at worst, parade itself as absolute truth.'

His voice is attractive but his accent is strange. His transatlantic drawling tone is often punctuated by slightly flattened vowels that started out, I'm sure, here in the north of England. It's a nice voice, all the same, soft-toned, hypnotic. The people here are hanging on his every word. He pushes a hand through his curls and smiles, suddenly looking much younger.

'For me the past continues to live in the present. Memory is one of the most valuable sites of study. For instance, how does the past figure in our present-day lives? How do we define ourselves and how do we place ourselves historically? Look at the great historical themes of this century, all within living memory – two world wars, a cold war, the great powers fighting surrogate battles in the Middle East and Far East, the changing tectonic plates of economics, the loss of one empire, the building of another empire, a torn-away Iron Curtain, a pulled-down Wall. The twentieth century is an historian's playground. It is our playground. My interest is how the past figures in the lives of the living, breathing individuals who have lived it, how they define themselves and place themselves historically. You might call it making memory respectable.' He puts a hand on the pile of folders beside him. 'There are several proposals here which invite this kind of approach. I've signed up to supervise them.'

Mine is one of them, I'm sure. What I want to do is interview the teachers and pupils in my old school about their perceptions of the Second World War. I have to say I thought my proposal would be thrown out as, despite being (in my view) so clever and original, it is almost entirely subjective and unacademic.

Dr Stephens is holding forth about these theories, his hand still on the pile of folders. I make notes automatically, relishing the thought that this man will be my supervisor, that I am bound now to become better acquainted with the fair man with sharp grey eyes who likes to row the river in the early mornings, even in winter.

Rosa's Tick Book

1954

Now I will write about Brock Carmichael my brother.

Brock became part of our family in Lancaster, in 1944 – I must have been four, I think. There were soldiers and tanks on the roads near our house. And in France our soldiers were creeping around the high-hedge lanes of Normandy, fighting village to village, pushing those Jerries back. In those days each one of us, in his own way, 'was fighting for freedom, fighting those Nazis to extinction'. My daddy, who was still alive then, wrote those words to us from his billet in Coventry, where he was doing electrical things to aircraft engines. He wrote letters to our house in Lancaster in his fine flourishing script. Even in joined-up, I could read it when I was four. I have read his letters a lot since then.

I was just a kid but I thought I was very old, even if my favourite thing was a teddy bear made by my mother from a cut-up blanket. Brock happened before I broke my arm and had to go to the VE street party as a Dutch girl with a pot arm. That was when my brother Charlie went to nursery and my mother, whose name is Kate Carmichael, was working late shifts at the mental hospital, fighting the Nazis to extinction in her own way.

My mother, Kate Carmichael, is very good at Looks That Kill. She just needs to have met one Nazi and he'd have been killed stone dead with one of her looks. Dead as a stone.

In those days Charlie and I came home to a prepared sandwich tea, which we ate watched by Mrs Cator, our neighbour, whose skin was like grey paper. Beside each small plate our mother, Kate,

17

always placed a small screw of newspaper inside which were folded two wrapped sweets. Nothing tasted as sweet as those sweets. It was like she, with her round squashy figure and her white skin, was there on the table for us to chew, like we could taste her sweetness, her motherness. We didn't mind so much that she wasn't there, because in fact there she was: wrapped in rustling newspaper and crackling Cellophane.

Anyway, this one day she was a full hour late from the hospital. Mrs Cator tapped our battered grandfather clock twice and clicked her false teeth together in a way that made you cringe. Then she went and stood, solid as a tank, staring out of the window. We asked to get down to play but it seemed like she didn't hear and we daren't get down. Not that we were frightened of her, but she would tell our mother. *That* had consequences. After all, we knew about *looks killing*. And she could smack. Once my brother Charlie took two pennies from the hall table and spent them at the corner shop. I can still hear him howling as she beat him.

When the front door finally did rattle, we all looked at the dining-room door, waiting for my mother to burst into the room with her usual gale of life and angry energy. But the door stayed shut. We could hear her light footsteps on the stairs. We looked up at the ceiling. She was upstairs shuffling and clattering, bits of her seeping through the ceiling and making us all hold our breaths.

Somewhere a cat meowed, but it wasn't our little cat, Blackie. He was out on his regular afternoon rat hunt in the quarry behind our street, which doubled as a dump for wrecked cars. Not the street, the quarry, that is. Me and Charlie usually went there after tea to play cops-and-robbers or Germans-and-English. As many as eight or nine lads played out there in full battalion formation. But Charlie and me were young and – worse – I was a girl, so we were most likely to end up being robbers or Nazis. They'd make us grit our teeth and face the inevitability of being defeated, captured, tortured, shot or otherwise executed. (Not as bad as the real thing, which I read about in the papers later.)

At last the door burst open and here she was, my mother, Kate

18

Carmichael, out of her nurse's uniform, dressed in her soft purple frock that stretched a bit across her chest.

'Now then, you two,' she said, eyeing us closely. 'Tea finished?'

Mrs Cator glanced at the clock. 'Kate, I don't think . . . ' Then my mother was hustling her out of the door, thrusting a shilling in her hand. Mrs Cator looked sour. Usually she stayed on a few minutes and talked to my mother about the hospital and the mad people. And the war.

My mother closed the door behind her and then, without looking at us, clashed the cups and plates on to the tray and carried it through to the kitchen. I knew something was up. You always did, with her. You could even tell from behind when you couldn't see her face.

We watched her, wide-eyed. She made these big movements with the tea cloth as she dried the dishes, then shook it out with a crack like a cowboy whip before hanging it on the rail on the back of the door. Then she turned to us. 'Now then, you two! Come here!'

We approached with caution and stood very still before her. I squared my shoulders, prepared for any onslaught. We were at war, after all. She'd been known to slap a person, being driven mad by all the shortages and my father not being there and all that. Look at Charlie stealing those two pence!

'Now, you two!' she said, her voice as sharp as rapiers. 'Can I trust you?'

What a thing to ask. Why should she ask us that? How could a mother not trust her children?

She took us by the shoulders. I can still feel her fingers biting into my shoulder. 'Do you trust me?' she insisted.

How could anyone not trust their mother?

'Yes, yes, Mum!' 'Yes, yes!' Our voices chimed together, Charlie's rising to a squeak.

'I'm going to show you something. And what you see you must tell no one, not one person. No one!' She gripped our shoulders harder. 'Do you cross your hearts?'

'Yes! Yes!' I gabbled, crossing my heart. 'I promise. Charlie does too.' My mind was whirling. What was this thing, this thing she wanted to show us? Perhaps she'd found some lost treasure on her way back from the hospital! A black velvet bag weighed down with diamonds, a Nazi pistol . . .

The painful pressure on our shoulders softened. I wanted her to sit down. I wanted to climb high on her knee and press my head on her purple-armoured breast till it cracked out of shape. I wanted her to smile.

Her mouth did begin to relax. 'Well then! Come on, you two!'

She led the way into the narrow hall and up the narrow staircase. Even after so many years I can remember every detail of that Lancaster house. It had a cellar. Before he went away my father kitted out our cellar as a workshop. He liked to play about with electrical things.

At last we saw the *something* she wanted to show us. There, on the bed in the bedroom Charlie and I shared, lay the narrow drawer from the built-in fireside cupboard. Nestling inside the drawer, wrapped in a white sheet, was the smallest most purple-faced baby you've ever seen. Smaller than a doll! It had this shock of greasy blackish brown hair. Its face was tiny, no bigger than the palm of my hand. Spit bubbled from its tiny lips. Tucked in beside it, just about the same size, was my blanket-cloth teddy bear.

I said, 'That's my teddy, Mum. What's that thing doing with my teddy?'

My mother poked me sharply in the back. 'You're too old for teddies, Rosa. Surely you don't begrudge the baby a teddy?' The words echo in my head today.

Charlie put his hand on the edge of the drawer and shook it. 'Is it a doll?' he said.

'No, it's not! And it's not an it. It's a *he!*' My mother's voice was sharp. She took Charlie's hand and put it on to the bundle. The two of them bent over the bed, their shadows joining in the fading evening light.

I remember putting my hands behind my back.

'Just touch it, Charlie! It's a baby. Warm.' She stood there. 'Flesh and blood.'

Charlie's hand moved to the scrunched purple face. 'What's it called?' he said.

There was a long silence. Then her hand covered Charlie's and she said, really quiet, 'Perhaps he's called Callum.'

I so wanted to feel her hand on mine.

'Not Callum,' said Charlie. 'Baby Brock. That's what he's called. Like a story at nursery today.'

The baby started to stir, mewing like a kitten. My mother folded Charlie's little finger into a knuckle and pushed it towards the baby's mouth. The red mouth opened like a fish and began to suck Charlie's knuckle. Charlie said. 'Crikey!' This was a forbidden word but she did not slap him.

She stood up straight. 'Wait here,' she said. 'Watch the baby.'

When she left the room I took a step towards the bed and stood at Charlie's shoulder, watching the baby as it made a big business of all that sucking. One time its face creased and crumpled as though it were about to sneeze, then it smoothed out and started sucking again. I leaned closer to see it more clearly. Its hair was greasy. Its skin was greasy as well, but smooth and red. One small hand clutched the edge of the sheet. Its fingers were tiny sea-things and the nails fragile and blue-rimmed. I put my face very close, then recoiled as its eyes opened wide – gleaming like washed bottle glass. He looked straight at me and I looked straight at him. I felt like someone had punched me in the stomach and for a second could hardly breathe. Then he closed his eyes and I could breathe again.

It seemed a long time before my mother came back with a steaming pudding basin containing a jug of milk in one hand, and this tiny plastic tube in the other, a bit like a fountain pen with no ink. She shouldered us to one side and sat on the bed.

'We'd better get him fed, or he'll die on us.'

This was ages ago but those words are still ringing in my ears. 'He'll die on us.' Then, and after, the papers were full of dying. There were these lists with name and rank and sometimes photographs. When he came home on leave from the factory my daddy would read those lists, his long finger running down the page while he mouthed the names of people he knew and people he didn't know.

Well, anyway. Our Brock didn't die on us. He's here with us to this day. But he's grown from a tiny wailing purple doll to the size of a young antelope. And now he's due in from school any minute so I'd better hide this tick book behind the wardrobe. There'll be war on if my mother finds it. It's taken me ages to write all this, which means I've read nothing today. Not a single book. And I haven't dropped off to sleep once. Come to think of it, I'm not even tired. That makes a change.

Bronwen's Experience of God

January 1991

Winter has its better points, I suppose. Bright hard mornings like today by the river, for instance. White slanting light that puts a crisp edge on people and houses, plants and trees alike. A satisfying need to huddle together with other human beings. But for me the worst, the very worst of winter is the darkness of the afternoons. Just after three o'clock the light fades and by four it is as though God has turned off the switch. This afternoon, after the research seminar and a book hunt in the library, I come out into the dark – streetlights full on – and take the short route back to South Street to my car, detouring just a little to walk through the cathedral.

The great nave is humming with other refugees from the dark. Even so, despite the clicking people, this place always weighs in on you as a house of God; other centuries, other incarnations hover only inches away in a veil of shadows. As usual when I steal five minutes from my homeward journey, I sit in a front pew. I have this trick where, if I lower my lids and put my eyes out of focus I can empty the place and silence the chatter and be alone there, made small by the monumental columns of Frosterley marble embedded with prehistoric seashells; rearing before me the elaborate carved screen that protects the tomb of St Cuthbert, above me rainbow light streaming from the miraculous rose window.

This quiet delight is the only fragment left in me of a great surge of religious feeling I had when I was fourteen years old, when – much to my mother, Rosa's, astonishment – I started going to church and got myself confirmed. Of course, this hunger for religion is not uncommon in adolescents. Look at these cult people now, who pick up kids at this stage, and make fanatics of them.

But for me my sense of history got entangled with a notion of belief. If it had been good enough for intelligent, inspired Christians for two thousand years I – as a wise child – felt there must be something in it. For two years after that I was an attentive Christian, relishing the poetry of the liturgy and feeling my heart race with the soaring joy of the music.

In the end this fragile and transitory sense of belief was blown away from me by the intervention of two men. One was the vicar, a distinguished, erudite man whose early exploits as a Battle of Britain pilot gave authority to his humane sermons. But one day he held forth on the inappropriate aspirations of women in this Age of Liberation. According to him it led to the Breakdown of Households and the Destruction of the Family. Of course, St Paul was quoted as his irrefutable authority.

Before that day I'd found this man accessible, interested in my adolescent journey to faith. But I was so angry at his sermon I caught him in the church porch and said that, really, I couldn't agree with what he'd said. Naïvely I waited for some intelligent discourse. He just looked me in the eye and said, 'Well, Bronwen, it's not up to you to agree or disagree; it's up to you to accept.' Then he turned and hurried away, the wind catching his white surplice, the sun glinting on his full head of silver hair.

The other man who pulled me out of that adolescent maze of magical hope and eternal possibility also worked for the Church. His name was Matthew Pomeroy and he came to our parish from some religious college at Oxford and was doing what we'd now call work experience in our church. A kind of mission among the natives in the North, perhaps. He was twenty-one, athletic, with the face of a chiselled stone angel. His mouth was full and generous, almost womanly. His voice was modulated, smooth, perfect. His faith, nurtured in the bosom of his family and his public school, shone from within him and made him even more attractive, not just to me but to the men and women in the congregation.

24

Matthew and I got on brilliantly. We clicked with each other. We talked about everything. The meaning of life. Social justice. Honesty and truth. Art. Family. The Women's Movement (with which he was much more in tune than was the vicar). Climbing and motorbikes, which he loved. Drawing and history, which I liked. My mother, Rosa – not at all religious, but ever loving and supportive – liked Matthew and welcomed him to our home. He would call quite late at night after church meetings or pastoral calls. His signet ring would click as he knocked on the sitting-room window and we knew it was him. My heart would lift. He and my mother would talk about the war and the Cold War and whether the Russians were truly a threat or whether it was all so much sabre-rattling. I joined in. Of course, I had my own distinct opinions, even then.

It was often after midnight when I saw him to the door. Before long he would give me a quick hug as he said good night. Then he would kiss me on both cheeks, like they do in French films. But, young as I was, I was not mistaken. The air between us was thick with possibility. The phrase 'pregnant pause' now comes to mind and makes me laugh.

Then one night Matthew called when my mother was away. She was down in London negotiating a very special contract for a children's story she had written. She was a teacher by trade but had always written children's stories. She was as excited as was possible for such a quiet person.

Matthew came late on that Thursday night and I made him a cup of tea as was usual. He took the cup from me and kissed my hand. Then he groaned and pulled me to him and kissed my cheeks, chin, lips, any piece of bare skin he could find. 'We shouldn't, we shouldn't,' he kept saying, kissing me all the time.

Then I kissed him back and the groaning was replaced by yelps of delight.

It took us quite a long time to get to the point of actually making love, as I only knew about this activity from reading books, and I don't think he knew much more. We had to find our way by trial and error but because of that it was all a delight, full of laughter, even the painful bit. 'It's impossible, it's impossible!' I kept saying. 'Just one more try!' he said desperately. 'Come on, Bronwen, just one more try!'

That did it. I've read since that it takes months, years, for women to achieve an orgasm. Well, this was a gold-standard orgasm in one. For him too. When it was over, he was sweating and astounded.

'I never knew!' he said softly. 'I never really knew. You are a wonder of the world, Bronwen. A wonder.'

When he had gone I had a long bath, then rolled into bed naked. Like Matthew I'd never really known about making love before. The distance between theory and practice was galaxy wide.

As I yawned, ready to drop off to sleep, I suddenly felt pleased that I'd finished my French and history homework before I heard the click of Matthew's ring on the window. At least I wouldn't have to get up early in the morning and could have a nice long lie-in.

That was the last time I ever saw Matthew Pomeroy. The next Sunday at church the vicar announced that Matthew had been obliged to shorten his sojourn in the North as he'd been called back to London, then on to India where his father, who taught at the university in Lahore, was seriously ill. I don't know whether it was my feverish imagination, or whether after that the vicar was particularly frosty with me. Perhaps it was my growing feminist sensibilities he objected to. Whatever the case, it didn't bother me, as soon after that I stopped going to church and joined a music appreciation group.

Matthew wrote ten times. I burned the letters unread. Matthew Pomeroy! He's there in the room every time I see my beautiful daughter with her carved-angel looks, her beautiful mouth, her quizzical eyes, every time I go to watch her play hockey or netball. Matthew is all there in her; she is a joyful creature borne out of a single golden moment.

After an initial flurry my mother just hugged me right through my child-pregnancy. And when Lily was here we got on with bringing her up between us and, as far as I can see today, we've done a good job between us. Having Lily put my education back a year, but I still went back to school, then on to get my degree and a decent job in a school. If I hadn't had Lily I might not have gone on to teach. I would have travelled, seen the world. But teaching is the most convenient profession and I've never regretted it.

My mother, Rosa, never made the connection between Matthew and Lily, and soon stopped asking questions. We got on with things and just occasionally she would ponder my missing out on teenage years when being a teenager was more than *Top of the Pops*. Then she would say I'd have to leave my adventures till later. And I have. This course in Durham is the first step on my own particular adventure.

My mother has her own adventures but they are mostly inside her head. They are the source of her children's books, which are much admired by people who know children. When I started work and the stories became modestly successful, Rosa finished with school to teach part time – always children with some kind of disability who had to learn at home. These days her commitment is to a child with spina bifida, who, she says, has a terrific personality and no number sense.

Of course Lily has asked about her father and I have pledged to tell her all about him when she's eighteen. *Sufficient unto the day*. That's one of my grandmother Kate's sayings. We hear a lot of Kate's sayings as she lives less than a mile away and one of us calls in every day. My mother told Kate once that we were going to make a list of her sayings and to put them in a book entitled *Kate Carmichael's World of Wisdom*. She glowered at Rosa from her chair. A powerful look, despite her great age.

'You think there's a book in everything, Rosa. Don't you be so sure! There's some things that just can't be said.'

She's right, of course. I know. The whole thing about Matthew – and Lily – comes neatly within that category of secrets that can't be told.

Anyway, that time in my life has bequeathed me three things: a beautiful, poised daughter, a love of churches as some kind of crucible of experience if not faith, and – rather sadly – the sheer inability to recreate with any man that golden orgasmic moment I had at fifteen with Matthew Pomeroy.

27

One thing is certain. I don't regret any of it. Not him, not Lily, not anything. Anyway, the older I get the more I realise that everyone has secrets. Despite the fashion for confession, for 'telling it all' and 'letting it all hang out', it seems to me that the glue that holds a family together, the lubrication that allows it to move forward, consists of individual discretion, holding back, and not telling all.

Rosa Keeps her Secret

1954

Here we go again. I've been dying to get back down to this. The thing is, I've had to put in an appearance at school for a couple of days. Then, at the end of chemistry, when Mr Blackett asked for homework marks to enter in his book, I just shouted out 'Six!' and he didn't seem to bother. Perhaps, with all those piles of books, he doesn't know who's done homework and who hasn't. That's worth remembering.

Yesterday I did a French dictation and an English comprehension in class, so at least those proper marks will go in the book. I always do all right in those subjects. Both of the teachers asked me how I was and didn't seem to be worried about the missing homework. Still I was as tense as a bowstring all day.

But today it would have been physics – Mr Lemon roars like a bull and bellows your surname – and biology – Mr Boardson looms over you and tugs your hair. And I am two homeworks behind with them. I've been thinking about how I'm trying to keep all this secret, this being off school and being so frightened all the time. Then that got me on to thinking about how we kept Brock a secret for a whole month before we went off to Coventry and took him with us. We didn't need to keep it secret at all then. Nobody knew any of us or how big our family was.

Enough about me, now. What I want is to write these stories from my family. I thought I should date them just to make it clear. So—

It was not that hard for us to keep my mother's secret about Brock. In those days, and ever since, my mother never mixed too much with neighbours. She looks down on that. Of course, she had to see Mrs Cator, who came to watch us eat our tea. But my mother paid her, so that made it OK. She says she never likes to be obliged. She was not interested in the neighbours, even though the neighbours were quite interested in her. They often came knocking on the door when they wanted some dead relative laying out or there was somebody ill or a baby on the way. But after Brock came to us she would give them the name of another nurse who would lend a hand.

To take care of Brock she had to stop working at the hospital for a while. She sent me round to the next road with a letter for another nurse to hand in to the hospital. After that it was like our house was a castle and the drawbridge was up. Every day Charlie and me went to school and came back, and for a few weeks our mother was there to watch us eat our teas. At these teatimes there were no sweets, and the sandwiches were thick bread with a thin scrape of margarine and a thinner scrape of marrow marmalade, a recipe she got off the wireless. You see, without her wages there were no treats.

The highlight of our week was the letter from our daddy. It was always long. Six or seven pages written on very thin paper. His writing was big and flowing. He talked about the war and his workmates, and people he knew who were fighting in France or some who had even died. 'Darling Kate,' he wrote. He talked about how much he loved and missed my mother. And he asked about me and Charlie and whether we had been good. He never talked about his work at the aircraft factory, as that was, we knew, Top Secret. Walls Have Ears. That was all over during the war.

I've read those letters so many times since he died. My mother keeps them in a mahogany box under her bed, with old bills and our birth certificates (but not Brock's) and her nursing diplomas.

My daddy's death certificate is there too. 'Bronchial pneumonia.' I looked that up. These days while I'm not at school and my mother's at the factory I can take my time to read those letters. But I've less time to do any of that now, what with writing this ledger.

(Oh, I do remember asking my mother if my daddy knew about baby Brock. Did she write about it to him in her letters? I remember her saying not yet, there was 'time enough' for that.)

On the second day Brock was with us, my mother moved out of the room at the front that she usually shared with my daddy, into a room right at the back of the house, beyond the bathroom. I asked her why and she said that Brock might keep people awake.

'Didn't you hear him crying in the night?' she said. I nodded. It was like the wild mewing of a cat. Worse than Blackie, our cat. 'We can't let them know our secret, can we, Rosa?'

I shook my head, warmed by the notion of me sharing a secret with her.

The room she now shared with Brock was above the scullery, looking down over the narrow strip of garden and the coal bunkers, then further out to the quarry, with its mountains of junk and its abandoned cars.

I'd always liked this bedroom. She had kept it neat and clean since Cy left, quite a long time before. Cy was a Canadian officer – RAF – who was billeted on us, my mother explained, just like our daddy was billeted on some family in Coventry. 'Both of them are working for the war, Rosa, and both of them need somewhere to lay their weary heads.'

If my memory is right, Cy was billeted with us in that time just before my mother went to work at the hospital. He was tall, nearly as tall as my daddy, and had smooth brown skin and soft hands. I remember hearing Mrs Cator asking my mother how she could do with a black man in the house. But I can't remember the answer. He wasn't black at all but sort of golden coppery creamy, if you know what I mean.

Anyway, Cy brought presents into the house – things like cheese and raisins, which were hard to get. Even now, every time I smell cheese melting under the grill I think of him. But all I can really remember is the tall figure, the officer's uniform and the gleaming tanned skin. There are no features. I could walk past him in the street and not recognise him. For months after he left, every time I saw a man with an officer's peaked cap, I thought it was Cy. My mother has told me that he was especially fond of me and even offered to take me back to Canada with him when he returned after his stretch of duty. How strange it is, then, that I can't remember his face.

We received long letters from Cy, with Canadian stamps, for years after the war, even up to the time my father died. There was always a special cross (meaning kiss) for me. My father took on the task of answering these letters. He was the letter writer. Funnily enough, none of Cy's letters survive in the mahogany box with my daddy's letters. I wish I had them here to help me now, when I'm writing this ledger about the times of our lives. If they're not in the box my mother's burned them or something. Why would she do that?

The day Peace was Declared we got back from school to find that Mrs Cator was back again with the tea and her folded arms. And no Brock! I saw Charlie open his mouth to ask where the baby was so I clasped my hand over it.

'We'll go up and wash our hands,' I gasped to Mrs Cator, and dragged Charlie upstairs.

We raced past the bathroom to the bedroom at the end. It was empty. The bed was neatly made, the drawers were dusted and there was no sign that a baby had ever been there. No Mam. No Brock.

Back in the bathroom I turned on the water and whispered into Charlie's ear, 'Don't say nothing about Brock. Nothing. Remember it's a secret.'

We washed our hands noisily then, and went down to eat our sandwiches and unwrap our sweets under the eagle eye of Mrs Cator. When my mother got back we had to wait until Ma Cator had gone to ask about Brock. But when our mother did get back home the two of them talked for ages about the war and mad people.

When Ma Cator had gone my mother sat us down side by side and loomed large over us. My nose was at the level of the buckle of the leather belt that pulled her uniform so tightly round her waist. She always looked so smart in her uniform. She told us then that she needed to go back to work for the money and a friend of hers near the hospital was minding Brock. 'For a fee,' she added wryly. 'The labourer is worthy of his hire.' I remember that. 'For a fee. The labourer is worthy of his hire.' Funny, seeing as it was a woman who was minding Brock, and would a woman count as a labourer?

'Will we never, never see Brock again?' said our Charlie. He had these round eyes. Still has.

She smiled faintly. 'Don't be silly. 'Of course we will. The war's over now and we're supposed to be joining your father soon. Brock'll come to Coventry with us.'

'Nobody'll bother at hearing him cry there,' I said.

She stared at me. 'You've got it, Rosa. We won't have to worry about anybody hearing him then. He'll be properly ours.'

'And will I be able to wheel him in the street?'

'I'm sure you will,' she said. She sat down. 'Now then, you two. We have to think what you're going to the party as.'

Party? It was the first we'd heard of any party.

'This party to celebrate the end of the war. Everyone has to go dressed up as something. There'll be balloons and paper hats.'

'Me, I'm gonna go as a cowboy,' said Charlie.

'Are you now?' She turned to me. 'And what about you, Rosa?'

I shook my head. She went into the front room and came back with a *Woman's Weekly*. (She still gets that when she can afford it.) She turned the pages until she came upon a picture of a Dutch girl among tulips, wearing a black waistcoat and a white turned-back bonnet. 'You can be a Dutch girl,' she said. 'You can symbolise the liberation of Holland.'

Symbolise! I didn't know what that meant then but I rolled it about in my head in delight, forgetting for a moment about Brock, who was now 'billeted out', just like my father and the Canadian Cy, wherever he was.

Victory in Europe Day came, and the street was draped in miles of home-made bunting. There was a brass band all made up of ladies. I went to the party as a little Dutch girl with her arm in a

33

pot because the day before the party I'd fallen off the low wall outside the house, trying to manoeuvre my way past the stumps of iron railings. (That's another story.)

My plaster pot won me a lot of attention, even among the Spanish dancers, the Italian signorinas, the miniature soldiers, the Red Cross nurses, and the flamboyant pirates. There were loads of children there, all faked up as one European thing or another. (Charlie said his cowboy outfit was for all the Americans in the war.) There were boys with balls, toddlers in pushchairs, babies in prams.

One old woman – she must have been a grandma – turned up with these twins in a battered old pram. Like the other kids, I peered curiously inside, but all I saw were two blue bundles topped with woolly pom-pom hats. Nothing so spectacular. The grandma seemed particularly keen that my mother should look at them.

'Come and see your handiwork, Mrs Carmichael. They're like as two peas in a pod.' My mother peered inside, nodded, then hustled us away as the three-legged race was about to begin and she told us she had Great Expectations of me and Charlie Aquitting Ourselves Very Well.

When the races and competitions were over, we had our tea at the long tables in the centre of the street where women with big jugs of lemonade were standing around ready to pour. I remember the tinny piping sound of someone's wind-up gramophone playing dance music. I remember the gritty bite of the paste in the sandwiches. But most of all on that day, I remember the end of the party and the sight of my own daddy striding down the road in dusty work clothes with a knapsack on his back: tall and film-star handsome with his big, downward-sloping eyes and his black hair slicked straight back from his broad brow. My daddy!

I clambered over the table and ran to meet him, shouting and shouting with relief. 'Oh, Daddy. So, so, here you are! Here you are.'

As I write this now I have been thinking that my daddy was everything warm and bright and comfortable in our lives, and when he went out of it, all of that went too. I've read about the attraction of opposites and I suppose that was those two. My mother is short and a bit fat, fierce and commanding, full of life and fire and echoing dark feeling, even in the best of times, which I now – too late – realise those times were. Daddy was dreamy and inventive, warm and comfortable, very loving and quick to touch and hug you. (I have made up my mind that when I have children I will hug them all the time. I will hug them till they're sick of it.) My mother must have liked all that touching too, as, young as I was then, I could tell she was happier when he was there, hugging her. Not so angry, which was a relief.

There is none of that relief for her these days. No hugging. I sometimes think she's been angry since the day he died, for want of a bit of hugging. There was the Canadian Cy, who came from Trinidad. I saw them hugging one time. I remember it. They leaped apart. And there were some letters from him that she kept in a locked box.

On the night of VE Day, or that weekend, I can't quite remember when, there was a street party for the grown-ups. We kids were allowed to go to it, but we had to stay in the shadows, to mind our Ps and Qs. They lit this huge bonfire on the edge of the quarry behind our house. During the day my daddy had vanished into his cellar and emerged after an hour or so with what looked like a bundle of wires. These turned out to be eleven cunningly contrived, extremely long, toasting forks for people to toast sausages and potatoes on the bonfire. You could tell that even though he was rarely there in the street, people liked him and his gentle, easy ways. They were more comfortable with him than with my mother, who had laid out their dead and comforted them when they were ill.

The day of the bonfire was also the day my daddy went off and scrounged a bicycle for her. I close my eyes and I see him now, teaching her how to ride it. He's holding the back of her seat and she's wobbling along and the bonfire's kind of spurting up behind them. They are laughing, and when he saved her from falling off, he kisses her on the cheek and he hugs her very hard.

That night, back at home, he seemed a bit tipsy and sang to her. 'If You Were the Only Girl in the World'. She wriggled from his grasp and shooed us upstairs to get ready for bed. Then he is there, sitting on our bed, reading us 'The Princess and the Pea'. He tucks us both in and kissed us twice, once on the hand and once on the forehead. I have a pain in my tummy now when I think of it.

I think she must have told him about Brock that very night because I remember shouting downstairs, and then there was silence. And then, oh delight, they are laughing again, and he is singing 'If You Were the Only Girl in the World' really, really loud. Our neighbours must definitely have heard him. The next morning my mother is smiling at breakfast and she tells us that the following week we're going to join Daddy in Coventry, because he'd kindly promised to find us somewhere to stay. Somewhere nice and snug.

Charlie claps his hands and says 'Is Brock coming with us?'

I freeze. Now there'll be trouble. The secret's out.

She smiles at Daddy. Smiles!

I remember she said this – 'Oh, yes, Charlie. Brock's coming with us. He needs a billet as much as any of us.' That day we collected Brock and walked in the Jubilee Park. My mother carried Brock till her shoulders ached. Then Daddy took over.

I've just done a little sum. On VE Day my mother must have been thirty-four years old, and my daddy would be thirty-five. I've read somewhere that these are a person's prime years. So they were in their prime and they were very happy.

And there was that man Cy. Every time those days sit in my mind, there he is, kind of a golden shadow.

A Kiss for Rosa

1945

Tangarete Road
Port of Spain
Trinidad

Dear Kate,

I said would write so here goes. Wasn't the war a real beast of change? Back here in the Trinidadian sunshine, your stone house with those bay windows seems to this lost soul now not just on another continent but in another time. Like that time when the Witchfinders stalked the land. You remember, Kate, all those ghostly tales I told you about the time I was stationed in Suffolk? Of course, that was before I made my long haul to your 'North countree'. How I did hate to be so roughly parted from my buddies at the camp! But then, your stone house, those fine breakfasts – you'll protest, I know, about the stuff I brought from the PX – above all, your gentle company and your bright talk of mad people – all these were the finest condiments for any meal. And now I can hear that chuckle of yours, rejecting 'overblown Yankee' praise. How many times in England had I to declare I was *no Yankee* and ram it down people's throats that I was as British as anyone there, albeit I come from these here islands and grew up in Canada and did not reach your gentle grey-green island till the ripe old age of twenty-five?

So here I am on my grandmother's veranda out of

uniform, sitting in the sun with the sand between my toes and I can't rid my mind of the thought of the stone house in the north of England, and its gentle people.

I've now applied for a job here, at Furness, Withy and Co – some shipping clerk's job. Even so, good old Canada is at the back of my mind. Life is faster there, and there's money to be made, I'm telling you. In my time in Europe all I wanted was to return to these islands and listen to the humming bee and get out my fishing line. Now I am getting restless. These islands are old-fashioned and those old ways still rule. My upbringing in Canada and my time in the air force have taught me to look any man in the eye. I'm telling you, even now that can get you into trouble hereabouts.

I hope, Katie, that this here parcel pleases you. There's a fountain pen for Rosa – I remember well the time she checked your letters to find out about real writing. A gun and holster for Charlie as I know he likes to 'ride the range'. A shirt for Rob, although I think the colours may be too bright. And French Rose perfume for you. Here I have a confession. Reality is I bought two bottles. Now every time I lift the stopper I think of you. And nylons. I thought you would like nylons.

Here in the sun I think of you.

Cy

X – a special kiss for Rosa

Port of Spain
Trinidad

Dear Friends Kate and Rob,

I thank you both for your very welcome letter. It warms my heart to hear of you and all your thoughts now that the war is finally over and you know that you and the little ones are really safe. Your work seems to be going full throttle, Rob, which must be a good thing. I read a piece in our local paper here that talked of fears of a post-war slump, but seems like that's not the case for you.

Now! You always told me that you couldn't properly bring to mind the place of my birth and I thought I would try in a letter to tell you a little. This here is the island of the hummingbird and the cascadura. The hummingbird, he lives the life of an emperor in our cocoa woods, on our savannahs, in and out of our waving sugar cane, and among all our wild fruits and fragrant flowers. I guess this old humming bee might just be ourselves, buzzing around in this place of waterfalls and fertile valleys, a paradise for some. For others, of course, this paradise is in their dream of the past, before others took their ancient lands and colonised their souls.

But the old fish cascadura, *Hoplosternum littorale*, that old boy is really the king of the island. He has bony scales marching down his body, big whiskers and almost no eyes. And the old boy thinks he's a man as he comes up to take a breath of air. Naturally, when the old boy does this the cunning fisherman snap him up in his nets. Everyone wants a bite of old cascadura. They say that once you've had a bite you'll always return to the island, wherever you may roam. Look at me! I am back here! But sometimes I think 'here' is not enough. My eyes stray to the horizon and beyond. The same for other boys coming back from fighting overseas. Paradise is not enough. They long again for the grey streets of London paved with gold nuggets. But Toronto is my choice because as you know I grew up there and went to school and college there. I have a welcome waiting.

But always here on my island I think of you. I will never forget the kindness I received at your hands, in the bosom of your family. I thought you might like this here picture of me with my brother in front of his house in Port of Spain. You must imagine the sea as blue, clear, crystal blue. Thank you for your photographs. I have them in my pocketbook.

My very kind regards to you both,

Cy

X – a kiss for Rosa

My Dearest Katie,

A message from a lost soul across the sea! I am now on the cusp of leaving my island. An RAF buddy of mine has promised me a job which looks very well. The excitement of my days in Europe is fading fast as reality cracks its whip. Now it's like I'm looking down the wrong end of a telescope at those times. I have a heavy stone of regret that will be inside me. Now I'm leaving them, the delights of Trinidad are more enticing than ever – the bright sun and sea – the cluster of alleys by the port – the patois here that reflects a dozen countries. My face here on the island is just one in a thousand. Different, but then we're all different here so we're all at home.

Did I tell you that the native Indian name for our island is the island of the hummingbird – *Jere*? I found this poem that you might like, and have copied it, seeing as – unlike you – I am no hand at poetry. I keep your lovely poem in my pocket book always. Anyway, here's this poem about the island.

TRINIDAD – JERE
Land of the Hummingbird

THOSE who eat the cascadura will, the native legend says,
Wheresoever they may wander, end in Trinidad their days.
And this lovely fragrant island, with its forest hills sublime,
Well might be the smiling Eden pictured in the Book divine.

Oh! the Bocas at the daybreak – how can one describe that scene!
Or the little emerald islands with the sapphire sea between!

40

Matchless country of Jere, fairer none could ever wish.
Can you wonder at the legend of the cascadura fish?

Katie, I will write with my new address as soon as I get to
Toronto.
I will always think of you.
Cy
X – a kiss for Rosa

HOSPITAL STORES
NOTE OF REQUISITION
(N.B. Requires two signatures)
Cy,
Dearest, the night is ending
Gone are our dreams divine
You must go back to your world
I must go back to mine
Back to the joyless duties
Back to the fruitless tears
Loving – & yet divided, all thro'
The empty years.
How can I live without you,
How can I let you go?
You that I love so well, dear
I that you love so well, dear
You that I worship so.
K. Carmichael

(Old song, copied to Cy's letter)

Driving Home

1991

When I finally escape the compelling magic of the cathedral and make my way to my car, there on South Street is Cali Vax draped over the bonnet of the Riley, smoking a cigarette, her white face glowing in the light of a streetlamp. She throws down the cigarette and grinds it into the soft path with the toe of her boot. An overnight bag lies like a tame animal at her feet.

'I looked for you, hon,' she says plaintively. 'And you weren't there.'

'You were off with the Ceolas Monkey boys and their bodhrán,' I say, unlocking the door. 'I went up to the cathedral.'

'The cathedral? All this time? If I didn't know you better, hon, I'd have said you were a religious maniac.' She throws her bag on the back seat and slips in beside me. The car fills with her prickly perfume.

'The bodhrán man's a sweet thing but he's into all that Irish stuff,' she says. 'God save me from sentimental politics. Anyway, his nose is too small. God save me from men with small noses. Makes them look like mean kiddie winkies.'

'You're always labelling people, Cali –' turning on the engine but letting it idle a bit – 'so how'd you label yourself?'

'Long nose and filled with the politics of love and life, hon, no more, no less.'

I know Cali's story, having heard it with embellishments many times. But I still wonder how someone of thirty-two can be so carefree, so in charge of herself and everyone around her. The stories she tells don't really speak of her life when she was Marjorie Rawlinson. There is no talk of family, of brothers and sisters. It's as though she was born at seventeen, thumbing a lift on the A1 at Nottingham. The only family she mentions is the family of friends accidentally engineered by life in a squat. Sometimes when she talks about that life, though it must have been very dingy, it seems to have a rosy glow, like some remembered paradise.

I manoeuvre the car into the narrow road. 'Where to? I see you've got your bag.'

'Well, that's it, old dear.' She lights another cigarette and draws hard on it. 'They wouldn't keep my digs because I wouldn't pay them over Christmas. So I am – temporarily, honestly – without a place to lay my weary head. I thought you . . .'

'Did you?' On this dark winter afternoon the lit windows gleam in the dark mass of the castle and cathedral on the other side of the river. 'Cali, love, we've been through this before. It's not a big house, and there's me and my mother and Lily . . .'

'A couch! A floor, hon! Just tonight. I'll sort something out tomorrow. I promise.'

'That couch, that floor are not mine to offer, Cal. It's my mother's house, you know that.'

Cali can be exasperating. She tried this last term, saying that we were 'such good mates, it makes sense to live together, darling. It's just a year, after all . . .' She was very persistent. She took some resisting and I was made very aware that I fell short of the natural rules of hospitality evolved in the squat culture.

Now Cali says, 'Your mother's a kind woman. A loving woman. She likes me. We got on famously.'

'So she'll say yes. And that's why we shouldn't ask her.'

We sit in rare silence. I feel embarrassed at turning Cali down. She is – I hope she is – embarrassed at putting me in that position.

Then she says abruptly, 'You'd better stop here beside the bus stop, Bronwen. I'll go back into town. If all else fails I'll stay at the County.'

That was it. She could do that, stay at the County. Cali's no impoverished student, although she likes to play poverty games.

She still has money in the bank from her time in the City. She can stay anywhere she likes. She can run a car. But she doesn't.

'There's posh.' I don't stop the car. 'I've this one idea, Cali. Just one. My Uncle Charlie lives at Croxdale on the bus route. He and my Auntie May run this little B & B by the railway line. They might just have a room. It'll be noisy, though. There are the London trains. And they have dozens of kids roaring around as well.'

I can feel Cali's grin. 'Noise I can stand, hon. All I need is somewhere to lay my weary head.'

At Croxdale, Uncle Charlie, very pleased to see me, cocks an appreciative eye at Cali, and sweeps us into the cluttered back room. He turns down the music centre, which was blaring some Buddy Holly song, shoves a child off one chair and a blow-up elephant off the other so we can sit down. There are children and toys in every room except the guests' parlour. May had three children when Charlie – a bachelor of forty-five – met her and they went on to have two children together. He says now that May will get a room ready when she gets in from the cash-and-carry.

'No room ready just yet, pet,' he says to Cali, smiling sweetly at her. It's funny to see your gentle uncle as a *man*. I can suddenly see Cali being charmed by those heavy-lidded eyes and the thick dark head of hair combed straight back from his forehead. And his nose is just about the right size. Just big enough.

He turns to me. 'Really nice to see you, pet. How's your mam? It's weeks since I saw her. Still working hard at those books? I saw a review of one in the *Guardian* children's section. Folks seem to like them.'

'They're good.' I can't resist it. 'You should read one.'

He shrugs. 'Not one for books, you know. Your mam could eat three books for dinner. Our Brock too. Our Rosa knows I'm not one for books.' He pauses. 'I haven't seen me mother either, for a while. Your grandma all right, then?'

'Kate's just the same.' You'd never call my grandmother just 'all right'. You wouldn't call a force of nature 'all right'. 'Never changes.' I stood up. 'We'll have to get on, Uncle Charlie. I'll take Cali home for tea and drop her back here.'

'Hang on.' He goes to a sideboard and pulls an airmail letter out of a long drawer. 'Here, it's a letter from our Brock, pet. I thought Rosa might like to see it. Mother too. They like to read his letters. There's a photo in there. Give my love to your ma. I really will come and see her.' He pauses. 'I kind of miss our Rosa, you know, but things do get hectic round here.'

On the way home I have to tell Cali all about my Uncle Charlie. How we don't often see him now, but how much I like him. How I know how much he loves my mother. How I sometimes wonder if that's why he waited so long to get married.

'Before he got together with May he was always at our house, hanging on her every word and doing practical things for her. He's a gentle soul. My mother always says Charlie's like their dad. He doesn't have the striving gene that plagues the rest of us. Of course, he's had a different life. He was a time-served toolmaker before Mrs Thatcher got rid of them. He worked in the cooker factory for years, and before he met my Auntie May, who worked on the lines there. Married seven years when he was made redundant, so they bought the B & B. They have some children still at home, others visiting every day and the whole family of children and grandchildren gathering every Sunday. No wonder he doesn't have time to come and see my mother . . .' I finished, my mind still on Charlie.

The B & B always roars with 1960s music selected from Charlie's immaculately organised and labelled tape and vinyl collections. He loves Elvis. Auntie May only just managed to stop him calling their B & B Heartbreak Hotel.

I went on, 'Charlie sometimes plays air guitar. And he plays a real banjo. He has this big shed out the back. And plays there in a scratch group with his mates. Need I say more? as Lily would say.'

I can feel Cali frowning. 'His voice is different from you and your mother and Lily. He sounds genuine, like the real thing . . . but you sound kind of posh northern, if you know what I mean.'

'No, I don't.' I make my voice sound threatening, to stop her blundering into this territory. One of my long-held bugbears is the way we are obsessed, *obsessed* in England, not just with categorising people, but pinpointing them with their accent. Not only is it crude and cruel, it's lazy and ignorant.

Heedless, she breezes on, 'Your uncle sounds really northern. Kind of authentic. Cute.'

I put my foot on the accelerator, having nearly overshot a right turn. 'Will you stop being so bloody patronising, Cali, or I WILL drop you at the next bus stop!'

We drive on, then, in blessed silence and I think about my mother and Uncle Brock's letter. She's always kind of tense when we get these letters from Brock. Even more inside herself than usual. And this time there is a photograph. What will she make of that?

All the Women Have Them

Rosa, 1954

Things are getting worse for me. Now I have to stay in the house even out of school time because I'm afraid I'll see another boy or girl, or – worse – a teacher, and they'll ask me where I've been all this time. My mother says I have a pasty look and should get some fresh air like the boys. They're always out in the street playing alleys or kick-the-can or British bulldog. But I tell her it's too cold. It makes my teeth chatter. She laughs at this, saying, 'The March wind doth blow, and we shall have snow, and what will poor robin do then, poor thing?' It's a nice laugh and makes me want to laugh with her.

Then yesterday she waits until the boys are out of the way, sits back in her chair and lights a cigarette. 'Do they teach you about menstruation at school?'

I really scowl at her.

'You know. Periods.'

'No. But I know about it . . .'

'Good.' She picks up her paper. 'Just remember. It's nothing to be frightened of. All women have them. Just remember to tell me if you get a sign.'

(A sign? A sign from God? A visitation in the night from the Angel Gabriel? Who knows?)

Back to these stories of my family. The more I write here, the more I remember. This one I will call

47

1947 School Run

That new house of ours in Coventry, according to my mother, was 'jerry-built'. I asked her once why they called it that. Had German prisoners built it? (I knew we had *their* prisoners just like the Germans had ours. There were tons of photographs in the papers of them – torture ones, which made you want to be sick even though they compelled you to catch them again and again, sideways, though, not front-on. Front-on would have been too much. These pictures were the only thing that made my daddy swear. 'Evil bastards!' I heard him say that more than once.)

My mother said no, it was that German bombing caused it. Another name for Germans is Jerries. While we lived there, it seemed the whole of Coventry was being jerry-built, having been flattened by German bombing. We did it too. Last November our German teacher brought this German man to talk to us, who had been there when we bombed Dresden. That was flattened too.

One day, when we still lived in Coventry, I was sure I'd lost my little brother Brock for good. I'd had my seventh birthday and was top of the class in the junior school. Brock's nursery school, attached to a church, was halfway between our new house and the school where Charlie and I went.

In the mornings my mother would walk with us all as far as the nursery and take Brock in there while Charlie and I went on to our big school. Every day after school Charlie would run home with his friends while I stopped off to collect Brock from the nursery. I quite liked this – fastening his red woollen hat and wrapping his scarf round his neck before walking home slowly, listening to his prattling voice and watching him skip ahead of me. You could tell the teachers at the nursery liked Brock. They talked about his fine fair curls and his bright grey eyes. He was very clever. He could talk in sentences at a year, could read at two and a half and write his name at three years old. My mother was very proud of him. I could do all of those things at the same age but she is proudest of all of him.

I've loved Brock since he first shone the beam of his eyes on me. I've always had to take care of him. When he was little, one of my favourite games was to stand him up on the sideboard on his own and go and stand at the other side of the room. He'd be all right for a minute or two but then he would look round and down at the floor far below him, start to panic. His big grey eyes would fill with tears and he would shout, Rosa, Rosa! And I would dash across the room and save him and he would cling so tight, so very tight. I liked to save him.

But there was this one day when I called at the nursery and Brock wasn't there. The place was empty. The big double doors were tied up with a chain and padlock. Fear rippled through me like a bolt of lightning and I walked round the back to see if they'd left him sitting on the steps behind. But there was no Brock and the door was locked. Now, my mind was somersaulting with panic at the thought of him in his red woollen cap wandering the streets, probably being run over by a bus or a man on a bicycle. There were lots of bicycles in Coventry, not like here in the North where there are hills round every corner and bike riding is too hard.

Well, I waited there at the nursery school door for a very long time, just in case there was some mistake. Maybe all the children had been taken for a nature walk along the canal, or in the park. But no one came. Not one child, not one teacher! In the end I set off for home, really cringing at the thought of how angry my mother would be. If Charlie got a hiding for stealing two pence, what would I get for losing Brock, the apple of her eye? As I trudged along I promised God I would never, never play the sideboard game again if I found him safe.

I stood outside our jerry-built house for ages before I dared to go in. When I finally crept inside, there was Brock on my mother's knee, reading the *Beano*! She was very sharp with me for being so late. But when I told her I'd waited all that time at the locked school for Brock, she laughed out loud.

'Rosa, you're such a dilly-daydream! Don't you remember? I told you not to get him. That's the worst of that nursery being Catholic. One of their blessed saint's days. I got him myself at dinnertime.' (I remember those words like they were printed on the inside of my skull.)

The truth is she'd not told me that. I don't say very much but I never forget anything. All this boiled up inside me then. I ran upstairs and locked myself in the toilet so she wouldn't see the tears rolling down my cheeks.

Later, when Daddy came in from his factory she told him about my mistake and they both smiled and he touched my chin with gentle fingers. 'Always in a dream, Rosa.'

When the tea was cleared away my mother went upstairs to get ready for her nightshift at the local mad hospital. During this time between tea and her going to work, the air always prickled with a kind of coldness and hard feeling. She and Daddy were so cross with each other. I would listen to their loud voices from the stairs, my body hot, their anger seeping through the door and lying across me like a dark cloak. It was something about her going to work.

These days I've got to understand that she loved the hospital and her work there, far more than being at home. You should hear her talk even today (when she's in a good mood) about her work at those hospitals in Lancaster and Coventry. Sometimes she tells stories about her times there, in which she is always the heroine. She says nursing is a 'vocation', not a job. Like a nun, I suppose. But then nuns aren't allowed families. Nowadays, of course, she has to compare her vocation at the mad hospitals with the drudgery of work at the factory (which she hates), here in the North (which she hates even more). And I'm in no doubt at all that it's because of us, because of Charlie and Brock and me, that she must Bear this Cross and be so cross all the time.

On those evenings in Coventry, when she went off to catch her bus to the hospital, when the door clicked behind her, it was as though the whole house breathed out with relief. Daddy would tuck Brock away in his bed, then Charlie and I would sit on the couch, tangled up with his long arms and legs as he tried to read his papers or listen to the wireless.

Sometimes he made us porridge for supper. I can remember him standing there at the stove, always stirring. 'A pinch of salt and a spoonful of honey.' He used to say it like a nursery rhyme. When

50

we'd had our supper, he'd get tired of our clamour and give us big, tight hugs and shoo us off to bed so he could get back to his newspaper and the wireless. Later, much later, he would creep into our bedroom, tuck us in and kiss us, once on our cheek and once on the palm of our hands, which tickled. I always stayed very still and pretended to be asleep. I thought if he knew I was awake it would break the magic.

You could always tell Daddy was not so keen on Brock as our mother was. He was nice with him like he was with us, but he didn't often really touch or hug him. Now I know more about things, because of all my reading, I wonder if this was about the way he was born, with my Daddy away and everything.

I've never really worked out properly how Brock happened. I have thought maybe my mother had given birth to him in hospital and brought him home in her bag that night. There are so many things wrong with that idea but it's the only one I can think of.

But Daddy's stiffness with Brock didn't bother him. Right from when he came into our family Brock was my mother's beloved, her ewe lamb. She doesn't touch him much more than she touches Charlie or me, but you can tell. Even in these really bad times in the North, she's gone into debt so he can have a bike, and she has promised him the earth if he passes for the grammar school this year. No shin-worn-through second-hand uniform for him, I bet.

I've thought a good deal about this. Am I jealous of Brock? Never? I like him. I like to take care of him, even if I do tease him a bit. He has that shining-bright character that attracts everyone. I sometimes feel I can warm my hands on him. He cheers me up – and I can get sometimes very gloomy. Oh my, yes!

But in those months, years after my Daddy died, Brock was the only thing my mother would lift up her head for. I made her endless cups of tea, told her of my good school marks, but she'd treat me to her usual blank, dark look. When Brock came into the room her gaze would brighten a fraction. Just a fraction but it was there.

I never play the sideboard game with Brock after I thought I'd lost him on the way home from school, so I suppose that's something. He's too precious to me.

From Monkeys to Eagles

Bronwen, 1991

My mother, Rosa, is pleased, as always, to see Cali, and when we are all settled – those two with their cigarettes, me with my coffee – she reads out Uncle Brock's letter. He writes only now and then but when he does write he always has something to say. He is vaguely educational, like all of us in this family. All of his letters, (addressed to Charlie or my grandmother, never Rosa herself), are kept in date order in an old chocolate box on a bookshelf in my grandmother's bedroom.

The top of the letter is printed with his name, C. L. Carmichael Ph.D., MBA. The address is . . . 'Hotel Ukrainia'. But it was posted in London. Brock often gives a letter to a friend on home leave to post when he lands. They're still obsessed with censorship, I suppose, even now when things are supposed to be better.

Rosa reads well, her quiet, even voice not pretending to be his.

Dearest Old Boy!

Yes I am quite safe, thank you for asking. These are wild times here, with states falling away from the Union like dead flies and this false talk of a Russia-centred Federation. Not much hope of that. The States will never agree to the reformulation of the S. Union under another name. Gorbachev is an ambitious old coot in trying to push through these changes – positive as they are, from my point of view – so quickly. He'll have to watch his back.

'The Times They Are A-Changin'.' Bob Dylan, is that right, Charlie?

Anyway, I'm quite safe and – like all the Westerners here – know that the changes will work to our advantage one way or another.

I hope you and the endless Carmichael and half-Carmichael brood are OK.

As I make my way along the grey corridors of the Ukrainia hotel, past the baboushka on the corner, and settle down for the night with my new toy computer (small but perfectly formed), and my bottle of whisky, I get some pleasure thinking of you being ambushed from all directions by those kids of yours, drinking strong electrician's tea by that Durham coal fire. To be honest, sometimes I'm touched by the barest tinge of envy.

But life here has its treats. Yesterday at a party in a flat on Myakovsky Street I met a woman who's just returned from America, where her family was exiled in the seventies. She works as a translator and a 'fixer' for us Westerners who are too dumb to make our way around. A friend took me to this capsule of a flat filled floor to ceiling with books. She reminded me so much of our Rosa. All those books. This woman, Katya, was born in 1953, the year of Stalin's death at the beginning of the Russian 'thaw'. Even then, it was still not really safe to talk freely and any joy at these changes – even at the people coming out of the gulags – had to be hidden.

Things even then, she said, were still very secretive. Denunciation and secret knowledge were old habits of mind. For a while as a little child Katya enjoyed freedom, but once she joined the adult world with its secrets, freedom was gone. Up to then, she said, even in her cramped flat, a single room housing three generations, she was surrounded by books and literature, and hers was indeed a magical existence. Books here – so long as they were classics or not banned – were cheap, freely available.

For this woman, reading was the key to inner freedom.

(How like our Rosa is that?) This woman said, 'When the child reads, the grandmothers rejoice. Through literature we were transformed from monkeys to eagles. Then we could soar in the sky.' For the grandmothers the children's love of reading and literature was their hope for the future, their only value in a life that had literally been pillaged and robbed throughout a whole century.

So far, so much history.

Not much more to say personally. You asked about Louise! Still sunning it in the house in France but young Anthony will be back at college in England, although between you and me I sometimes dread to think of those proselytising monks. But Louise was very keen, and after all, I have to bow to her wisdom regarding Anthony, as I am so rarely home.

Greetings to Mother, to our Rosa, Lily and all the young ones. I have a conference in London in November so thought I might hike up to see you all somewhere near Mother's birthday. Eighty is quite a landmark.

Fraternal affection,

Brock

PS. Here is a photograph of me with Katya, my fixer. It's Red Square, of course, and the mausoleum holding the remains of Stalin are to the right although we were not allowed to photograph it.

Rosa hands me the photograph and I lean across to share it with the eager Cali. The dense, winter light has bleached out the colour and rendered the photo in sepia. Brock towers over the woman. He wears a high fur cap and his lady friend's hat (surely silver fox?) stands out like a dandelion clock in the cold air. It's hard to tell whether this Katya is young or old, and Brock's trim blond beard completes the sense that they are both somehow in disguise.

'Very *Doctor Zhivago*!' says Cali.

Rosa smiles her slight smile. 'Brock always did like to make a mystery of himself. Always in disguise. Masks when he was little and a beard from the minute he needed to shave.'

'Why's that?' demands Cali. 'Why disguise? What is he hiding from?'

Rosa laughs. Strange to say, she's blushing. 'Brock? Never. He likes to pretend to be other people. Here he looks like he's pretending to be a Muscovite. He can pick up an accent like assuming a skin, brilliant at languages. When he came back from Oxford he talked with a *plahm* in his mouth,' her own accent changes into a parody of 'posh' as she describes him, 'although he can drop back into the vernacular when he talks to our Charlie . . . So many years.' She takes the photo from me and smooths it gently with her fingers. She looks up at Cali. 'He talks French like a native because, as far as he lives anywhere, he lives in Normandy. No more nor less than a chameleon, our Brock. The international man.'

'So Brock's the favourite?' The words shoot from Cali. 'Is he your favourite? Is he your mother's favourite?'

I have to rush in. 'Cali, I don't really think—'

Rosa waves me to silence. 'Well, Brock's certainly our mother's favourite, always was. And me, I have a soft spot for him and all his adventures. Kind of vicarious travelling, I suppose. I always wanted to travel.' She shakes her head. 'We're not supposed to have favourites, but if I had a favourite it would have to be Charlie. He and I were always comrades. Always. He used to get into trouble when he was young but he's one of the innocents and they are to be cherished.' She tucks away the letter and the photo, a signal that such talk is finished. 'Now then, a meal. Any ideas, Bronwen?'

As we rub shoulders in the kitchen, rustling up a meal, I wonder at my honest mother telling a lie. A blind man on a flying horse can see that Brock – even the absent Brock – is her favourite. Cali, as she often does, has hit a nail on its head.

Dancing in the Dark

Rosa, 1954

Today, as I sometimes do when I've finished reading, I closed the curtains and pushed back the couch. Then I put the wireless on and danced. As usual I do my positions, a couple of 'pliés' and an 'entrechat', but then I start whirling and whirling to the music, making the movements up as I go along. I did this today until I got tired and flopped down on the couch. I was suddenly very hungry, so I went and made myself some toast as that was all there was. The toast was hot and I got margarine all over my hands so I had to wash them before I settled down with this ledger. I'm trying to keep it clean and true.

The dancing makes me think of my next story

1948 The Escapologist

My daddy always loved reading newspapers and was a hoarder, so his newspapers sat in the corners of the sitting room, stacked in date order, until he died. (They were all cleared out when we moved North. Three years of newspapers.) When he was at work, and my mother and the boys were out, I'd sometimes sit on the floor and work my way through the papers, being forced by fear to look sideways at the worst photographs. As well as the concentration camp pictures and dead buildings and all that, there would be pictures of Coventry as it had been, an old, old town with beamed houses and narrow streets, the aeroplane factories that made the Jerries bomb us.

Our new, jerry-built house was in a long meandering road which was half pre-war bay windowed houses, half jerry-built infill. At the top of the road was a surviving aircraft factory, the target of many of the raids.

We used to catch the Number 2 bus, which rumbled through the suburbs to the centre of town. It was full of pre-fab shops and bomb sites. But there was a bubble of excitement in the air. My daddy said Mr Churchill had promised that Coventry would be the City of the Future. Mr Churchill himself promised it. 'The old city was going to be brand new. This might seem,' my daddy said, 'to be a contradiction in terms.'

I could see all these changes on my bus journey into the city every Saturday for my dancing lesson. I loved to dance. I used to dance to music on the wireless even before I had lessons. My daddy caught me at it one day and persuaded my mother that I should have some lessons. He promised to keep Brock and Charlie by him, to help him dig over the new garden. She could go down the Crescent to do her shopping, and I would go into town to learn to dance at Miss Hathaway's dancing school.

I loved that dancing class, even though Miss Hathaway was even fiercer than my mother. She wore green trousers, smoked cigarettes through a black holder and had black hair smoothed back like a tango dancer. In spite of her I began to think that dancing was like reading: the more you learned the more you were free to make it up yourself.

So, on Saturday mornings, my mother gave me my bus fare and two shillings for the lesson. After that, she forgot all about me. Happy to be forgotten, I put my nose to the window of the bus and watched the world go by. Old. New. Old. New. Wrecked buildings and bomb sites. Windows opening on to thin air. Pre-fabricated shops. People on bicycles. A few new-built cars. I loved it. It was exciting, it was the Future.

To get to the dance studios you had to get off the bus and cross the city centre. One day, as I walked across Broadgate, my way was blocked by a crowd on a dusty bomb site. I squeezed through to the front of the people to see two men, younger than my daddy, stripped to the waist, wearing dirty army trousers and muddy boots. One of them was marching backwards and forwards in front of the crowd with a dusty sack over one hand and heavy rattling chains in the other. The other man was standing in the centre of the circle, his hands on his hips. He was not looking at the crowd. His eyes were half closed and he seemed to be looking right into himself.

The man with the sack shouted and rattled his chains. I don't know why, but I couldn't make out his words. It was as though I'd somehow strayed into a foreign country. Then suddenly the shouting man threw the sack over the other man's head and lowered him to the floor. He started to wrap and tie him in the sack, all the time shouting out these words I couldn't understand. He finished his task with a click of this big padlock and then sprang to his feet. The sacked figure lay still on the ground. The crowd went quiet.

Then the man took a watch out of his pocket. 'One minute, ladies'n'gen'lmen.' His words were clear enough now. 'In one minute Corporal Frost'll be out of those bonds. See how he escaped them Nazzies from one of the worst camps in all the war. Starting . . . now.' He kicked the inert figure and it started wriggling and convulsing. Then, one by one, the chains slipped down the body. The whole crowd breathed in and out with every movement. As the chains slackened and slipped, it came to me that the sacked figure looked like a chrysalis a teacher brought into school one day. She told us that very soon a butterfly would crawl out of it and stretch its wings and fly away.

At last the chains were off. The crowd held its breath and finally the man wriggled out of the sack and leaped to his feet. His face was dirty from the sack and there were patches of red flesh where the chains had pressed on to his skin. The crowd cheered and instantly the timekeeper started to make his way among them holding out his battered army hat. People were throwing money in. He got to me and pushed the hat so hard against my chest that it hurt. His eyes were black pebbles. I reached in my pocket and pulled out the two-shilling piece that was my dance money. He nudged my hand and the silver coin seemed to leap out of my hand and into the army hat.

My heart really thumped in my chest then! I waited till he had gone round the rest of the crowd and the people had drifted away. I wanted to tell him that I'd given him my dance money by mistake. But he and the other man were lounging now on a half–demolished wall. They seemed to have this iron cloak around them that prevented me approaching them. I was invisible to them.

Then another crowd began to gather and the man took up his sack and the chains and began shouting again.

I turned and went across the town centre to catch my usual bus home. I didn't tell my mother or my daddy what had happened in town, or that I'd not been to my dance class.

When I got to the house Charlie was wheeling Brock up and down the garden path on a sack–barrow and my parents were busy putting up a hen run. It seemed my daddy had decided we were to have our own hens and our own eggs. My mother was holding wire netting as he nailed it to a wooden framework with his big hammer. I could see the muscles in his wiry arms. They were laughing together and in the blending of their voices my mother's sounded as young as a girl's.

'Hold it steady Kate, love,' Daddy was saying. 'Hold it steady.'

I can hear that laughter even now, so many years later. Both of them. His and hers. Together.

So they barely noticed my return, and there were no questions about the dance class, or the missing two–shilling fee. I suppose I really learned something that day about the keeping of secrets. And here I am now in the middle of another big secret!

Lily

1991

When I get back from delivering Cali into the welcoming arms of Uncle Charlie at the B & B I get the usual flip of the heart to see Lily lying on her stomach on the hearthrug, turning the leaves of the *Daily Mirror*. Rosa, sitting on the couch with her bare feet tucked underneath her, is peering at the *Guardian* crossword, pencil in hand. They look up as I enter, identical looks of disinterested enquiry on their faces. Physically these two are entirely unlike each other, my mother fine-boned and slightly worn but with her pale skin and her long bobbed hair she is still attractive. Lily is beautiful, big-boned and rangy, radiating that special gloss that only youth can give. That and her father's genes, of course. But Lily is so like my mother in gesture and attitude. When she was born those two took one look at each other, fell in love, and have been boon companions ever since.

Of course, I had to go back to school as soon as Lily was born; then university, then work. My mother was still teaching then, as well as writing her books and articles, but she fitted all this round Lily without apparent strain. Rosa is a quiet person, but has always been very loving with both Lily and me, generous with her hugs and quiet words of affirmation and reassurance. We're left in no doubt that we are loved. This is strange, because my mother and her own mother, my grandmother, Kate, are very touch-me-not with each other: mild to the point of being cool.

'Hi, Mum,' says Lily, sitting up and closing her paper. 'First day back at school OK? Er, sorry, I mean university . . .'

'OK.' I nod. 'How about yours?'

She groans. 'Usual cr— rubbish. More work. Dire warnings about standards, grades. Those teachers need a dose of joy. I sometimes think they hate coming to school. Half of them are on Valium; drag themselves around the place like junkies.'

I have to object. 'You're exaggerating.'

'You'll see.'

So I will. I've managed to fix it to do the field work interviews for my research in Lily's school: how do twenty pupils from the fourth year, their teachers and parents define and think about the Second World War? Lily is vaguely embarrassed about my project but interested too. She keeps feeding me little bits of what she thinks might be interesting and was very disappointed when I told her she wouldn't be allowed to hear the tapes of the interviews. Well, not till she reaches the Age of Reason.

I step across Lily's legs and sit down in the chair opposite my mother. She closes her newspaper. 'So, you got your supervisor, then?'

'Yes. This man's from Harvard on some kind of sabbatical.'

'Trust you,' says Lily. 'Did they have to get him from America specially for you?'

'Is he good?' asks Rosa.

'I don't know. His reading list's very ambitious, if that's anything to go by. I've got a meeting with him tomorrow, so I'll have some idea then.' For a second I am back on the river-path leaning on the tree, feeling the damp bark on my back, looking across the black water at the rower letting his oars trail and glancing across and meeting my eyes.

I get back to the present to find that the atmosphere in the room has changed. Lily sits forward and clasps her arms round her knees. She glances across at her grandmother. 'Gran and I have been talking . . .' Her voice fades.

Rosa takes it up. 'Lily and I have been talking, Bron. She wants to talk to you about what people have to do to go on the Pill.'

I feel a blow on my chest, a clutching on the heart. 'Now? You're too young . . .'

'I never said I was going on it.' Lily smiles softly at me. 'But, like

I said to Rosa, you can hardly say that to me, Mum.' The fact hangs in the air, unspoken. *When you were my age I was one year old.*

'Why?' There is desperation in my voice. 'Why now, Lily?'

'I want to know how to avoid unwanted pregnancies, of course.'

'Of course. But why now? Is there . . . ?'

She shakes her head. 'No boyfriend. I don't have time.'

'Then why? Why now?' My mind's scrolling back through the young men she's known. 'Who?'

'No one. I might not be doing the practice but I want to know the theory. Everyone else is on it, Mum. That's except for Sharon Ingleton. Now she's pregnant. I wouldn't want to take the remotest risk of that.'

'I think Lily's being very sensible,' my mother puts in, and I flash her a hard look. This is too much like a surgeon's knife cutting far too near a major vein.

I turn and flee upstairs and throw myself face down on my bed. And now I'm no longer Bronwen Carmichael, briefly Bronwen Drury, mature student, teacher, mother of one, I'm Bronwen Carmichael aged fifteen who has missed her period and been sick. I have to think through what has happened before I tell my mother. I didn't cry then, but I cry now for that fifteen-year-old, that young innocent still deep inside this mature student, this teacher, this mother of one.

Lily's ring clicks as she taps my door. I feel the bed move as she sits on it beside me.

'Really, I didn't mean to set you off, Mum. I was just thinking it was all so logical. I'm not tangled up with some lad, but then neither was Sharon. Just a thing of a moment, at a party. It happens sometimes.' She paused. 'I'm quite aware that's how I came on the scene and I'm jolly pleased to be here.'

'I'm not sorry I had you, Lily. Even then I wasn't sorry.' My voice is muffled by the pillow.

'Me? I'm glad about that.' A soft hand rests on my shoulder. 'Things are different now, though, Mum. You know that.'

I roll over, sit up and pick up the pillow to dab my streaming eyes with its loose corner. 'Well, what d'you want me to do?'

'There's a clinic. You could come with me. Just to check it out. Just in case.'

I reach out and hug her tight, the pillow between us. 'Of course I'll come.'

I'm being reasonable and rational, but I recognise all this for what it is. We've come through a door. The room of her childhood is now behind us. We can peer back inside but we can never re-enter it. I suppose Rosa felt like this when she found out I was pregnant. I've never thought about that till today.

Discovery

Rosa, 1954

Crisis! A letter has came in the post from my form teacher about my absences, asking my mother to go to school and give an explanation, or send a letter with a doctor's note. Funnily enough, I now really, really feel it would be all right if I could go back to school properly without any comment, without any consequences. But that's not possible now, just to go back. So I've dug out some of my mother's letter paper and will write a letter myself. Something like this:

Dear Miss Burston,

   I am sorry Rosa has not been much in attendance this term. The doctor cannot find a valid basis for this persistent debility. He has been giving her iron tablets and these have been having an effect. So now the debility seems to be fading – no, say *receding* – and I have high hopes of her being able to return to school on Monday.

   Yours sincerely,

   Katherine Carmichael

I'll copy this in my mother's writing style that I imitate off her letters. And post it. That should do it. Now, of course, this means I'll have to finish this ledger quickly, at least up to the present, and get back properly to school on Monday. I can't believe it but I'm looking forward to going, specially doing history and English and French – I can always drop back into them dead easy. But physics and chemistry with the bellowing, nipping men! Yucagh! I blanch at the thought. But how can I avoid it? I read of this boy who cut his wrists so he needn't go to school. Maybe I'm like that but not that brave.

But somehow just this morning I can feel the energy to face them. Maybe it's because of the tick book. Maybe not. Anyway, there's only two weeks left till the summer holidays. Then, next term a fresh start with no physics and chemistry. I can drop them, glory be! As for the rest, I'll show them how really clever I am. I will.

Before that there are a few further things for this ledger.

Next Story!

1949, Mrs Walters and the End of Lushness and Love

By the time he was five years old our Brock had pulled Charlie into the magic circle that seems to surround him and our mother. When she wasn't at work she'd take Brock and Charlie everywhere with her and would call them 'my boys' to the few people she met in the street whom she knew. Charlie was three years older than Brock but she still dressed the two of them exactly alike. Of course, this emphasised how different they were – the delicate, fair-haired Brock, so tall for his age, and Charlie, so compact and dark. Charlie was a practical boy, but our Brock still kept this habit he had from when he was little of talking to people who weren't there, and playing games with imaginary friends. So when he did that our mother would call Charlie in to play with him, to get his little brother out of the habit of playing with thin air.

So when I think about those times now, I think I was mostly on my own in that jerry-built Coventry house. After Daddy had made our breakfasts and gone off to the factory I was responsible for the house. The boys went off to school together and I had to wait for my mother to come in from her night shift before I could follow them. Once she got in, pale and tired, she would hustle me off to school, keen to be on her own.

65

I was still early. In those days on the way to school I used to call for a girl called Judith Meadows, who lived three roads away from us. Usually I had to wait while Judith and her parents finished their breakfast. I sat on a chair by the wall, taking in the smell of cooked bacon and Lavendo polish, as the three of them held hands and thanked God for the privilege of fine food and good fellowship. You really felt on the edge of things in that house.

One rainy day as we walked on to school I asked Judith if she believed in God and all that, and she said yes, there had to be a Beginning of Life and Everything, and hadn't God helped us win the War? God was Love, after all. She asked me if I believed in God and I had to think about that for quite a long time. 'Well?' she said. I had to admit that although I closed my eyes and prayed in assemblies, I didn't believe in God because my mother had told me for certain that He didn't exist.

Judith hauled me to a stop there on the pavement and pulled me round to face her. It was hard to see whether it was rain on her face, or tears. She asked why not. She said she didn't know any grown-ups who never believed in God. I had to explain then that before my mother had me, she'd had twins and they'd died and she was so angry with God she didn't believe in Him any more, in spite of her sisters being big chapel people in the North.

'My mum told me she knew then there was no God. And I believe her.'

We set off again, heads down against the rain. Judith said in a very low voice, 'You should believe in Him, you know. You should pray for your mother if you love her. God is Love, Rosa.'

Love? I couldn't think of a single thing to say to that, so we just plodded on, splashing through puddles. We arrived at school soaking wet and had to sit by the radiator until we steamed dry.

A girl called Melanie Walters went to that school too. I liked her much better than Judith. I played skipping and hopscotch with her in the playground. She was taller than me and quite fat. She was often in trouble at school for being late but she took the blame with a lowered head, without letting the teacher's hard words bother her. She told me that her mother had a problem getting up in the morning and was sometimes even too late to remember to give her a note. Melanie always had sweets. She was very generous with them in the playground, which stopped her getting knocked about as sometimes happens to fat kids or poor kids, even now. Being scruffy and down at heel in recent years has led to a bit of bashing for me here in the North, I'm telling you. Name-calling is the least of it.

Melanie's mother was fat and blousy too, but very clever. I knew that because I went home with Melanie for tea after school a couple of times. The table in that house was always groaning with sandwiches and bought cakes, and there was usually jelly afterwards. It was a feast. Mrs Walters would sit at the table with us and tell us tales of when she was young in Leamington Spa after the Great War, and in a place called Caen in France in the 1930s. She could speak French and everything. (I sometimes wonder if this is why I like French so much now.) Mr Walters never showed up although he was in the house in a room they called his study that was off the half-landing upstairs. You could hear the floorboards creak and the rustling of paper overhead.

Then one day that spring I gave Judith's mother, the God-loving Mrs Meadows, a bit of a shock.

I'd been off school that day and the day before. (I was *never* off school then! I even walked to school waist-high in snow in the bad winter of 1947. Mother insisted, 'If you can walk you can work.' One of her favourite sayings.)

It was a Tuesday when I gave Mrs Meadows the shock. On Friday the week before, as I sat on the chair in her kitchen, I did wonder whether I should tell them that my daddy had been taken to hospital in the night, but it seemed a bit rude to interfere with their prayers and their family conversation with God.

By Saturday our own house was full of my grandmother, my aunts, even some strangers. Brock, Charlie and I had to sleep in one bed, top to toe. Our mother vanished from the house with our grandmother and my aunts fed us treats like cream buns and currant bread until Brock was sick. He had hysterics because our mother wasn't there and in the end Auntie Fran locked him in the bedroom, still screaming. I unlocked the door and lay on the bed with him, wrestling with him until he was still. (Auntie Fran is my daddy's sister and is not in the least like him. She smells of sour lavender, like Mrs Meadows' house.)

My mother and grandmother still weren't home when Auntie Fran put us to bed. By that time Brock had quietened down. After a bit of horseplay and too much giggling, the boys fell asleep. I forced myself to stay awake until I heard the front door click and the rattle of my mother's high heels on the hall floor. Then I crept down and sat on the stairs, listening to their voices rising and falling: my grandmother's voice was deep, almost like a man's; my Auntie Fran's light and shrill, just this side of crying; my mother's voice was clear and very cross. 'For God's sake, Fran, have you always got to be the drama queen, the centre of attention?' Then I heard the click of her heels on the lino and, touched by terror, fled back upstairs.

On Sunday the aunts from the North – my mother's sisters – arrived, and Charlie and me were sent upstairs with toys and drawing books to be quiet while they all moaned and groaned downstairs. Brock was allowed to stay downstairs on our mother's knee, like some kind of shield against all these people that were invading her house. He looked very pretty, wearing a Fair Isle jumper, which she'd knit for him herself on three long night shifts.

On Monday morning, when we were finally allowed to come downstairs, the house was eerily quiet. My mother and the rest were out. Auntie Fran was on her own, stirring the porridge. At the smell of the porridge my heart clutched in on itself and I wondered if Auntie Fran and my daddy had learned to make porridge together when they were little.

She sat us down and dribbled honey over our porridge and then said, 'Little loves, I have to tell you all something.' Tears welled up in her eyes.

Funny to see a grown-up crying. We sat watching her, our eyes wide, our spoons poised.

'Well, my loves, I'm afraid you won't see your daddy again.' The tears were flowing down her cheeks now.

'Not ever?' said Charlie, shoving a spoonful of porridge into his mouth.

I remember Auntie Fran's black curls trembling as she shook her head. 'No. Not ever. Not in this world, anyway.'

Not in this world? I thought of the sky where the Kingdom of Heaven was located, according to Judith Meadows. I put down my spoon and didn't eat my porridge, although the boys ate theirs and Charlie finished off mine. We were kept off school that day, a long weary day with lots of coming and going. I spent the day in the garden down by the hen-house, wrapped in my coat and scarf, hunched in against the sharp February wind. I looked up at the sky and thought how very, very far away the Kingdom of Heaven must be.

The next day – it must have been the day of the funeral, though no one said – Auntie Fran put me on a bus and told me to get off after five stops and look for Mrs Walters. It was all arranged. Melanie's mother was there at the bus stop, a green cloak flowing over her fat body, my friend Melanie beside her.

When I got off the bus I was clasped into the green cloak and Mrs Walters' voice was in my ear. 'So sorry for your loss, my dear.' Then, arm-in-arm we were walking briskly towards their house.

In the hallway Melanie squeezed my arm. 'A day off for me too!' she said, obviously delighted.

That day the three of us made pancakes, drew pictures, went for a long walk in the park with the Walters' ragged dog, Scruff, and even sang songs while Mrs Walters played the piano. I remember Mrs Walters sang '*Frère Jacques*' to us. Then, while she made the tea, Melanie and I played with a doll that Melanie usually kept in a cabinet, still in its box. It had three sets of clothes and we took turns at dressing and undressing it. Even then I was keen on books and had never been keen on dolls, but I remember distinctly what a pleasure it was to dress and undress this little doll. I know I thought of Brock when he was very tiny. Before I went home Melanie insisted on giving me a brand-new skipping rope with red handles. 'Mummy and me chose it for you yesterday at the shop.'

Later, as we stood at the bus stop, Mrs Walters touched my cheek. 'Your daddy'll always be there, love,' she said. 'Always watching over you.'

I remember those words even now. I looked up at the February sky but it was too dark to see a single thing.

So, to get back – it was when I was skipping home from the bus stop that I gave Mrs Meadows this big fright. She was leaning over her garden gate. I let my skipping rope lie still.

'Oh, Rosa!' she said. 'How is your father now?'

I smiled helpfully. 'Oh, he's dead, Mrs Meadows. I think his funeral was today.' I had just a glimpse of her shocked face before I skipped on.

And that was the end of it. The end of lushness and love. The end of tangled legs and arms on the couch. The end of news being read from the rustling newspaper directly into your ear. The end of the night-time kiss on the brow and the palm of the hand. Fat Mrs Walters' touch on your cheek at the bus stop on the day of the funeral was the last time anyone touched you in love. That was years ago and now you are fourteen.

Phew! I had almost forgotten that. Writing made me remember. Funny, that.

The Big Clear Out

Bronwen, 1991

My grandmother Kate Carmichael's council bungalow is as clean and clear as a nun's cell. It used to be cosy; to be honest it was really cluttered, but when she had her seventy-seventh birthday things changed. She began to gather carrier bags full of clothes, books, ornaments and leave them by the kitchen door. Then, when one of us was leaving, she'd ask us to drop the bag in the Oxfam shop in the precinct. Then, the week after her seventy-ninth birthday, she asked young Lily to come and help her. Between them they ended up with thirty-three bags of books, ornaments, clothes, kitchen utensils, tools, cutlery. These were also destined for Oxfam but Lily thought otherwise.

'Kate and I,' she announced (she could never manage 'Great-grandmother'; that's how all this Christian-naming began), 'have decided to take the stuff to the car-boot sale at Newton Aycliffe and make some profit, which will go into my bank account.'

'I suppose,' I remember taking a really deep sigh, 'the car boot involved is mine.'

'You've got it!' said Lily. 'We'll all help, though.'

And we did, even Rosa. After an hour of Lily's cajoling, she said she'd come, as it might be good copy for a story some day. It was she who packed flasks and sandwiches and patiently sat and priced every item. Lily and I did the selling while Kate held court in a garden chair clutching the money-handbag on her knee. My mother kept tidying and organising the table as the things were sold.

71

Back at Kate's, Lily added up the money and announced we'd made one hundred and eighty-nine pounds. My mother said she'd top it up to two hundred to go into the bank. Kate really objected to this, as she said it ruined the point of the whole thing. There ensued an almost wordless tussle between them, which Kate won. Lily banked a hundred and eighty-nine pounds.

In this way Kate's bungalow has been stripped of nearly everything that gives the place its identity. The bland 1960s teak furniture, bought when she moved in, betrays nothing about its owner. Her wardrobe now consists of four changes of everything, even down to knickers. She has two handbags, one in black and one in brown, a winter coat and a summer coat. On top of the wardrobe are two woolly hats and one each in black and aubergine velour. Her bookshelves are stripped except for the current library books, two dictionaries, a three-volume encyclopaedia and a bible in the King James version. The single picture and ornament allowed in each room give nothing away about its occupant. Three photographs survive. The one in the sitting room is of Lily and me when she was four years old. On Kate's bedroom table are photographs of my grandfather Rob Carmichael, handsome in his work overall, and a fuzzy bespectacled image of Uncle Brock – a tall figure in his doctoral gown with a strange cap on his head. He had a beard even then. She's so fond of him even though she sees nothing of him. But he's present in our lives in the cards and presents that he sends at appropriate times, and in the letters he writes to her or Uncle Charlie, all of which end up in an old chocolate box by the bed.

One of my errands this morning on my way to university is to bring Kate Uncle Brock's letter, as well as a shepherd's pie my mother has made for her.

The routine of Kate's days is equally stripped down. Each day she reads the *Northern Echo* and a library book; listens to Radio 4 during the day, takes a walk as far as the precinct on any fine afternoon and returns to watch her black-and-white TV at night till her bedtime at eleven o'clock. Her meals are equally simple: cereal and tea for breakfast; sandwich and tea for lunch and for her six o'clock dinner whatever dish Rosa sends round by me.

Sometimes she varies it by having the dinner at lunchtime and the sandwiches at teatime.

So my grandmother has cleverly balanced her shrinking energies into a simple life and is self-sufficient, if not blatantly happy. However, according to my mother she's never been what you might call a happy person, so no change there.

I get on with Kate far better than my mother does. My grandmother was kind, even indulgent with me when I was growing up. When my father was dying and my mother was visiting hospital for six weeks, I stayed with Kate and we cemented a kind of friendship that has endured. That time with Kate is all I remember of my father, and the smell of hospital on my mother when she finally got home.

Truthfully, there had been very little of my father in our lives. When my mother married she remained Miss Carmichael at school, and Lily and I still go by Carmichael, which is our middle name. I could suspect that my father has been air-brushed out of history, like Stalin's disgraced comrades, but knowing Rosa I just think it has been expedient.

But then when my Lily was born, Kate really fell for her and, despite the two-generation gap, they've always been very close. She's said more than once that Lily reminded her of Brock, 'who was always such a lovely kid. Very special.'

My mother heard this once and raised her eyebrows towards me. I asked her afterwards if she minded. She shrugged. 'Brock was always her favourite. Ewe lamb and all that.' Still, I could tell that she did mind.

Today Kate takes off the clingfilm, peers at the shepherd's pie and puts it into her half-empty fridge muttering, 'Your mother has a nice touch with shepherd's pie, Bronwen. I always say she turned out such a good cook because I didn't cook. Never did.' Her voice is much lighter, breathier than it used to be. Her walking is not brilliant but she totters on.

Taking credit for things, even in such a perverse way, is an old habit for Kate. She loves to tell hospital tales in which she is the heroine. She takes credit for Brock's outstanding career, citing her early advice to him to get out of the North, as there was nothing for him here. The fact that he never comes home doesn't seem to worry her a bit. She also takes credit for my mother, Rosa's, success, talking about all the sacrifices she made to put my mother through college. In fact I know she made few sacrifices as my mother won a County Scholarship and had generous grants. When I voiced this opinion to Rosa she said wryly, 'What Kate means is that I didn't go straight to work from school and contribute to the Brock fund. Of course, I did that later when I started teaching.'

Today Kate puts on her glasses and keeps me waiting while she reads Brock's letter through twice. 'That Brock!' she says, a slight smile on her face. She peers at the photograph. 'Another girl! There's always a girl, with our Brock.'

'She's his fixer – his interpreter,' I say helpfully.

She laughs at this, her face blooming into a thousand wrinkles. 'They're always called something, dear.'

I am curious about this. 'Don't you mind? Don't you mind if he . . . well . . . he has these women?'

The thin shoulders shrug under the Crimplene dress. 'Human nature, dear. His wife doesn't travel with him, a good-looking man like that.'

I have to laugh. 'That's very liberal of you, Kate.'

'Wasn't born yesterday, dear. Don't imagine your lot have invented everything.'

'Well, I . . .' I start to get up but she waves her hand and I sit down again.

'Tell me, that course you're doing at the college, what's that about? What did you say it was?'

'It's an MA in history. Research.'

'I see. Not something useful like our Brock's? Will you end up a doctor like him?'

'I might, if I keep going. If I want to.'

She sniffs. 'Get as high as you can, pet. It's the only way to get away from here. So what is this research, then?'

'Well,' I look for a straightforward way to describe it, 'it's about how people see the war.'

'The Great War?'

'No. The last war.'

She laughs at this. 'That's not history, pet, it's the here and now.'

'It's fifty years ago.'

'Like I say, here and now. History's only when people are dead.' She sniffs. 'I'll be history soon.'

'There are people in the History Department who would agree with you, Gran. About history being about dead people. And dead writing.'

'Everyone was alive once,' she says.

My hands itch to applaud. 'Exactly.'

'So what will you ask these people?'

'I'll ask how and what they know about the war.'

'And they were all in the war, these folks?'

I shake my head. 'No. Some of them were not even alive then.'

She shakes her head. 'Queer history.'

'Like I said, lots of the professors would agree with you . . . So, Kate, what would you say if I asked about the war?'

'I've told you dozens of times. Old Hitler. The bombers coming over. The news on the wireless. Your granddad building aeroplanes to beat the Nazis. The Russkis saving us on the Eastern Front. VE Day and all that. The people coming back from the camps. Despicable. And the rationing . . .'

Her voice goes on, repeating the well-rehearsed mantra typical of her generation. If my research can't break through this, it will achieve nothing. What I need is a time machine so I can talk to my grandmother as she was during the war, what was happening to her minute by minute.

Her voice subsides and after a decent silence I stand up. 'I really have to go, Kate. I have an appointment at eleven o'clock with my supervisor. I'll be late.'

'Is he any good?'

'I don't know. He's from America.'

'Yanks! Everything's from America these days.'

'Well, he's not really from America. He's from England before he went to America.'

'The brain drain? I heard about that on the wireless. Well, that's not so bad then, if he's drained back.' She hauls herself up by the arms of her chair. 'I've got something for you.' She vanishes, then returns with a bulging Co-op carrier bag. 'Here.' She thrusts it into my hand.

'Oxfam?' I say.

She shrugs. 'You can take it there if you want. But there's stuff in there – my nursing certificates, a few photos and letters, some stuff of Rosa's. It all goes back to the war.'

'Then I'd better keep it.' I say. 'Too precious for Oxfam.'

The irony was lost on her 'You might be right,' she says. 'Now, pet, if you'll just shut that kitchen door on your way out. You left it open last time and it let in a gale.'

I race down her path. I'm in a hurry now. I have to call at Uncle Charlie's for Cali, get to Durham, park the car, and get to Richard Stephens' study by eleven. It will be a race and even then I will be late.

Living in the Here and Now

Rosa, 1954

Further crisis. I did not go back on Monday. In the end I decided I should tell Miss Burston in the letter that it would be *another* week before I could go back to school. I've this children's version of Pepys' Diary to finish and return to the library. (It has this wonderful bit in it about the Fire of London.) And I want to finish this ledger. This time the letter to Miss Burston took ages to write, as I couldn't quite get my mother's script right. Five drafts! So I've had no time today yet to read or to write. But now it's done and in its envelope. I've cashed in two Domestos bottles to buy the stamp.

Now – My Next Story about a very important person.

1950 Charlie

I've been thinking I should write something here about Charlie. There's more to Charlie than getting a thrashing from our mother for stealing two pennies, even more than being Brock's chosen playmate. Right! Here goes.

For a boy our Charlie is very good-looking, but not a beauty like our Brock with his frail blond curls. (*His* hair was black when he came to us as a baby, but it turned white.) Charlie's like our daddy. He's strong, getting tall now for his age, and has this head of thick black hair like Daddy and wide blue eyes with that same downward slant of the lid that makes them both look just a bit mysterious. Or used to make Daddy look serious. Of course not now. Charlie's not, really. Serious, I mean. He's crazy for music, Frankie Laine and all that. When he hears him on the wireless he stands in front of the mirror and pretends it's him singing, him playing a guitar. His best dream is to get a record player. Our Charlie's as clear as the day and he's a gentle lad, and because of this quite easily led. He's frightened of our mother, of course. More frightened than I am, because at least I can escape into my own thoughts, into my own head, whereas he lives in the here and now.

Charlie is just as you see him, with no deception in him. But because of his naughty friends he catches my mother's wrath like a jumper snagging on a hedge. In that matter of the pennies, he was egged on then by Ferdy Smith, a big lad who lived beyond the quarry. Then there was that time in Lancaster he got trapped in one of the wrecked cars in the quarry itself. My mother clipped him on the ear and locked him in his room for a whole weekend.

The worst thing, since we've been here in the North, was when a tweedy policeman brought our Charlie back home and said he'd been caught with some other boys inside locked licensed premises.

'Your lad here was Thieving, Missis, Scrounging Around. I've Taken his Name and Address and have been instructed to Write a Report on Him and His Background.' He kind of Talked In Capitals.

The policeman was thin enough, but had that slack skin that seems like it's waiting to be filled with fat. I knew he was eyeing the cold, sparse front room of our tiny house with contempt. I was dying to shout that this was not really us, that we were only poor because our father died, that our house in Coventry had been warm and filled with furniture and was much nicer than this. That it had modern fires and sinks and things, even though it had been jerry-built.

I didn't say any of this, of course.

The policeman was clutching my brother by the shoulder. Charlie shrank, trying to peel away, to make himself invisible.

'Measures Will Have to Be Taken, Missis,' the policeman growled. 'This lad of yours is on a Slippery Slope.' He sounded like a character from one of those *Friday Night Theatre* plays on the wireless, or one of those dog-eared books you buy for pennies off a market stall.

My mother, my stout, strong mother, sat in a chair before this growling, shambling creature. I could see she was mortified, crushed by him standing in her house, in her private space. I wanted her to stand up to him, to say one of her dismissive words, to give him one of her dark, extinguishing looks. But she didn't. I was very disappointed in her. So I went and stood beside her and looked right into his watery eyes.

'Did our Charlie take anything from that place?' I said.

The policeman's slack mouth tightened. 'That's not The Issue.'

'He's only nine,' I said. 'That's not very old.'

Now I had his full attention. 'But you're not nine,' he snarled. 'You should know better than Set Up Your Cheek . . .'

'I didn't take anything,' I said. 'I wasn't there.'

I could see his hand, the one not clutching Charlie, curling into a fist. Distinctly. I saw it. I waited for him to punch me.

'You!' he exploded. 'Cheek! If you're not careful I'll get The Policewoman down to you!'

My mother looked up to me, her face white. 'Go away, Rosa! Go upstairs.' She gave me a shove. 'Go!'

Of course the policeman didn't do anything. He'd only come to frighten my mother. And he succeeded. After that she didn't speak to either Charlie or me for a whole week. Oh, she'd chatter on with Brock, though. It was like having an open sore that itched and hurt you all the time, that made you flinch at the very air. Charlie walked around for days with tears in his eyes. In the end I got down on my knees and begged her to speak to us again. Her mouth moved into a brief smile and she told me not to be silly. Of course she was not *not* speaking to us, just a bit disappointed in us. We'd let her down. After all, the police were just waiting for a chance to take us away and Put Us Into A Home. I've heard that threat more than once. But I know she doesn't mean it. For her it was all down to ending up in the Bloody North.

The Bloody North! I can't really remember just how Charlie and Brock and me got up to this North. A long-distance bus, maybe. It couldn't have been a car. If it had been a train I'd have remembered it. But I *do* know that when we travelled north my mother wasn't with us. I know we were swept up by the strange northern aunts who had been at the funeral. We stayed in their houses, which were too hot, their fires piled high with concessionary coal, the rooms cluttered with brass objects and religious pictures, the air always smelling of bleach, ashes and Lavendo polish.

The aunts made a pet of Brock and left Charlie and me to our own devices. They fed us and watered us and only paid us close attention when Charlie wet the bed we shared. They started us off in a strange school and didn't say anything when Charlie came home with a bruised cheek inflicted by a boy who told him to stop talking bloody funny like a toff. So Charlie mimicked their northern speech to save himself from the beatings and settled in at school. Nobody beat me at school but then I didn't say much, so my voice could stay the same.

I do remember that my mother came north later, in the van with the furniture. (How can I remember that, and not remember how me and Charlie and Brock travelled?) When we got to our new house the furniture van had gone and our mother was there. There was the fire burning brightly in a big iron fireplace. She greeted her sisters and, when they turned down the offer of a cup of tea, she showed them to the door. She turned and hugged Brock although she didn't touch either me or Charlie. 'Well, then!' she said, quite brightly for her. 'Home sweet home. A poor thing, but our own.'

It *was* a poor thing. It *still is* a poor thing! You come straight off the street into a front room. In the corner, high on the wall, is an electricity meter in full sight. Then you go through a door to the scullery, which has a turning staircase that leads up to two small bedrooms. Out of the back door is a square yard, in the corner of which is a privy. A zinc bath hangs on a nail on the wall.

'Where's the bathroom?' said Charlie as we came back into the house.

She shook her head. 'No bathroom, Charlie,' she said. 'We just lift the bath into the kitchen.'

'You've brought us to the slums!' I said this as a fact.

My mother gave me a really hard look. 'Not my fault, Rosa.

Circumstances alter cases.' (Another of her sayings!) 'Your father dying like that . . .' She went on then in this hard voice, about ending up with so little money that this house was all we could afford. She blamed him for dying. You could tell. And she protested that she hadn't chosen the house. The aunts had found it and it was all the money ran to.

'Didn't they know we wouldn't want to live in the slums? Did they think this was really good enough for us? Their houses are not like this.'

She frowned. 'They were only doing their best, Rosa.'

Just then Brock began to moan about being hungry and she told us she'd bought cakes and pop to celebrate being together again. The boys were happy enough and it hardly matters what I think. For me this a dark place and always will be.

Our Charlie was not half as bothered as me about being here. He liked our first school and doesn't mind the grammar school where we both go now. He likes the street we live in, where the boys always play out. He specially likes the walk across the town to the aunts' houses. To get there you have to walk a narrow path through these big mine spoil-heaps that from the first day he called 'cowboy country'. Now he goes down the heaps with friends to build camps and conduct wars between the Germans and English, dodging between the scrubby underbrush and challenging, 'Friend or Foe?'

In those early days in this house I used to dream a lot. In one dream I was sitting on my daddy's knee and he was reading to me from the paper. In another I was in my dancing class and people were clapping my 'Sugar Plum Dance'. In another I was helping my daddy to feed the hens in the hen run. Then I stopped dreaming these things – the dreams were too real and were just memories that I knew could never again be real.

I don't know whether Charlie dreamed about the old times. We never talk about these things. But he's good, our Charlie. I know he likes me and that's something for me.

End of Charlie's story.

Know the Book, Know the Man

Bronwen, 1991

Dr Richard Stephens' room is in one of the old buildings on the Bailey, the cobbled road leading off Saddler Street and on towards the river. The In/Out board by the door tells me his room is on the fourth floor. Twenty minutes late, I hare up four narrowing flights of stairs to a landing in the eaves, which has two doors, on one of which is impaled a scrap of paper with Richard Stephens' name scrawled on it in red projector pen.

I have to knock twice and wait a full minute before a voice instructs me to enter. The room is low with all the walls sloping inwards to the ceiling, but it stretches twenty feet. The floorboards creak. There is a desk under one window that's impossible to reach because of the pile of boxes scattered across the room like a mountain range. The other low window has a cushion on the sill, which is wide enough to sit on.

'I guess you lost your watch?' The drawling voice comes from behind the tallest mountain of books and boxes.

For some reason I'm more angry than apologetic. 'I'm sorry, Dr Stephens. I had to take my grandmother a shepherd's pie and then the traffic on North Road was . . .'

A head appears over the ridge, topped by red-gold curls. A muscular figure in a black T-shirt rises like a surfer breasting a wave. Grey eyes sparkle with amusement.

'*A shepherd's pie?*'

'It's an English dish . . .'

He shakes his head, the lines of his face deepening. He's older than I thought. But now that doesn't matter. My heart's still pounding.

'I know what shepherd's pie is, Miss Carmichael. I *even* know about Lancashire hot-pot.' His grin tells me he's just joking. But even so, I blush.

To ease my own tension I look around the room. 'All these boxes. Full of books, I suppose.'

'Books, files, notepaper, computer paper, a computer. You name it. I don't know whether I'm on my arse or my tip.' Now he's staring at me. 'Are you *very* busy today?' he says, his head on one side.

God, he's so attractive. If the course itself was my first adventure here comes my second. I feel it in my bones.

'Well, I'm here to talk about my dissertation, but if it's inconvenient . . .' What a stupid thing to say. I have an appointment with the man, for God's sake!

'It's most definitely not inconvenient. We have an appointment, don't we? But I'm not sure I'll be that coherent in the middle of this mess . . .' He glances round at the piles. 'You know? Difficult to focus? I wondered if . . . perhaps . . . you'd take pity on a poor expat and help me sort this mess out? Of course, if you are too busy . . .'

Neatly put. If he had demanded my help I'd have turned him down flat. 'Well, after this, I *was* going to the library . . .'

'Right, right. Find a perch and we'll talk about your dissertation in the middle of all this mess.' He sounds sorrowful, dejected. What a ham!

This makes me laugh out loud. 'Oh, come on then!' I put down my book-bag, take off my cape and push up my sleeves. 'It had better earn me a few Brownie points.'

He grins and my heart lurches again. 'You betcha! Thousands of them.' He pretends to roll up his non-existent sleeves. 'Brownie points, whatever they might be.'

The next two hours are fun. Working side by side, our shoulders occasionally touching, we get the books on to the empty shelves in author order – themed for fiction and reference – the box files on shelves, the hanging files into the cabinet, and the rather dinky

American computer set up and connected. Richard Stephens, in black T-shirt and shorts, sports socks and trainers, is better dressed for this work than I am. By the time we have finished, my jeans and sweater are veiled in book dust, my nose is smutty, my hands are filthy and my hair feels gritty.

But as we work together, although we speak very little – checking titles and the order of things – we become intimate. It is better than any conversation. I get used to the way his body turns and stretches as he reaches for a shelf; I learn that his hands are narrow, his fingers rather well manicured for a man's. Sometimes he runs his hands through his hair. I love that movement. I like the way he peers, then puts on his rimless spectacles to read the small print on the files. The way he sits on the floor cross-legged like a child to arrange his books on the lowest shelf.

He tells me about his battered copy of Graham Greene's *Stamboul Train*. 'School prize. The first intelligent novel I ever read, and the first I ever owned for myself.'

I hand him a well-thumbed edition of Jung's book on dreams.

'Do you dream?' he says.

'Every night,' I say. 'Every single night.'

'Have you ever tried analysing them?'

'I can't. They fly with the day. Do you? Dream?' I say.

'Yes.'

'Do you remember your dreams.'

He frowns. 'Yes. They're very mundane. Not worth analysing. Mostly about things I did – or might have done – with my brother when I was young.' He laughs and my heart lurches again. 'One time, when we were young and shared a bed, he woke up and told me he'd had this great dream about us being cowboys and riding through some golden hills. He told me to change pillows and I would have the same dream.'

'And did you?'

'Strangely enough, I did. We changed pillows and I had his dream.' He laughs. 'Power of suggestion and all that. Now then, Miss Carmiahcael, where do I put this copy of *The Turn of the Screw*?'

★　★　★

84

I feel sorry when it's all done, when the floor is clear, apart from a pile of box files in the corner. Despite all this book-laden intimacy now I know he'll have to sit on his side of the desk, and I have to sit on mine. But this doesn't happen. He vanishes and returns with two beakers of coffee, hands me one of them and slips down on to the low window seat, his long brown legs sprawling before him.

'Now then, Miss Carmichael,' he says. 'Where were we?'

'My dissertation . . .' I say. My heart begins to hammer again.

'You know, I looked for you on the river this morning,' he interrupts. 'I thought you might be there.'

'I told you. I went to my grandmother's to take—'

'The shepherd's pie. Yes, the shepherd's pie.' He sips his coffee. 'Do you walk by the river most mornings?'

'If I'm here in Durham. If it's fine. When it's wet I—'

'Are you married?' he interrupts again.

I frown at him. There's direct and then there's *direct*. 'No. Yes. My husband died ten years ago in the Lebanon. So no.'

He frowns. 'He was in the army?'

'No. He was a teacher there. There was a bomb.'

'Bombs. There are always bombs. I'm sorry. Were you there? Were you with him?'

'No, we never went with him. My daughter was at school.' I am calm now, angry at this catechism.

'Your daughter?' He stands up, ducking beneath the sloping ceiling. 'It must have been hard for you. And your daughter, her father dying like that.'

'He was not Lily's father. She barely knew him. Our getting together was a thing of the moment. We knew each other only two years, and one year of that he was in Beirut.'

Why am I telling this man all this? a) Because, in a second, with a glance, he has ensnared me. b) In that same second I know I have ensnared him. And c) After this morning sorting his books I am too bloody comfortable with him. You might say know the books, know the man.

'So how old is Lily?' He persists, lowering himself into the chair behind his desk.

'She's seventeen.' I watch him. Many people have that look on their face when I tell them about Lily. That counting-back look. The how-old-were-you-when-she-was-born look.

He opens the file before him and flicks through my papers. 'I like this project of yours, Miss Carmichael. Looks good. Intricate and interesting. Some flaws in the structure, but we'll soon iron those out. Have you got the permissions in the school for all these interviews?'

'All fixed.'

'And you'll get at the parents and the grandparents and they *will* talk to you?'

'I think so. I can only find out.'

'The study could fall down without that data.'

'I know that. I'll get those interviews. I will.'

He smiles broadly. 'That's my girl.' He leafs through my proposal again. 'Of course, some people here who would say this is not verifiable, not history, not significant.'

'Do you think that? You seemed to say otherwise yesterday.'

'I think it's valid. But you'll find that the data will be the least of this study. The largest part will be an argument about the validity or otherwise of oral history. You'll have to justify your approach before you present your data. Did you get my reading list the other day?'

I nod.

'Well, that's a starting point.' He looks at his watch. 'Do me an essay justifying oral history as research, then get back to me with that next week. It'll give you the basis of your introduction. And do make a start gathering the data. We'll need to keep an eye on emerging issues there.' He sounds academic, efficient, a far cry from the comrade he was when we were sitting on the floor together. He stands up, his eyes serious, a stranger now.

That's it then. I feel like lead inside. I throw on my cloak, pick up my bag, and make for the door.

'And, Miss Carmichael . . .'

I glance back at him.

'Thanks for all the help.' He pauses. 'Do you know whether you'll be walking by the river tomorrow?'

'Like I said, I come in that way if it's fine.'

'Do you ever bring a flask? So cold there on the riverbank.'

I take a breath. 'What are you saying? Are you asking me to meet you there?'

He smiles and looks me directly in the eye. My heart starts to thump again. 'Well, I'm saying if you happen to be there and you happen to have a flask it would make my day.'

Making my way down the narrow stairs and out on to Saddler Street, I wonder what I am doing acting like a star-struck teenager with this man, twenty years older than me, who one minute acts like a serious academic and the next like some lovesick swain.

I do know one thing. As my second adventure this is hitting the spot. I find myself almost skipping down the street to make my way to South Street, back to my car.

A Rare Event

Rosa, 1954

Our Brock has won his Scholarship to the Grammar School so there is something like celebration in this house. He was the only one from his junior school to go to the grammar school, just like I was. There were three when Charlie passed but, being so clever, Brock passed a year early. As a reward, my mother has got Brock a two-wheeler bike from the bike shop. On tick, of course. It's second-hand but looks new. She's got herself a night job at the dog track to make the weekly payments. You would have thought our Charlie, who has only a real old bone-shaker, would have been huffed about it but he's far too nice for that. He looked at this shining two-wheeler but didn't say a bad thing. Just clapped Brock on the back and said, 'You did good, Brock, son. Real good.'

Now about me. Because of forging the 'official' note from my mother I'm relaxing a bit this week. Not tired. I've read an English translation of *Le Petit Prince* and two Agatha Christies and a book by someone called Norah K. Strange, which is, in fact very 'strange'. There was proper 'sexual congress' in it. Made me feel all bubbly. As well as this I've looked through my French, German and history books because of my new certain feeling that I must return to the fray next week. I've not bothered with chemistry and physics (Yuagh!!) because I can't make head nor tale of them. Never could. They'll bellow at me and pinch me anyway, whatever I do.

But in spite of all this swotting I've still left time to get on with this ledger. No time to sleep now in the day, but I'm not so tired.

Today I thought my best thing was to write here about the Queen's Coronation. A Momentous Event. Like the Fire of London for Mr Sam Pepys.

The Coronation happened last year about this time. My mother, who loves anything historical, calls it history 'in the making' – a bit like the Blitz or, like I say, the Fire of London – and said we were privileged to witness it through the magic of the wireless. I've kept the *Radio Times* and all the newspapers from that week. My mother looks at my pile of papers and says I'm going to end up a hoarder like my father. But she says it sadly, without blame.

1953, A Royal Romance by Rosa Carmichael

One of my mother's reasons for coming north was that we would benefit from the support of the Northern aunts in what they called our 'moment of dire need'. They talked about the concessionary coal from our miner uncles. 'At least you never need be cold, Kate, lass.' But in the end we never seemed to get any of this coal so my mother got a gas fire because it's more convenient with her working. So now there is this constant battle to be sure we have shillings for the meter. Sometimes there are no shillings because my mother has no change. Sometimes there are no shillings at all because she has no money till payday.

Just everybody in the world was 'off' for Coronation Day. We were off school and our mother was off work. There was this big build-up in the papers and at school. Some streets had bunting. According to the paper, in some places they had permission from the ministry to roast oxen. *Oxen!* At school we even had some pictures on the wall in the history room: one showed the Queen and Prince Philip as stiff as decorated dolls. Another showed the family tree of the whole Royal Family, who in fact are mostly Germans and had to change their name in the First World War to one that sounded more English so people didn't think they were The Enemy and put them behind barbed wire.

Three kids in my class boasted that they'd be watching the

Coronation on their new televisions. I said I didn't need no television because I could imagine it all from the wireless. They smirked at that in a way I've got to know. But I turned away and left them to it.

In the morning my mother cleaned through the whole house (how rare is that?) while the wireless blared out about the crowds building up in London, and how many people had come from as far away as Australia and America to be there with hundreds of thousands of others to watch the procession. The crowds were so huge and some of them brought periscopes. Of course, we had to explain to Brock what a periscope was. My mother said if our daddy had been here he'd have made us one, just to show us how it worked. That made me ache inside but no one saw.

She cut some chips and let them stand in cold water beside the bowl of eggs. Egg and chips for dinner. Sandwich spread sandwiches and fruit salad for tea. She certainly pushed the boat out that day. It was like the Queen herself was coming to join us. On that rare day my mother was really kind of brisk and bouncing, more like her old self when our daddy was here.

Sounds came out of the battered Redifusion box in the corner and pictures streamed into our heads. In London, like here, it was wet, dripping with rain, but you wouldn't have known it. The man on the wireless said that the fairy-tale golden coach with its scarlet postilions was 'the greatest jewel of all', and talked of the 'tiptoe moment' when the crowd could see the Queen, 'radiant in her golden dress'. And he referred to the procession coming through Admiralty Arch as a 'glittering necklace of pomp'. Oh, how you could just see it. The anointing with oil of 'oranges, roses, cinnamon, musk and ambergris' – those words stick in your mind. They make a poem, don't they?

Brock asked what ambergris was, but none of us knew, not even our mother. I looked it up in my daddy's old dictionary, the one we still use. 'A wax-like substance of ashy colour found floating in tropical seas, and as a morbid secretion in the intestines of a sperm whale.' I think that is wonderful. Like I said, the words stick in your head.

By the time I was setting the table for our dinner we were up to the Queen being crowned with St Edward's Crown. Three hundred years old! 'A priceless object,' the man said. And in the Abbey the Queen was wearing a cloak of cloth of gold. Just think of it. It just felt like the edge of that robe was touching us here in our living room.

We sat down and ate our egg and chips and Brock had egg yolk dripping down his chin, which my mother wiped off with her apron.

The crowned Queen was just coming out of the Abbey when we ran out of gas and the fire died. The room was instantly cold, reflecting the grey world in the street outside. My mother said the problem with gas fires was that there was no residual heat. 'Residual.' Only she would use that word. She looked at her purse and shook her head. Nothing.

On the wireless there was another man's voice now, describing the Blues and Royals riding with the Queen's coach, their uniforms glittering, to the cheers of the crowd.

'Oh, Rosa, make us a cup of tea,' my mother said. 'Good job the cooker's electric. And we can always put our coats on.'

So we ended up that afternoon clustered round the wireless in the corner with our top-coats on, oblivious of the mean, cold room, munching sandwich spread sandwiches. It was wonderful. We warmed ourselves on pictures streaming into our heads from that small brown box in the corner, of a fairy gold coach making its way through the crowds of posh folk following on in coaches with their hoods down against the rain. But there was this other great queen, Salote of Tonga, standing up uncovered in her coach, acknowledging the crowd. There were sailors lining the route, the powder-white on their hats softening and dripping down to stain their smart uniforms.

I can see it all now.

When things slowed down after tea the boys went out to take turns riding this old bike that Charlie had bodged together from two older ones, and my mother sent me across the town to one of my aunts, to borrow half a crown.

When I got there, to this hot house where you fall over furniture all the time, it was full of friends and neighbours, there to watch the Coronation on the new television. The sideboard was covered with all these empty plates and a single left-over meat pie. They must have had a great tuck-in.

'It was great, Rosa,' said my cousin, a boy I never much liked. 'Yeh shoulda seen it! Television. Nowt like it.'

'I saw it,' I said.

'Yeh didn't,' he said. 'Yeh dinna have neh television. Yeh're scratchin' poor.' His face was looming, like the boys' faces loom at school.

My aunt's face was as blank as a sheet of paper. She held out her hand palm up. The half-crown glittered.

'I saw it! I tell you I saw it,' I shouted at him. I grabbed the half-crown from my aunt's hand and fled. As I made my way back through the slag-heaps that Charlie called 'cowboy country' I wondered whether the auntie had invited us to watch her television. My mother wouldn't have told us if she had.

In any case, I was really pleased we spent the day at home all together. It *was* a bit chilly there but the pictures were much better.

I see from my pile of papers that another thing happened that day. Edmund Hillary and Sherpa Tenzing Norgay climbed the highest mountain in the world. At least we weren't the only people suffering from the cold on Coronation Day.

Uncle Charlie's Banjo

Bronwen, 1991

Cali catches up with me at the end of South Street on my way to the car.

'I hoped I'd catch you here, Bron. I need a lift again.'

I'm pleased to see her, to feel her blast of normality. My head is spinning with images of the low attic study, the boxes of books, and the proximity of the rower Richard Stephens. I open the car door and throw in my bag.

'So, where to today, Cali?'

'Back to your Uncle Charlie's. Nothing doing in the town as far as rooms go, so I rang him and booked his room for the term.' She smells of patchouli slightly overlaid with hops.

Her decision really surprises me. Uncle Charlie and Auntie May and their cluttered house are as uncool as you can get. A week staying there will choke Cali Vax. I try to tell her this.

'Surely, Cali, the B & B's full of fourth-grade reps and . . . well . . .' I put the car into gear and gun the engine.

'Bronwen Carmichael! You snob! Your own uncle.'

She has me on the back foot. 'It's not that at all. I love my Uncle Charlie. I just can't imagine you there in that house, Cali. At Uncle Charlie's! And what about getting to college? I know there's a stop in the road there but the bus is slow. I suppose I could give you a lift, but I usually go in at the crack of dawn and that wouldn't suit you. And this term I'll be working from home a lot anyway. You couldn't rely on me.'

'No probs, darling. The bus was OK this morning. In any case,

I met this guy in the Union today whose mate is selling his motorbike, so I'm buying it. It's a battered old thing, so it won't get pinched.'

I don't need to ask. *Of course* Cali can ride a bike! She can drive a car. She can even pilot a plane. She might not have a seventeen-year-old daughter but she's done quite a few things in the last seventeen years. She has had her adventures. 'I just can't imagine you there at the B & B, Cali.'

'I like it there. Charlie says he'll put me a work table under my room window.'

This sounds impossibly romantic for Cali and I can't think of anything to say. My silence drives her on.

'I do like him, your Uncle Charlie. Do you know he made the most divine lasagne last night for my supper? Did you know he was a great cook?'

'Well, I know he's better than my mother and me. She says that all we cook is the books. All she can do is a few Durham dishes she learned on a WI course.

'And he has this wonderful collection of sixties 78s *and* this dinky player with a needle that he plays them on. Oh, yes, he's cool.'

'Mmm. He's obsessive about those records. Lily calls him a proper anorak.'

I can feel her turning to look at me, very hard. 'I'm surprised at you, Bron. Not like you to sneer. And did you know he plays the banjo?'

'Oh, yes. He just messes around . . .'

'No. He doesn't mess around. He plays. He told me one time he "used to mess around". Then when he came out of the factory he started to play properly with this group of guys. One of them plays the ukulele. Can you credit it?'

I just have to shake my head. It's news to me. 'They perform, these men?'

'Well, not really. They get together and play. They do an odd gig as a favour. Charlie played one of their sets for me and I got out my penny whistle and we played together till the early hours.'

I can't quite imagine it, those two playing in that cluttered house. 'I bet Auntie May liked that,' is all I can manage.

'She was in bed. She knew nothing about it.'

I bet she does, but I don't say that. I just drive on.

Now Cali starts on about missing me at lunchtime. 'Left me high and dry in the Union, you cow.'

'Well, I suppose you were sitting in the corner like a shrinking violet?'

'Of course not. I had a great time, as it happens. So many nice young things looking for the . . . er . . . mature point of view. That's how I got to know about the man with the bike, so all was not lost. Of course, they look at me like I've just landed from Mars.'

We've talked about this before. It seems to me that the young undergraduates view us with amusement. They think anyone over twenty-two's an old trout. It's not surprising. They seem very young to me. After all, some of them are only six months older than Lily.

When I said this to Cali she told me to speak for myself. 'Some of us didn't join the adult world quite as soon as you, darling.'

Now she fiddles with her cigarettes, then puts them back into her bag. 'So, my darling. What kept you, what made you stand me up?' She's very tenacious.

One part of me would love to tell her in detail how my meeting with the rower had set my head spinning; how somehow there was recognition between him and me that was not just about time and place; how I came out of that low room more alive than when I went in. How I know – I just know – it's not just me. That he feels the same. Ironic that I think her impossibly romantic about Charlie and his B & B.

I just say, 'I had the meeting with Stephens. About my project.'

'Well, I had a meeting about my project with the divine Dr Devine but that lasted half an hour, not two and a half hours.'

'I stayed to help him sort his books. They were all in shipping boxes. Thousands of them.' This sounds so lame and defensive that I am annoyed with her for making me feel this way.

'I'm sure he was very grateful,' she said, fiddling with her cigarettes again.

'For heaven's sake, Cali, have a cigarette, will you?'

'Great! You're a doll.' She sighs with relief and makes a great business of lighting her cigarette. 'So what's he like, this Lancashire Yank?'

'He's OK. Cool, though. He was wearing shorts and a T-shirt.'

'Crikey!'

'It was hot in there, right up in the eaves.'

'You weren't tempted to strip off yourself? To make him feel more at home?'

I have to laugh, 'You are so predictable, Cal.'

She takes a deep drag on her cigarette and fills the car with smoke. 'You don't understand, darling. It's my great mission in life to see my favourite Miss Icy-pants melt.'

My lack of involvement with any man has been a great puzzle, even a challenge, to her in the six months we've known each other. She once told me she'd wondered whether I might prefer women. But then, according to her, her delicate antennae, darling, told her otherwise. If I had been that way inclined she might make a bid for me herself. So she decided to settle for pure friendship and consoled herself that at least it lasts longer than passion.

Now I say defensively, 'It's nothing like that, Cal. It was just strange, being up there in the eaves with a half-naked man.'

'Did you find out anything about him? How old is he? Does he have a family?'

'I found out that he's interested in dreams, quite likes Renaissance painters and has a weakness for British fiction and American thrillers. And that was just from sorting his books.'

'And you know he likes to keep fit, or else why would he row in the dark of the morning? So how old do you think he is? Forties? Fifties? Sometimes hard to tell with the ones who work out.'

'You talk some rubbish, Cali.'

'And weren't there any photos of wife and kidlets?'

'No. But that doesn't mean there aren't any.' In fact I had looked for evidence of such things and there weren't any images except one of him up a mountain somewhere, clutching ski-sticks. He was wearing a ski hat and sunglasses and was almost unrecognisable. He said, 'How did that get there?' and took the picture from me and put it in the back of a filing cabinet.

'Go on, Bronwen. Say! Do you like him?'

'Sometimes, my good woman, you not only sound like a teenager, but make the mistake of thinking I'm a teenager too.'

'Sometimes, Bron, you sound like a crabby old dame who needs a good seeing to.'

To my great relief we are at the B & B. I turn off the engine. 'Sometimes, dear Cal, your vulgarity becomes you. Sometimes it make you seem like a sad case.'

She leans over for her bag, then kisses me hard on the cheek. 'Are you coming in?'

'No. I'll leave you in Charlie's good hands.'

My uncle is there at the gate, grinning and waving. He's not wearing his usual corduroys. It looks as though he's treated himself to a rather sharp pair of new denims. He's obviously been looking forward to seeing Cali again. It crosses my mind that she should have a safety warning pinned somewhere about her person. Probably to her knickers.

It's a relief to be away from her. Sometimes my friend and her insistence on intimacy can be very wearing. Despite the pressure to do so, I've never been tempted to tell her about the odd encounters I've had with men since Jacob died in Beirut. She'd have made me suffer a lot of teasing about the clever, very married headteacher whom I'd met in secret over five years. There would have been much speculation round the fact that our relationship ended when he saved his wife's life in a house fire. And Cali would have gone to town about the beautiful builder with whom I had the greatest fun, but just that. In truth there had been no one really, since Jacob, except Lily and Rosa. For Cali that is, I know, very stick-in-the-mud.

When I get back to the house my mother's out at a Labour Party meeting and Lily is in the dining room where she has covered the table with postcards, sketchbooks, bits of fabric, paints and crayons (all material from her trip to Paris with the school in November), with which she's creating a very elaborate collage. I sit and talk to her about this for a while, but I can tell that she wants to get on, uninterrupted. My mother has this quality too – an occasionally intimidating self-sufficiency.

97

I drift off upstairs to peer into the dark little study at the back of the house, my mother's workspace. The room is crowded with bookshelves and papers, the table with the pile of drafting paper and her electronic typewriter, her new word processor beside it. I straighten her curtains, then close the door tightly behind me, feeling guilty for spying.

I make my way back down to the kitchen, intending to assemble some food for me and Lily. In the doorway of the kitchen I kick over the carrier bag I dropped as I came in, the bag Kate gave me this morning. Abandoning any idea of food, I take the carrier back up to my bedroom and place it on the bed. I pull out the certificates and the photos and lay them side by side. Then there are some letters with a West Indies postmark. The last thing to come out is an old-fashioned long ledger that smells of time and damp. Scrawled on the front in black capital letters is says, 'The Life and Times of Rosa Carmichael'.

Times. Time. I know about this. I'll start here.

Facing up to It

Rosa, 1954

Another crisis. It's Monday and I'm ashamed to say, despite my good intentions, I'm still here in the house! Last week I thought for certain that I'd be back properly to school and face it all out. But I couldn't manage it. I pressed my skirt and I put my socks through two washes and dried them on the mantelpiece above the gas fire. I brushed my hair really hard to get the tangles out. I put my pencil case and jotter into my empty satchel.

Then, when the boys left for school I looked round the empty house, my safe haven. And the thought of going out of the door, and walking the half-mile up the hill to school became impossible. *I could not face it!* So I put down my satchel and rooted in the back of the sewing machine drawer for my secret stash of shillings, acquired through judicious raids on my mother's purse and exchanging old pop and Domestos bottles at McAllan's for money.

I put a shilling in the meter and turned on the gas fire. I made myself some toast and sat down to read *Mrs Miniver*, which I've just now finished. Then the sun came out and I turned off the fire and came back here on to the back step to write this ledger. I printed on the back, 'THE LIFE AND TIMES OF ROSA CARMICHAEL'. Like Samuel Pepys.

The yard walls are high here, so no one can see me. I've rolled up the sleeves of my school blouse so I can catch the rays of bright June sunshine. In the yellow light the uneven dusty bricks which floor the yard cast narrow shadows like graph paper. On my right is the coal house, now redundant, filled with buckets and brushes and now Brock's new bicycle. Beyond that is the privy, which is my mother's eternal shame. I occasionally hear her muttering furiously, 'In-this-day-and-age . . . In-this-day-and-age . . .' I sometimes think the privy is why she never lets anyone over the threshold. I've always wondered why the aunts couldn't get us a house with a proper toilet. Perhaps the privy is their revenge on her for going away and trying to better herself. 'So are the mighty fallen!' There'll be some phrase like that in their Methodist hymn books.

As school is very much on my mind today I thought I'd write about teachers I have known. So, not quite a story but a comment about

The Great Profession!

There was the headmistress of my junior school in Coventry, Miss Brown. She had these bright blue eyes, was tall as a birch tree and always wore pearl grey. One day, new to the school, I was walking along a narrow corridor and found my way barred by Miss Brown, who was talking to an older girl. The only gap was between them so I made myself very small and crept through that gap. A large hand grasped the back of my jumper and hauled me back.

'Manners! Manners!' she boomed. 'What's your name, child?'

'Rosa Carmichael.'

'Well, Rosa Carmichael, it's the worst of manners to crash through people like that.'

'There was no space to go round, miss.'

'In which case you catch the eye of the people concerned and ask to be excused before you go through.' She sent me right back down the corridor with instructions to return and excuse myself before I went through. I did this and slipped behind her as she continued talking to the big girl. I suppose I learned something that day. I've certainly excused myself to people a lot of times since then.

Then there were two of the teachers at the junior school here in the North. One was Miss Johnson, who was tall and thickset. Her face was always slightly red and she kept her black hair under a hairnet. She told us once that she was born with the century, which I thought was a wonderful thing to say. I had always read any book that I could get hold of, but she showed *Piers Plowman* to us, and Lamb's *Tales from Shakespear*. She made us learn Keats' 'Ode to a Nightingale' by heart and that became my party piece when my mother wanted a bit of entertainment. 'O blithe newcomer . . .' Miss Johnson loved words and language and spent too much time on all that kind of thing, rather than teaching us the tricks to pass the scholarship.

The honour and the privilege of being judged in the top fifteen per cent of all eleven-year-olds in the whole country faded when I encountered The Grammar School. I must have been clever then because I went straight into the top stream. But everything at this school felt like trouble. The assemblies are noisy and very long, and when I first went I kept fainting in the middle of them. The senior mistress kept asking me what I had for breakfast and I kept saying toast, which seemed to make her very annoyed and she told me I should have a proper breakfast. 'Tell your mother to give you eggs. Porridge . . .' The 'porridge' made me think of Daddy. I swayed again and she pushed me roughly down on to a seat. How could I tell her there was only bread in the house? That my mother went out at seven fifteen and that it was me who made the toast for my brothers?

In my third week the same angry senior mistress hauled me out of the corridor into her room, got hold of the collar of my blouse and demanded what did I think I was wearing?

'It's a blouse, miss.'

She pushed me so I nearly fell. 'Don't be cheeky. Uniform is white blouse. That blouse is nearer brown. Don't come back here wearing that. White, Rosa Carmichael. White.'

The blouse was one of a pair sent over by one of the aunts who, in a rare burst of generosity, had had them made up from a length of cloth she had lying around. They were a shade of pale biscuit, but my mother said that would never be noticed and, anyway, beggars couldn't be choosers. That night, though, when I told her of my humiliation at the hands of the senior mistress she was very angry. She took the blouses and tore them into shreds and didn't speak to me all night. It was as though it were my fault.

They aren't all bad at my school. The French teacher is a clever, gentle man, who manages to teach us French entirely in French, which makes him a genius. The German teacher is a big bluff man who looks German with his short-cropped hair and tells us funny tales of his student days in Germany before the war. He makes Germans human to us, which is also clever, because nobody really likes the Germans, what with the war and all that. The English master is very handsome in spite of wearing glasses, and reads poetry like an actor on the stage might read it, which I like. He once wrote on one of my compositions, 'Good syntax'. I looked that up. It means the way a language is structured. I like that. Being good at that.

But now, in your third year, you have to endure those nasty science teachers who pile meaningless fact on meaningless fact and lose you in three sentences. They shout, they pinch, they look at you like you are stupid. You are afraid of them. More afraid than you have ever been in your life. You wish, wish your daddy were here to tell them where to get off. Them and the boys who call you Medusa. Medusa the Gorgon.

THAT'S IT THEN. TOMORROW I DEFINITELY GO AND FACE THEM. I WILL.

It's boiling hot out here in the yard. You can smell the privy and the chickweed that grows in the cracks between the bricks. There is bleach and steam in the air. Washday Monday in other people's houses. My mother doesn't do washing that often.

I've just been reading through this ledger. This old tick book. Not exactly Samuel Pepys but it's a funny kind of life I've had, when you think about it. As I was reading through the pages here I started to cry. Great tears plopping on to the paper, making the ink run. I cried for my daddy, and I've never cried for him before. I think, as well, that I cried for me. Funny, that, sitting out here on my own, crying. The page is blistering with my tears. I quite like that.

But now I've made up my mind properly to go back to school tomorrow. I'll do it. I'll grit my teeth and do it. The exams are over and there's only a week or so to go until the summer holidays. Next year I can drop the sciences and those bellowing teachers. From a great height if possible. A clean slate, that's what I'll have.

AND THEN I'LL SHOW THEM!

Part Two

Modern Times

Landing Stage

Bronwen

My grandmother Kate always says I'm 'backwards in coming forwards'. But the morning I met Richard again by the river I have to say I felt very forward. I found myself putting a flask of coffee in my book-bag alongside my notebooks and Rosa's ledger, now protected — like the treasure it is — in bubble wrap.

I had spent the night before poring over the photos, the letters and ledger from Kate's carrier. I was in tears at the thought of the young Rosa battling her way unseen through what looked like a nervous breakdown. Nowadays there are lots of theories and ideas about truancy and school refusal, but then, then they were all in the future. I was amazed — although I shouldn't have been — at Rosa, so young, being able to express even her terrible experience with such beautiful power and restraint. I was amazed at this image of Kate, so vengeful and so unthinking, even uncaring. I was intrigued by Rosa's tale of Brock. And this Cy. Who was he?

When Rosa came upstairs to ask if I cared to join Lily and herself in a bit of supper, I moved quickly to the door, not wanting her to see the things spread out on the bed. It was hard to know why I did this. But I felt some kind of betrayal in the air. One set of secrets was begetting another.

As we went downstairs I watched my mother's straight back, her long, well-cut bob. Just who was this person? Never again would Rosa be the familiar, tranquil woman, briefly married, teacher of children, respected writer of stories, occasionally somewhat distracted: a transparent, easy-to-read person. No, this person was a holder of secrets and was a secret in herself. I saw, deep inside her now, this distant child Rosa, younger even than Lily, battling against a hard world, dealing with her mother's dark character and her own depression. And writing all that down. The sheer loneliness of it was almost too much to bear, even at this distance. I gave her an extra hug at bedtime and she looked rather confused.

Driving to Durham the next morning I began to focus on what I had learned, not just about Rosa, but about Kate, from both the ledger and the letters: Kate in her thirties, little older than I myself was now. Those sweet letters from the Canadian or Trinidadian, whoever he was. The poignant poem that Kate had written out on the hospital paper. The wasteful, regretted death of Rob. And such anger. So much anger.

And at the centre of it was the puzzle of Brock, the child who had turned up in the middle of the night and lodged himself right at the core of Rosa's family. He couldn't be Kate's own child. But just who was he? Who is he? I know I saw him once when I was very small, but can't remember any details of a face or a figure. All I know are fuzzy photographs. Always with a beard of one kind or another.

I've heard Kate laugh about this. 'Always in disguise, our Brock, even when he was little. Pretending to be Batman or Zorro or some Arab sheik. Would only look at himself in the mirror if he had something on his face.'

I thought of the *Dr Zhivago* photograph that arrived with this week's letter from Moscow. Who was *that* man? Of course he was my Uncle Brock, the one who wrote the letters. He's Rosa's lively, clever brother; Charlie's beloved Brock. According to Kate he's the child who heard voices and could speak in any tongue. He's the clever one who really became something in the world, an example to others. But Brock is something else, something unknown. Perhaps he is the son of the Canadian? What on earth had Kate *done*?

And, I thought, as I settled down on a seat by a river landing, what on earth am I supposed to do about it all? Did Kate realise what it was she'd handed over to me, or was it really just another bag of clutter to be stripped out if her diminishing life? You had to watch Kate. She might play the old woman but she was sharp and clear. Nothing around her happened by accident.

The morning was dry and fine but still very cold, the surface of the water veiled in limpid mist. As Richard Stephens' boat clicked against the battered boards of the landing, all thoughts of Kate vanished from my mind. Here we go again, I thought.

He had a sweatband round his thick hair and, despite the cool morning, his neck and upper arms glowed with sweat. He tied up the boat, took a thin sweater from a sports bag in the bottom of the boat and pulled it on over his singlet and shorts. Then he came across to sit beside me, his trainers squeaking on the boards. I could feel warmth and energy flow from him.

His face split into a grin. 'I guess you forgot that flask?' he drawled.

'Well, you guessed wrong!' I dipped in my bag for my flask, poured steaming coffee into one plastic cup for him, one for me. I handed him the cup and our fingers touched. I knew then I was not mistaken.

He took a sip and breathed a deep sigh of satisfaction. 'Nectar,' he said. 'Pure nectar.' He handed me the cup and I turned it round and took a sip myself, avoiding where his lips had touched. I had a wild unbidden thought that this was the first of many intimate gestures between us, vibrating into the future. He was watching me closely, his face hawk-keen, redder-skinned and older after his early morning labours.

I handed him the cup.

He took another great gulp and emptied it. 'I should thank you for your efforts yesterday, Miss Bronwen Carmichael. You made a real difference. "After the chaos, the order." Now at last I feel at home. It's been quite a leap. Can I call you Bronwen?'

It was an old-fashioned courtesy: perhaps as much American as a mark of the age difference between us. I nodded. 'Only here,' I said, meaning: only when we are like this, alone together. He stared at me and I knew he understood.

I poured more coffee and started to sip it. 'How long have you been across there, in the States?'

'Nineteen, twenty years, man and boy.' He stared at me for a moment. 'Cards on the table, Bronwen. My whole life is across there. I qualified there. My dear wife, Maria, I met her there. I have a house there, and a hut out in the woods where I go to write. I'll be going back there at the end of this sabbatical.'

My dear wife. Unambiguous. 'There is just you? You have no children?'

'O-oh, yes. My two boys are just in college.'

I took a breath. 'And will your . . . will Maria join you here?' I cared about this even if she was *my dear wife, Maria.* There would be no adventure with her around.

'I shouldn't think so,' he said. 'She's a very busy woman. Has a real estate business there, and then there are the boys.'

I suppose I should have felt guilty at the relief that flooded through me but somehow I didn't. 'So how old are they, your sons?'

'Nineteen.'

'And the other one?'

'Nineteen,' he grinned.

'Twins, then. Are they identical?' I felt myself blushing. 'I'm sure everyone asks you that.'

'Yeah, they are. Monozygotic. Single cell. As a matter of fact I did my undergraduate dissertation on the history of twins.'

I frowned. 'To be exactly like another person! How strange that must be.' It was a relief to be talking about something like this, at one remove from the burning immediacy of us sitting side by side in the chill of the early morning. And the ghost of *my dear wife, Maria.*

'Part of one's taken-for-granted life. One's world view.'

'Well, I can see that being their father you'd know that.'

'I'd know on my own behalf. I'm a twin myself.'

Now I was doubly fascinated. 'And your own twin, is he in the States too? Does he teach too?'

He laughed at this. 'Hardly. I wish he were. I miss him every day. No, Pete's a very wise guy but the academy is not his thing. He lives up a hill in the Lake District, not across "the pond". And I miss him. I really miss him. That's one reason why I agreed to take this sabbatical. To see him.'

'What does he do across in the Lake District? Is he a scientist, a teacher?'

He laughed. 'Pete would howl with laughter at that. He climbs trees. He works for the Forestry Commission. His wife's a farmer.'

'And does he look like you?' (That same crass question.)

He laughed. 'Well, except for the hard hat and the steel-capped boots, I suppose he does.' He stretched out his legs before him and looked at his sock-less feet. 'You can make up your mind for yourself. I guess I'll have to take you there one weekend.'

It was an odd thing for him to say, but it made me relax. He was telling me this was not just about now, today. We both knew that. I had never been so certain of anything.

The day lightened; the rake of birdsong was competing with the wind in the trees and the distant sounds of traffic on the bridge.

I poured him some more coffee. 'I wondered if I might ask you something.'

'About Pete?'

'No. It's about my research.' I hesitated, shy suddenly at mentioning Rosa. 'I've been given this journal thing . . . a kind of personal diary by a fourteen-year-old girl. It was written in 1954, but it casts back to the war years.'

'Is it a publication? A transcription?'

'No. It's the real thing. Handwritten in a kind of account book. I wondered whether I might use it somehow in my dissertation. It's retrospective, I know. But no more retrospective than will be the case with the people I'll be interviewing.'

'Your idea is to cite this diary as evidence?'

'I can't quite see that. It's so personal.'

'The things the people will tell you in interview are all personal. The personal is the political is the historical. The thing that's important here is *the way* you will treat their world-view as evidence. Something about respect.'

'Well, this writer does mention a lot about the war. The home front – even though it's across in Lancashire, not round here. She talks about school, in the war and in the years after the war. There's an amazing perception of the Coronation, for instance. And there are some letters as well. Images.'

'Is this person still alive?'

'Very much so.'

'In that case it's all a matter of verification. Interview the writer, and anybody she mentions. Burrow underneath the material to get multiple points of view. It could be that you might use this data as a little case study, to illustrate the first part of the research where you justify the way you're writing this?'

Even as he spoke I wondered whether I should have brought up this thing about the tick book. How could I burrow like this into Rosa's life? Into Charlie? Into Brock? How could I set about cross-referencing Kate's view with Rosa's? What kind of betrayal was that? What was I thinking of? I was beginning to think perhaps I'd just brought the ledger along as some kind of trophy, so I could talk to Richard Stephens about *something*.

'Do you have it? Can I see it?' he said quite urgently.

It was burning a hole in my bag. 'No,' I lied. 'I don't have it here. It's at home, I don't have permission to use any of it yet. I just thought I'd ask you.'

Richard moved the flask and cup to the end of the bench and eased himself across so that our shoulders were touching. I could easily have moved away but I didn't. His shoulder burned against mine. On the river in front of us another rower was cutting his way through the water, head down.

'Well, now, Bronwen. What about this?' he murmured. 'What about this thing that's happened here?'

'I don't know . . .' But I did. I wanted him on any terms. Even with *my dear wife, Maria* hovering around us in space.

He took my left hand and peeled off my white woollen glove. 'As I said, Bronwen, cards on the table. You know all about me. We both know it's complicated. And I have to tell you I don't ever do this kind of thing. Never. But the weirdest thing. I have to tell you I've never stopped thinking about you since Monday, when I first saw you here on the riverbank wrapped up in your scarf. I nearly telephoned you twice. It's like I recognised you standing there,

110

leaning on that old tree. Like I dreamed you up, somehow. Or I knew you from another time, another place. Like I say, I never do this, but now this has happened.'

I let my hand lie in his. Things were moving very fast. In one part of my mind I could hear Cali sneering about predatory tutors but that's not so here. I knew it. In another part of my mind I considered my own certainty about these events: at the way they all somehow fitted together to lead in one direction; about my sense of this as my second adventure. Recognition. That was it. I knew I felt the same as he did. Richard Stephens had been on my mind since I first saw him. I had even been prepared in some mad way to sacrifice Rosa's secrets to make a connection with him.

I have to admit the first real gesture was mine. I put up my other, still-gloved hand on his face, turned it towards me and kissed him, not opening my mouth, but pressing my warm lips on his cold ones, feeling the roughened, cold flesh of his face against mine. He put his arm around me and pulled me to him, and this time we kissed properly, eagerly learning the contours of each other's face, the softness of each other's mouth. Then we could hear the splashing of another boat on the river and the shouting of a coach careering along the riverside path towards us on his bicycle.

We wrenched ourselves apart just before the bicycle ground past us. Richard leaped to his feet, untied his boat and clambered aboard. He pulled off his sweater and tucked it into the sports bag. Using his oar, he pushed away from the landing and settled down in the boat. He looked at me and winked. 'Thanks for the coffee, Bronwen. As I said, it was pure nectar.'

I smiled faintly, my eye following at the streaming wake of his boat as his oars struck the water cleanly, decisively. What with Rosa's journal, Kate's letters and Richard Stephens, the tectonic plates at the centre of my life were certainly moving. I'd never kissed a man unasked. As well as that, I had lived a long time under the illusion that I knew everything about my own mother and my own grandmother.

I picked up my book-bag and stood up, thinking I needed to

go to the Royal County for breakfast, and gather my scattered thoughts. I wondered if Cali would be there, ready to take up the tease about Richard Stephens. That didn't worry me now. Any excuse to talk about him, however obliquely, was welcome.

Running in Marble Halls

Cali was there in the Royal County, stirring the tea in the big silver teapot. She poured me some, before pouring one for herself. Rather disappointingly, there was no teasing about Richard Stephens. She launched into how good a time she was having at Uncle Charlie's and how, despite herself, she envied me my family.

Her own notion of family, she went on (repeating something I already knew) was somewhat limited. At fifteen she had run away from her parents – a retired Baptist minister and a science teacher 'of implacable and unendurable domesticity'. Since then she'd never lived as part of any family, unless you counted her squat-commune in the eighties. But here she was, enjoying the warm welcome and informal style of Charlie's home.

She'd learned so much in the few nights she'd been at the B & B, much of which I didn't know. Most of the guests – reps and transient skilled men serving the local factories – occupied the upper front rooms that faced the main road. Cali's privilege, as what May now called 'our permanent Pee Gee' (she'd got the label from a story in *Woman's Own*), was to occupy the large room at the back, overlooking the fields and villages of South Durham.

May's relations – Charlie's stepfamily – bridged three generations, and came and went at idiosyncratic times through the week. May was fully occupied by this lively crew while Charlie was relatively untouched by them. His contribution was doing the major chores such as vacuuming right through the house, cleaning windows and making breakfasts and an occasional dinner. May's favourite thing was to go to the cash-and-carry, to Stock Up.

'So Charlie,' Cali concluded, 'can concentrate on his passion for music, which is mostly consummated in the shed – a long stone place out the back. It was stables once, d'you know that?'

As we stood up to go my mind went back to the Charlie Rosa talks about in her tick book: the little boy who made do with an old bike he'd built himself and did not begrudge his little brother a much grander nearly-new one. Cali accepted my offer of a lift and, after I'd picked up my books at the library, and she'd checked something about her boring Victorian philanthropists, we went home together.

My mind was still on Charlie when I stopped at the B & B to drop Cali off so I thought I might call in to say hello; perhaps make an appointment with him to do a proper interview about the war years. No one answered the front door so we went round the back. Charlie was in the back hallway, carrying his banjo. He beamed, obviously pleased to see us.

'I'm going across the shed. D'ya fancy a look round? Go and get your whistle, Cal. Mebbe we can have a bit tune.'

Going into Charlie's shed during the day was to experience the transformation of day into night. The windows and the walls were masked and soundproofed with foam-filled panels painted black.

'All fixed without metal nails to avoid problems of sound conduction,' said Charlie when I commented. At one end, yards of old wartime blackout curtain were glued on top of the panels, adding insulation and atmosphere.

Halfway down one wall was an immaculate, probably out-of-date, recording console; beside it was an ancient upright piano. Charlie picked up a duster and passed it across the gleaming surface. 'Never been out of tune, this beauty!' he said fondly. Beside the piano was a long bench divided neatly into boxes to take generations of cable, microphones and boxes of small gear. Stools and chairs sat around the room in neat ghostly groups, and in one corner stood a wooden-legged couch and stained teak coffee table that probably in the sixties had enjoyed pride of place in the window of Doberman's furniture shop. The whole space was lit by two long fluorescent tubes and a swirling spirit lamp just above the gear table that glowed green and yellow.

Cali told me later that three times a week Charlie's friends Stan Smith and Theo Cartwright, nodding genially to any man, woman or child who crossed their path in the house, would carry their guitars through the house to the back. And once they were in the shed and the door was shut, the soundproofing was so good that nothing more was heard of them until they emerged, blinking, into the day.

May, who was not very original, called the shed 'the Starship *Enterprise*'. And now and then, when the house was empty and her galloping mothering impulse was reined back, she would ask Charlie which galaxy he and the lads had played on that night.

'It's bigger than you think,' gasped Cali, coming in behind us, clutching her whistle.

Charlie grunted, 'Our May calls it—'

'The Starship *Enterprise*. We know.'

I wandered over to his mixing desk, which was past its best, more clunky and mechanical than the kit that is around these days. Still, it was immaculate, its white levers were shining like scrubbed teeth.

'You actually record your stuff, Charlie?' Now I was ashamed about how much I didn't know.

He shrugged. 'We mess around, like. Make our own backing tapes. They want a bigger sound in the clubs these days, even the small venues. So we use the tapes.'

Our voices were strangely finite, without resonance in this padded space.

I fingered a white lever. 'Just backing tapes? Not performance tapes?'

He grinned. 'Persistent? You? Aye, there's one or two tapes with our stuff on them.'

'Demos? D'you send them out?' said Cali

He laughed out loud at this. 'You gotta be jokin', love. Thirty years too late for that. No. We lay them down just for our own vanity. To listen ourselves. To see where our stuff works and where it doesn't. To "make a *record*", I suppose – in the other sense. So I

115

can see where we've been. Mebbe even get some ideas about where we might go. The tapes are the history of this crew, I suppose. Archive. *My* obsession, like. The lads aren't bothered. They just like to play.'

'Can I hear some of it?' I said, eager now.

'Yes,' said Cali. 'Show us what you're made of.'

He consulted his battered pocket notebook, then went to a wooden shelf unit mounted above the gear table. It was lined with rank after rank of neatly labelled tapes. He took one out, slotted it into the desk and fiddled with a couple of levers.

He murmured absently, 'I suppose what we do is kind of traditional. When we play out there the young lads have quite a laugh at us. It's traditional but it's our own kind of traditional. Sometimes we write our own stuff. Now then, listen! This is one of them.'

The sound was clear and hollow: piano and guitar and an occasional bizarre banjo riff. The first voice sounded young, squeezed. Halfway through the first verse I realised it was a man's voice swooping high into falsetto. The song was about two miners torn apart, finding themselves on opposite sides in the 1984 strike.

> He set me on at work when I was seventeen
> Giant in the sun, a giant in the sun
> Shoulder to shoulder, crouching in the seam
> There in the dark, in the dark, in the dark
> Shoulder to shoulder, walking home
> Laughing like brothers, strangers to hate
> Now a shadow in my life, a shadow in my life
> He spits on my cheek as I go through the gate
>
> Shoulder to shoulder crouching in the seam
> Shoulder to shoulder walking home
> Now a shadow in my life, a shadow in my life
> He spits on my cheek as I go through the gate

'Bee-utiful,' said Cali.

She was right. The song was simple enough, the harmonies

116

straightforward. The chorus was two voices, one apparently young and light, one deep and sad. Much older.

'Well,' said Charlie. 'That's that, then.'

'It's very touching,' I said, hoping it was the right thing to say.

He didn't need my cautious evaluation. 'Not brilliant. Not even good. Not angry enough. It should be *very* angry,' he said. 'Whatever. Folks seem to like it. They like to hear about themselves. Only human.'

'Will you sing that song for us here? Now?' I said suddenly.

He looked at us, from one to the other, then went across to the keyboard and gave himself a note. He started to sing. His voice was pure and young, hardly matching the middle-aged man before us. At the end of the second line Cali's whistle swooped down into the melody. He nodded his approval and his voice took on some strength with the second chorus before he returned to the first verse. When they had finished I clapped, my applause vanishing without resonance into the padded walls.

After that Charlie played us a song about a boy who was bullied at school and when he grew up returned there to wreak vengeance by setting fire to the school. A very modern theme. Then he sang another song, this time comic, about a man who volunteered for the army because everyone said it would 'make a man of him', and was turned down by the army. So he realised he was 'no man, no man'.

Every song had a message.

Next he made Cali play two of her whistle solos and then he asked her about the poems she performed at her gigs. Surely they were lyrics? Surely she could sing them?

She laughed. 'They're too short and far too rude, Charlie.'

'Believe her,' I said. 'I've heard them.'

'Say one for me now,' he said, his voice mild. 'Go on!'

She was already shaking her head. 'They need a complicit audience.'

'Complicit!' he said. 'Well now.'

'So much *innuendo*,' I said. 'It means nothing said cold without an audience to anticipate the joke.'

'I can see that,' Charlie said placidly. 'You'll want tea, I suppose?

Coffee?' He nodded at a battered, neatly arranged trolley in the corner, complete with electric kettle. 'Coca-Cola?'

'What? No smokes? No hash?' said Cali cheerfully.

He looked at her under his strong brows. 'Yer must be jokin', lass.'

Not knowing whether or not *he* was joking she cracked a can of Coca-Cola.

'And what about Rosa?' I said. 'What does *she* think of your music?'

'Our Rosa?' He raised those brows. 'She knows nowt of all this.'

'I'd have thought . . . there is so much of you here, in all this. She would have wanted . . .' said Cali.

'Aw! You know families . . .'

'No, I don't.' She shook her head. 'That's the point.'

'It's like this, pet. Me and our Rosa, we've always lived our own lives. She knows I like my music, always have. But all this?' He flung out an arm to encompass the whole shed. 'She'd think . . . why, she'd just smile. Mebbe even be embarrassed.'

I could see what he meant, but Cali didn't get it. 'She wouldn't smile,' she said. 'Seems to me she's a very nice person. Kind.'

'Aye, she's that, all right, our Rosa. But we keep things separate, me and her. For safety, like. Those stories of hers, I've never read them. Not one.'

Of course, Cali made it her business to read all of Rosa's books in the weeks after she had met me. Then she couldn't rest until she met Rosa to say 'how . . . well . . . how *good* they are.' Even when she said it you could tell she felt embarrassed, as though she'd made a *faux pas*.

Now she said, 'Why on earth not? Why haven't you read her books?'

He shrugged. 'Mebbe I'm frightened I'd not like them. Then how'd I face her? Same with her. What if she winced when she heard my music? Would I ever be able to look her in the eye? Or she me? Families don't work like that, Cali. You've got to keep space between you, to go on together. To get on, like. It's the spaces that tie, the secrets that hold.'

118

I always thought my mother was clever, but there in the shed I suddenly realised just how wise Charlie was.

Cali persisted. 'Old Mrs Carmichael too? Kate? Does she not know about this? Your music?'

'Ah!' he said. 'Different kettle of fish, me mother.' He poured himself some tea in a thick blue mug. 'Nah. Kate likes my old banjo. Sometimes I take it down there when I go and see her. I sing her songs from the war, "White Cliffs of Dover". "I'll Be Seeing You". Even one or two of my own. Saves talking, like.'

'I've been there,' I said. 'You have to see them. They sing along.'

'And Kate likes it?'

'Oh, yes. Like I say, she sings along.'

'Now that surprises me.'

'Ah! That's 'cause you only know about her from Rosa or our Bronwen. Me, I reckon each of us is different to different people. Remember that. Rosa has her own ideas about me mother, her own memories. But I remember Kate as really stalwart, like, sticking to us through thick and thin, through the highs and lows. You know? When me dad died her world fell apart. But still she kept going. She worked at the factory all those years, even though she hated it. Got me set on there, didn't she? It was a great place to work, I'm tellen yer. Me, I loved it. And Kate saw our Rosa through teaching college and our Brock through university. Kate's a heroine to me, love. Pure heroine.'

'What about Brock, Uncle Charlie?' I said quietly. 'Isn't he the big wheel in finance, wheeling and dealing with the Russians as we speak? Does he know about all this, about your music?'

'Wheeler-dealer? That's our Brock.' He nodded at Cali. 'Didn't you tell me *you* did that kind of thing, Cali? Down in London?'

She laughed. 'I was a much smaller cog in somebody else's wheel.'

'Didn't you like it?' He started to adjust the strings on his banjo. 'Packed it in, didn't you?'

She sipped her Coke. 'All right for three, four years even. Heaps of money. Good times. Bubbly. Loved all that. Got me the money to take the time off so I could do this course. But the work was bo-oring. Darling, the people were so boring. P'raps your old

Brock wheeling and dealing with the Russians is not so boring. More life and death, I would think. Dangerous perhaps, but not boring.'

'Our Brock seems to like it. Not just the money, though there's plenty of that. Not the money. I don't think so.'

'It's you that Brock writes to, isn't it? You really know most about him.'

'You could say that. He writes now and then. And I send him compilation tapes – all the current stuff. Music I like. Still some decent stuff coming out, even now. Sinead O'Connor, Madonna, Elton John. And I send him the odd tape of me and the boys. He likes our music. Or says so. But he would say so, wouldn't he? What he really thinks is a mystery. Always was.'

'And he never comes home?' said Cali.

'Home? Why, this isn't his home now, love. No. He's never here. Not back since he was out of university. He's been a busy man since he shot up that ladder.' Charlie caught the sceptical look on Cali's face and shook his head. 'It's not like that, love. Our Brock's not grown out of us. Not got above hisself. When he goes home, he goes home to his wife and kid in France. Proper little Frenchy that kid is. No. Brock has this busy life. May and me have been to France to visit them a few times. Lovely place. They really make you welcome.'

'Don't you think it's odd that he stays away so completely?' I said. The tick book was back in my mind. I wanted to know more about Rosa and Brock. There were so few clues about that.

He nodded. 'Yer right there, pet.' He shrugged. 'I think it was sommat to do with him and our Rosa in 1968. That year there were all those demonstrations. Everywhere. Here. In France where Brock'd been studying. He'd just got some extra qualification and we were all celebrating at Kate's. Then whoosh! Brock was gone, days before he'd intended. Sommat to do with him and Rosa. Never knew what. I thought they must have had a row but that's not like our Rosa. She never rows. Sometimes I think she should. Too buttoned up, is your mother. May says that. Too buttoned up!'

Cali laughed. 'Bronwen too. All buttoned up. Chip off the old block, maybe?'

120

My murderous glance was lost on her. She was watching Charlie tune his banjo. The chords were sucked in by the soft walls of the shed.

'But that's what it's like with us,' he said. 'We all go our own way, like. No playing happy families. But in this queer way we're, like, wired together. Old Brock's letters do the rounds between us. You might say they *resonate* between us.' He played a chord. 'No words needed.'

Then he shook his head. 'Now then!' He put down his banjo, went across to his tapes and selected one.

'Here's one called "Beauty and the Beast" by an American, Jane Yolen. It's a poem, like yours, Cali, and mebbe this needs a complicit audience too. She speaks this one. Doesn't sing. Just you listen!'

The clean dead space of the shed was filled by this rich, pure voice laced with tragedy. Spoken lace on ragged velvet. The poem/song told the story of the Beauty and the Beast in old age.

> . . . Though sometimes I do wonder
> What sounds children
> might have made
> running across the marble halls
> swinging from the birches
> over the roses
> in the snow.

It was suffused in sadness and loss. When I looked at Cali her eyes were full of tears. When the tape stopped we sat on in silence, becoming too conscious of each other in the echoless space of the Starship *Enterprise*.

Then the tension broke as the door swung open, bringing in a slash of universal outside light and Charlie's friends Stan and Theo, clutching their guitars. The two men laughed, seemed quite pleased to see us. They persuaded Cali to sit in on their rehearsal for a forthcoming gig at some firemen's social club up the dale. That was a fortnight away and had been the focus of all their energies for a week. They wanted me to stay too. An audience – even of one – would sharpen them up, Charlie said.

121

I turned down the opportunity to be that audience of one and got up to go. I leaned towards Charlie and he gave me a kiss on the cheek – the first time that had ever happened.

'Give your mother my love, pet,' he said. 'Nice to see you down here.'

My head churned like a tumble dryer as I drove the last few miles home. Swirling around in there like some helpless flailing garments were the tick book, images of young Rosa and Charlie and Brock; of the older Rosa and Charlie in the flesh; the photograph of Brock looking like Doctor Zhivago; Cali playing the penny whistle with Charlie; Charlie kissing me; me kissing Richard Stephens; that tragic voice intoning 'swinging from the birches/over the roses'. Talk about overload!

I had quite a headache when I got home and had to take two paracetamol and lie down before I could get on with my work.

A Matter of Verification

Over the next few weeks I had to concentrate on my work to get together the data for my study. Engrossed in my research, I went less into Durham and saw nothing of Richard Stephens. So, after a while, there were no more half-chaste early morning meetings by the river, no piercing glances as I passed him in the corridor, no discreet conversations in other people's presence.

I worked from home, arranging my project in the school and embarking on a schedule of interviews with the pupils and teachers. I planned to leave the parents' interviews until I had analysed the in-school interviews – Richard would advise me on how to proceed with that. I rather treasured that thought.

The ledger and its contents started me thinking more about the details of my mother's life, things that had slipped into the background of our lives together. How, after my father died, Rosa had stayed on at Arran Lea, the roomy comfortable house that we all shared now.

And how supportive Rosa was when I, just a child myself, had a child of my own. She was amazing. She asked a few questions, which I didn't answer, so the matter of Lily's father was put to one side. Then there was the way she'd invited me back to Arran Lea when Jacob went off to Beirut. And the way she comforted me when Jacob was killed. All this made more difficult by our tacit knowledge that all had not been right between me and Jacob.

She and I both knew it was a guilty kind of mourning. On the day of Jacob's funeral we talked long into the night about our loss and the irony of history repeating itself in two generations. Three, I reminded myself now. Because Rosa's father died when she was nine. It was there in the tick book.

So our life together had proceeded peacefully enough. Lily went back and forth to school. I did the same, going backwards and forwards to school, until just this year when I embarked on this course. Rosa moved in and out of Arran Lea, seeing friends, giving lectures, posting her letters and manuscripts, and on one day a week she went to teach young Cherie Bostock, who had spina bifida.

Sometimes Rosa would share with me a rare anger at this intelligent child having to be in a wheelchair, not growing. She'd tell me tales of how Mrs Bostock liked to go dancing at the working men's club. If no babysitter materialised, Mrs Bostock danced to music tapes in the house with little Cherie as an appreciative audience, keeping time with her curling hands. This reminded me of that passage in Rosa's tick book, where she would draw the curtains and dance by herself in the cold front room of that house.

I feel privileged that Rosa shared the secrets of the Bostock family with me. A rare thing. Mrs Bostock was preoccupied with the problem of having a teenage girl and keeping up with the fashions. 'They grow out of things so quickly, don't they?' she would say. But although she was thirteen, Cherie had stayed the size of an eight-year-old and was never in a position to wear out her clothes. She and her mother had slept in the same bed since Cherie was born. This despite the fact that Mrs Bostock now had a beefy young husband and a new baby.

Rosa's books have always been the mainstay, the steady centre of her life: a flow of children's stories that seemed to fit the niche in literature between childhood stories and the bolder shores of teenage life. They've had some critical success and must have struck a universal chord as her study is always littered with Spanish, Norwegian, Japanese and German editions of her work.

All this drummed through my mind as I sat there, working my way again through the tick book. Then for a while this private, accomplished mother of mine became mixed up in my mind with young Cherie, a child in aspic, and with Rosa as a girl, existing in a different, difficult world, filling the ledger with her neat writing, outlining what was effectively an unobserved breakdown.

I steeled myself several times to confront Rosa with the ledger and – in the role of researcher – ask her about the post-war world it described, but each time it seemed impossible. There was no space in the routines and customs of our lives together for such deep questions.

But Rosa's ledger, closed now on my desk, still dominated my mind as I went in and out of school with my tape recorders, asking my questions. The data that was emerging from the school was engaging but not unexpected. The ledger and how I might use it was beginning to seem too important to neglect.

In the end, one day I came in from school to a thankfully empty house. I went up to my bedroom, took an empty spiral-bound book and labelled it: 'Research Questions: Aspects of Verification'.

I tipped out the contents of Kate's carrier bag on the bed and listed them in my book:

Photographs

1. Brock in Moscow

   Write to Brock?
   Ask Kate & Rosa about Brock

2. My grandfather Rob in suit and tie with other workers from his aero-unit

   Ask Kate about Rob & work
   Check factory/public record

3. Rob, bicycle in background.

   Is this the bicycle from the Tick Book?

4. Rosa and Charlie and an angelic Brock in studio photo. Round-eyed, bright faced

   Where? Why?

Letters

From	To	Comment
1. Brock	Charlie	What is Brock like?? Why does he stay away?
2. Cy	Kate & Rob	?Relationship?
3. Cy	Kate	?Relationship
4. Cy	'Darling Katie'	Affair?

Kate's poem. Draft. Was it sent???
Emerging question. Who was Cy? Would it be possible to trace him? The Canadians over here during the war. Just how does he relate to Kate? And Rosa (see tick book . . . and letters. 'A kiss for Rosa'.)

Ledger written by Rosa Carmichael (Aged 13)

– Written in 1954, reflects on period 1944–54
– Perspective on a life during the war and after – refers:
1. D-day
2. VE Day
3. Wartime food
4. Canadian troops' presence. Billeting of troops on civilians.
5. Coronation Day
6. Schooling during and after the war
7. Writer's state of mind: worldview

Emerging Questions:
1. How could a child play truant this long and not be discovered, even then? (N.B. this was NOT during the war, when I know attendance was difficult to monitor. And not today when truancy is more common.)
2. Why did Kate not see Rosa's pain? (Personal, not research question.)

3. Where on earth did Brock come from? What on earth had Kate *done*?

4. Does Cy have anything to do with 3.?

So many questions!

Next! – go and talk to Kate.

I had just closed the notebook and put it in the carrier bag with the other stuff when the phone rang down in the dining room. I pushed the carrier bag inside my wardrobe and raced downstairs.

It was Richard. 'Hi, Bron!' It was so good to hear his quiet voice. 'Missed you lately.'

'I've been working very hard.'

'Sure you have!' I can see his slight smile.

'Interviews with teachers, beginning tomorrow.'

'I have a voice-activated recorder I could lend you . . .'

'I have a perfectly good recorder.'

'Don't you feel like coming in so we can go over your method one more time?' He sounded quite plaintive.

'No. Honestly. I know what I'm doing. I really will want some help when I've done the transcriptions. But that'll be weeks away.'

A dramatic groan at the other end of the line. 'Are you sure you don't fancy one more walk by the river? One more cup of coffee?'

'No. Honestly. I really need to concentrate on this.'

'Well, why don't I come and see you there? Visit?'

'No!' I know I spoke too quickly.

There was a silence. Then, 'Is there something you're hiding there, honey?'

'No . . .' I looked for an explanation. 'I don't like things to be complicated. I can do only one thing at a time. The one thing now is getting all this stuff into some kind of order.'

His voice was even. 'OK, Bron, if that's how you feel . . .'

I spoke quickly then, to stop him putting down the phone. 'I have another problem here, which I need to check out. Not the research, but that ledger I told you about. The tick book. It's taking a bit of untangling. Very personal to me.'

'Ah, the ledger!' His voice warmed up again. 'Now you may have something there.'

127

'I tell you what,' I was desperate now for him not to get impatient, 'I'll come in early on Friday to talk to you about it, then I can get back here for my first school appointment.'

'Gee, ma'am, thank you for that.'

'Don't be sarcastic! I'll be there by the river at seven fifteen.'

'No,' he said decisively. 'I'll tell *you* what. Come to my eyrie and join me for breakfast at seven fifteen. I'll open the outer door. See you, honey!' The phone went dead.

See you, honey! I wondered if Cy had said that to Kate, the last time he left. *See you, honey!*

Kate's Best Truths

'So what is this thing you're doing at the school, pet?'

I put Rosa's chicken casserole in Kate's fridge and sat down opposite Kate in the pristine sitting room of her bungalow. 'It's just about the war, Kate. You know, the children in school have to learn about it now, for their exams? Well, I interview them and record the interviews. I get them to tell what they know about the war. Their idea of it as a real thing, not just textbook stuff. Then I transcribe the recordings and see what kind of truths they tell. Not about the war but their own perceptions of it.'

'Truth?' Kate pulled her skirt straight and touched her hair, pure grey now but still plentiful. 'So it's just the children you talk to? What do children these days know about the war?'

'Well, I'm talking to the teachers as well. Of course, lots of them were born after the war. Then I talk to the parents. Perhaps even the grandparents. They should remember the war personally.'

Kate stared at me with bright eyes in a face that, like the bungalow, had been shorn of extra clutter. 'And what good will that do, I ask you? Kids, mothers, grandmothers – just a jumble of opinion. Not fact at all. How do they know the real truths about war? They're not scholars. They might have seen and done a lot – more than the men who write it down – but them men who write it down can stand back and look at it all and make proper conclusions about all that jumble. Then they become facts.'

'Women write it down too, Kate.'

129

'Well, whatever.' She fluttered her fragile hands.

But she's so sharp. Many people in what Richard Stephens called 'the academy' would agree with her. I tried to counter my view against hers, and that of people like Dr Devine. 'If it has any worth it might show the best truths about people's perceptions of the war, not just conventional academic conceits and sentimental notions.'

'Mmm. Best truths? Conventional conceits? You've lost me there, pet. All this jargon.' She was being polite. 'Myself, I'd have thought history was fixed. The kings and queens, the Boer War. Florence Nightingale. The Great War. Things you knew for certain. Hard facts.'

'Yes. But you could argue that they're not hard facts. It all depends who's telling the story. There's no fixed truth. Only best truths from an individual perspective.'

Kate shook her head. 'Best truths? It's beyond me.'

I hesitated. 'I wondered if I might talk to *you* about the war, Kate.'

She sat back in her chair. 'Ask away. I expect you to tape-record it, mind. You might forget things.'

I set up the recorder, then delved into the Co-op carrier bag. 'This stuff you gave me last month, Kate.'

'Stuff? I gave you no stuff.'

'You did. In this carrier.'

'Just rubbish for Oxfam. Clearing out. You never know when . . .' She often said this, but she never finished the sentence.

'For instance, these.' I pulled out the Canadian letters.

'What are they?' Kate reached for her heavy-rimmed glasses. 'Let me see.'

'No need, Kate. I'll read them to you.' I started with the address. ' "Tangarete Road, Port of Spain, Trinidad . . . Dear Kate." '

It didn't take long to read the letters. Kate put down her glasses, shot me a hard look, then sat back and listened in silence. When I was finished I looked up to see a faint smile on my grandmother's face.

'So who was he, this Cy?' I said.

'He was from the air force. Canadian on some kind of

130

attachment . . .' Her voice faded, then got stronger like a radio that had tuned itself in. 'He was billeted on us in our Lancaster house. You know, when your mam was a little girl.'

'Didn't you mind, having someone like that in your house? A stranger?'

She shrugged her thin shoulders. 'Everyone was doing their bit. That's what they called it. "Doing your bit." And we had that spare room, out past the bathroom. We got some money for it. You only had to do bed and a bit of breakfast. The "boys" ate in the mess.' Her face lit with a rare, open smile. Years dropped away from her. 'In fact many a time *we* ate *from* the mess. Cy brought home a lot of stuff, off ration, from the PX or the NAAFI or whatever it was. We ate like kings, those three months.'

'And what was he like, this Cy? What was his other name?'

Kate reached across and took the letters in her hand, and stroked out the paper creases on her knee. 'Ah, he was a bonny lad, Cy. Smile like stars in the night. And he was elegant. I never knew another man who manicured his nails. He called me "ma'am" until I stopped him.'

I thought of Richard. *See you honey!* 'Anything else?'

'He was what they called "coloured", then. Can't say it now. They tell you on the wireless. You have to say black, although nobody is really black, are they? Just like there's nobody really white . . .' Her gaze wandered to her brightly patterned curtains.

'And . . . ?' I said.

Kate turned to stare at me. 'Do you have that recorder on?'

'Yes. Go on about Cy.'

'Cy didn't like the "coloured" thing even then. Said what was he – pink, purple, green? I told him he was sky-blue pink with yellow dots on. He really laughed at that.' She smiled into herself. 'Anyway, he told me his grandfather was a free negro, a farmer, and his grandmother was Spanish, but he told me *her* grandmother was a full-blood Indian, off that island where he was born.' She paused. 'He had skin like beaten copper and as far as I could see he was a gentleman . . .'

'And?'

She chuckled. 'He hated being called a Yank! Hated it.'

'And did he keep writing, Kate? There're only three letters here.'

She shrugged. 'Well, there were others. A pile. He wrote when we moved to Coventry. Your Granda Rob wrote back. He wrote these long letters. He was a good writer, Rob. Like the newspaper. That's where your mam gets all her writing from. Not me. Anyway, Rob checked on the map where Cy was from. Trinidad. Then Ontario, where he was living.' She sat still and quiet for a full minute. 'Then Rob died and we came North. Nothing was the same then. Everything was finished. Cy might well have written but we weren't there, were we? I burned a lot of the letters.'

'So that was it?' I couldn't ask her about the poem, those passionate, heartfelt verses on hospital paper, about 'joyless duties' and 'fruitless years'. I couldn't ask my own grandmother if she'd gone to bed with this man she so obviously admired. One more try. 'Nothing else?'

Kate's thin shoulders moved under her cardigan. 'Well. Not quite. It would be the early sixties, maybe 'sixty-three. All that *kerfuffle* then, over President Kennedy being killed. Anyway, Cy went to Coventry looking for me . . . for all of us. A woman there who belongs *here*, but was visiting *there*, told me she'd seen him. But I wasn't in Coventry, was I? I was here. And in no state for anyone to visit. In a terrible place, that house we lived in. Terrible, the way we had to live, Bronwen. You'll never know. A slum. I wanted nobody to come North for me. Not even him.' Her voice had lost its power.

'Is there nothing else you can remember about him, Kate?'

'He was very fond of your mother. Quite taken with her. She used to dance for him.'

'I can see that from the letters. He was always sending her kisses.'

She smiled. 'Our Rosa was a quiet, appealing little thing. She took a real shine to him and he to her.' Kate squinted at me. 'You're not asking if Rosa was more to him in some way? You don't think she was *his*?'

I blushed.

She sniffed. 'Are you asking if there was anything between us,

132

between him and me? Maybe you think you're asking questions about your own grandfather.'

'No . . . no.' A long silence. I couldn't think of anything more to say.

Kate sat forward in her chair. 'These days, in the wisdom of old age, when all things are equal, I regret to say, pet, that there was nothing between me and that Cy. I've thought long and hard about this, believe you me. We did hold hands, Cy and me. There were a few cuddles. And we danced to the wireless – that was really lovely. A few declarations were made. But nothing! No courage. You see? He was such a gentleman and I was . . .'

'And if anything *had* happened?'

She laughed, the years stripping away. 'Well then, disaster, pet. I'd have left Rob cruelly and gone away with Rosa and Charlie. Mebbe to Trinidad. Cy was keen enough.'

Now that was a shocking thought.

Another thought struck me. 'Of course, Brock wasn't there then, was he?'

Kate's laughter faded. 'No, honey, our Brock wasn't there. Not just then.' She shrank back into the skin of a very old woman. 'Now, pet, I think you'd better go. You've worn me out with all these "best truths" of yours. Quite worn me out.'

It was only when I was outside my grandmother's door that I realised that Kate had not told me Cy's surname. So I couldn't track him further. Not just yet.

And the truth about Brock would have to wait for another day.

Butterfly Net

'What now?' I slipped into Richard Stephens' eyrie. The narrow door off the steep street was ajar. The staircases were deserted, paper notices lifting as the draught from the street door joined forces with some fugitive breeze to make its presence felt throughout the building.

'Now, Bronwen?' Richard stood up behind his desk. 'Now I return the compliment and feed you coffee.' He nodded towards a high-tech espresso machine perched on top of a wooden filing cabinet. Beside it were chocolate biscuits on a china plate. Such welcome domesticity melted the misgivings that had been mounting in me as I parked the car and made my way through deserted streets to the department. Perhaps this was why I had been putting this off.

I moved across the room, avoiding the tutorial chair opposite him and sat on the low windowsill. He stood up to depress the lever of the coffee maker, watching intently as the coffee dripped through. I could see at close hand the spare planes of his face, the slight gathering of ageing flesh on the jawline that contradicted the youthful contours of his body.

He gave me the first small cup and depressed the lever again.

I looked into the dark heart of the coffee. 'An improvement on my flask,' I said.

'Like I said, your coffee was nectar.' He took his cup and sat cross-legged on the floor in front of me so he was looking up at me. How clever. He sipped his coffee and looked at me over the rim of his cup, his pale eyes very bright, the flat early morning sun catching his bright hair.

Suddenly he looked young, sitting there at my feet. I liked that but still I couldn't think of what to say. Then the tension between us was broken by a pigeon landing on the outer still, making me jump. The bird side-eyed us malevolently and fluttered away.

'Well, Bronwen Carmichael. What now?' he said.

I sipped my coffee. It was so strong it made my jaws ache.

'*What* are you thinking?' he persisted.

'I was thinking how different this is from the riverbank.' I paused, glancing at the window, then the door. 'That beady-eyed bird. Less free, somehow.'

He leaped to his feet and turned the ancient key in the door, then resumed his gnome-like stance. 'Well, I suppose in here we have no river and very little sky but we do have privacy.' He leaned across to offer me a chocolate biscuit. 'And we have chocolate.'

'Wonderful!' I had to smile. 'But what I was thinking is why are we here? Why am I here?'

He raised his brows. 'Very existential. I asked you. You came.'

'But *this* is not me. I hardly recognise myself, creeping around.'

'You have free will. You're a free person.'

Silence. Then I asked the question that was haunting me. 'Do you do this everywhere you go?'

He frowned. 'What?'

'Choose someone and pull them in with your butterfly net?'

He put his cup on the desk, his cheeks reddening. 'What do you think I am? Who? Some kind of collector? Like the guy in that John Fowles book?'

I shook my head. 'I'm just trying to work this out. I am . . . we are . . . attracted. I know that but . . . ?'

'What has happened is that I saw you there on the riverbank and felt I'd seen you there every day for twenty years. You too,' he said determinedly. 'Something happened to you. And I don't know about you but this has never happened to me before.'

I finished my coffee and put my half-eaten biscuit on the windowsill. 'Why you, why me?'

He reached up and tugged at my hands so that I slid from the

135

low sill and was kneeling on the floor in front of him. He leaned forward and kissed me properly. It was as good, as strange, as electrifying as the last time on the river, when it was me who did the kissing. Then he took his lips from mine. 'That's why you, Bronwen. That's why me,' he said softly.

Then we kissed again and somehow we slipped down, and were on the theadbare carpet, sealed like positive and negative magnets. I could feel the hard edge of his thigh and the wiry strength of his shoulder as he held me so tight. Then he rolled away from me and stared at the ceiling.

I was suddenly bereft.

He spoke to the ceiling. 'I think, I think I might be in Heaven. I am in England. In Durham City. The lovely Bronwen Carmichael beside me. A man can ask no more.'

I lifted myself on my elbow and looked down into his gleaming eyes. 'You could give lessons in teasing,' I said.

He grinned, stretching back. '*You* have to make the first move. I made the coffee.'

So I made the first move. I pinioned him by the shoulder with one hand and with the other stroked his face from brow to chin. He closed his eyes. I placed my face and upper body across his and kissed him. His eyes snapped open and he groaned and twisted so that it was he who held me. Now he was kissing me, on my face and on my neck, on my shoulders under my loosened blouse, on my wrists and then back to my face. Then we were both scrambling to loosen and discard clothes so that more and more skin could be touched and savoured. Then he groaned, and pressed me closer, more urgently. Still he touched and kissed me until I needed him as much as he needed me.

Afterwards, our sense of relaxation and trust was complete. Lying there in a fuzzy trance with Richard breathing deeply beside me on the threadbare carpet, I thought how much this act changed everything. This was not flirting. It was not perfunctory attention. It was not just an answer to a physical need, like an ice-cold beer conquering a thirst. It was the kind of transformation that turns a chrysalis into a butterfly, an egg into a bird. The first and only other time this had happened was that single time with Matthew

Pomeroy, when, for good or ill, my life had been transformed when Lily was born. Making love to Jacob had been resolutely untransforming. With him the act was cool, perfunctory. I always stayed absolutely myself. After that, my other desultory affair was a mere matter of reassurance, that I was still alive and functioning, not a marionette on a cardboard stage.

Richard's voice broke into my thoughts. 'A revelation. Unique. You are so special.' He murmured. '*We* are something special, dammit!'

I sat up and started to pull on my blouse. He tried to pull me back down but I resisted. 'I have to go, Richard. People will be coming.'

'Fuck *people!*' he said. But still, he kissed me on the cheek and set about pulling on his shirt.

When we were both fully dressed he asked me if I wanted some more coffee. I shook my head. 'No, I'll go to the County for breakfast. Gather my thoughts.'

He stared at me. 'Gather your thoughts? Look, what are you doing later?'

'Well, I'm going to the library to check on some sources. Then I have to be back in the school for some interviews at one thirty.'

'Come here at eleven thirty.'

I looked down at the threadbare carpet.

He laughed. 'No, no, not that. Honestly. The working day has started. Bring your stuff and we'll do a "work so far" on your research. Did you do anything with that material you told me about? That ledger?'

'I haven't brought it with me.' I made for the door.

'Well, we can talk about it, and about how the interviews are going. You never know,' he added drily, 'I might have something relevant to say.' He came across to turn the key in the door. 'That was extraordinary, Bronwen.' He put his arms round me and kissed me on the lips.

I kissed him back, savouring the new familiarity between us.

'This is unique,' he said. 'I have to tell you this is absolutely unique in my life.'

I had to laugh. 'It's very unusual in mine.'

137

He opened the door. 'See you at eleven thirty?' he said.

'See you at eleven thirty.'

As I let myself out at street level it struck me how much this thing with Richard was like the thing with Cy and Kate. A powerful meeting between strangers, somehow existing out of time.

Enterprise

In the first week in March I went into Durham early three times to spend time with Richard in the eyrie. The third day that week, as I was returning home, I caught sight of Cali's motorbike sitting in the gravelled front patch, beside Charlie's battered Volvo. It felt like ages since I'd really seen Cali so, on impulse I turned the Riley at the next roundabout and went back to call on her.

In the back lounge the telephone answering machine was blinking in mute reproach. 'Cali?' I called into the echoing space. 'Charlie?' I went through the back hall, cluttered as always with coats and boots, through the kitchen and across the yard to the shed. I lifted the green dragon knocker and rattled it hard. There was no response and I was about to turn away when the door creaked open and Charlie stood there, blinking in the natural light.

'Here's our Bronwen! Now here's a surprise.' He opened the door wide and, in a gust of the prickling sweetness of cannabis, nodded me in. Inside, Cali was sitting cross-legged on the sofa, smoking. She waved her roll-up at me, grinning. 'Oh my God. Caught in the act!'

As the door thudded shut the interior space was restored to its state of echoless night. For the first time in my friendship with Cali, I felt embarrassed. Uncle Charlie seemed comfortable enough with it. Their very ease with each other filled the space. But why should I feel embarrassed? They were good people, nice people and they were good friends. That was all there was to it.

But Richard and I were not 'just friends'. Perhaps that was why

139

I'd not yet invited him home, in spite of hints he had dropped. I was not sure it was because I felt embarrassed about my own unusual relationship, or whether I didn't want to be seen in context, as Rosa's daughter, Kate's granddaughter, or even Lily's mother. I wanted to be the stand-alone person he first spied on the riverside, who made love to him in the mornings and argued with him about social constructions and situated perceptions in tutorials; the one who passed him in the library corridor with a cool sideways glance, and with delight that not one person around us knew our secret.

'Jeepers!' Cali rolled back her eyes. 'The lovely Bronwen has discovered us in *flagrante musicalio*!'

I grinned. 'Not at all. I just saw the bike and came calling.' My glance strayed from Cali's spliff to Charlie's more conventional cigarette.

'Don't worry, darling, I'm not corrupting your venerable uncle. We are just the best of friends. Isn't that so, Charlie?'

Charlie was not quite so laid-back. He coughed. 'We've been laying down some tracks using Cali's whistle,' he said. 'D'ya like a cup of tea, honey? A Coke?'

I perched on the sofa beside Cali. 'No, thanks. Like I say, I just saw Cali's bike and thought I'd have a word. Days since I've seen her.'

Cali waved her spliff. 'You and the rest of the world, darling. Been buried in the library. Those bloody philanthropists. Boring as hell. Dead fish.'

'Cali here says you're recording interviews with the kids, about the war,' said Charlie. 'What kit're you using?'

'Just bog-standard kit, Charlie.' I looked around. 'Nothing like this stuff.' I nodded towards his console.

He sniffed. 'Out of the ark, my stuff. But I'm used to it. Nice dirty sound.'

Cali sat forward. 'For your information, darling, in this case "dirty" means lively, natural, not over-refined.'

'Well, that's a relief.' I wondered about the protocol of asking to hear Cali's tape, then decided against it. I stood up. 'Well, I see you're busy . . .'

Cali shook her head. 'Nah. Just hanging out.' She stood up. 'I'll walk you through the house.'

As we stood by my car I couldn't resist one question. 'Cali. You and Charlie. You're not . . . ?'

Cali tossed her mane of hair. 'And why shouldn't I? If I were . . . I mean.'

'Well, he's my uncle.'

'He's not mine.'

'He's my mother's brother. Nearly fifty!' Even as I said it I thought of Richard Stephens.

Cali kept smiling. 'Oh Bronwen. Think of Charlie Chaplin and the youthful Oona!' Then the smile faded from her lovely face. '*If* we were on like that, darling, it'd be nobody's business but ours. But it so happens that we're not. I like him. We are just special friends. I'm just luxuriating in the warmth of Charlie's high esteem. And he likes to be with me. Likes the chat. He's a change from those children at the university. We gell together, he and I. He's that rare thing, a person who seems to like me and wants nothing from me. I come away from him feeling enhanced. Charlie and me embody the Platonic ideal. Is that enough for you, dearest Bron?'

'May . . .' said I.

'May wouldn't notice if we were making love on her hearthrug stark bollock-naked.' She paused. 'Well, perhaps she would. But that isn't going to arise so the theory will not be tested. We're great friends, that's all. I value him, he values me.'

I rooted in my bag for my keys. 'So. Your dissertation? How's that going?'

'Oh, that! All those books and articles sitting in reproachful piles! I do have a date with the fragrant Dr Devine on Friday so I'll probably burn the oils of inspiration on Thursday. How're you getting on with the enigmatic American?'

'Dr Stephens? Well, for one thing he's not American. For another he's been helpful so far. Even so, it's a quagmire, this quali-tative stuff, this talking with messy human beings. You're better off with your books and journals. Stephens talks of "celebrating doubt" and "becoming fierce with reality" and stuff.' I was aware of using the jargon to stop her questioning me as closely as I had catechised her about Charlie.

'"Fierce with reality"! Cripes!'

'You said it. So I'd better get back home and transcribe another interview and juggle with all this doubt. At this point you're lucky just to have those boring old articles.'

'Aren't I?' said Cali complacently. 'Now then, darling, robbed of the bonding in lectures we need to get together properly. A pizza or something. I've been in the County a couple of times, but you weren't there. You're less predictable than you were, darling. But then, of course, that's a good thing. You're making progress.'

A very good thing. I thought of the coffee and the biscuits and everything else that happened in Richard Stephens' eyrie. Three times in the last week. It beat early morning tea at the County into a cocked hat.

'Tomorrow night?' I said. 'Come to my house.'

'Great,' said Cali. 'It'll be nice to see Rosa. Now there's an enigmatic woman, if you like.'

Enigmatic? Cali was right. Always something unattainable about my mother. 'Yes. Let's do that.'

On my way home I contemplated the strange pairing of Cali and my Uncle Charlie. Worlds apart and yet cosily together in the sealed world of the stone shed. Even their names were alike. Charlie and Cali. They were such good friends. Cross-gender, cross-age friends. A good thing. Like Richard and me were a good thing, for quite a different reason, and even though he was barely younger than Charlie.

I got home to find Lily and Rosa laughing as they pegged out washing in the garden, battling with the March wind. I sat on the wall and watched them. When the two lines were full, Rosa slotted the plastic baskets inside each other and lifted them on to her hip.

'Just watch!' she said darkly. 'Ten minutes and it'll be raining.'

Back in the house, Rosa asked me about school. 'I was at the university, seeing my supervisor.'

'Was he pleased with your work?' Rosa used the same tone of voice as she had when I was at school: 'How was the exam?' she used to say, as though it didn't really matter.

'Was he?' she repeated.

I thought of Richard's lips on my bare shoulder. 'Oh, yes,' I said. 'He said he thinks my research is going well.'

'Good,' said Rosa. 'Now then, I've got some proofing to do, so you two will have to scratch around for your teas.' She smiled faintly. 'Now there's a surprise!' She glided to the hall and vanished upstairs.

I thought how insubstantial my mother was, hardly with you even though she was with you. Even as a child I always knew she usually preferred to be alone. That in turn taught me to relish my own company. Lily was the same. Now the three of us seemed to glide around the house without bumping into each other either physically or psychologically. It had always been a quiet house. But good.

I was not hungry so Lily made herself a cheese and jam sandwich. She came from the kitchen, balancing it on one hand, picked up her schoolbag and made for the stairs. I stopped her.

'Did you visit the clinic, Lily. Get that information?' I realised guiltily that I had promised to go with her but had forgotten.

Lily nodded. 'Yep.'

'D'you feel all right about it?'

'In what way? Safer? More prepared?'

'Well, I suppose I mean both.'

'Suppose so.'

'Good.' I stared at her. 'Lily. Is there anybody? Is there a reason for all this Pill thing?' It felt so improper, pressing Lily like this.

Lily shook her head. 'I'm the only one I know who hasn't tried . . . it. Done . . . it. And I thought if the opportunity arose I might like to try. But safely.' She put her plate on the stairs and stood up straight. 'Is there anyone for you? I noticed in the bathroom, there are Pills there.'

I felt myself blushing. 'Maybe I feel a bit like you. If the opportunity arises . . . Better safe than sorry. I've started to think I should live in the world. Not closeted from it.' I stumbled on, aware that I was protecting my own secret, perpetuating the family habit. 'It's just that I wanted to tell *you* it was all right, Lily. There's no point bursting with blooming youth and having no . . . life.'

'*Life?* Is that what they call it?' Lily picked up her plate and started up the stairs. Then she threw the words behind her like grenades. 'Really, the Pill is *not-life*. Isn't that true? I suppose that seventeen years ago it would have been *not-me.*'

'Oh, Lily!'

Lily looked down at me and then grinned, calling off the attack. 'Really, Mum, the whole thing is because we were talking to Miss Dent – you know, who teaches physics? She must be at least your age and she's getting married in August. She's really excited; said, "I've had a great life and I've got all my life before me." That made me think of you . . .'

'. . . with all my life behind me?'

'No, no . . .' Lily surveyed her sandwich. 'Well, I've got chemistry and a French translation to do . . .' Her tone was kind.

I stood at the bottom of the stairs and felt deserted, bereft. My own mother and my own daughter: both of them preoccupied and entirely independent of me. I felt suddenly heavy, as though I was made of clay. Mud was seeping through my veins instead of blood. I felt so heavy that it seemed to take ages for me to go to the dining room and pick up the phone.

I rang his home number. 'Richard? Is that you?'

'I . . . wait.'

I heard a door click.

'Now then, hello, Bron honey.'

I couldn't think of what to say.

'Are you all right?'

'Yes. It's just . . . I feel so old and useless.'

'Old?' he laughed. 'You should look at yourself through my ancient eyes.'

Another pause. Then he said, 'So, what are you doing this weekend?'

'The usual, I suppose. And yet more transcription of these interviews.'

'I'm visiting my brother near Carlisle. Why not come with me? Stay across there on Saturday night?'

I had made up my mind not to do any of this. I liked this secret thing, this relationship confined to the eyrie. It was my choice. He had wanted to meet outside but I wouldn't have that. Now that decision seemed perverse, juvenile.

'I don't see why not . . .'

'You don't have to be so enthusiastic,' he said quietly.

I laughed. 'I mean, yes, Richard! Yes! That will really give me something to look forward to. Now I have to go and have something to eat. I'm starving.'

Now I was not made of mud. Now I was made of quicksilver. A weekend with Richard. Wonderful. I'd have to say something to Rosa and Lily. So what? It was about time.

But first I needed to tackle Rosa about the tick book.

We Are Mysteries, One to Another

I knocked and entered my mother's study: a tight, interesting room that had been carved out of the end of the top corridor. Three of the walls were stacked with books, some of them two deep. The other wall was a fluttering litter of lists and plans, enhanced by images from papers and magazines, torn up artwork and page proofs of her own books: a literary compost heap. In the centre of the room was a draw-leaf oak table that served as a desk. This was neater than the walls. The two chairs were dedicated to different activities. One chair faced Rose's word processor, which had a neat stack of typed pages to its right and a scribbled-on hardback notebook to its left. The chair on the other side of the table was set towards the page proofs of a book, half done, red pens and markers stuck in a Spode mug beside it.

Rosa herself was sitting by the window, her feet up on a long garden chair. She smiled and swung her legs to the floor.

'Bronwen!' she said, as though it were the first time she'd seen me that day.

'Can I speak to you?' I looked round, then planted myself on the desk chair nearest the window. Rosa's room was not equipped for visitors.

Rosa smiled again. 'It's come to a strange pass, love, if you need to ask that.'

I thought that remarkably disingenuous. Despite her mildness Rosa lived her life with a kind of drawbridge pulled up around her.

I said, 'Kate gave me this carrier bag of stuff . . .'

Rosa smiled. 'Kate and her carrier bags! I reckon we must have taken three hundred of the dratted things out of that bungalow last year.'

'Well, this wasn't clothes or bags or crockery. It's full of papers, photographs, letters.' I paused and then took the plunge. 'And there's this big ledger. Like a shop ledger. You call it a tick book.'

Rosa was suddenly sitting very, very still.

'It's a kind of diary. Dated 1954. You . . .'

Rosa frowned. 'A diary?'

'Written by you, I think. You would be fourteen.'

Rosa glanced through the window at the garden outside. 'That? The tick book? I'd quite forgotten about that. An object from another world. I thought it had gone out when Kate moved to the bungalow. I looked for it but it wasn't there. I imagined it on the garden tip. Burning.'

I waited for my mother to say more about the diary, but she didn't.

'And there were letters in there from Trinidad. From a man called Cy. You get a mention there. At the end of the letter he says, "Kisses for Rosa".'

Rosa smiled and looked back at me. 'Ah! Cy! I can't really remember him, you know. What I remember is missing him when he was gone. A kind of absence of warmth. He must have been a good man. I feel that even now.'

I took a breath and said, 'Really, there are two kinds of letters from him.'

'What do you mean?'

'Well, there are newsy letters, the kind of letters a man sends to his friends. And then there is a love letter.'

'Is there now? Well, that doesn't surprise me. I've sometimes wondered whether that loss I felt as a little girl was really Kate's loss, somehow transferred to me.'

'So d'you think they were lovers?'

Rosa raised her fine brows. 'How would I know? I was just a tiny child. I just know it was nice and warm when he was there. And cold when he was gone.'

'And, according to your ledger, Brock arrived after Cy had gone.'

'Ah, I see what you're getting at. I don't know about that. There are things we don't know. We're mysteries one to another. But no, I don't think Brock has anything to do with Cy. I certainly don't think that.'

'So what has he to do with?'

Rosa shrugged. 'I can't think what you're talking about, Bronwen. Your Uncle Brock is my brother. He's always been my brother. The child of my mother and my father.' Her tone was wary, flat.

I changed tack. 'You know that this study I'm doing is about perceptions of the war?'

'Yes. Your dissertation.'

'Well, there are things here, in the ledger and letters, that kind of fit into my theme. I was wondering if . . .'

'You could use them?' Rosa paused. 'It seems a bit grubby to me, poring over other people's letters and diaries.'

I blushed. 'Mother, I—'

'You mean with my name on it? With Kate's name on it? I wouldn't like my name scrawled all over anyone's thesis.'

'You'd be anonymous.'

Rosa looked out of the window again. 'Well, love, you do what you want.'

'Would you like to see it again? The ledger? Could I ask you more specific questions about it?'

Rosa was already shaking her head. 'Oh, no, dear. I don't want to see it or talk to you about it. Why would I want to see something from the worst part of my life? I was a child in the Slough of Despond. The fashion these days of revisiting your own pain to expiate it seems to me as cruel as thumbscrews. That tick book was my private audit of my life at that time. It is finished. The line is drawn under it.'

'But me using it? You don't mind?'

She shrugged. 'Suit yourself, love. I just don't care. That little girl is not me. She is a stranger.' Her voice had a rare grim note. 'I just don't want to see that book.'

As the door clicked behind her daughter, Rosa sat very still for a while. Then she stood up and took down a pristine hardback notebook from a pile on the shelf behind the desk and, pushing the proofreading to one side, she sat down at the desk.

She opened the notebook and on the flyleaf wrote: 'Rosa Carmichael 1991'.

The Day Before the Bomb

From the road above Bluestone Dyke Farm, the house looked deserted. Rampant ivy had woven a tight mat across its front elevation, covering most of a door that clearly hadn't been opened for many a year. But everything changed when the Riley nosed its way down the side track and through a gate propped open with a defunct ploughshare. Fresh hoof-prints crisscrossed the muddy track that led to the distant cow byre. Hens pecked away at the chickweed that pushed its way through the slabs of Lakeland stone that lined the farmyard. A tethered pig snuffled in a trough by the ivy-clad wall. In a chicken-wire run against one wall two black and white collies quartered their bleak space, tails swishing.

A tall, beefy figure detached itself from the dark kitchen doorway and strode across the yard towards us, a yapping border terrier at its heels. The industrial boots and the vast dungarees suggested a man, but the generous bosom and the long braids were all woman.

'Hey up, Richard! How are you?' The woman put her arms around him and almost swung him off his feet in a muddy, byre-scented embrace. 'Good to see you again, love.'

'Sophie! It's impossible, but I swear you've grown!' He gave her a big smacking kiss on the lips, obviously delighted at her greeting. The little dog leaped up at him to share in the affection, to participate in the excitement.

Richard extricated himself and turned to me. 'Honey,' he drawled, 'this Amazon is my sister-in-law Sophie Stephens. Queen

150

of all she surveys, best farmer in the Northwest, the tenth generation on this land and a miracle with cows.'

'Get away with you, Richard!' Sophie landed a blow on his shoulder and chortled her appreciation. Her face, weathered to a gleaming nut brown, was broad and open, her nose commanding, her lips generous and her large eyes bright and knowing.

'And this, dearest Sophie, is Bronwen Carmichael, a buddy of mine, also a student of mine, who happens to have that rare thing, an original mind.'

'Student?' Her glance dropped from my face, down my suede jacket, past my neat cords to my Doc Martens (borrowed from Lily, who said they were *de rigueur* on farms). 'By, they breed 'em long in the tooth these days, students. When I was a student across at Houghall, where they thought they knew about farming, there wasn't one of us over nineteen years old.' Her critical words belied her warm tone as her large hand clasped mine. 'No offence,' she added.

I laughed. 'None taken.'

'Come in, come in then!' She led the way through a cluttered vestibule to a long narrow kitchen, dominated on one side by a black iron range that would not have been out of place in Beamish Museum, and the other by an elaborately carved chaise longue that someone had rather roughly upholstered with yellow padded plastic. There was a long narrow table in the middle of the room and at the end was an enormous dresser haphazardly littered with food tins, half-used cheeses, thick pottery chargers, mugs, cups, and a pile of newspapers with a black cat draped across like a feather boa.

Sophie told us to sit ourselves down on the couch, then hitched her bottom on the table and surveyed us. She proceeded to talk man-talk with Richard about the car journey in terms of time and length; whether he was leasing a car for his year here or buying one; about the ups and downs of farming and her perpetual worries about market prices and the paperwork a farmer was obliged to do these days, which was the bane of her life. She spoke of Peter and his work with the Forestry Commission and how excited he was that his twin was coming.

151

'He was that excited he didn't know whether he was on his arse or his tip this morning. The bugger went off in the wrong shirt,' she grinned. She might have been talking about a favourite son rather than a respected spouse.

I sat back, at ease as they talked away together, showing me the warmth, the sheer comfort of their relationship. I learned about Sophie and Peter, and Richard himself. Of course I'd learned a lot about him since we'd met, from our own private jokes, our wide-ranging conversations, our intense lovemaking, but there was so much more to learn. And I knew he was keen to know everything about me, hence his thinly veiled resentment that I wouldn't take him home. Perhaps this trip to the Lake District was more pressure from him to let him get closer to my own family.

I sat there thinking that when you fall in love with someone when you are young, it's just you and the beloved and that's it. When you're older, you're interested in the beloved's context, not just who he is, where he has been, where he is going. That was the very opposite of the 'pure present', which was what I was desperately trying to focus on in this relationship with Richard. But people do have pasts, which make them who they are. Just look at Rosa's ledger. The fashionable word these days is 'baggage'. And here was his 'baggage'. Illuminating.

Clearly Richard was extremely fond of this mountain of a woman. I went on to wonder if attraction were some chemical thing, some genetic predisposition. If this were the case, then he, like his brother, would be attracted to Sophie. A strange thought.

Sophie began to ask Richard about Maria and the boys, but there was no cross-reference to her own offspring. I concluded that Peter and Sophie had no children. Perhaps, as is the tender case with many childless couples, they were each other's children.

Sophie caught my thought. 'D'you have young, Miss Carmichael?'

'Call me Bronwen, please.' How gentle this woman was. 'Yes. I have a daughter, Lily. She's seventeen.'

A barking laugh rippled through Sophie's frame. 'Well, Bronwen, you're either a miracle of nature, or you were a child yourself when you had that bairn.'

I beamed. 'Me? I'm no miracle. But I *was* a child when I had her. And she's the miracle.'

'Lucky you. Some of us canna seem to manage it, young or old.'

The brief hiatus was broken by a concatenation of dog-barking outside. Richard stood up, moving from one foot to the other, like a child waiting for a treat. Then Peter Stephens, a bearded, booted facsimile of Richard, blew into the room, a black and white collie at his heels. The two men held each other like lovers. Over Pete's shoulder I saw the tears in Richard's eyes. I truly loved him at that moment.

Sophie stood back, like a fond mother surveying her beloved children. She glanced down at me. 'Two parts of the same egg,' she murmured. 'Can't see how Richard hacks it, out there across the ocean with no Pete.'

The two men turned, faces sparkling – one with the pop of golden hair, the other with cropped beard and cropped hair covered by a thick wool cap – towards me.

'And this,' announced Richard, 'is my friend, my student, Bronwen Carmichael.'

Peter looked across at me with his light grey eyes and I shivered. He said, 'Yes. So I see, Rich.' Then he pulled off his thick wool hat, came across the room and shook me firmly by the hand. Now I really knew that the theory about chemicals and genetics of attraction must be right. Holding his hand, breathing in his scent of bark and pine, an instant recognition flooded right through me and I felt I knew him almost as well as I knew Richard, and that was as well as I knew anyone.

'Wonderful,' said Pete. 'How wonderful this is. Welcome to Bluestone Dyke Farm, Bronwen.'

I had thought he would talk like Sophie, but his voice was softer, more articulate, laced with a Lancashire lilt.

Then Sophie broke the tension by announcing that they should all have a spot of lunch as she had 'a very decent stew' in the oven. In the afternoon she proposed to show me her farm while Pete took Richard off to his forest, where there were trees and other things to talk about.

Although I am no countrywoman, it was a delight to walk the

bounds of Bluestone Dyke with Sophie, who knew every stick, every stone, every hedge, every field. She recounted the varying history of each field – the hard work her father, grandfather and great-grandfather had done to improve them. 'Real men, they were,' she said. 'Me, being a lass, was a disappointment for me dad. He'd much rather've had a lad. But by the time I was fourteen he told me and anyone who'd hear that I was as good as – and better than – any lad.' This was sweetly, confidently said. No *angst* here.

She showed me tumbled stones that had been a sheep-shelter hundreds of years before. She used the tip of her boot to point out some incisions on the stones. 'Roman,' she said. She nodded to the horizon. 'Roman road to Carlisle, just a mile over there. Me dad used to say our ancestors were Roman camp followers. Then he'd always say, "No! Our Sophie could only be British, riding along wi' knives in her chariot wheels."'

Sophie was as much part of this landscape as the dry-stone walls and the hedges. And just as beautiful. No wonder Peter fell for her. She was a force of nature.

I asked Sophie how she and Peter had met.

The big shoulders shrugged. 'Our dad had this stand of woodland and some of them poor old buggers were dying. Peter came across with his boss to talk about it, help with the new trees, like. Anyway our dad and Pete took out the dead 'uns and planted new. The new fellers are doing well now, twenty years on.' She took hold of my arm. 'See! See across in that dip? Growing on nicely now.'

So they were. A mantle of bright spring green was sitting on their branches, shimmering in the afternoon haze.

'Well,' Sophie went on, 'after that time, old Pete was never away. He brought their Richard across once, him being over here in England for some conference. I must have passed muster with him, like, 'cause me and Peter was married before Richard's leave was over. Richard was our best man. Still is our best man, if you see what I mean! I tell you one thing, though. My Pete has as good a head on him as Richard. Richard chose schooling, Pete chose the forest. Still, they understand each other, those lads. Pierce one, the other feels pain even across continents.'

We turned and set off back down to the farmhouse.

'And you, are you wed, then?' said Sophie.

'I did have a husband but he died. He was a teacher in Beirut. There was a bomb.'

Sophie stopped in the path to turn to look at me. 'Pity, that.'

'Yes.' I wish I could have told her that marriage had been a short thing, a flight of fancy, which made it somehow even sadder when Jacob died. I could say none of this to Sophie here, on the hill, the crisp westerly wind lifting my hair and picking at my scarf.

We walked on. I wanted now to ask about Richard's wife. It seemed possible to do this here, out in the open. I wondered if Sophie liked her sister-in-law.

Sophie spoke up suddenly on cue. 'That Maria of Richard's. She's a right beauty. She has a good head on her too.'

'Richard told me she was very clever.' I tried not to sound defensive, or territorial.

'I think so. But then we hardly know the lass. Pete and me's been across there a couple of times to see the boys, and they've been here too. But "here" for Maria was just a jumping-off spot for Edinburgh or Glasgow. Once it was for the Isle of Skye where her ancestors come from. She's nice, very polite, the way those Americans are. But as hard to read as a June sky. Clever, though.' She paused. 'But mebbe walking the bounds would have been a bit out of the way for her.'

I was saved from saying anything further by the need to concentrate on climbing over a gate and making my way down a last narrow track, back down towards the house. When we reached it, through the flapping hens and the barking dogs, the house seemed deserted but somehow still listening. Peter's Jeep was missing.

'They've gone off again, those two,' said Sophie, placidly. 'Now then, Bronwen, I need a couple of hours to do the byre so maybe you could unpack and have a bit of shut-eye. The supper'll be ready about half seven. Men'll be back by then and we can have a good old time.'

She showed me up to my room, which was so far into the back of the house that it was wedged into the hill behind, its windows

155

level with the ground. One of the windows was an arrow slit that looked down into the yard, and I peered through it to see Sophie let out her dogs and, whistling and calling, go off to bring down her cows from the field.

I turned round to look at my room, which was dominated by a large walnut bed. A mirror on the larger windowsill served as a dressing table. The well-ironed, pale green bedlinen, the neatly mended flowery curtains and the white-painted floor demonstrated Sophie's discreet welcome. The woman was a wonder.

I climbed on to the bed to try it out and stayed there to close my eyes, tired after walking the bounds. I slept, and dreamed again of my conversation with Kate. In the dream Kate, younger now, was shouting angrily at me in words I could not hear. It was a relief to wake up to the quiet room and find I had slept nearly an hour. But I remembered the dream. A rare thing.

I stripped off, pulled my hair out of its clip and brushed it down over my shoulders. Then I slipped into my cotton wrap, found the bathroom and had a quick bath. That done I was just hanging my clothes on the iron bed-end when there was a knock on the door. I went to answer it but there was no one there. The knocking persisted, coming now, I realised, from the cupboard in the corner. I opened that to find Richard standing in front of me, a whole room behind him. It was a door, not a cupboard.

Richard grinned. 'Adjoining rooms! Some old nursery arrangement, d'you think? That brother of mine reads my mind.' His hair was still wet from the shower and he'd changed into a black T-shirt and dark red linen trousers.

I thought of the forthright Sophie. 'I don't know whether Sophie—'

'Sophie knows what she's doing. There's another room at the front with views right across the valley. She could have put a whole house between us if she'd wanted to.' He came and sat down on the bed. 'D'you have a good walk?'

I stayed where I was. 'Wonderful. Sophie's a great girl. Where did you go?'

'We drove into the forest. Pete always likes to show me his work just as I like to tell him about mine.'

I pulled out a long silk skirt from the bag and shook it out.

'Are you getting changed?' he said. 'That's a pretty skirt. Can I watch you getting into it?'

I didn't know whether to laugh or be angry.

He caught my feeling. 'Does that seem perverse? I don't mean it to be. It's just that I want to savour every moment here.' He paused. 'Pete likes you.'

'He doesn't know me.' It was ridiculous to be angry. But Richard's attic eyrie at the university was one thing. This place was another. The pristine hills. The radiant devotion between Sophie and Peter. Even the high bed that dominated the room and had probably seen many consummations. Births, deaths, God knew what: all so purposeful, all imbued with commitment.

'I have no desire to do any striptease, here or anywhere else,' I said. 'If you really knew me you would realise that.'

He reached up, pulled me down beside him and nuzzled my neck. 'I didn't mean . . .' he said. 'Oh, honey . . .'

I sat up straight, my knees tight together. 'This is too strange, Richard. What about Peter and Sophie? They—'

'Will be quite happy about this. Nothing will be said. They already know that you are not just my buddy, or my student.'

'Did you tell them?'

'I don't need to.' He hesitated. 'Look. I wouldn't have brought anyone else here. They know that.' He pulled back my wrap and kissed my shoulder. 'Honey I must be getting old but I've been so lookin' forward to the *bed*!' he said glumly.

I had to laugh at this, and relaxed against him. 'You're not so old. Well, not very. This is such a beautiful place, Richard. Out of time. I think Sophie is quite wonderful. Like some Celtic goddess.'

He hugged me. 'I can see that you *get* her, as they say. That you see how very special she is. Not everyone would see that.' He paused. 'And what do you think of Pete?'

'How couldn't I like him? He's like you, only up trees!'

He was playing with my hair, tucking it behind my ears. 'Maria didn't get them, you know.'

I didn't know what to say to that. I couldn't even imply criticism of his wife. I wouldn't. That would be too easy. Then,

157

'Perhaps, being American . . .' What was I doing sitting here, half naked, talking to some man about his wife?

He laughed. 'You've got it. She's a great person, Maria, but here she suffered a double culture clash, I suppose. First England, then Cumbria, which is like another country. Like I'd dared to take her up into the Appalachians.' His American intonation had vanished altogether. 'I could see that she might not *get* Sophie. A universe of difference. But Pete? Illogical that she doesn't like Pete. Chemistry would say different.'

I scrambled in my head for some rational idea. 'Perhaps, seeing how close the two of you are, she felt, well, excluded. Outside . . .' I pulled myself out of his grasp. 'This is ridiculous, Richard. I can't sit here talking to you, criticising your wife.'

We sat on in silence. Then he said slowly, 'Stupid of me. Crass. It's just . . . I've known her, loved her for twenty years. But then our lives were full of other things and I jumped at the chance of coming here. And now I've fallen for you, who are so much younger, and I'm worried about looking like some predatory older man . . .'

The tension was splintered by a loud, piercing whistle from downstairs. I imagined Sophie putting her fingers to her mouth and calling in the cows.

'Bronwen . . .' he began again.

I put a finger on his lips. 'Just don't talk to me about Maria,' I said. 'Don't! Let's just live for the day, like it was the day before the bomb.'

He frowned. 'You're very unusual,' he said.

'Thank you.' I stood up and he leaped to his feet beside me. 'Now I really need to get changed.' I surveyed my bare feet. 'No floor show, mind!'

He kissed my cheek. 'Take your time, you strange person. I'll wait in my room. Give me a knock.'

When we got downstairs the murmur of voices led us through to a dining room off the square hall beside the never opened door. The square table was covered in darned white linen and dressed with silver and crystal. Places for four were set at one end, and a silver branch candelabra at the other end burned brightly with seven candles.

Peter and Sophie were standing hand in hand by the broad window that looked across the hills to the mountains. Peter was wearing a black T-shirt and dark red linen trousers. I wondered whether he and Richard had consulted over their clothes, but instantly realised how ridiculous that thought was. When I saw Sophie I was really pleased I had taken the trouble to change. She was wearing a long ruby velvet dress that skimmed her generous curves and swept down almost to her ankles. On her bare feet she wore black embroidered mules. The yoke of the dress was exquisitely embroidered in green and yellow silk. Her long hair was piled in a fairly haphazard fashion on her head and held there by carved wooden combs. She wore no make-up on her nut-brown face. The effect was timeless and regal.

Richard kissed her on the lips. 'You look absolutely gorgeous, Sophe!'

'What a beautiful dress,' I said.

Sophie beamed. 'D'you like it? I made it myself. Only way to get anything decent, for me.'

'I tell you, there's no end to the talents of this woman,' said Pete, hugging her to his side. Then he went to the sideboard and picked up a bottle of wine, already opened. 'Now, kids, if you sit yourselves down, you can try this. The man down Carlisle says it's a good label.'

Sophie went off and came back with a big mahogany tray laden with a great joint of lamb and a vast blue earthenware dish of vegetables.

'Dinner! The prodigal returns!' said Pete, slapping his brother on the back. 'Welcome home, mate.'

The dinner was hilariously convivial. And even in this celebration of family solidarity I was not neglected. In their very direct fashion they asked me about my studies, my work as a teacher, my family. We talked about all the changes that were shaking the world, the drawing back of the Iron Curtain and the coming down of the Wall. Richard talked of some students he'd had, who had travelled to Germany and taken possession of stones from the Wall.

I mentioned my Uncle Brock, out there in Moscow even now,

drumming up joint ventures with the Russians as they loosened off the tight bonds of the past.

'There was a bit in the Sunday paper about the Mafia-style Russian gangsters,' said Sophie. 'Now that's a big shame, I say.'

Later, she seemed really interested in Rosa and her children's books and her work with the young Cherie.

Then she took the spotlight from me and went on to talk about the perennial problems of farming and the moral responsibilities in forestry. They spoke of the South American rainforests and the ecological balance of the world. All three of them talked with unforced, rapt interest. Each had his or her space to talk. I thought about the boys with their conch shell in *Lord of the Flies*, before the children's fall into the darkness.

Peter questioned Richard about his sons and their plans. Richard told me that Castor – whom they called 'the younger one', because he was born thirty minutes later than his brother, Paul – was coming to Cumbria for a year to work with Sophie on the farm when he finished his first degree. Apparently Paul was going to India for a year to help build a hospital. After that they would both go to Harvard to do law. 'Allegedly . . .' Richard finished with a laugh. 'Who knows?'

It would be the first time the boys had been parted from each other. Peter and Richard reminisced about the time that happened to them, after they had finished their first degree and Richard went off to do his doctorate in America.

'It was like physical pain.' Richard looked at me, suddenly serious. 'The tearing of flesh.'

'No matter,' said Peter. 'That way you learn that it doesn't really matter. You're in each other's heads and hearts anyhow.' He looked at his brother. 'Doesn't bother our Sophie here. But some women can't take it, the way me and Richard are.'

For a second Maria sat at the table with us.

Sophie broke the tension. 'Just look at 'em, Bronwen. There's the evidence. Turn up at the table in identical gear! It happens all the time. Two minds with but a single catalogue.'

The men laughed comfortably. 'Same genes, same jeans,' said Richard.

We sat on, still and quiet, having reached that point in any long conversation when there is nothing more to be said. The clock in the square hall chimed twelve. I stood up and started to pick up the pudding dishes.

Sophie yawned. 'No, you leave them, love. Me and Pete'll do them, won't we, Pete? We like that, don't we? Messin' about in the kitchen till late. After that we'll go and check the dogs and the stock. Great thing to do, last thing at night. I used to do it with me dad every night the good Lord sent us from when I was five.'

It was so easy that night, to fall into bed together and make love one, two, three times, waking and sleeping, moving around that vast high bed at the points of the compass, as though we were mapping the world.

The clock downstairs was striking four when we finally settled. Richard pulled the blankets up around us and tucked himself behind me. His sleepy voice was in my ear. 'The day before the bomb! It really works, honey.'

Rosa Carmichael:
Her New Notebook

(What pleasure it is to write with ink and pen . . .)

Well, that old tick book! What did I write in there? I wouldn't open it now, much less read it, no matter what Bronwen says. What tastes and smells of those times would fly out? It's a Pandora's Box of a book. A Pandora's Box of a time. I can't really remember what I wrote. Oh, yes I can. I deceive myself. I can remember. Thank God for blessed change. Those times, these times. Me at fourteen. Me now. That house, this house. That old tick book taking an account of that time. This new book with its clean-paper perfume. The compulsion to write. Oh dear.

My mind is in a turmoil now, about Brock. First his letter. Now this bag of tricks from Kate, handed on to Bronwen. How could she? Talk about throwing off life's mortal coil! I met her neighbour, Mrs Novelli, who informed me that Kate is now going to church and what a good thing that was, even if the church was only a Protestant one. The old needed to think of The Hereafter, she said. Needs must when the Devil drives, as Kate would say.

I have never been one for church. There was the time Bronwen 'got' religion when she was in her teens when she had a crush on that young curate. But that was short-lived.

I wonder if there are some of Brock's letters in that bag. Or has Kate hung on to them? They always compel your interest, Brock's letters. Colourful. (I say so even though I only ever read them second-hand – or should that be second-eye? – from Charlie.)

I can just imagine Brock there in Moscow with his 'fixer'; of course, she's one of a long line of fixers. My mother was his first 'fixer', fixing up his life so that despite our dire circumstances he flourished. Unlike me and Charlie, our Brock never lacked books, or money for school trips, or a decent change of clothes. She made sure of that. She grabbed overtime at the factory, night work at the dog track. She spared no effort, large or small, on his behalf.

And he was never in any doubt that he was worth it. That charm of his! A natural, invincible charm that saw him through school, through university, into those high-level jobs, into many beds – I take a breath here – including mine.

That word – charm – is strange, with its implicit allusion to both magic and a certain shallowness, a febrile quality that makes one wary. But those negatives never seemed to soil Brock's brand of charm. His charm has, well, had this openness, this honesty. *Insouciance*. (The French word defines him. He would like that.) He looks into your heart with those long grey eyes. When we were young he could – and would – wind you round his little finger with no devious purpose. His wants became your desires. He would focus on you with that clever, intense concentration and drink his fill of everything you had to offer. There is nothing so seductive as such close attention. We felt it. His teachers felt it. Brock had this magic. The magic of '*other*'. The enchantment of a changeling.

His absence leaves us all out in the cold. The gap he left behind nearly thirty years ago yawns chasm-wide in this family. My mother is bewildered by his staying away but says nothing. She feeds off his letters. Charlie talks about him as though he is still here, waiting behind some door.

And me, I am bereft. I can't go on about this, so I will write about Lily. I've been wanting to do this for a time. To capture something of Lily as she is now.

Lily has this certain quality. She's cool – in more than the modern sense – but still she has charm: she's self-possessed, yet exciting to be close to. She draws friends to her like the ceanothus in my back garden entices bees. Her happiness draws people to her. Unlike me, that young Rosa, who was so unhappy that she drove people from her. And the quiet, reserved Bronwen, who is just now coming out of her shell. (She's a different girl these days. That's good to see.)

Of course, Lily has grown up here in this house at the centre of our lives. How different is this house from that cave, that dark place where that thirteen-year-old Rosa wrote in the tick book. No dirty back yard, no privy. Here we have garden running round the house front and back, for goodness' sake! Two bathrooms! A very different house.

I think a lot about Bronwen and Lily. I know she loves her daughter but I sometimes wonder whether Bronwen really *sees* her. Of course, I know I am *projecting*. Kate never really *saw* me, what with her grief over my father, her obsession with Brock and her preoccupation with getting Charlie out of scrapes. I was too invisible – perhaps too hard to think about – in that crowded mind.

This thing has been on my mind: unbelievably Lily is older now than Bronwen was when Lily herself was born. And here's Lily today twice as worldly-wise as was that young Bronwen; infinitely more cushioned and loved than me, that young Rosa. The generations do not replicate themselves in a boring cycle. Thank God for that.

Take this thing about birth control. She made up her own mind about that. Just made it up. Plenty of boys call here – especially Simon, who often stays over. Girls too. There is a lot of music and laughter. Strident opinions. Smoking at the very least. But still Lily makes up her own mind about that and other things. She won't fall into any boy's bed unprepared.

Of course, getting pregnant was not Bronwen's decision. The classic accident. But the way she dealt with it was entirely *her*. So quiet on the surface, she's very instinctual underneath. And – like the rest of us here – she knows how to keep a secret.

And on. Sitting here with my soft fountain pen, reminding myself of my own pain laid out there in the tick book, I realise that in writing that book I learned to write consistently for the first time, a habit that has stayed with me all these years. (Without it, would I have become a writer?) I suppose these modern counselling gurus would say that when I wrote in the tick book I managed to 'externalise the deep scars and somehow heal myself'. (I can hear a vaguely transatlantic accent.) How little do they know. In all probability, fixing that time in words is the reason why time and again I cling to the enclosed world of childhood in my stories that so many children read. Not entirely healed, then. It merely shows that I've spent most of my life in some kind of dream world, at one remove from reality. Not a grown-up way to go about things, you might say.

Recently I heard Melvyn Bragg speak at the Durham Library. Tall and boy-faced, elegant in his pale city suit, he told us that when he was fourteen he spent a term truanting, walking the Cumbrian hills instead of going to school. He defined it as an 'unseen nervous breakdown'. So that's what it was. I could have gone up and hugged him, but obviously I didn't. Might have creased that suit.

I've often thought that Bronwen having Lily so early – too early – in her life was probably down to me living in this dream world. The whole thing happened before I really noticed. I've often wondered just who was Lily's father. But Bronwen has been entirely successful in covering his tracks. Not a whisper. There is no trace of this boy, this man – whoever he was – in her life. At the time, covered with guilt, I talked to the people – teachers and children – from Bronwen's school, but they were as baffled as I was. Her best friend. Baffled. They hadn't noticed her with any particular boy. No boy had ever hung around here at the house and made himself felt. Oh dear, what a thing to say!

It did cross my mind that she might have been, well, raped. But she was far too tranquil, too undisturbed for that. At least I knew her that well.

In my own mind I sometimes conjure up another life for my Bronwen: in this other life there is no Lily, and, of course, there is no hurried, makeshift education, no Jacob, no staying at home way beyond the age any daughter should stay around her mother.

In my story this different Bronwen goes to France to learn more French – she was so good at that when she was young. Then she gets a good degree and on to France for a higher degree. Once there, she marries a French professor who writes erudite books. (A bit Charlotte Brontë-ish?) Perhaps she becomes a translator, like that nice girl who translates my 'Pippa' books. Then – quite late – she has a boy, a half-creature: half-French, half-English. And all the more interesting for that.

Oh dear, I am circling back now to Brock and his Louise: his very late marriage and his children, who – like my Bronwen's dreamchild – are mermaid half-creatures. And all the more fascinating for that.

But in my life I have the real Bronwen, not the one storied up by me: this one is the good quiet mother, the clever woman growing more attractive as she gets older. Branching out at last, what with this course and this research. Not hiding away in her school. With a bit of luck now perhaps she won't go back there to become spinsterish and over-contained by the world of children. (Like me?) Perhaps now, with Lily grown, my Bronwen can pull herself out of her particular bowl of aspic and start to grow. Not that she will learn French and meet that erudite *professeur*. But she's at another branching pathway. Now she can walk on and become her real self. I have noticed a quiet relish about her these days.

I am determined she should leave this house. Otherwise, she'll stay for ever and the arid mother-daughter cycle will repeat itself yet again. How much things tumble down in families. Only Bronwen knows just who Lily's father is. Of course, there's no such mystery about Bronwen's own father, who has been equally absent from her own life, my own short, convenient marriage not lasting much beyond her fifth birthday.

So here we are Kate – Rosa – Bronwen – Lily: a prison of inheritance, mother-daughter-mother-daughter. A chain that has to be broken. I think Lily could be the breaking of the chain.

(Of course I might have broken that chain with the one person who could have smashed it with me. But that would have been a disaster. I am not alone in my suffering. I read somewhere that in the kibbutzim communes in Israel there is an incest taboo on unrelated youngsters who have been brought up together.)

My hopes are on Lily but it's not impossible now that Bronwen will find the means within herself – or the person – who will help her break the chain. It never seemed possible that I would do it. Of course Duncan Carmedy, Bronwen's father, entranced me when I was eighteen. All that book learning, all that verbatim quotation of Shakespeare. The house, the comfort. It was just too easy to marry him and revel in his support when I trained to teach after Bronwen was born. He didn't even object when I contributed to Brock's expenses at university. But he did not help me to break the chain. Marrying him was no bid for freedom. He was more rooted here than my mother and would never contemplate leaving. I grew to hate him so much for that. Sometimes I think my bad feeling poisoned him, somehow caused him to die. But even he would laugh at that. His voice echoes in my head sometimes. 'Your problem, Rosa, is you think too much.'

I suppose at least he got me out of my mother's house. You might say the achievement of my marriage is this comfortable house, this haven that has sustained Bronwen, Lily and me for all these years with such warmth. But then in the comfort of this house, caring for Bronwen, with Duncan's grave haunting me, I still couldn't get away. Of course that was when I began to look inside myself for change, for excitement. My stories and the way I research for them – these are my great journeys. Now I no longer feel the need to escape. I am beyond that. But sometimes – just sometimes – like my mother, I do contemplate the 'Bloody North'.

All this brings something else to my mind: young Cherie and *her* mother. The closeness of those two is almost palpable, as though the umbilical cord was never cut. The intimacy between them is complete, and miraculously it diminishes neither. Mrs Bostock confides in Cherie as though the child were twenty, not thirteen years old. She asks Cherie's advice about food, complains to her about her neighbours, the government, the council, the vagaries of her young husband. She pours her opinions into Cherie's finely

167

curled ear. Occasionally these opinions emerge – unmodified from Cherie's mouth – about the way things should be and what precisely is wrong with the world. Bizarre.

Although she is so small, Cherie has had no childhood. It seems she was born old. Am I happy or sad about that? I suppose I should be happy as, in my experience, childhood is no happy place.

Another thought. I do love my mother, Kate, with deep passion, but even at my age I fear her and tend to avoid her. And I remember my childhood too clearly to trust her entirely. The shadow of her unhappiness made – and still makes – me long to please her. But she delights – even now – in wrong-footing me. I suppose that's why I see so little of her, sending Bronwen and Lily as my surrogates. They both have a lot of time for Kate and feel no fear at all. There is satisfaction in that. Time, even now, has moved on.

But I must go and see her soon. There is her landmark birthday this year. A birthday party! From his letter to Charlie it appears that Brock actually intends to come for her birthday. There are certainly things for Kate to talk to him about. Perhaps she has forgotten it herself. But no! The tick book. Of course. She gave it to Bronwen. Kate's no fool. She's clearing up her life, just as she's cleared out her house.

Why do I watch her so closely, think about her so much? Even now! Perhaps it's I who need my life clearing up. Perhaps it's I who need to see Brock. And perhaps in writing in this new book – no tick book this – I can contemplate the scars and get on with things, just as I did after I wrote all that stuff down in the tick book when I was fourteen. And if someone reads this in another forty years' time, see if I care!

Stone Window

Bronwen

I looked around Dr Devine's study. What a contrast there was between Richard's eyrie and this spacious, high room with its ornate fireplace and tall, stone mullioned windows looking out on the narrow street below. Devine's desk – an elegant Georgian table – stood at right angles to the window. Behind that was a very modern chair, all gleaming chrome and red leather, a match for the low chair and couch beside the fireplace. Her books were in regimented rows, pulled right to the front of the shelves. No dust.

On the desk were two neat piles of files and a single book with a leather marker: Antonia Fraser's *The Weaker Vessel*, subtitled *Woman's Lot in Seventeenth-Century England*. I remembered Dr Devine's famous lecture on the role of women during the Civil War in my first term on the course. It was a fine, erudite piece of work.

'Sit down, won't you?' Dr Devine glided past me and placed a black patent-leather briefcase on the table.

I looked at the humble wooden chair this side of the table, then across to the low chair beside the fire. Dr Devine solved her problem by sitting on the wondrous chrome and leather on her side of the desk. I sat on the wooden chair.

Devine leaned back in her chair and surveyed me for a long minute. Then she extracted a file from her case, placed it carefully in front of her and opened it. 'Dr Stephens tells me we have a problem, Miss Carmichael.'

I felt the colour stain my cheeks. 'Well, not exactly a problem,

Dr Devine. Richard and I . . .' My voice trailed away. We had talked about it in the car on the way back from Carlisle: the impossibility now of his supervising my dissertation. Not after our time at Bluestone Dyke Farm. I tried to say it would make no difference, that we could keep the two things separate.

Richard had laughed at that. 'After the weekend we have had? After you have met Peter and Sophie? I don't *want* to keep this a secret, Bronwen. Aren't we adults? I want to flaunt it. Don't you? In any case we'd be in hot water with the good doctor. And the university. It would do your dissertation no good.'

Devine broke into my thoughts. 'We do have a dilemma, Miss Carmichael. We are all adult here. The presence of mature students inevitably blurs the lines between teachers and taught. Things were easier before.' She left that hanging delicately on the air. It was clear she had liked it better that way. 'But we have to deal with it.'

'I thought,' I ventured, 'another supervisor, perhaps?'

A small frown marred Devine's smooth brow. 'There you have it, Miss Carmichael. Your subject, this history-in-the-present *malarkey* . . .' her voice dripped with contempt '. . . is controversial in the academic field, to say the least. The theories are gaining ground, I admit it with some reluctance. However, appointing Dr Stephens was our attempt to come to grips – however temporarily – with these new ideas. So he was the obvious choice to supervise you. And now . . .'

Looking at Devine, I was suddenly struck by the thought that they must be very close in age. Why was she so intimidated by someone who was no older than herself? It was ridiculous. I had to smile. 'Oh dear, I see I've blown it.'

Devine frowned again. 'I see no reason to rejoice, Miss Carmichael.'

'Well, there must be a way round it, Dr Devine. We can put man on the moon, we can excavate individual identity with DNA. This matter of supervision can't be insoluble. Why can't *you* supervise me?'

Devine's glance dropped to *The Weaker Vessel*. 'I don't see how I . . .'

'What if Richard supervises me and you sit in on the supervisions? You can challenge him. You can see if his ideas hold academic water in your terms. I'd learn a lot. Perhaps even—'

Devine cut in. 'Don't you *dare* say *I'd* learn a lot, Miss Carmichael! The reverse would be the case.'

'Well, it would be one way round this problem. I'm halfway through this project and can't stop now. I won't stop now.'

Devine stared at me. 'Pity. I had this rather appealing idea about the role of women in the Rising of the North.' She permitted herself a wintry smile. 'Don't worry! I won't insist.' She stood up. 'Very well. We will go with that. But I *will* supervise in consultation with Dr Stephens. I'll make a note on your file to that effect, and inform him.'

I stood up and made for the door.

'Miss Carmichael!' The quiet emphatic voice came from behind her.

I turned round.

'I am aware that it's no one else's business, Miss Carmichael, but you do realise that Dr Stephens is very much married?'

I blushed. 'As you say, Dr Devine. It's no one else's business.'

I shut the heavy old door and leaned on it. 'Cow,' I muttered fiercely into the weathered panels. 'Dried up, academic cow! *Weaker vessel*, all right.' But even as I said it I knew I wasn't being fair. Devine had dealt with the matter quite well, all things considered.

Twenty minutes later, in the Royal County, Cali choked over her toast when she heard the story. She laughed about Devine but she was more intrigued by the thing with me and Richard Stephens.

'I suspected it, of course, but really, darling, he's absolutely too long in the tooth for you. What would you say if I ran off with Charlie?'

'Are you going to do that?'

'Well, I do love the old boy to death, darling. I *get* him. He is special. He's my precious friend and always will be. But carnal knowledge? Ugh! Ri-diculous. Young flesh is my preference.'

'A cannibal. I always thought you had cannibal tendencies. Hanibella Lecter, you.'

'Thank you. That's the most exciting thing you've said to me in weeks. Now I realise why. You've been seriously, humungously, preoccupied. Makes me realise, darling, that despite being so decrepit the old boy really must be good in bed. A laugh with Charlie Chaplin? A brush with Picasso? Is that how it is?'

I resisted the temptation to say that it was much, much better than that, but instead told Cali to mind her own business. 'He's not decrepit. I can vouch for that. Anyway, Hanibella, how is the music?'

'Fab. Oh! I was going to say. We – that is Charlie and the boys with me taggin' along – have a gig in a place called Crook. The Elite Hall. Spelled E-l-i-t-e. But they say "Ee Light"! Strange place, this is. Strange way of saying things. Sometimes since I've been in these parts I feel like Alice in Wonderland. Anyway. Why don't you bring old Stephens along to the gig so he can see Durham life in the raw? And what about Lily? Has she ever seen her uncle on full banjo? Should be a laugh.'

'May . . . be.' I gathered my book-bag. 'Have to go, love. Got to talk to somebody's grandfather about the war. I love these stories that I have been hearing. Whether they'll do for the study I don't know. What about your Victorian philanthropists? How are they coming along?'

Cali groaned and rolled her eyes. 'So boring, darling. So unutterably boring. God save me from self-made men. I've met a few in this century. So fucking full of themselves.' She caught my sleeve. 'The gig? You'll bring the American to the gig?'

I pulled myself free. 'Only if he really wants to come, Cali. Might be just a bit too "life in the raw" for him. He's only this very genteel elderly American. Might be just too much for him.' I leaned down and kissed Cali on her soft cheek, breathing in the scent of patchouli. 'I know! I'll tell him you're just an old-fashioned girl. Singing sweet old songs. Seeing as he's such an old guy he might just enjoy it.'

The Tiger in the Corner

Summer 1991

More in this new notebook. Here goes. This writing down is compulsive.

About Brock. After he went off to university, Brock came home only briefly – bulkier, longer-haired and more of a genial stranger at each visit. He worked through most vacations – taking all manner of jobs in Scotland, in London, in Canada, in Namibia. He did this not just for the experience (which he did relish), but for the money. In his first year at St Andrews he met this boy from Eton – not of the first grade academically – who knew all about money. He'd gambled on the Stock Exchange since he was eight. Ran a gambling syndicate at school. This chap saw money as a religion, a pathway to secular power, and he showed Brock the way.

At St Andrews and later at Oxford, Brock studied French and Russian. But alongside the attraction of the language and politics of the USSR, he was driven by a fascination with what he called 'the juggernaut politics of capital in that changing continent'. That's in one of his letters. I don't know what Charlie made of it.

Each time Brock came home he seemed more solid, more alien, more *himself*. He was 'the little brother' no more; he was a stranger, heavily built, horn-rimmed glasses . . .

His very last visit home was just before he went to Moscow to take up some research for the British Government, supposedly some kind of attachment to the British Embassy. That period presaged a lifetime of stints into and out of a USSR that almost became his second home. He watched the Cold War change temperature, watched the USSR stumble and evolve into the world as we know it with no Berlin Wall, where Capital is King.

I know all this from his letters, which I have read so many times.

But before all that, there was this time he was home, to celebrate getting a very fine doctorate. The two of us went out together to a little Italian restaurant on Clay Path in Durham City. It was popular then, even exotic. Every time I smell that combination of burned wheat, garlic and tomatoes I think of that night with Brock.

He had set it up for us to go alone. Bought Charlie a seat on a bus trip to the Fiesta Club in Stockton where Engelbert Humperdink was singing. And he'd dropped Kate with a toy-laden Bronwen off at one of the aunts for their occasional whist-cake-and-tea nights. He took them a bottle of Fino sherry, I remember.

In the restaurant he lounged back easily in the smoky light, and fixed me with a very Brock-look over his glasses, no longer horn-rimmed but small and round with metal frames.

'Well, Rosa, how are we these days, apart from enlightening the great unwashed in that school of yours?'

'Don't be so bloody patronising!'

'Owch!' He held up a hand before his face as though to fend off a blow. 'Just something to say, Rosa.' His voice, stripped of all sound of the North, laced with the clipped tones of the establishment, the BBC, the Diplomatic Service, had become the voice of a stranger.

I remember I said. 'You don't sound like you, Brock. I'm sitting here and I don't know who you are.'

He took my hand then. 'I am Brock, Rosa. I am me. See that scar in my thumb? That's where I cut myself on some wire in Tudhoe Woods where we went to watch the Pitch and Toss. Do you remember?' He tapped his bearded cheek. 'And this one's where Sam Brooks broke my cheekbone when I was giving him a hiding for bullying our Charlie. It's me, Rosa, under all this.'

'All right then.' I unclasped his hand. 'Even if it really is you those scars give you no right to insult me and the children I teach.'

'*Mea culpa.*' He bowed his head. Then he was looking at me, his silver-grey eyes gleaming in the candlelight. 'No. I was trying to get you to tell me about this story thing . . .'

'Story thing!'

'Sorry. Kate tells me you have been writing stories . . .'

Then I told him about the children's story that had just been taken. Sold. Actually sold. For money! Over our pizza he made me tell him the actual story. It was half made up and half about that real time when the policeman came to frighten my mother about Charlie's misdeeds. It involved theft and secrecy and had a good resolution. Brock nodded as the story unfolded, then demanded to hear what the woman from Corgi had said about it.

He leaned across the table and clasped both my hands. 'Great stuff, Rosie. You'll be famous and I'll be rich. How about that?'

I left my hands there, between his. 'Writing children's stories will never make me famous, Brock. Most definitely not rich'

That was when he leaned right across the table and kissed me full on the lips. I could feel the glances from the dark booths all around. Then he stood up, threw some notes on the table and almost hauled me out of the restaurant, up the hill and down the narrow alleyway that led to the car park. There in that narrow place we kissed like teenagers against the wall and held on to each other as though we were drowning. I told myself that I could allow myself this, just this. But then we were in the car and he was driving like a maniac, my hand in his, and we stopped at this place, one of the new motels on the A1. And we spent the night there. Together.

Neither of us mentioned the forbidden nature of what we were doing, but it was there in the room between us like a tiger in the corner. Only I knew that it was the innocent guilt of the children of the kibbutz. *He* thought it was the other thing and I couldn't enlighten him. Perhaps I should have told him then, of the night in Lancaster when he came into our family. I longed to tell him all this was all right. That he wasn't my brother. Not in blood. I can't say – even now – why I didn't tell him. It would certainly have changed our lives. But it wasn't my secret to tell. It was Kate's, and she wasn't telling anyone.

We got back at three in the morning, just before Charlie.

Bronwen and my mother were fast asleep. The next day when I got up he was gone. And that was the last time I saw him, except for the increasingly alien photographs that come with the letters he sends to Charlie and my mother. With the letters, the French wife, the merman child, the cars, the boats, the small château, the fixers who make life easier for him wherever he goes.

But now he'll come. He'll come for Kate's party. I know it. I don't quite know if I can bear that. But of course I will, because I have to. But part of me just wants to see him. Brock in the flesh after all these years.

Sweet and Sour

'Of course, pet,' said Kate, pushing her bit of pork from the sweet part of the sauce into the sour. 'You're not a bit like your mother or your grandmother Rosa.'

'Why's that?' said Lily. She was standing on her head, her slender feet nearly reaching the low picture rail, her T-shirt slipping past her small tight bra and scalloping down about her neck, revealing the tender button-like navel. 'Because I like to see the world upside down?'

Kate chewed carefully at her pork, contemplating in passing the miracle of still owning quite a few of one's own teeth. 'Don't be daft, pet. Now let's see. Your Grandma Rosa? Well, our Rosa's always been kind of folded in, like a pillowcase. Born in the war, you see. It didn't leave anyone unscathed. People were left with lots of problems. It's all there in the newspapers. Post-traumatic and that. New thing. Like shell shock in the Great War.'

Lily flopped gently to the floor and sat with her back to the wall, relishing the gravity-rush of her blood coursing back down through her body. 'And you, dear Kate? Did the war *scathe* you?'

Kate put down her fork. A smile glimmered around a mouth made thin as string by old age. 'Me, pet? Why, me, I had a *good* war.'

Lily frowned. 'Good? What's good about war? Didn't you see that stuff on TV? That horrible stuff in Slovenia and Croatia. And those air strikes in the Gulf. "The hand of Thor striking from the heavens" – that's what this philosopher who came to school to tell us how to think calls it. How can people do that thing? Rain down destruction on other people? Shoot them? Burn them?'

'Well, pet, you didn't have television then. Not in your homes. You never really saw it, all that raining-down destruction. I tell a lie. You saw bits of it at the pictures. Pathé News. All edited like a film itself with a voiceover telling you what to think. Not the same as now, with those reporters in army jackets dodging bullets, playing at being heroes themselves. We were all for victory and beating Hitler then. Seemed simpler, pet.' Kate started to eat again with her usual thoroughness.

'Even so, how could anyone say they had a good war?'

'Well, I suppose it stirred everyone up, pet, reminded them they were alive. I read in a newspaper that you are never more alive than the moment before you die. Soldiers have always known it. But in our war we ordinary people knew it too. Us people down here below, us people back at home. I suppose those people in Croatia know it. All that raining down.' She pushed her plate away. 'All I know is that for women it made everything different. We got out of the house. We drove trucks, we built tanks and shells. We danced, we shopped – mostly queuing, really – we cooked up miracles – well, that's what they say we did – we "made do and mended" like we were told. We were all shook up. After the war our Rosa used to dance to a song called "All Shook Up". She did like to dance. Funny, her being so quiet. Anyway, that's what we were like in the war. Suddenly anything was possible. We were "all shook up".'

'Did *you* drive tanks?'

Kate shook her head. Then she smiled. 'No. I didn't cook miracles either. But I did nurse mad people. Well, the ones who were shut away. There were mad ones outside but they had their uses, in war. Anyway, the folks in my mental hospital didn't really know there was a war on but even so they were still "all shook up". Their condition, you see. It was all going on inside.'

'But Grandma Rosa didn't have a good war?'

More shakes of the head. 'Grew up after the war, really. Always had her head in a book. Or a newspaper. All that stuff about the camps! Enough to depress anyone. I had to take them away from her in the end.'

'And her dad dying like that. She told me once. Rob Carmichael. My great-grandfather. He died.'

Kate sniffed. 'Rob? That too, I suppose. He'd have liked you, Rob. He was always very fond of Rosa. She him. I could see she missed him but what can you do?' She paused. 'Now then, pet, can you just mix me some of that Instant Whip? Strawberry. There are two packets left. Use the big whisk, now! If you get pockets of powder it's like biting grit.'

Lily waited till Kate had finished her Instant Whip before she pushed the conversation further. 'And my mum? What's your theory about her?'

'Bronwen? Oh, our Bronwen's a treat. Nobody nicer, I always say that . . .'

'But . . . ?' supplied Lily.

'But . . . d'you ever see that programme on TV about amber, how it oozes from the trees and sets for ever? They showed you how insects crawled into it, thinking mebbe it was something sweet, like honey. And they get set for ever. They never really perish.'

'And when Mum got me, she was set for ever?'

Kate's gaze faltered. Crepe lids lowered over bright eyes. 'I wouldn't say that, pet. Mebbe once she herself crawled into this family there was no escape.'

'Determinism!' announced Lily. 'We discussed it with the Philosopher. I don't believe in it.'

'You make it sound like a religion,' said Kate.

'No, Kate, it's you that make it sound like a religion. An insect crawls into a bit of amber and it's Jesus Christ.'

Kate sat back in her chair, closed her eyes and then opened them. 'Crikey, Lily, every time we have one of these chats you lose me off. I thought I knew a thing or two. Known for it. But you have brains. Your dad musta been something special, whoever he was. All I can say.'

'*Crikey?* Who says that these days?' Lily grinned, grabbing the fragile bony hand and squeezing it. 'Oh, Lady Kate, you're a peach.'

Kate let her hand lie there. She clasped Lily back. 'Now then, let's get to easier things, pet. Tell me all about this surprise party they're planning for me birthday.'

179

'I'm not supposed to say. It's a surprise party.'

'Surprises are bad for me. This heart.'

'Well, Uncle Charlie's band are going to be stationed on the first landing in our house and will play a set. Mum's friend Cali is playing the penny whistle. Nostalgic stuff. You know.'

Kate groaned. 'Someone on TV the other day said, "Nostalgia isn't what it used to be." Can you imagine?'

'Har–har!' said Lily gloomily. 'The old ones are the best.'

'What else?' demanded Kate.

'Well, Rosa's got a new hairstyle – shorter cut – and this new dress that makes her look no more than forty. Well . . . forty-one. I keep trying to get Mum to have her hair cut. That horrible plait. Yuk.'

Kate scowled. 'I never see much of our Rosa these days.'

'She makes the casseroles. She sends us. She says my mum and I are her surrogates. Now why don't I clear away? I'll just—'

Kate clung on to her hand. 'Surrogates? No you won't clear up. Leave them, I don't want no surrogates washing my pots,' commanded Kate. 'I like to wash me own. People are so careless these days. No wonder they're dropping like flies left right and centre. Germs everywhere. Now then, pet, this party. What else?'

'Mum's bringing her new boyfriend. Some teacher from the university. And his brother. They're twins.' She shuddered. 'How weird is that?'

Kate stared closely at her.

'So where does that put your theory about her being an insect in amber?' demanded Lily.

Kate shrugged.

Lily went on. 'Think of it, Lady Kate, after all these years the insect is crawling out, full of life . . .'

'. . . And twice as natural.' Kate finished the phrase that she had used since Lily was a toddler, bursting through the door in a gust of life. 'That it, then? For my party?'

'Well, not quite. According to Uncle Charlie, Uncle Brock's definitely coming from Moscow. Stopping off in France, then here. Stopping off? How cool is that? But then he says Uncle Brock has been coming before and has never landed.'

Kate loosened her hand from Lily's. 'We all know about that, pet. We'll take our Brock when he lands. *If* he lands. Good job he writes a decent letter or we wouldn't know him from Adam, would we?' Her voice had lost its edge.

Lily stood up. 'Gotter go, Lady Kate. Playing tennis with Simon this afternoon.'

'Sport!' snorted Kate, hauling herself to her feet. 'Now that's a new one in this family. Whoever your pa might have been, pet, he brought a breath of fresh air into this house.'

Lily, long used to casual mention of her unknown father, let that slide by.

As she locked the door behind Lily and made her way back to her seat by the fire, Kate dwelled upon the idea of Brock's return. Every time her son failed to turn up in the last twenty-odd years he'd managed to postpone the inevitable. Well, now might just be the time to say something. Though perhaps it was best to let sleeping dogs lie. Really. What harm was there in that? He didn't need to know. Did he?

Least Said

'Full turnout for this show of Charlie's, then?' said Rosa drily. She was standing in the doorway of the bedroom that had been mine since I was small, before it had evolved into a marital bedroom and then shrunk again into the bedroom of a lone woman. Rosa sometimes called it my Prioress's Cell.

'What's that?' I was peering into the mirror above the fireplace, applying a second coat of mascara.

'This outing to Charlie's show. According to Lily, she and I are going. As well as – er . . .'

'Me and Richard, and his brother, Peter, of course. As you say, Charlie and Cali really want a good turnout.' Sophie had sent Peter across to Durham to spend some time with his brother. I could just imagine her shoo-ing him away like she shoo-ed her chickens.

'Are they exactly alike, those two men?' said Rosa. 'Or should one not ask?'

I shook my head. 'Richard says people are always curious about it. Since you ask, they are and they aren't alike. Size and shape, yes, although Peter's much bulkier. Sense of humour, yes. Way of walking, yes. Voice – in tone, yes; in accent, not quite. But the thing that strikes you about those two is their sheer joy, their sheer delight in being together. Very unusual in grown men. But not surprising when you think that for their first twenty-odd years they were each other's mirror. I've begun to understand that they're each to some degree bereft, when they're apart – which is most of the time.'

'Bereft? I felt like that for years after my father died,' said Rosa, her voice suddenly bleak.

I turned to look at her. 'You can tell that from the tick book. How bereft . . .'

Rosa's eyes were glassy. 'I haven't read it again, you know. Don't need to. Poor little girl, that young Rosa. Quite, quite desperate.' She turned and walked swiftly along the landing.

Turning back to the mirror I wondered briefly just what sort of can of worms I'd managed to open with my curiosity about the war. Then I turned my thoughts to Richard, which quite often happened now when I was alone. In the last few weeks, without the burden of discretion, we had relished our time together: in his eyrie at the university, in his rooms at college. Impromptu breakfasts when I arrived in Durham in the mornings. Midday feasts brought in bags from Marks & Spencer. Talking our lives and making love. Always making love.

It was always the day before the bomb. We lived in the present. Only once did Richard allude to the future. He'd found a small Celtic brooch in the market, a blunt cross set with polished coloured stones. 'The guy said it was more than fifty years old. I guess it could last another fifty.' He pinned it to my blouse when we got dressed again after making love early one morning.

I didn't object to this living in the present. It was my idea, after all.

Now I looked at my watch. Half an hour early. I sat down at my table and put on my earphones, conscious that I had to grab every moment for the laborious transcription of my tapes. Transcribing the tapes took much longer than doing the interviews. Analysis seemed a long way away.

I wrote at the head of the yellow sheet: 'Mrs Eileen MacIntosh, 82, the great-grandmother. Kelly MacIntosh, 15 (Year 9).' After a few minutes the woman's ragged, elderly, over-used voice began to take on pure, young tones as the image of her younger self emerged. One section caught my particular attention.

'Those days you lived right on the day, pet. My lad went overseas six weeks after our wedding. Never saw him again till after the war. But round here, you just live day to day. Queuing and shopping for me mother. Working across at the ROF making shells. Long hours, but all right really. Good pay to tip up for me mam and a bit over for my Post Office book. The ROF lasses were good. Never a dull moment. We went dancing Friday and Saturday nights. Soldiers came over from Barnard Castle. Not from round here, those lads. Taller, generally. From Devon and the Isle of Man. Funny talkers, them. There was this really nice lad from there. Good manners. I remember thinking it was funny that our lads had gone over to Italy and these lads came here. And even these new lads vanished just before D Day, like. Just like water rushing for the plug hole.' The voice on the tape went on, became even younger. 'I fell wrong, like, with that Isle of Man lad. I called the bairn William James after my husband.'

Then I heard my own voice, bland and neutral. 'So what did your husband think about the baby, when he got back?'

The woman's voice went on, 'Billy? Well, they took a bit of time to get on together. But that happened all over, when the men came back to their families. But they soon made up. My Billy was a good father to William James. And the other two that we had ourselves. My Billy was like a string-bean when he got back home, but he soon filled out. He used to take our William James for walks down Tudhoe Woods. Fresh air did them both a lot of good.'

I cringed, then, at the prissy tones of my own voice. 'Didn't he mind about it?'

'About what?'

'About where . . . how William James came . . . he was away.'

There was a distinct pause on the tape.

'Why, pet, he never mentioned it and neither did I. Least said, soonest mended. He was pleased to be around at all, after his time in that bliddy camp. And I was pleased to see him.'

'So this child William James is Kelly's granddad?'

'Yes . . . well, he *was*. Got picked off by cancer in 1980. The doctor said, was there any in the family? And I just said never. Never before. I wouldn't know about this Manx lad.'

Then I heard myself breaking the research rule of no assumptions, no preconceptions. 'And when did you tell William James about it? About where he came from? How . . . ?'

The woman's laugh was like the twittering of birds. 'Now, pet. I'm no idiot. Why should I tell him? There was no harm. Like I said, least said, soonest mended.'

'And Kelly and her dad don't know?'

'Kelly and her dad? No. Why should they? Nothing spoiled . . .'

I clicked off the tape and drew a line through the last page of the transcript and put the sheets in a fat ring-binder. That last page was unusable, inexpressible except in the most common generalisation about the statistics on illegitimate births during the war. But my thesis was not about common generalisations. It was about a close-in, almost magnified, focus on the individual's unique perceptions of their wartime experiences. I could not use the involuntary disclosures of an eighty-two-year-old woman, of facts that her own family did not know.

I rewound the tape, returned it to the rack and closed her file. There were so many drawbacks to this way of working. In putting a line through Mrs MacIntosh's words about William James, I was airbrushing his Manx father right out of that family history. I wondered now where these thoughts left me in relation to Matthew Pomeroy. Wasn't saying nothing about him to Lily just the same as lying?

'You shouldn't frown, Bronwen.' Rosa was standing in my bedroom doorway. 'You tend to look your age when you frown. Did you say your friends will meet us at this hall?' She came across and put her hands on my shoulders. 'To be honest, darling, I don't know whether I'll looking forward to our Charlie and his banjo, but I'm really looking forward to meeting your friend Richard. Lily too. She's very intrigued.'

I didn't know whether I was looking forward to it. Much to Richard's frustration I had delayed bringing him home to meet my family. It was quite contrary to my rule of living in the present, the day before the bomb. I knew that letting him in would involve the past and the future. Quite how true that was I could never have anticipated, not in a thousand years.

The Emperor of Rome

At the Elite Hall Richard half rose in his seat when he saw us and raised a hand. He and Peter were sitting on one of the corner banquettes, pints of bitter ale before them. They wore roll-neck shirts under leather jackets: Richard pale blue under black, Peter white under brown. Their similarity was distinctive, although Peter's shorter hair and bulkier frame marked the difference between them.

I heard Rosa say, 'Good grief!' as we made their way between the crowded tables to the corner. The two men stood up as I made the introductions. Richard shook Rosa by the hand and grinned at me. 'Nice bloke, your uncle. He came over with drinks before he went out back. Cool. He left some under the counter for you.' He strolled off to the bar to find our drinks. Lily, Rosa and I sat in silence for a moment, then I asked Peter about Sophie, saying how much I enjoyed her company and what a pity she wasn't here.

Peter's face lit up. 'Aye, she's a big miss, is our Sophie. But what would her livestock do without her? The very trees would weep.'

'Is she the proper farmer?' said Lily. 'Herself? It's not you?'

Peter shook his head. 'I can drive a tractor or get the beasts in, but the farm? The land, the livestock and the seasons? All that's intricate, love, like a clock. Old Sophie's had that mechanism bred into her through the ticktock of three generations.'

'So what do *you* do, then?' said Lily, tilting her head, concentrating on him.

'Me? I work in the forest. Trees, not livestock, is the rhythm that

I live by. Twenty-year seasons in a forest. Hundred year turnaround.'

'So how d'you get into trees?' said Rosa, staring at him intently.

'Climbing?' said Lily. And we all laughed.

Peter looked at Rosa. 'After we'd met your Bronwen, our Sophie bought some of your books in Carlisle, Mrs Carmichael. And we read them. We don't have children but we read them ourselves, over a few nights. Sophie told me to say to you how much we enjoyed them. How really nice they were and how she wished they'd been around when she was a kid.'

This was very direct. Rosa flushed. 'That's very kind of you . . . her.'

'Kind? It was a privilege . . .'

They were interrupted by the return of Richard with the tray of drinks, followed by a bustle out front as Charlie and Theo Cartwright set up on the raised area at the end of the room. They were dressed in pale yellow T-shirts and working jeans. On his feet Charlie wore well-polished brown loafers, but Theo wore his scruffy 'lucky trainers'. Theo's hair was slicked back in his Elvis sweep and Charlie had had his usual short back and sides. He glanced over towards our corner and winked, somehow achieving the wink with his whole head, not just his eye: a kind of whole-head twitch, generous and inclusive. We all waved at him and some people turned to look at us.

Then Stan Smith plodded on to the stage like a great bear, followed by Cali. She looked quite odd. The only Cali-like things about her were her high boots and her bird's-nest hair. Like the men she wore a yellow T-shirt and jeans, although her T-shirt was ripped down the front and tucked in to show a decent bit of cleavage. Surprisingly she looked a little nervous. It occurred to me that the clientele here were a different kettle of fish from the more pretentious but less demanding audiences she'd met so far at university gigs.

They were set up. Stan Smith placed his bodhrán carefully on the stool beside him. He tucked his fiddle under his chin. Theo slipped the strap of his guitar over his head. Cali fingered her whistle. Charlie made a play of adjusting the microphones one

187

more time before sitting down with his banjo. The stage lights brightened. The other lights dimmed slightly, though not so much that it would be hard for any customer to find their way to the bar to replenish their drinks. Business was business.

The audience dropped into silence.

Charlie stood up and spoke quietly into the microphone. 'Here's one for those of you who know your pigeons. There must be a few in here . . .'

A small cheer bubbled from the back by the bar.

'It's about courage and fortitude and about grace. It's called "The Emperor of Rome".'

Charlie sang the song like conversation, merely keying his voice to the music. It told the story of a racing pigeon in a long-distance race, who got home when everyone thought he had not survived the journey. Cali did a short solo on her whistle before the last verse, at the point where it seemed as though the pigeon was lost. When the song was finished there were murmurs of appreciation from the audience.

After that they performed the song I'd heard in the shed, about the miners' strike and the pitman brothers, followed by one or two older folk songs. Then Charlie did a banjo solo, intricate and without words, which raised appreciative applause. Then they did an Irish song featuring Stan Smith's virtuoso playing of the bodhrán. Then Charlie sang 'Danny Boy' as a kind of duet between his voice and Cali on the whistle. The audience applauded warmly and as the band took their bows there were shouts of 'More'. In response Theo came centre stage and performed a version of Elvis Presley's 'Old Shep', an innocent parody, much appreciated. After bowing to the appreciative applause they trooped off and the room was a-clatter with people replenishing their drinks and the sudden surging thump of music from the DJ's cabin in the corner.

Through the noise Rosa leaned towards Peter. 'I have this peculiar feeling I've seen you before somewhere.'

He exchanged glances with his brother. 'Often happens. Rich's theory is that people take us both in at a glance and register familiarity and that somehow transforms itself into a sense of having seen one or other of us before. Human *déjà vu.*'

'Weird!' said Lily.

'Try living it,' grinned Richard. He had manoeuvred his chair beside me and was holding my hand. I could feel Rosa's glance, knew she was paying close attention.

Charlie and Cali came in through the exit door, followed by Theo and Stan Smith, who made their way straight to the bar. Charlie tucked in on the banquette beside Rosa, and Cali sat beside Peter. Rosa put her mouth to Charlie's ear. 'That was so good, Charlie. I didn't know, didn't realise . . .' she said.

He grinned. 'You never asked, pet. Pleased you liked it, though.' He nodded across towards Richard and Peter. 'What about these lads? I couldn't keep my eyes off them, even when I was up there strutting my stuff.'

'Soon wears off,' said Richard. 'Believe me. That set of yours was really good. I loved "The Emperor of Rome".'

Charlie nodded. 'A great song, that. Of course, old Cali here did her bit.'

We all turned to Cali and she squirmed under our benevolent gaze. Not 'cool' but warm. I thought of our talk about family. Perhaps this evening she was brought right into its heart.

Then the music from the DJ's console swelled and talk became impossible. The dance floor was filling and everyone except Rosa got up to dance: Charlie rock and rolling with Cali, Lily doing some kind of awkward twist with Peter, me happily in Richard's arms improvising a kind of rock foxtrot. Rosa was sitting and watching tapping her foot. I thought of the thirteen-year-old Rosa with the curtains drawn, whirling and whirling in the daytime-dark, to music from the wireless. And I thought of her missing her dancing lesson to watch the man escaping from his chains. All there, wasn't it, in the tick book?

Our party broke up just before closing time. Charlie went off with Theo in the van and Cali roared away on her motorbike. Richard and Peter left in Peter's four-by-four. Lily and I piled into Rosa's car.

Richard had whispered to me to go back with him and Peter but I refused. I could have squared it with Rosa but I didn't really want to be with the two of them. Not on my own. With Sophie there it would have been different. He pulled a face, then kissed me on the nose. 'Oh well. I've met them and that's something. Your family, Bronwen, like you, are unique. Brilliant. Phone you tomorrow?' And then and there, by the car, in front of Lily and Rosa, he kissed me properly.

'Well,' said Lily as I got into the back seat. 'He's got it bad, hasn't he? Are you sure he's the one for you?'

'Oh, shut up, will you!' I slid down in my seat.

'You two are an odd pair,' said Rosa from behind the wheel. 'Sometimes you'd think you were the mother, Lily!'

Odd? Takes one to know one.

Always the Worst

Rosa was quiet in the car on the way home from the gig. She drove efficiently, peering at the narrow night road, oblivious to our chatter in the car as Lily persisted, firing more questions at me about Richard and Peter, about where Richard lived in America, and about Sophie and the farm in the Lake District. She said what must it be like for those two men, with the Atlantic between them? They certainly did make you uneasy, with that strange likeness. But they were likeable. She did like them. Really.

As we opened the hall door the first thing that hit us was the red eye of the telephone winking at us. Rosa looped her handbag over the newel post, picked up the phone, listened to the message, then started dialling, her back rigid.

'What is it?' I said.

Rosa put up her hand, listened, then put down the phone and dialled again. She put it down for a second time. 'It's Kate. A message from her saying she's fallen. And now she's not answering.'

We turned back to the door. Rosa said Lily should stay behind to listen for any more messages, but Lily refused. In five minutes we were at Kate's bungalow, which was in darkness. Rosa used her own key to open the door and, flicking lights on as we went, we walked through the rooms. Kate wasn't there. The bed was disturbed. In the sitting room a low table was lying on its back like a dog with its legs in the air. I felt a chill at the nape of my neck. Lily clutched my arm.

We rushed back into the hallway. There on the glove shelf, held down by a snow-scene of Blackpool was a note in a neat schoolboy hand. 'Mrs Carmichael has been taken to Bishop Auckland Hospital. Please find her there.'

The hospital lights were low and grey, and the corridors echoed with subdued voices and the click of hard heels. When we got to the ward, the sister, a tall hawklike woman, would not let us visit Kate in her side ward. She led us to a small window so we could see Kate in the dim reflected light from the corridor. The figure under the neat cover could have been a seven-year-old. Her face, cradled in her hand, was bony and spare. Her hair a silver spider's web across the pillow.

Rosa clutched my arm.

'I believe she fell,' said the sister. 'Something to do with a mat in the bathroom. She's had a sedative and is tucked in till morning.'

'Is she injured?'

'Nothing broken, as far as we can see. Bruising to the side, the hip, the cheekbone. They'll do X-rays in the morning. She told us in no uncertain terms that there was nothing the matter with her even though it was her who got the ambulance. Forceful lady.'

'She was a nurse herself,' volunteered Lily. 'Years ago.'

'They're always the worst,' said the sister, smiling to show this was a joke, not an insult.

'So we can come and get her in the morning?'

'I should think so. But leave me your number and I'll get the day staff to telephone you when she's back from X-ray.'

'And we'll be able to bring her home?' said Rosa.

'Depends on the doctor, of course. As long as there's no break. Of course, she's very fit for her age. Well nourished. Can't say that for all the old people who end up here.'

'That's my Grandma Rosa's casseroles,' said Lily earnestly. 'Meat and two veg. Every day. And the multivitamins.'

The sister glanced from one to the other. 'So you're the old lady's daughter?' she said finally to Rosa.

Rosa nodded. 'I'm the said grandma.'

'She mentioned you. Said you'd turn up. Said you'd take care of things. Like I say, she's a lucky woman. Plenty of the old dears who get in here have no one. Crying shame, I say.'

In the car on the way home Lily broke the silence. 'I never thought of Kate as a person who might die. Not Kate.'

'She's not going to die,' I said. 'She just fell down. She's OK.'

'We're all going to die,' said Rosa abruptly.

'Mother!' I said.

Lily giggled. 'I've never heard you call Grandma that before,' she said. 'Sounds like a radio play.'

Later, I was already in bed when Rosa knocked on my door and waited for an invitation before walking in, balancing a teacup in her hand. She sat down on the low chair beside the blocked-in fireplace. 'I'm too awake, Bron. Can I sit?'

I sat up straighter in bed. 'You're worried about Kate. But just think! She's tough as old boots. Just look how she managed even this crisis. She let us know, got herself an ambulance, sorted that old sister.'

Rosa stared at her. 'Kate's fragile, Bron. Like the rest of us. But she's never admitted that. Now she'll have to come and stay here for a few days at least. She won't like that. I suppose once she perks up there'll be no keeping her. That's a blessing.' She took a sip of her coffee. 'What a strange evening it's been, Bron. Me, I was so surprised at Charlie. So touching. I hadn't expected that. I thought it was all rock and roll. Delayed youthful excess. A bit sad. That kind of thing.'

'According to Cali he writes lots of those songs. That thing about the miners is his own. Did you know he wrote things himself?'

Rosa shook her head. 'I thought he just played for laughs in that shed of his. Didn't even realise he performed. He was different in that hall. Not diffident. Sure of himself.'

'And you're surprised by that?'

'Isn't it terrible? To me he's just cosy old Charlie who used to be a bit of a mischief but who settled down to work at the factory, met a merry widow and set up house. He's kind, is Charlie. Nice to our mum. Undemanding. And there he was, performing to hundreds of people, singing his songs and moving grown men to tears. Made me feel again that we never really know anyone, even our own.' She drained her cup. 'So this Richard, Bron. Is it a serious thing?'

'Well, we're seeing each other, as they say. As for serious. I don't really know.' I wondered if I should tell her about Maria.

Rosa stood up. 'He seems very nice. That wry charm. And that remarkable thing with his brother. Very difficult to carry off, I would think.'

'I don't think they worry about carrying anything off.'

'The age difference doesn't worry you?'

'He's forty-seven, Rosa, not sixty-seven.'

'Now there's a thought.'

'He does have all his own teeth, you know.'

'Me too.' Rosa looked down at her. 'I had quite a jolt when I saw him, you know.'

'Why? Because he's so long in the tooth?'

'No. I can't really say why. Probably the twin thing. How much the same they are. How different. How alike but unalike. I keep thinking, feeling I've dreamed this before. Have you ever had that feeling? Oh, leave it. Your mother's going potty, dear.'

I grinned. 'I suppose this is where I tell you that he's married. Happily, so I'm told.'

Rosa raised her eyebrows. 'Oh, well.' She stood up. 'And I suppose this is where you tell me you're a grown woman in full command of your senses and I should mind my own business.'

'Something like that.'

At the doorway she said, 'I'll go for Kate tomorrow. We'll have to clear a space in the boxroom and move Lily in there. I hope Lily won't mind but it'll only be for a few days. Kate will want to go home as early as possible. She does like her own front door.'

'Lily was cut up to see Kate like that,' I said.

'She wasn't the only one. It made me realise I need to talk to her about something. Get something clear. I was reminded of it with the tick book surfacing like that.'

'Reminded of what?'

'Something I'd forgotten. Or buried very deep.'

I waited but Rosa turned and vanished along the dark landing. The door clicked behind her.

Just then my bedside phone rang. A thought fluttered through me about Kate so I was relieved when I heard Richard's voice.

'Where have you been, hon? I've rung you four times.'

Swallowing a flicker of resentment at his possessive tone I explained about Kate. He was very sympathetic. 'She'll be fine,' I concluded. 'Kate's as tough as old boots.'

'Will I get to meet her, this Kate?'

'If you play your cards right. You'll like her. She's a treat.' I paused. 'So, why the late call? What do you want?'

'Do I need an excuse to ring you?'

'At this time of night, yes.'

'Well, I've just tucked up old Pete in his cot and thought I'd like to say good night to you and tell you that it had been a great evening. And how even now I'm missing you and how much I wish you were lying here beside me in my cot with that thin strap of your gown slipping down over your shoulder.'

I laughed. 'You're incorrigible.'

'Seriously, I loved it tonight, seeing you among your own.'

'My own? That's the first time I've been to that club. I knew no one there.'

'You know what I mean. Charlie and Lily and Rosa. That Charlie! What a great guy he is. Different. Twin souls with your buddy Cali, as far as I can see.'

'It's just souls with those two. Remember that.'

'I kinda saw that. No less deep, though.'

I stayed silent.

'But with you and me, though, it's body *and* soul, Bronwen. Be sure of that.'

'If you say so.' I had made up my mind to be severe with him, telephoning so late, but I couldn't stop the smile in my voice.

'Don't you wish you were here in the cot beside me?' he said.

'No. I have a very comfortable bed here, thank you.'

Another silence.

'You have a very beautiful daughter, honey.'

'Thank you. I think she's lovely as well.'

'And your mother . . .'

'Rosa?'

'. . . Well, she's lovely too. But enigmatic. Very distinguished but very hard to read.'

195

'Are you fishing?'

'Fishing?'

'For what she thought of you?'

'Perish the thought, as Sophie would say.'

I left another tantalising pause.

'So, then, she thought I was a klutz?'

'She thought you were attractive. I told her you had all your teeth and were kind of funny.'

'That all?'

'Well, like you say, she's enigmatic.'

'Bronwen?'

'Yes?'

'*Are* you wearing that gown with the narrow straps?'

'No, I'm wearing some of Lily's pyjamas. They're printed all over with images of Winnie-the-Pooh.'

He groaned. 'I . . .'

'Richard. Go to sleep.' I put down the phone, switched off the light. I slithered down in bed and leaned my head on the pillow. It had been a long, long night. But as I turned over and snuggled down to sleep I was smiling.

Revolt

In her small room tucked in between Rosa's study and Bronwen's bedroom, Lily Carmichael hears the late murmur of conversation and tosses and turns in her narrow bed. Her room, christened the Tardis in the early days, has a big calligraphed notice pinned on the door saying 'NO GO!' The notice has been there since she was fourteen when she rebelled against over-enthusiastic cleaning of what she saw as her personal space. It is a small space, no more than ten feet square, but it works for her. When Lily was fifteen she threw out all the little-girl furniture and designed her own storage, covering two walls with industrial shelving on which sit baskets and boxes that contain all her possessions: books, pens, papers, files, ten years' worth of battered diaries, magazines, hats, socks, sweaters, T-shirts, jeans, cotton trousers, shoes, boots, school reports, dancing and ju-jitsu achievement certificates. A small sound system with racks of tapes and CDs. A miniature television (Christmas present from Kate – never used).

There are no photographs.

Two open shelves display a collection of ammonites, a musical dancing girl, three dressed Sacha dolls – boy, girl and mop-haired child – and eleven glass-globe snow scenes, which were Lily's obsession as a young child.

There is no mirror. Her toiletries are kept in the second bathroom down the corridor and her coats and jackets live in the downstairs cloakroom. There is no room here for a chair or a desk, but the bed, piled with cushions like a rajah's couch, does service as both. When she works she sits against a stack of cushions with an art board on another cushion on her knee.

From the age of seven up to the age of fourteen, Lily did all her homework in a little desk in her grandmother's study, working back to back with Rosa in companionable silence. Occasionally she checked a word or fact in one of Rosa's reference books, or chatted with Rosa about problems or ideas as they occurred to her. There in Rosa's room she learned to work fast and efficiently, finding study as natural as breathing. At school she was called gifted, but Lily knew it was all about the habits of study she learned in Rosa's room.

At the age of fifteen she transferred her study habits to the redesigned Tardis, building her own collection of reference books and only occasionally going next door to tussle through some new idea with Rosa. She did use Bronwen as a sounding board and consultant but it was Rosa who remained her study partner. It was from Rosa that she learned the power of books and the joy of finding the exact word to say what she meant.

This hot-housing has meant that Lily is top in her year at school in every subject without too much trouble, and is on her way to a Cambridge scholarship for certain. It has also meant that when she was younger, she was teased by both teachers and children (who for a short while labelled her 'Silly Lily'), for being slightly quaint, with her grave, grown-up language and mannerisms. But now this teasing has come to an end, as those around her see this interesting, grown-up Lily emerging, in whom these characteristics seem more appropriate, even attractive.

Teachers like her and treat her somewhere near equal. Friends now invade the Tardis – which seems to have the capacity to expand like its namesake – to listen to music, talk, and spin outrageous collaborative dreams. She has a best friend, Simon, who will never be her lover. From time to time some other boy will lounge on the rajah's couch with her, arousing in her feelings that few reference books can truly explain. It is all, Lily has begun to think, very good.

But tonight has not been very good for Lily. Tonight she has encountered mortality. She tosses and turns, throwing her cushions across the room, dislodging a million-year-old ammonite off a shelf.

Usually she is busy, contented with her life in this house, amused at the way that Rosa and Bronwen create and re-create the warp and the weft of their seamless lives. She is charmed by Kate's eccentricities and impressed with her total selfishness. She is quite aware that she herself is in transit, that *this* is not all there is, and that she is on her way to something much more exciting.

But for now, she is content. Which is why she was quite happy to join the oldies tonight for their quaint evening at Uncle Charlie's gig. But it didn't turn out too well, really. First there was that Richard Stephens. American. Besotted with Bronwen, anyone could tell. But he was an old man. Older, even, than Lily's head-master. And besotted. Chance was, he'd whisk Bronwen off to America and that would be that. And where would she and Rosa be then?

His brother, though, was all right. Less taut. Kinder-looking, less alien. In the car Rosa had gone on about how alike they were, the brothers. But Lily thinks they were not alike at all. Quite different. Now if the forester were besotted with her mother, that would be quite a different thing.

But even worse, what about that music? Dire! Posey sentiment. Sturdy Uncle Charlie talking sentiment, sweet and low. Mortifying. And Cali with her penny whistle and her yellow T-shirt! What was she thinking of? Lily rated Cali as reasonably cool in the past. But now even that would have to be rethought.

Of course, Lily now thinks with hindsight it was a mistake to go with the oldies anyway. Perhaps *she* was the freak, going with them. Most of her friends think it's weird that she has time for her family at all. And they've always found the Christian-naming thing weird. Lily is sick of explaining that when she was young, hearing Rosa call her mother Bronwen, she copied her. And when Rosa talked of herself to baby Lily she referred to herself by name: 'Rosa will take you for a nice walk', 'Rosa has made a nice cake for you.' 'Rosa' was much prettier than 'Grandma' and it stuck. And then, when she found out Kate's name she insisted on using that. Sometimes, if she was feeling especially respectful, she might call her Lady Kate. So in time Rosa called her own mother Kate and in the end Bronwen adopted the same first-naming habit.

But all that is past. Tonight Lily realises that she will have to stop this fraternising with the enemy: she has to decide which side she is on: the present and the future, or the past. There is really only one choice.

She turns over again on the bed, dislodging another cushion, and closes her eyes. But behind her eyelids now she has a vision of Kate's still, childlike figure under the hospital blanket. Kate. The best of them all. The most *herself* of all of them. The freest spirit. Not wrapped up in herself like the inward-looking Bronwen and Rosa. Kate's so full of herself she's not interested in wanting any part of you. But now there she is, on that narrow hospital bed, looking as if a hard breath would blow her right out of this world. Kate could die.

Lily turns over yet again, leans up and slots in a Jimi Hendrix tape, keeping the volume low. She lies back, her eyes closed. Now she's thinking of that unseen, unplumbed side of herself, the progenitor of the lively sperm that ignited her own life – the life of Lily Carmichael Carmedy always known as Lily Carmichael. She's quite aware that she herself is caught in the warp and weft of Bronwen and Rosa's lives, but she herself is neither warp nor weft. She is different from them. And that is down to *him*, whoever he is. There is no photograph of him anywhere. Lily has looked.

Now is the time, she thinks. Now is the time. I don't want Kate to die before I find out who he is, my *progenitor*. She is suddenly angry with Bronwen for not telling her, for not – never – saying a single thing about him.

Her bedroom door opens and there in the doorway is the object of her anger, wearing Lily's own cast-off Winnie-the-Pooh pyjamas, blinking and yawning.

'Are you all right, Lily? I heard your music.'

Lily sits up and turns off the tape. 'I'm fine,' she says shortly. 'Just restless . . .'

'I know,' says Bronwen. 'Kate . . .'

Lily leaves it at that.

Bronwen still stands there. 'Rosa says that Kate will need to come here for a few days. We thought if we sorted a bed in the boxroom for you, Kate could sleep in here.'

'No,' says Lily firmly.

Bronwen opens the door wider, letting in more light from the landing. 'Lily, I don't think you—'

'Have the right? Well, thank you very much.'

'Well, why not? Why won't you lend Kate your room?'

'Bronwen, it's the only space I have in the world. The only space that is really *me*. Kate wouldn't want to take it from me. I know it.'

The books rustle, the clock ticks, the tape deck hums in the long silence that follows. Finally Lily breaks it. 'Why don't *you* give Kate *your* room? Why don't *you* go in the boxroom?'

Bronwen stands up straight. 'I'll do that, Lily. No reason why not.'

I shut Lily's door behind me with a click and hear from inside the room, the Jimi Hendrix tape start up again. I climb back into bed and put out my light. During my daughter's life I have waited in vain for the 'terrible two-year-old temper tantrums', the 'pre-teen angst', the 'adolescent rebellion'. Lily has been almost too good. Now here it was, the Revolt. The first signal that will lead to irreversible change. About time too. I nuzzle my face into the pillow. The revolt! It is quite overdue when you think about it.

Data

Following the gig, I did not manage to see Richard for nearly a week. With a grumbling Kate installed in my bedroom I had to take over the dining room for my work, spreading my books, cards and transcripted interview sheets over the extended table and the four chairs. I played tapes of wartime music while I worked: songs and anthems so familiar that they were bleached of meaning and did not disturb my thinking.

The transcription of the tapes – a long, laborious process – was now complete. I placed Rosa's tick book and photographs alongside the transcriptions. My method of analysis was initially simple. Take quotations from the transcripts that related to the main themes that had emerged from my extensive reading of the literature. They were all there in the transcripts: Justification of the War. Perceptions of the Germans. Women at Work. The Government. The Germans. Law and Order (e.g., Black Market). Making and Mending. Military in the Community. The Moral Climate. The Bomb. Soldiers Coming Home. Each theme would make a chapter – a short essay on a theme, illuminated by direct quotes from my data. It linked very neatly the local attitudes to the national and international events. There was further work to do as I sorted through the cards again and again, looking for new insights. I needed to do some more thinking and reading about propaganda.

And on and on.

I worked on the material day and night, so that in the end I felt as though I knew the long transcripts by heart and could hear the voices of my interviewees in my sleep. Richard told me weeks ago, 'Lose yourself in your data, honey. Know it backwards, forwards, and upside down; the answers will be there. Then step back.'

Having stepped back I decided I needed to do some work on post-war films and literature. How much of the received wisdom emerged from that, rather than actual or handed–down family experience? And newspapers. Think of those references in Rosa's tick book.

And then there were the anomalies. Children whose grand-fathers had come from Poland or Lithuania during or after the war, whose fathers and mothers had come to work at the factory that dominated the town after the 1956 uprising in Hungary. And where, in the midst of all this, would I put Cy, Kate's Canadian?

I muttered resentfully about this in one of my late-night conversations with Richard. 'These anomalies!'

'Just another chapter, honey. Track back your historical research and references for anomalies and formulate another chapter.' He warned me that Dr Devine would be much more interested in my academic research and my bibliography than my human material. It would, he said, have been the opposite with him. 'Just play along with her. It'll still make a great paper.'

On some nights I was too tired even to talk to him, and he took his cue and kept the conversation short.

One afternoon Cali called round, dark rings round her eyes, to exchange tales of dissertation horror stories. 'These fiendish philanthropists, those voracious Victorian millionaires.' She moaned. 'Give me Jean Paul Getty any day. Those jumped-up, mealy-mouthed millionaires thought they were missionaries. Give me my decadent twentieth-century greed–is–good guys any time.' She sat up straight. 'Anyway, it's done now. I'm finished.'

I eyed her wearily. 'Finished?'

'Just about. Devine's passed the draft. Charlie's stepdaughter's typing the final draft on her work computer. State of the art, apparently. I'll be ready for submission at the end of the week.' She grinned.

I scowled. 'Have you seen this thing in the magazines about "no visible pantylines"?'

'Seen it? I live it, darling!'

'Well, I think you have perfected the "no visible work line".'

Cali rolled her eyes, 'Why, thank you, darlin',' she said. 'Now then,' she went on briskly. 'I've got a suggestion. Have a bath and wash your hair.'

I opened my eyes wide. 'Do I smell?'

'Like a sweet pea, my dear. No. But you look a wreck. You're hardly a member of the human race and that's no way to do research. You wash your hair and I'll cut off those split ends and blow-dry it for you. OK! OK! The plait can stay. I know you like to keep it long, darling, but this is ridiculous. There is long and there is *long and ratty*. The latter is unacceptable in a grown woman. So I'll do your hair and give you a manicure and return you to the land of the living. Then you can finish your paper.'

Later, shouting above the sound of the hair dryer, Cali said, 'Charlie has been a wonder, Bron.'

I took the dryer from her, turned it off, said, 'Are you getting too fond of him, Cali?'

Cali laughed. 'Can a person be too fond of another person? I feel comfortable with him. More than I ever was with my mother and father. He's my friend. Just like you are. When I go away from here I know I'll have two friends I'll always want to come back to. Charlie and you.'

I flinched. 'You're going?'

Cali nodded. 'I'm lighting off to London when I've put in my dissertation.' She brushed my hair vigorously, then wove it into its loose plait.

'London? Where will you go?'

'I have a friend who's forsworn the corporate world and is dabbling in some kind of charity to do with Yugoslavia. He has a spare back room that I can have for free in return for a bit of leafleting. And he has this scratch band called Lulu's Dog. Sounds like a laugh.'

'Oh.' I stared at her in the mirror. 'Good. That sounds good, just your ticket.' I sighed. 'Lucky you. But I'll miss you. Charlie'll miss you.'

Cali shrugged. 'What'll *you* do?'

'Me?' These days I barely thought beyond the next week. Researching. Writing. Seeing Richard. Beyond that everything was a blank. 'Probably go back to school . . .'

'Back there? After all this? I can't believe it. You could come to London with me and we'll kick up a storm.'

I was already shaking my head but Cali was right to be incredulous. How could I go back to that after this year? It was not just Richard. It was Cali and breakfast in the County. It was Durham and its river and the monumental buildings on the peninsula. It was the library and the books and rapt conversations in dusty rooms. It was even the intense Dr Devine. And it was, it was indeed, Richard Stephens. No denying that. I had the ridiculous thought now that I was really like those women on my tapes, talking about the war. Nothing would be the same again. Nothing. Richard would go back home. I would go back to school. But nothing would be the same.

'Hey! What's this? Tears?' Cali swung me round in my chair and put her hands on my shoulders. 'Don't worry, darling, I'll come and see you on visiting days. If they let me through the gate.'

I clung on to Cali's hands then, and started to laugh, tears streaming down my cheeks unchecked.

'Hey, Hey, lover! Stop this,' said Cali. 'Stop it this minute, put on your coat and come out with me. These prison walls are crowding in on you.'

I grabbed a tissue, mopped my face and shook my head. 'No, no. I've too much to do. Another day and this draft'll be finished. Then I'll breathe out. Go on, woman! Go away! It's good to see you and you've done me a world of good but go! You're a proper stop-work, as Kate would say.'

Cali pulled on her fingerless gloves. 'How is the old girl?'

'Pulled away from death's door. She's been here at Arran Lea for a week, looking sideways at my mother in this peculiar way, smiling at Lily, raging to be back home. Actually, she's fit as a flea, barring a couple of yellowing bruises. Rosa's taking her home tomorrow.

She's already stripped the bungalow of loose mats and things, for safety. The place is getting more spartan by the day but I think Kate quite likes it that way.'

'Think about what I suggested!' said Cali. 'When this is all over you come to London with me. It really is time to cut the cord, darling, don't you think?'

I laughed this off and five minutes after Cali had gone I made my way downstairs to the dining room and sat at the Amstrad to convert more of my notes and cards into chapter seven.

I had just got past the first paragraph when Lily sailed into the room, in her hand a tray, laden with a mug of coffee and a cream cake.

'Cali dashed out and brought the cake for you.' She grinned. 'Actually she brought two, but I've eaten one. She said you needed a sugar rush, or something.' She put the tray down carefully to one side of the computer and looked around. 'This all looks very interesting. Bit of a paper blitz, but interesting. What does it mean?'

I went through the points that I thought I was discovering. My argument sounded surprisingly clear and conclusive, unlike the muddle I thought I had in my head.

'You clever old thing,' said Lily, her lips curling into a smile.

I bowed my head over the cream cake. 'Why, thank you, dear daughter!'

Lily sat down on the floor, as there was no space on any chair. 'Bee, I wanted to talk to you.'

'Talk away.'

'You know I've kept off this thing about my father?'

I saved the chapter and closed down the Amstrad. 'I noticed that.'

'Well, now I'm on it. I've asked Rosa about it and she swears she knows nothing.'

'She doesn't,' said I. 'Not for the want of trying, I might say. Particularly in the early days.'

'Well now,' said Lily firmly, 'you have to tell *me* about him. Now.'

I hesitated. Then I nodded and gave in. 'Well . . .' I told Lily about those distant days that now seemed somehow outside of time. I told her how brilliant Matthew Pomeroy was. How kind. How unusual. 'But young! Not much more than a boy himself. Hardly older than your friend Simon. I see this now. I didn't see it then.' I paused. 'He knows nothing about you, I'm afraid.'

'Nothing?'

'Absolutely nothing.'

'Where is he now, then?'

'I have no idea.'

Lily's eyes narrowed. 'Well, if he's still in Holy Orders he shouldn't be too hard to find. With a name like that. Pomeroy! Jesus!'

'Quite. But I've never looked for him, Lily. I don't want to find him. And I don't want you to find him. Not yet.'

'When?'

'Just wait.'

'He might have died.'

'I don't think so.'

'You can't tell me not to look for him.'

'No. I can't do that.'

Lily stood up and rubbed her hands down the front of her jeans. 'You know I have this time before university?'

'Yes. Done and dusted a year ahead. Clever girl.'

'I'd like to go somewhere.'

'Not in search of Matthew?' I couldn't bring myself to say 'your father'.

'I don't think so. Can't say. Abroad somewhere. Everyone's going to India but I don't fancy that.'

'What about money?'

'I have my savings. And Rosa's promised me two grand.'

'Rosa?' I shook her head. 'When?'

'Ages ago. We had one of our heart-to-hearts. But I don't want to miss Kate's party.' Lily paused. 'And I've started to worry about her dying.'

'Don't. She's as tough as old boots. I told you. You go on your journey. Wherever.'

Lily drifted to the door. 'Thanks, Mum.'

Mum! That was new. 'Thanks for what?'

'For talking.' The door clicked behind her.

I turned on the Amstrad again and waited for it to boot up. One more day should see this draft done. One more day!

The Return

Rosa's Notebook

Kate has just been in to say that she's quite well now and is leaving the house at two o'clock today if anyone can be bothered to take her. If it's too inconvenient then she'll 'get the bus and one of you can drop off my case when you can spare a moment'.

The relief I feel is almost humiliating. How many years is it since I've been under the same roof as Kate? Not since that dark house in Butler Street. I think I only married Duncan to get away from there, first to here, to Arran Lea, then (I once thought) much further afield. London! Manchester, even. Duncan soon disabused me of that, of course. Then when he died it was somehow too late. I had to make myself content to remain here, not a mile away from Kate, creating other kinds of distance between us to make it all tolerable.

When she came here from hospital Kate was quiet. The hospital had shocked her more than she would admit. That and the accident, and then having to come here. Then the next morning she was up at her usual time and in the kitchen before I got there. The table was set, the cereals were standing to attention on the table and she was stirring porridge in the pan.

I remembered my father in Coventry stirring porridge in the pan. And how happy I was then. Before she came in from nightshift. And how in the bad times at Butler Street there was no breakfast because she was depressed and anyway had to be at the factory by seven thirty. And how I fainted in Assembly.

Anyway, on that first morning of Kate's stay here I fled upstairs without any breakfast, mumbling something about getting on with my work. I sat here at my desk and told myself that at my age I shouldn't be running away from my mother.

The mornings since then I have managed to eat the porridge before I flee back upstairs to my study. But here I am, still disturbed by the sound of her talking to Bronwen and Lily, the click and clatter of her moving my things here and there. The sputtering roar of the Hoover. When I go downstairs the place will be shining and shaved clean and all the ornaments will be very slightly out of place. There is no doubt about it – with Kate here *I* am slightly out of place!

I'm put out as well because I'd intended to use this time when she was here to tackle her about this thing about Brock. But I've not built up the courage. But Brock really is coming for her birthday and something should be said. It could be the last time she sees him. The last time any one of us sees him. Of course, she started this herself, by letting Bronwen have that bag of papers with the tick book in it. She knew what she was doing. She doesn't miss a trick. She knows what's in there. She always knows what she is doing. Tick book. Ticking bomb! Here am I, sailing along, quite content, then boom! It is all flooding back. Those years are on my mind again. Hiding in the house like an injured rabbit. Dancing behind closed curtains. And writing down in the book my memories of how Brock came. Battling with secrets. I weep for the child that was me. Bronwen has asked me twice what's the matter and I have told her it is nothing. She probably puts it down to the menopause. That seems to be the catch-all explanation these days. Not that I am menopausal. The curse that is recorded in the tick book is very much with me.

I will talk to Kate today. About Brock. When I take her back to the bungalow. Two o'clock. She specified two o'clock. I'll tackle her today.

The Princess in the Forest

I stood in the doorway and waved at Rosa's car as she set out with Kate. I was just about to go back inside, when Richard's car, driven too fast, sprayed gravel into the air as it ground to a stop in front of me.

He leaped out, then stood before me, his hair glinting in the afternoon sun. 'I am the mountain!' he grinned.

'You can say that again.'

'The mountain coming to Mohammed. Where the hell have you been? It's been more than two weeks.' Then he shook his head. 'No. You don't quite look like Mohammed.' He leaned forward and kissed me, our mouths barely touching. 'You don't taste like Mohammed.'

I pulled him inside and shut the door behind him. I was conscious of music – some kind of modern jazz – emerging from upstairs. Lily.

'What are you doing?' I whispered fiercely, leading the way to the small back sitting room.

'I missed you. I don't care if you are working. The telephone is not enough.' He glanced round. 'Now, this is a very nice house. I was curious about where you lived. Now this—'

'It's not my house,' I said, hurrying to disabuse him. 'It's my mother's.'

'Were you born here?'

'Well, yes, but—'

'Then it's your house.' He glanced round the small sitting room, orderly and quiet, the fire laid to light now the evenings were colder. 'Why don't you show me your room?' he said. 'Where d'you spend most of your time? I'd love to see that.'

'I can't show you my room. My grandmother's just vacated it. It's not really mine until . . . until . . .'

'You've lit some votive candles to clear the atmosphere?'

'Don't be silly.'

'Go on, Bronwen! Humour me. Let me see. You can't know how much I missed you.'

He was very appealing.

'All right. But Kate's stripped the bed. My room is really not itself.' I led the way upstairs, then stopped at Lily's door and knocked. When Lily shouted I opened the door and went in. 'Lily, Richard's here . . .'

There was no room for Richard to follow me in. Lily was sitting side by side on the bed with her friend Simon, looking at a book on a cushion on her knee. She put aside the cushion and kneeled up on the bed to greet Richard. 'Hi. Welcome to the Tardis,' she called over the music.

Simon just nodded, his white-blond hair lifting in the air.

Richard glanced round. 'Fascinating. Elegant,' he shouted. 'Not like . . . well, not like a teenager's room.'

Simon giggled.

Lily bowed from the waist, just saving herself from falling over from her kneeling position by grabbing Simon's shoulder. 'Why, thank you, sir.'

Richard eyed her. 'D'you know there's a field of research that takes the contents of a person's room and can analyse their character with remarkable precision?'

Lily shrugged. 'Well, that doesn't surprise me. Not one bit. They do research on which way a flea will jump these days.'

'Lily!' I said. Then I turned. 'Well then, let's see what your research would make of *my* room, what Kate's left of it.'

Lily sat back shoulder to shoulder with Simon and pulled the cushion and the book back on her knee. 'That's not fair, Bronwen. Your room's immaculate. Never been so tidy.'

'That's what I mean.'

In my bedroom the bed was stripped off right down to the striped mattress, and the duvet and pillows were stacked neatly against the bed head. My work table and bookshelves had all been dusted, the photographs and ornaments repositioned and the books had been made to stand upright. The documents and books on my table had been restacked and placed at right angles to any convenient straight edge. On the mantelpiece was a glass vase filled with flowers from the garden. The sun streamed through the windows on to the polished floor. I had to admit that apart from the bed, it all looked very nice − neater and smarter than it had for a long time. But it did not look anything like my own space.

Richard sat down on the bare mattress and leaned back against the stacked duvet and pillows. 'This is all very nice.'

'It looks terrible with the bed like that. You can't analyse me from this place because it is no longer mine. It's been hijacked by the spirit of my grandmother.'

He patted the mattress beside him. 'It looks very nice to me.'

I rejected his invitation and sat down on the chair by the table. 'I've been struggling with this analysis,' I said, nodding at the piles of file cards that Kate had stacked so neatly. 'Most of the stuff is downstairs in the dining room. I had to decamp down there.'

Richard swung his legs down from the bed and sat up straight, almost to attention. 'You want me to go through the data with you?'

I shook my head. 'Dr Devine has her own ideas.'

'Honey, I told you. Just make sure the literature's sound and make the theory five to one to the data. She won't be too interested in your data.'

'I realise that. But there are those anomalies to deal with. And then there's the way my own family seem to be tangled up in all this.'

He nodded. 'Yes. That ledger thing. What'you call it? The tick book.' He stood up and glanced around. 'Can I read it?'

'Do you want to read it because you're curious, or because you want to help me?'

He shook his head. 'I'm probably curious. I don't think you need my help, and anyway, you should get your help from Devine. She's your supervisor and will be your apologist at the meeting. I guess I have to admit I'm curious about your family. Just like I'm curious about everything in your life.'

He looked so earnest I almost laughed. Then I went downstairs and returned with the tick book wrapped in bubble wrap, and handed it to him. He placed the book carefully on the desk and examined it, turning it this way and that, then lying it flat and turning the pages. He glanced down at me. 'I did think I might come here and you and me might make love right here in your own space.'

'Really, Richard! This is just not the—'

'Time or the place. I see that now. I'm stupid. So what say you if I sit here like a mouse and read this? It will be interesting to me and might be some use to you. And I promise I'll be quiet, real quiet.'

This made me smile. 'All right then. And what's inside is all confidential. I want no clever comments. This is far too close to home for that.'

'Promise!' He moved round on the bed so he was sitting against the headboard. Then he eased down a pillow from Kate's pile and placed the book on it, on his knees. I thought of Lily in her room along the landing with *her* book on her cushion on *her* knees.

I went downstairs again and brought up my tapes and the rest of the cards from the dining room. I sorted cards on the table while he read the book. Our silence was companionable. Trusting. I liked that.

When he had finished he looked up at me. 'And this is your mother, honey? The lady I met at the gig?'

I nodded.

'Jeepers. Wonderful. Precocious. A tender writer, even then. She knows her own experience. Marvellous stuff,' he said quietly.

'But you can see I can't use it in anything except the most general way. I wouldn't want to. On the other hand, there's this other stuff.' I played him the tape on which Mrs MacIntosh

214

casually revealed that her son never ever knew that his father wasn't his father. 'Can't use that except in broad generalisations and if that's the case why bother with all this kind of research?' I nodded at the pile of tapes, the stacks of file cards.

He came and placed the ledger carefully on the table beside me. 'Because, my love, doing all this close-in research makes the researcher feel and think in a more complex way, so that when she comes to the literature and encounters the received wisdom of these great events of our time her mind is open, not closed. And in that way she'll get to open other minds.'

He tugged at my thick plait and leaned down and kissed my cheek. 'Now, honey, you need a break. I want to put my arms round you but can't, with all these ghosts living and dead walking around. Peter's here again. Been back every few days, filling my rooms like his forest. I love him dearly but I need some air. And I think you do. Why don't we go have a brown bag lunch at the eyrie and talk? Or something. Come on, Bronwen, you need a break from all these cards and tapes and smoky memories. From this house. And I need you. Just to be with you.'

When he said that I knew that was just what I wanted, just what I needed to do. It was a relief to say yes. I shouted goodbye to Lily on my way downstairs and followed Richard down. In the car he asked me if Simon was Lily's 'beau'. I laughed. 'Those two have known each other since they were born. Simon is her soul mate, her *alter ego*. If he were her boyfriend — her *beau* — it would not be right, somehow.'

Much later, after we had made love in the low shadowy space of the eyrie, he said, 'I can't believe this, Bronwen. The more I know you, the more all of this means to me. I've never felt like this, never. I promise you, never. I love you.'

I laid back and closed my eyes tight. I wouldn't ask about Maria. I wouldn't. And I knew if I answered him in kind I would be lost. The only way I had been able to manage this thing was to deal with it entirely in the present. I thought of the story of the princess in the briar forest, woken by the kiss of the prince after twenty years. But that prince wasn't on a year's sabbatical and he didn't have a wife and two children back in his kingdom across the sea.

215

If I told him I loved him I would break the spell. Instead I put my arms around him and drew him to me, and there on the floor of his eyrie I slept more soundly than I had done for a week. The future would have to take care of itself.

Snowflakes

Kate's bungalow was cold, and Rosa found herself insisting that her mother should keep her coat on until the central heating kicked in. Kate threw off Rosa's restraining hand. 'Cold? You've never known cold like I have. That house on Butler Street was as cold as Christmas.'

'I know, Mother,' said Rosa quietly. 'I was there. It rained in at this time of year in Butler Street. And in December there were ice snowflakes on the inside of the windows.'

Kate frowned at her. 'Yes. Yes. I know you know. But you were little. You'd hardly notice. Children don't.'

Astounded as always at her mother's unknowingness, Rosa said, 'Yes, Kate. But we're all used now to being warm inside, aren't we? In those days we were cold inside the house. So now, when it's cold you really feel the difference. Reminds you of that cold inside.' She watched Kate sit down on her narrow sofa. 'Never mind. By the time I've made some tea the place'll have warmed up. It doesn't take much to take the chill off. It's small enough.'

Kate looked up at her. 'Different to that place of yours, of course. And you keep that place too hot, if you ask me. Germs breed in that heat. Everybody knows that.'

Rosa let that go and went into the kitchen to sort out the hot water, leaf tea, the teapot, the cups and saucers. Her mother liked things laid out properly. Think of those teas supervised by Mrs Cator in Lancaster. Think of the times later when she herself used to make Kate a tea tray at Butler Street, in a desperate, childish effort to lift her mother's gloom.

When she got back Kate still had her coat on and was rubbing her face with the palm of her hands. 'Cold in here,' she said.

Rosa pulled out the smallest of a nest of tables, put the tray on it between them, and poured tea into the cups. 'It'll soon warm up,' she said.

'That Brock *is* a terror, isn't he?' Kate announced in a conversational tone, as though they had just been talking about him.

Rosa almost dropped the teapot. 'What d'you say?'

'Our Brock. He's a proper terror.'

Rosa frowned. 'Now what makes you say that?'

'Well, love, I know about this secret thing, this party. Our Lily told me. And about our Brock coming.'

'Did she, now? She had no business to do that.' Rosa handed Kate her cup. She was not too troubled about that revelation of the party. This was an unimportant secret. Bound to leak out. Anyway, an out-and-out surprise would be bad for Kate at her age.

'And I know the other secret. The one about our Brock coming. Our Charlie let that one out. But then I sent Brock a card and told him to be sure to come. Not down to Charlie at all.'

Rosa took a breath. 'Well, then, so now that's out. Not a secret. It doesn't make Brock a terror. Nothing of the sort. So there is a party and Brock might come, though I can't think why Charlie asked him after all these years.'

'Not just Charlie,' said Kate composedly. 'Like I said, it was me sent our Brock a card.'

Rosa breathed hard again. 'Did you, now?'

'When *is* my birthday, Rosa?'

'Next month.'

'Well, that's a while to go. So what's our Brock doing lurking around here now? If he's here he should come and see me, not lurk around like Banquo's ghost.'

Rosa thought the fall must have shaken Kate up more than she had realised. 'He's not here, Kate. I was talking to Charlie on the phone just yesterday. He's on his way, but it's a long journey.'

'All right then, I've seen his ghost. His living ghost. I'm losing my marbles, like those old women I used to nurse.'

'I don't think so, Kate. Never met a woman whose marbles were so intact.'

'Well, why am I seeing him all over the place?'

'He's on your mind for another reason. Because he's coming here and you're getting ready to tell him something before it's too late. To tell me. To tell us all.'

'Tell?' Kate glared at her. 'You do talk some rubbish, Rosa. All those fairy stories must be addling your head.'

'They're not fairy stories. But it was you who started this. You gave Bronwen that old ledger that I wrote in when I was young. I'd forgotten about those things, after all this time. Stopped even thinking about it. It reminded me of something I knew about even when I was so young. About Brock.'

'Oh, you!' Kate crashed her cup and saucer down on the little table. 'You! Think you know everything and what you don't know you make up.'

'Young as I was, I knew Brock was not really my brother.'

'Of course he's your brother! He's the best of all of you!' Kate almost shrieked the words. Then her tone softened. 'Except for our Lily. Now she's a real pet.'

'Kate, listen to yourself! That's a very unkind thing to say.'

'Is it now?' Kate picked up her cup.

'But why should I be surprised? You can be very hard.'

Only the clink of teacups broke the long silence that followed.

'Well?' said Rosa.

'Well what?' said Kate.

'Aren't you going to tell me?'

Kate shrugged her thin shoulders. 'Nothing to tell.'

Rosa felt an uncharacteristic rage grow inside her. She restrained herself from shaking her mother, very hard, even injuring her. She thought of the old woman in 'Hansel and Gretel' being bundled into the oven by Hansel. She put down her cup carefully and clasped her hands tightly together in her lap. 'Kate, if you don't tell Brock when he comes, then I'll tell him. I'll show him the tick book with those very clear memories. How when I was just four you brought him into our house. I'll tell him he's not really our brother, not really your son.'

'Tell him as much as you like. He knows you make up things. Tell fairy stories. Always did.'

Rosa breathed in very deeply. 'You can be so irritating, Mother.' What a weak, wailing thing to say.

Kate grinned, showing all her yellowing teeth. '*Mother*! Sunday name, is it? You must be cross, Rosa. But you're right, love. I am rather irritating, aren't I? Privilege of old age.'

'So you won't tell him?'

'Nothing to tell, love.' Kate hauled herself upright. 'Now then, can you help me with this coat? It's getting steaming hot in here.' She slipped out of the sleeves of her coat and held it out to Rosa. 'There's a wooden hanger on the back of the door. Can't abide those wire ones you have in your house. And, oh, on your way out will you turn down that heating? No good wasting good money on a fine day like this, is there?'

Threesome

Peter, used to rising very early on the farm to do chores for Sophie before he went to the forest, was taking advantage of these Durham sojourns to sleep on in bed. Today he had finally risen to join Richard and me for lunch in a rather nice restaurant built into the old Elvet Bridge.

The men hugged each other closely when they met, then Peter grabbed me, held me close and kissed me. He smelled and tasted like Richard, which made me blush. I wondered suddenly just how much these brothers shared, whether Richard told Peter of the times I had spent with him in the eyrie. How I shouted at certain times: a strange thing for someone so shy. How he loved what he called my 'cognitive sexuality'. While lying back after one encounter he had sleepily held forth on his view that all good sex began and ended in the head. Rather good, for a man, I thought then. But now I wondered just how much these brothers shared. It occurred to me again how close Richard was to Sophie. So much closer than you would expect of a brother and sister-in-law.

Then as Peter kissed me soundly for a second time I decided that I didn't really mind. Then I wondered if Peter was so open with his American sister-in-law who would only stay in the North long enough to jump off for the Isle of Skye. Had Peter hugged her so tight? Had he kissed her on the lips so soundly? Then I dismissed these thoughts, reminding myself of my resolution to live in the day, focus on the present. Not the past. Not the future. Just the here and now. Like the people on my tapes said about their experience of the war. You just had to live in the here and now.

.I chose pizza, the men chose pasta and we all looked on as the neat young waiter poured Chianti into our oversized glasses. We tackled our food enthusiastically, Richard and I because of our energetic morning, Peter because he'd had no breakfast. When he was halfway through, Peter sat back and took a sip of wine. 'So, young Bronwen, what are you thinking?'

I had been thinking about Richard and the room under the eaves, but I said, 'I was wondering about you two. What it was like growing up there in Cumbria.'

The men exchanged glances. 'Cumbria?' said Peter. 'Not Cumbria, love. Manchester, Barrow, Lancaster, Carlisle. We were all over the place.'

I was taken aback with the vehemence with which he said this. Richard reached across the table and grabbed my hand. 'Talking about growing up, honey, how about that family of yours? That cute daughter, that elegant clever mom, that hip uncle, that neat snug house. Everyone lovin' each other . . .'

'How would you know that?' I said, wrong-footed with the spotlight back on me. 'You don't know that.'

Peter was digging into his pasta.

Richard smiled. 'It was there in the very hang of the curtains, honey. In the way your daughter greets you. In your talk of your mother and your grandmother.'

'It's all very ordinary,' I said. 'And we are all women, except for Simon.'

'That's young Lily's *alter ego*, Pete,' said Richard, scooping up his pasta.

'*Alter ego*?' said Peter. 'Isn't that you and me, mate?'

Richard waved his fork at his brother. 'Tell her, Pete. You tell her about us.'

'Well, love, your house of women is nowt like me and Rich here were used to. We brought each other up, us two. In care – *care*! You wouldn't think they'd call it that, would you? Foster care. Group homes. One time they wanted to split us up with two lots of foster parents, but Rich here fought them on that. Talked to the committee himself. Swallowed a dictionary very early, did Rich.'

'And Pete fought on the other fronts, didn't you, buddy? The bigger lads who fancied their chances . . .'

'Aye, mebbe I was too busy fighting to do my homework. That's why Richard here's the brain and I'm the brawn.'

'Not as simple as that, is it?' Richard coughed. 'The main thing is, Bronwen, that it was always him and me, and that's the way we liked it.' His earnest tone, no longer laughing, emphasised the trust, the confidence they were sharing.

'But how—'

'Did we end up there, in care?' said Richard. 'Well, we were the youngest of eight children, only one of them a girl. Either the social services or our mother thought she couldn't cope, but we were in care by the time we were eighteen months.'

'So do you know them? Your family?'

'We never knew our mother. She lit off, after the war,' said Richard. 'Never knew our brothers and sister. Well, really half-brothers and -sister as our father wasn't our father. That was the trouble, I think.'

'Brainbox here got all the facts,' said Peter. 'Our first name was Ballantyne. And we went to take a look at the Ballantynes, which was a weird experience, I can tell you. We peered through the window. We did just that, peered through the window! But we never met them. It was scary. Noisy, mucky. There were rabbits running round inside the house. And two dogs. Decided we were better off in the group home. Our family was each other.'

'So you went to college and training from there?'

'Oh, blimey,' said Peter, grinning. 'Weren't we the stars? They loved us. Pictures in the papers. Lads succeeding from care and not landing behind bars. Unique. See what our dear mother had missed!'

'You are stars! The pair of you.' I wanted to leap up and hug them both indiscriminately. Perhaps Sophie felt like this about them.

'It must have been hard when you went away.' I looked across at Richard. 'To America.'

He shook his head. 'Once he'd met Sophie I knew the lad here was all right. I came to visit, saw her, went back. We do visit from time to time. Me and the boys, anyway. And we talk all the time on the phone.'

'And anyway,' said Pete emphatically, 'we're in each other's head and heart and that means you can teleport, like they do on *Star Trek*.'

I must have looked startled because they both laughed uproariously.

Then the waiters came to clear the table and present the pudding menu and the talk moved to more general, even more important things. The weather. Global warning and the threats to the rainforest. The outrage of pop stars covering upland hillside with conifer forests as a tax loophole. The crumbling USSR, Departmental gossip. They didn't talk about wives, husbands, children, the past, the future. They talked about the here and now.

At three o'clock Peter stood up. 'Well, mate. I'm off now. Time I was home. Sophie's getting the tea for five o'clock and is pining for the delights of my company. I need to get on the road.'

Richard stood up and hugged him, full body contact. Then Peter came to me and took my face in his large hands. 'Eh, lass, a time of delight. You make the old boy happy. I can see that. And that's all that matters. You could make him get a decent haircut, but that's a different matter.'

Richard walked him to the door of the restaurant, then came back, rubbing his hands. 'Now, honey, an Irish coffee to finish? Or what?'

I shook my head. 'You told me Peter was going tomorrow.'

'He was. But I think he's missing old Sophie. He's a funny guy, our Pete. He might think I'm the bee's knees, but I don't hold a candle to her. Not even a taper.'

We spent the rest of the afternoon in his rooms in college. He made coffee as I leafed through his books; we watched *Stage Coach* on his portable television; we got into an argument on whether cowboy films were America's equivalent of the European fairy tale. I thought not, saying the Western myth was all about powerful men, whereas in Europe women got a look in. Richard named films where this was not the case. I told him about my mother's new project, taking a feminist view of fairy tales.

'So would your Rosa call herself a feminist?'

I smiled. 'Not so cool nowadays to say so, I know, but yes, I'm sure she'd say that. Part of the protests in the sixties, but – like everyone – she's less vocal about it now. I think she'd say that she lives the life now. She doesn't need to flap the banner.'

'She's certainly quiet. Not loud like you'd expect.'

'Like *you'd* expect,' I said.

I tried to steer the conversation to what he and Peter had talked about this afternoon.

He shrugged his shoulders. 'Really, honey. We were all right. Think how many people there were not in care, in families, who were worse off than we were. I told you we went to take a look at this family, though we didn't meet them. But when I saw them I knew me and Pete were better off where we were.' He paused. 'But there were two of us, really close, watching each other's backs, sometimes literally. We were better off in care, the two of us. Peter would fight to the death for me and I would argue to the death for him.'

I raised my eyebrows.

'Honestly, all in all it was quite a decent time. We were kind of mascots because we were clever. Most of all we had each other.' Then he reached out for me and kissed me. 'Too much talking,' he said.

We made love then. And later. And later still. As I held him I tried in vain to blank out images of two brave bleak boys clinging together for dear life.

Part Three

Family Ties

Tyne Princess

The next day Cali rang me to say she'd finished her dissertation and, yes, she did know it was still a month to the deadline but the bloody thing was so boring she had to get it finished as quickly as possible before she turned into stone. She wanted me to read through it for her before she handed the final package over to the fragrant Dr Devine.

'I know it's finished but be a love and do take a look for me. Could you pick it up at the B & B, as I'm without the bike at the moment? And while you're on the road could you possibly drive me to Gateshead?'

'Gateshead?'

'Stupid me. I left the thing last night on the quayside. Wild night dancing on a boat. There was this leisure boat called the *Tyne Princess*. Had a wonderful time, darling. Hanging out, dancing . . .' The down side was that in the early hours of the morning she'd felt too far gone to drive so she'd cadged a lift from some boys from Darlington, who'd dropped her off at the roundabout near the B & B. 'I do realise that you've got your head down over those blasted tapes of yours, Bron, but could you spare me some time?'

I looked at my table, still too orderly from Kate's scourge, at its centre my yellow drafting pad already displaying one paragraph of the chapter entitled 'Anomalies: The Myths and the Lived Experience'. This chapter was today's work. 'What about Charlie?' I ventured.

'He's taking that hapless stepdaughter of his to hospital.

Something about her allergies. May won't take her because I think she wants to keep him away from me. I fear May's finally got her eye on me. Nice woman, but lacking in imagination. Thinks I've set my cap at him, or whatever they say in these godforsaken regions. But it's friendship, pure and simple.'

The rare tone of desolation in her voice made me decide to forget my own work and go to her aid. On my way to the B & B it dawned on me that in my fever about Richard, Cali had somehow fallen off my radar. So much for friendship. Typical adolescent aberration to dump your friends when you got a boyfriend!

At the B & B I jumped out of the car and gave Cali a big hug before opening the car door for her. Cali, with her motorbike leathers over her arm, was pale even under her white make-up. But she warmed to my guilty affection.

'Steady on, old girl. The lovely May'll think I'm even stranger than she thinks I am already.' She nodded at the twitching lace curtain.

She was quieter than usual as we drove along. Finally I said. 'So there's trouble at t'mill, then?'

Cali shook her head. 'Well, everything was fine at first, darling. Back then, May just saw Charlie doing his thing with Theo and Stan. As though it were some hobby, like keeping greyhounds or going to football matches. And she didn't mind me because I was business to her, her *Pee Gee*. She's a shrewd businesswoman. She has a family to keep, after all.'

But it seemed now May had started to pressure Charlie about spending so much time in the shed, and making more of these gigs than they deserved. Neglecting his family.

'She's kind of belittling him and it sticks in my craw because he's my friend. Nothing else.' She wound down the car window and lit a cigarette, only afterward saying, 'D'you mind, darling?' She drew on it deeply. 'The worst thing is, I can't say anything. Me! If I said anything it would imply that I had an eye for him, that I was a threat to her.'

'And are you?'

There was a silence. 'I keep telling you, Bron. I'm not into families, as you know. But families have been on my mind lately.

And I've come to think that every family, however oddly constructed – and Charlie's family is not your conventional two parents and two point four children – every family has its own style. Any outside intervention – a foreign body, if you like – upsets the balance and either it has to adjust to the intruder or the intruder is expelled. Spat out. In the case of the B & B I am the foreign body. And I have a feeling I'm in the process of being spat out. May is giving me piles of this fried stuff that I can't eat. Even Charlie is silent and furrow-browed.'

'Not a bad theory,' I said.

'Mmm. I bet you even as we speak some geeky person is writing a paper on it.' She took another long drag on her cigarette.

'So what're you going to do?'

'Well, first you're gonna read my dissertation and tell me it's brilliant . . .' she pulled it out from under the leather coat on the back seat, '. . . and then I'm going to thrust it into the eager mitt of Dr Devine. Then I'm gonna light off.'

'Where to? What'll you do?'

'You know what, darling? I think I'll do what I said and put on a suit and make some money. Go down and help my mate to save Yugoslavia. There at the B & B, I've begun to think I'm between the devil and the deep blue sea. To be perfectly honest I felt positively ancient, dancing among those kids last night. They treated me with *respect*, like I was from another planet. And then in the B & B I'm treated like I was some predatory teenager. Can't stand it, darling. So I think it's time I made some money again. All my gifts have gotta make me a good bet in the dark satanic halls of the City, don't you think?'

'You'll succeed wherever you go, Cali.'

'But . . . ?'

'Seems to me you're always on your way somewhere. It's always a journey.'

'As opposed to what? Staying put, like you?'

I had to laugh. '*Touché*. You're right. As opposed to me who has never ventured anywhere.'

'Talking about staying in one place, how's the thing with this American and his brother? Eerie, those two.'

231

'Nothing eerie about it. All they are is brothers. I like them. Particularly Richard.'

'Well, the American certainly has a thing for you. Clear as a bell the other week at the gig.' Cali threw her cigarette out of the window and closed it. 'Talking about going places, where is this *affaire* going – anywhere?'

I was already shaking my head. 'Nowhere. He goes back to America at the end of the year.'

'To his wife and family?'

'Just so.' She had made me say it. She had pulled me out of the present and made me think of the future.

After that there seemed little more to say and we stayed quiet until we reached the edge of Gateshead and Cali directed me down to where her bike was parked, heavily chained to an old dock bollard just along from the *Tyne Princess*. The ship was in permanent dock, serving as a dine-and-dance venue in her extended retirement. At night, with fairy lights from stem to stern, the *Tyne Princess* took on a look of romance and adventure. By day she looked a bit battered and old: a lady in reduced circumstances.

'Look at those chains!' I pointed at the pinioned bike. 'Where d'you get hold of them?'

'They were in the helmet box. Better safe than sorry.' Cali laughed. 'Doesn't that make me sound sad and old? Like I say, it's time to quit this scene, while I'm a fraction ahead.' She jumped out of the car and leaned back in and touched her chunky dissertation. 'Go back to your nest and read that, will you, darling?'

'You sound really very confident, Cali.' I thought of me still scrambling with these hard ideas.

'To be honest, Bron, I've done harder things. I picked that subject 'cos it looked easy. If I'd picked something harder it might have been more fun.'

I watched her unchain her bike and roar away, then set off myself at a more sedate pace. For a moment I contemplated the thought that I might put on a suit and try my luck in London with Cali. Of course, that was impossible with Lily to think about, and Rosa, and Kate.

But it might be fun to go with Cali, to give London a try.

Of course, Richard wasn't the problem. He would be gone by the end of the year, after all. I would have to keep saying that to myself, to get used to the idea. That was the penalty for falling for a married man, even if you know, you're quite sure, he has fallen for you.

Lily's World

Lily Carmichael is very pleased that she has Simon. The day after they started nursery school she bit his nose, caused havoc, and they became great friends. When they were seven they played doctors and nurses briefly, to find out just what *was* the difference between boys and girls. Simon exclaimed in amazement that she had a 'crack' and said he was sorry that she lacked the real thing. At ten years old they decided that they would get married and have a fairy-tale wedding like Princess Diana, even though they would have to wait until they were sixteen. When they were twelve they called the wedding off and decided they would be blood siblings, inventing an intricate and briefly painful ceremony to celebrate their new status.

Since then they have been as close as any girl-friends, as any boy-buddies. They study together, they read together, they listen to old-style music together – differing only on the comparative merits of Jimi Hendrix versus the MJQ. Occasionally they sleep together, bundled and innocent on Lily's narrow bed. Each of them has strayed, from time to time, into quite compelling outside relationships. But these relationships always founder on the fact that in no case has any other boy or girl understood what Simon and Lily have together. They have been subject to vicious episodes of jealous ranting and, in one case, accusations that they are the queerest pair of queers.

For quite a long time now they have talked about Breaking the Barrier: having sex for the first time. Those first outside crushes involved attempts to tackle this hurdle but neither of them ever went the whole way. 'Too ridiculous! Gross!' was Lily's description of the experiment after she had first tried French kissing and endured above-the-belt fumbling, before having to fight off a frantic boy who'd at first seemed cool and attractive.

In the end Lily and Simon have escaped ridicule at school by letting their friends think they are probably doing *it*, and this 'buddy' thing is all an act. Simon has grown up through spotty adolescence to blond glamour and these days there are girls who envy Lily.

After puzzling over the problem for some time they decided to do it 'As and When' and 'Be Prepared'. Hence Lily's research into birth control. But now, having thought further, they have decided to leave Breaking the Barrier until they are both away from here, when they leave school: Simon at Warwick University, Lily wherever she is in her year out before she goes to Cambridge.

Perhaps only Lily realises they can, *will* only do it when they are away from each other. She thinks privately that the barrier can only be broken with a stranger in a strange place.

So through this summer and into the autumn they have lived in each other's pocket. After all, they know that this is the end of something. They want to stretch their togetherness right till the end. This year they have walked together, climbed together, gone to two raves in Yorkshire together, tried hash together, but drawn the line at coke. Lily has watched Simon play cricket for his local team, taking a book to read in the boring bits. Simon has been to the Edinburgh Festival at Lily's urging, and watched plays that defeated him, then dragged Lily to see two comedians on the Fringe who were much more to his taste.

A bout of bad toothache meant that Simon missed the night out at Uncle Charlie's gig but Lily has filled him in with the gory details, not missing out on the strange case of two grown men – quite old, in fact – who look and seem almost exactly alike.

'Eerie! And worse! My mother's going out with the professor one although I think the tree one is nicer. Even so, they're both ages older than her. They're both fit enough, but think of someone fifty years old with their clothes off! Yaagh!'

'You'd better believe it,' Simon says gloomily. 'My Dad's fifty-one and – clothes off – he's second only to that geek in *Nightmare on Elm Street*. Sagging white flesh.'

'Gross,' says Lily. She is lying across the bed with her bare, long-toed feet up on her shelves. 'Although these two weren't as bad as that. Tanned and muscular, for a start. That is, one of them has bulging muscles, the other wiry. And they were kind of funny. They made me laugh. Bronwen seems to like them both. I have to say my mother's coming out of her shell. Sometimes I worry about her being on her own when I'm gone. It would be nice for her to meet somebody. But,' she adds thoughtfully, 'when you reach her age I suppose there's not a lot of choice.'

'How old is she?'

'About thirty-three.'

'That's not so old, really,' says Simon, closing his eyes. 'Not compared with the geek from *Elm Street*. We'll be that age ourselves in sixteen years' time.'

'Yaagh!' Lily turns up the music with her toe and closes her eyes, letting the music move through her body and take her under. That's what's so good about Simon. She doesn't have to talk to him. She read this piece in *Cosmo*, where it said that in any relationship – even a friendship like hers and Simon's – one person is always 'the lover', and the other is 'the beloved'. She knows Simon will always be 'the lover' – enamoured, dying to please and always willing to fit in. And she herself will always be the 'beloved' – loved without needing to strive for it. After all, that has been her experience. All her life at the centre of her mother's, grand-mother's, and great-grandmother's lives, she has been able to take love for granted.

But as she lies there shoulder to shoulder with Simon in the Tardis, it occurs to her that there is one person who can't love her. He can't love her because he doesn't even know her. It comes to her now that this person *should* know her. He should love her. Not because she is bereft, or needs yet another person to love her. But because she is curious about her father and wonders now whether, with him, she will be the lover or the beloved. Or nothing.

The thought builds up in her head. Yes, she really should find this man. Perhaps she should save Breaking the Barrier until she has met him. She can't Break the Barrier until she knows who she really is.

She turns the music up yet another notch and the Tardis is filled with layers of sound and words beating against her skin. And she forgets everything except the urgent pulsing sound and the camomile scent of the lit candles on her windowsill.

Vox Pop

Dr Devine pushed the manuscript across the desk. 'It's very well written,' she said. 'But of course good writing can disguise shoddy research.'

My heart sank. 'Are you saying my work's shoddy, Dr Devine?'

'I didn't say that Miss Carmichael.'

Many university tutors these days used Christian names, but Devine, though comparatively young herself, still stuck to the old courtesies. I waited, telling myself that this woman, self-assured to her manicured fingertips, is only two years older than I am. And she doesn't bite.

The professor pursed her lips. 'We knew from the start that this style of research was not my cup of tea, Miss Carmichael. I said as much in a rather long conversation with Dr Stephens.'

'But you did agree to supervise it, Dr Devine.' I kept my tone even.

'So I did. And I've tried to read it with an open mind. As well as this, I say I've discussed it at length with Dr Stephens. And somewhat reluctantly I have to agree with him that it has interest. It has some merit. But I can't escape the feeling that this kind of enquiry smacks of journalism. The flotsam and jetsam of current fashionably derived information. A kind of vox pop, if you will.'

I could feel myself going red. 'I've been very careful to justify the method, Dr Devine . . .'

Devine put up her hand. 'You justify yourself and the study

quite well, Miss Carmichael. In line with certain contemporary approaches, what we have here is a substantial small study at this level. I just wish today to reiterate my discomfort with this kind of work at this level. Work with documentary evidence is a much safer bet, even today, at this level.'

I thought of Cali and her *boring* Victorian philanthropists. 'I do believe there is a relevance to this kind of work, Dr Devine . . .'

Devine stopped me. 'Relevance! Relativity! You're participating in the death of true scholarship, Miss Carmichael.'

I took the bull by the horns. 'What I like about it is that at least studies like this acknowledge the role of ordinary people in the great movements of history, allow their voice to be heard.'

'Ah!' Devine flashed her teeth. 'Vox pop? D'you see? I see there is more than pillow talk between you and the very modern Dr Stephens.'

I was consumed with the desire to hit her, to wipe the smug smile from her face. I curled my hands into fists on my lap. I managed a very sweet smile. 'Is being offensive your way of saying that you think my work is too shoddy to go for submission, Dr Devine?'

Devine stared hard at me, then shrugged and sat back in her chair. 'Not at all. Far from it. As I said, it is very well written. The theoretical justification is good as far as it goes. You need to look at the ordering of the bibliography. Three sources are out of order. And seven of your footnotes are not properly cross-referenced.' She pushed the manuscript across the table with the tips of her fingers. 'I've highlighted them.' She stood up. 'When you've done that it's done. Miss Carmichael, I have a busy morning.'

I almost waltzed out of her museum-like study. Done! No matter how reluctant, how mealy-mouthed Devine had been, the thing was done. I felt like that man who discovered the Victoria Falls. My first adventure had reached its best outcome. Now there was just the other one to tackle, the one with Richard. But just what ultimately counted as the desired outcome for that journey, for that adventure, I was still not sure.

But I was only a few yards along the pavement when I was hit again by Devine's patronising attitude to me, her rudeness about Richard. I had to fight down the desire to go and tell her what I thought about her. My delight about the dissertation drained away. I needed to talk to somebody about this. Not Richard. I would look for Cali.

Letting off Steam

I made my way to the Union where Cali was sitting at a corner table, holding court with two members of her group Ceolas Monkey.

At Cali's table they were drinking Snakebite, a foul mixture of lager and blackcurrant rejected by cooler students as naff and common, and approved by Cali for the very same reason. The boys looked vaguely bored, as though all the jokes, of whatever vintage, had been told yet again.

Cali smiled across and beckoned me over. 'At last! A mature mind.'

Ming, the lanky guitarist, made room for me beside Cali, who gave Hardy, the drummer, a fiver to go and get me a beer. I shook my head at the offer of Snakebite.

Ming put his hand on mine and thrust his face close to mine. He was a nice-looking boy but his good looks were rather spoiled by his aura, a rich mixture of hash and rolling tobacco and boy-sweat. 'Sit here and talk sense to this woman, will you, Bron? Whad'ya think? Desertin' us just when we got this good gig in Edinburgh.'

I slid along the bench to sit beside Cali.

'Did you know about this?' demanded Hardy, a small boy with the eager face of a border terrier. 'Did you know she was going? Deserting us?'

Cali slid her arm through mine. 'Bron knows as well as any of us that Ceolas Monkey doesn't need a penny whistle.'

Ming scowled. 'Whereas,' he drawled, 'it makes an awful difference to those working chaps you've been gigging with upcountry. Rather extreme mode of exploring authenticity, if you ask me.'

'Hold on, you!' I said sharply 'One of those working chaps is my dear uncle.'

Ming afforded me a military salute (long perfected in his school army corps, in his pre-pacifist stage). 'Politically correct! How *that* are you, darling?'

Cali felt my tension. 'Ming, you're just too bad. Get lost, will you? Go and play with your other nursery friends. Go! The lot of you.'

The boys scooped up their drinks and made to go. Hardy winked at me. 'Don't worry about old Ming. He's miffed because his den-momma's deserting him. Queer old codger is Ming.' He drew back his leg to avoid Cali's boot. 'And he has a serious need to score.'

Cali and I sat in silence, watching the boys pick their way through the scattered tables. Then Cali said, 'What is it, darling? You look as though you've just eaten an egg with the shell on.'

I told her about Devine. How I was pleased she'd approved the draft but how I loathed her attitude. 'Leaves a sour taste in your mouth.'

'Snooty cow.' Cali squeezed my hand. 'She's jealous of you and old Stephens.'

'Jealous? Women like her are too full of themselves to be jealous. It's more as though I've broken some arcane rule, that I've stepped over some precious line of hers. She's out of the ark, that one, despite her Armani suit, and despite being only two years older than me.'

'Even so, she didn't say you shouldn't submit the thing, did she?'

'No. She kept on saying how well written. But it was like she was talking with tongs. Like those you pick up dog turds with.'

Cali chortled. 'Good one, that, Bron.' She paused. 'But honestly, darling, get the thing sorted and to the printers and put it in and forget it. Take it from me, darling, the feeling's wonderful. You'll feel as free as a bird. Ready for the next chapter in your life.'

I sipped my beer. 'And that's it for you, Cali? You're really ready to turn the page for the new chapter? You really are going?'

'Mmm mmm. Can't wait. A new adventure.'

'And what does Charlie think about this?'

The smile faded from Cali's face. 'The old boy seems a bit down, to be honest. Talking about jacking the band in. Says he feels now it's a bit ridiculous to go on with it.'

'Does he *really* think it's ridiculous? Perhaps he thinks that's what you think. Perhaps you've come into his life and broken something that was not even cracked.'

'Don't say that, Bron. You underestimate him and me. He knows I dig what he does. *Dig!* God, that dates me! I'm his friend. He knows that.'

'Are you sure of that? That he doesn't think you've been on him and now you're going off him? How can you be sure?'

'I'm sure because I told him to come to London with me. It would be a laugh. There's plenty of work there in bars and things.'

'You must be joking. He might think he can play, but he's not good enough for that. Not down there.'

'Not *that* kind of bar work. I was thinking of pulling pints. That sort of thing.'

I withdrew my arm clear of Cali's. 'You are impossible, Cali. You can be so cold. So selfish.'

'Now, darling, don't you go all huffy on me. This is who I am. I am urging Charlie to have his adventure just like I urge you. You're my friend. He's my friend. Charlie gets it. He likes it. If I'd been some mumsy live-alike I'd never have got out of Bristol in the first place.' She examined my face carefully. 'Don't worry, darling. I'm a brilliant judge of men. He'll like thinking he has a choice but he won't come. And May can keep her old buddy. And he'll still gig with Stan and Theo, churning out the same-old same-old. They're good. And he enjoys it all too much to give it up. This little episode with me around has been a giggle for him. A ring-fenced adventure. Why should age be a bar to that or any adventure? Or any friendship? If it is I'll drive my bike into a tree on my fortieth birthday, see if I don't.' She put her hand on my arm. 'Don't you go off me, darling. Not you. I'm darting away

243

soon, but I'll be writing postcards from the edge to you when I'm eighty.'

I laughed. '*The Times*, 2038: "Elderly woman found dead in central Sahara. Lover survives",' I said.

Cali lifted her glass in salutation. 'You've got it, darling.' She drained the glass. 'Now. What about you and the pouting professor?'

'He doesn't pout.'

'I love to alliterate. You know me. I rather liked that brother of his, at the gig. He had this aura.'

'Aura?'

'You know. Like a priest. Oozing pure goodness.'

I shook my head. 'You're spooky, Cali, d'you know that?'

'Whereas,' went on Cali, as though I had not spoken, 'your professor-guy is different, even though he may look the same.'

'No virtuous aura?'

'No, he's had his virtuous edges rubbed off somewhere. He's more world-weary, more dissatisfied. That's why he's with you.'

'Well, thank you, dear friend, but I think that difference is one reason why I I-like him.'

'L-like? Listen! What about him? Why is he here, half a world away from whatever he's left behind? For a whole year?'

'Perhaps he relishes an adventure. If Charlie deserves one, he does.'

'Is that what it is? I though it might be true *lurve*, darling.'

'You're such a romantic soul, Cali. Truth is, he came to the UK to see his beloved brother, his mirror self. He misses him.'

'Even so, what's this thing with you? What's the future for you and lover-boy?'

'No future. Just here and now. Simone de Beauvoir would approve.'

'Bully for her. But all that does, darling, is play into the hands of the men who want to own the past, present and the future. In other words to have their cake and eat it.'

'As a free spirit, you're a bit of a cynic, Cali.'

'Lessons from an adventurous life, darling. Believe me.'

'He's not like that. Not like one of your *lessons*.'

'I see.'

'No you don't. I don't think even I *see*.' I picked up my book-bag. How could I explain to her when I hadn't properly worked it out myself?

'Well, there's one thing,' said Cali.

'What's that?'

'Besides me dying in the Sahara at the side of my mourning lover, and him living a world away from his wife and falling for you, a scratchy old madam like Devine fades into absolute insignificance. So don't give that Ugly Sister a thought.'

There it was. This was why I came to find her. I stood up and grinned. 'If you say so, Cali.'

Cali stood up and kissed me on the cheek. 'I *do*!'

I turned to leave, then turned back. 'You're not going off on your adventure before next weekend, are you?'

'I don't know. Why?'

'My grandmother's birthday party. I want you to come. Rosa asked whether you would be coming. Richard's coming. And the angelic Peter. He'll be back across here again. Charlie, of course. You've been so much part of us this year. You should endow Kate's party with your own special brand of anarchy. Kate'll like that. And Charlie will be pleased. Your swan song with your penny whistle.'

Cali grinned. 'Course I'll come. How could I resist an offer like that? A professor, a forester, an old rocker and the Carmichael coven of white witches. Irresistible.'

I just shook my head at this and as I strode out of the union I passed Ming and Hardy, glasses in hand, making their way back to Cali's table. My mind was on Richard. We had a two o'clock appointment.

Tour Guide

I was barely through Richard's door when he swept me up in his arms, pressing kisses on my cheeks, nuzzling my hair, pulling at the tape that held my thick plait in place.

I wrestled myself free. 'Stop! Let me get through the door, will you?'

He relinquished his hold and held his hands out in front of him, palms up. 'So what's this? Don't you love me any more?'

I clicked the door shut behind me. 'I never said I loved you. I never said that. Never mentioned the word,' I said this with more vehemence than I intended.

He groaned and smote his brow. 'Look, honey, I missed my run this morning, I've been marking papers all morning, then a harrowing meeting over lunch with the Devine Doctor. And all I could think of was two o'clock and you coming through that door.'

I sat down on the window seat. 'Did Devine say anything about me?'

'Why d'you ask?'

'She gave me a very jolly roasting about my dissertation. Handled it with tongs, as though it were poisonous. Talk about damned with faint praise!'

'Now that's strange, honey, because she did corner me and mention it, right at the end of the meeting. I shouldn't say this but she said something about it being remarkably sound for a study "of that type". Then, having heard it all before, I had to stand for ten minutes and listen to her drone on about "that type" of research. She's remarkably intelligent but somewhat blinkered. Not because she's a woman,' he added hastily. 'But she's just that kind of academic.'

'See what I mean? Tongs!' I said.

'Listen, honey. It's been very fair of her, considering.'

'Considering what?'

'What do you want from her, Bronwen?' His voice was losing its humour, taking on a chilly edge. 'She said your work was sound, well written. That's a great concession from her. It should pass. She won't block it. What more do you want?'

'Nothing! Nothing! I stand corrected. Or, I *sit* corrected.' I stretched out my legs before me.

He squatted down in front of me and pulled off my long boots and socks. He held my heel in the palm of his hand started to massage my instep. Then he kneeled up and kissed my cheek.

'Look, honey, I can see I was too full-on when you got here. Didn't stop to take the temperature,' he murmured. 'But this is the way you've got me. This you–and–me–thing has got to be more important than your research and the Devine Doctor and this venerable institution.'

'Has it?' He moved to sit beside me so we were sitting shoulder to shoulder. 'Tell me, Richard. Talk to me about what it's like at home. What it's like to be half a world away from the American Richard Stephens. Who are *you*, when you are back home?'

I could feel his shoulder stiffen against mine. 'So why now, Bron? Why d'you ask this now?'

'Well, you've seen me at home with my family. I've seen your Peter at home with Sophie. Being in someone's home tells you about a person. So I really know more about him than I know about you. Now you've been invited to my grandmother's party. And you'll see us all. My mother, my grandmother and my daughter. You'll see all of this family that ties me up, ties me down, that makes me who I am.' A smile forced itself to my lips. 'Cali called us the Carmichael coven this lunchtime.'

There was no smile, no word of response.

I went on. 'Look, I only know you here in the eyrie, or in your

247

rooms, or down there splashing your way against the flow of the river. All I know is this side of you. The Durham side.'

'And it's not enough?' he said quietly.

'I don't know. I don't know if it's enough. Perhaps it's enough for now. And if now is all we have perhaps it will have to do.'

He was about to say something when there was a loud knock on the door and a rattle as someone struggled with the awkward iron catch. We scrambled to our feet and to our chairs in front and behind the desk, in positions more suited to academic encounter. Richard ran his hand through his hair and I pulled on my boots, put my socks in my pocket, picked up my book-bag and clutched it on my knee.

Richard coughed. 'Come in!' he said.

Seconds later the door burst open, letting in a crowd of people who only turned out to be three: a short neat man and a tall pretty woman in matching brand-new Burberrys, and a lanky boy of perhaps fourteen wearing a baseball cap and rimless glasses.

'Harry! Leonie, honey!' Richard leaped round the desk and greeted them with hugs of genuine affection. He punched the boy on the shoulder. 'And Baker! Ain't you just a foot taller than last I saw you?' He surveyed them. 'I didn't expect you so early.'

He sounded American again. Like he did when he first arrived.

The man called Harry grinned. 'Wa-al. We're staying at this cute hotel called the Royal County Hotel. And they fed and watered us right early and it's only a step away. So we thought . . .'

'Yes, yes. That's fine. Fine,' said Richard.

Then they all stood there and three pairs of bright eyes moved to me, as though their owners were about to eat me.

'Oh, yes.' Richard leaped into the breach. 'Harry, Leonie, Baker! This is Bronwen Carmichael, a very accomplished student of mine. Bronwen, this here is Harry Crossfield, an old faculty friend, and Leonie, who teaches school, and Baker whom I've known since he was in diapers.'

They shook hands with her. Harry's grasp was firm and positive, Leonie's was delicate and papery, Baker's was damp and fishlike.

Duty done, Leonie turned to Richard. 'I promised Maria we'd look in on you, see that you were OK. And,' she said blandly, 'I can see you are. She was telling me you're flourishing here, seeing your brother and all. And such an opportunity, this fine old university.'

'It's been excellent so far. Stimulating. Even life-changing,' murmured Richard. 'I have no complaints.'

I felt the hair on the back of my head raise a little. I stood up, and hauled my book-bag on to my shoulder. 'I think I should go . . .'

Richard gestured me to sit down again. So I sat down.

'We thought we'd take you up on your promise,' said Harry, 'to show us round this fascinating city. The view from the train was je-est amazing.'

Richard rubbed his chin. 'I have an even better idea. Bronwen here's a native. Knows this town inside out. Why doesn't she show you her city? I have this meeting at three, but then I could come and meet you all up at the cathedral. There's this cute café there, just off the cloisters.'

A native? Is that what I was? Just a bit of local colour? 'I don't think I can do this,' I said firmly. 'I have a stack of books to return to the library, and some photocopying for my dissertation . . .'

'I'll drop your books in at the library on my way to my meeting,' said Richard. 'And you can do the photocopying any time, Bronwen.'

'Oh, please, Miss Carmichael.' Leonie put her hand on my arm and looked at me earnestly. 'It would be su-uch a privilege. We've been in this country for a week and have only talked to waitresses, chambermaids and doormen. One feels so outside the loop.'

Behind her Baker snorted. '*Outside the loop!* Jeez!'

'Baker!' warned Harry.

I had to smile, warming to Baker. 'Well, put that way . . .' I unloaded my books on to Richard's desk. 'If you would just drop them into the library, Dr Stephens,' I said demurely. 'It's good not to have to lug them up hill and down dale.'

'*Lug!*' said Baker. 'Jeez!'

We made our way down the steep stairs, me in the lead. Really, from the moment they had disturbed Richard and me, I'd been prepared to dislike the Crossfields. But there was an attractive innocence about them, a certain charm. And as we walked through

249

the town I warmed to them even more. Harry exclaimed with delight at the way the river curled round the mass of cathedral and castle on the peninsula. Leonie was delighted at my tales of the prince bishops and their Northern fiefdom. Even Baker grunted some attention when I told him of the nearby site that witnessed the bloody battle of Neville's Cross and the capture of the Scottish King. The cobbled streets, and the tall narrow houses, so random in design, so settled in their elegance – they all won approval. The Crossfields did not even complain of the sudden heavy deluge of rain as they stood on the North Bailey. They merely congratulated each other on their foresight in buying the Burberrys in their one-day stop in York.

They gasped as they turned into cathedral square and were enchanted with the cathedral, comparing it very favourably with that in York. 'More – er – homey,' declared Harry. Once inside he cricked his head towards the great ceiling of the nave and murmured, 'Wa-al, Miss Carmichael, we may have the *space* but you certainly have the *time*.'

'Nine hundred years,' said Baker. '*Jeez!*'

The boy even betrayed another flicker of interest when I told him of the Scottish soldiers imprisoned in the cathedral, who lit campfires to keep themselves warm.

Leonie wrinkled her nose. 'Think of the smell, honey. The smell! In this beautiful place too.'

'*Unclean, unclean!*' A note of irony in Baker's young voice. It crossed my mind that teenagers were never what they seem. Any good teacher knows that.

Then Harry, Baker in tow, wandered off to take a look at the clock tower and the military chapel with its threadbare banners and books of the glorious dead.

Leonie went and kneeled in a pew. She crossed herself and bent her head in prayer. I looked up towards St Cuthbert's tomb and my favourite rose window that glowed with filtered light even on this dingy day. I thought of me and Richard, and wondered if a prayer to an unknown and unbelieved-in God would be any help.

Leonie stood up. 'Always a help,' she whispered. 'Are there candles here, or is this place too Protestant for that?'

We found the candles and Leonie lit one. 'For our little Alex,' she whispered to Bronwen. 'Gone to Heaven when she was just four. I miss her still. She's always in my heart. Now we just have Baker. He sure is a pickle at times. But we treasure him.'

Even the taciturn picklish Baker exclaimed when we came out into the cloister. 'Ca-aint you just see those old guys marchin' round and round in their hoods? Pure Goth, a-ain't it?' He said this to his father as though he were the first one in the world to have noticed it. '*Jeez!*'

The café, when we got to it, was clattering with voices that echoed up to its stone arches and down to its stone-flagged floor, but was still half empty. Even so, there was a queue at the self-service counter. 'Queues!' said Leonie. 'The English and their queues.'

We took a table in the corner, Leonie fussing, finding a spare chair for the absent Richard. She sent the men off to get some coffee and some of those 'cute English scones', and settled down to talk to me. She leaned forward, her well-maintained teeth gleaming an affable enough smile.

'So, what about you, Miss Carmichael? How do you happen to be a student here at . . .'

'At my age?' I explained my situation. Leonie was even interested in my research. Her father had been stationed here during the war and her grandmother was a GI bride from Norwich. 'My dad and Uncle Rube were at Omaha beach for the landings. Lucky to get back home. After that my dad always said we were on borrowed time. Not just soldiers at war but all of us.' She grinned. 'Praise be the old boy's still ticking over.'

I thought of the letters from Trinidad in Kate's carrier and wondered if the man called Cy was still 'ticking over'. He could very easily be dead. I glanced at the queue where Harry was still only fifth in line.

Leonie went on, 'So, Miss Carmichael, what d'ya think of our good friend Richard?' her sharp eyes boring into mine.

I cursed the colour surging into my cheeks. 'He's a clever scholar, much admired here, I believe, even though he's stirred things up a bit.' Red cheeks or not, I was proud of my even voice.

'We're all so fond of him back home, despite his bohemian ways. Not like Maria! She's so elegant, organised. Such a clever woman. We are all in awe of her. Leading family. Leading firm. A full partner. What do the French say? *Formidable!* I have to confess that when she's around even *I* feel in the shade.' She touched her immaculate hair and I was suddenly aware of my loosening plait and the halo of escaping hair that always asserted itself at this time of day. No competition for a *formidable* woman.

Leonie nodded. 'I always say those two complement each other. He so clever and so – how should I say it? – untamed. And she so sophisticated. And those wonderful boys! Any parent would be proud.'

It took a lot of effort for me to look away with Leonie's kindly, concentrated gaze on my face Of course Leonie knew I was no mere student; that it was no tutorial consultation that they had disturbed. It was a relief to see Harry and Baker at last, making their way across the floor with their trays.

I sat with them long enough to drink halfway down my cup, then stood up. 'I'm really sorry but I have to go. Dr Stephens will be here any minute. My daughter will be wondering where I am.' Of course this was not true. I had no idea where Lily was. Off with Simon somewhere, no doubt.

The Crossfields exclaimed their dismay but I was firm. 'I must get home.' I forced a smile. 'It has been wonderful to meet you.'

They all stood up and shook my hand again. This time Baker's hand was less clammy, more firm and friendly. As I walked back through the cloisters and the nave I reflected on the kindness, the appreciative manners of the Crossfields. They were genuine people. And I shouldn't be surprised that Leonie Crossfield was so defensive, just now, over her friend Maria.

I met Richard just outside the great door. He grinned. 'Away already? Where are you off to?'

'Up to South Street. The Riley's parked there. I have to get home.'

'And Harry and Leonie?'

'Well, I've given them the tour like a *true native*, had coffee with them and now I'm going. They're waiting for you in the café.' My glance strayed to one of the long gravestones, worn with age, its dedication obliterated.

Richard took me by the shoulders and made me look him in the eye. 'Oh dear. Are we miffed? *Mea culpa!* I shouldn't have called you a native.' The glimmer of laughter in his eyes made me even angrier.

'I was worried that they would find me lacking. No war-paint and feathers.' I shook my head. 'It's not just that, Richard. Did you think I've nothing better to do, that my time is less valuable than yours?'

He frowned. 'I just thought you might like to show off this fabulous city of yours, honey.'

'The Crossfields are strangers to me, Richard. Not only that, Leonie guessed – well, guessed something. She was keen to let me know that they were no strangers to you. Or Maria. That she knew you *both* very well. I was embarrassed.' I pulled myself free of his grasp. 'Anyway. I have to get back. Lily wants me to look at some travel brochures with her.' What was I doing? I'd never used Lily as an excuse, not even when she was little. Not ever. 'Anyway, I'm going.'

I turned and walked steadily down the old path. He didn't come after me. I turned back at the end of the path but he wasn't there. The great weathered door with its sanctuary knocker had closed behind him.

A Question of Sex

'Of course all this blew up then, didn't it? In the 1960s.'

Lily is sitting at the little desk in Rosa's study, where for many years she did her homework.

'What? The Bomb?' says Rosa. 'I'd have thought the point was it didn't blow up the world.'

'No. Sex. The Pill and all that. Women's Liberation. Didn't you march and all that?'

'I was in a group in Durham – well, I was taken up by these university types who were into it. A trophy, if you like. A real live working-class girl with only a smidgin of education.'

'Didn't you like them?'

'Well, I couldn't quite put my finger on it then. They were very kind and enthusiastic. Smiles that could blind you. Such intellectual energy.'

'Were they lesbians?'

'Oh. Stereotypes, darling!' Rosa laughs. 'A few of them actually were. Some more in style than substance. Lesbian-style was quite chic in those circles.'

'Did they ever come on to you?' Lily is used to being very direct and open with her grandmother.

'It wasn't like that, love. For me it was more an education in how normal those women were. How innocent. How very nice. How – in some cases – you could be friends. There was one, though . . .'

Lily leans forward. 'What about her?'

'She'd already graduated and was a social worker round here. Up on the estate.'

'Good sort, then. Brave to venture up there.'

'She thought so. Anyway, one morning she calls here at Arran Lea for coffee and I ask her what it's like working up there, knocking on doors on those landings. I knew from school how tough a place it was.' She pauses. 'Well, she says the people are fine. Putty in her hands, she says. All you need, she says, is to smile at them and look them in the eye. And she switches on this glorious, blinding smile, the smile that she had used on me in that first meeting, the smile that made me feel so welcome.' Rosa wrinkled her nose. 'At that moment I saw it was so patronising, so inauthentic. Like her clients on the estate, I was an *object* to her! Someone to be won over in the cause. By feminine wiles, if you like. So inauthentic. Inappropriate, given the cause.'

'Were you attracted to her?' says Lily.

Rosa shakes her head. 'I don't think so. I did like her. I was pleased she seemed to be my friend. But really I learned she was cold and manipulative.'

'So, *did* she come on to you?'

Rosa laughs heartily. 'Oh, sweetheart, it doesn't always come down to that, you know.'

'But did she?' persists Lily.

'I suppose she did.'

'What did you do?'

'I pretended I didn't notice.'

Lily laughs out loud. 'You are so good. The iron hand in the silken glove.'

Rosa smiles, the rare confidence obviously at an end. She glances down longingly at the manuscript and her jar of red and green pens.

Lily is having none of this threatened withdrawal. 'I really want to ask you about sex.'

Rosa laughs. 'Be direct, won't you? Well, love, I'm no expert. I'll have you know I abstained until I got married – but I was just eighteen, I suppose. Not that everyone abstained to that age. What a virtuous myth that is.'

255

Lily persists. 'But you're always *watching*, Rosa. You observe. You have feelings. You build theories.' She pauses. 'So what's your theory about this? About this matter of sex?'

Rosa frowns. 'You can't theorise about it, love. You just have to respect yourself, go gently and you'll know when it's right, and you'll know what's right. All I can say is that when it's all synchronised – oh, Lily! It is exciting, profound, exquisite, powerful.' She breaks off for a moment. 'Lily darling, I'm not sure I should be talking to you like this . . .'

'Who else, Rosa? I love my mum but how embarrassing is this to talk to her about? And now she's on with that professor . . . How embarrassing is that?'

'So it's all right talking to me because I don't have a professor in the background? Because I'm not participating?'

'Well . . .'

'Well!' Rosa echoes. 'Do you have anyone in mind for this great experiment? Simon?'

'Simon?' Lily laughs. 'That would be so wrong. He's my friend.'

'I see.'

Lily stretches her long legs in front of her. 'Some of the girls at school, they say just do it with anybody for the first time just to get it over with. One girl did it with her brother.' She shuddered. 'How gross is that?'

Rosa's eyebrows rise up into her fringe. 'Like squeezing a spot, you mean?'

'Just about. Like I say, some of them have already done it. Very cocky about it. But they seem no better for it, to be honest.'

'So you'd not do it for that reason?'

'Like I said. Sordid.'

'So all that investigation of the Pill was mere research?'

'I just thought . . . what intuition? Spontaneity?'

'I don't think being intuitive and spontaneous are the same thing. Meet someone, get to know them. Get in tune with them. Follow your intuition. Make love to them. I assure you that doesn't happen in twenty-four hours.'

'But it seems to. That's what the girls say. And in novels and magazines it seems to happen like that.'

Rosa is already shaking her head. 'I might be wrong, m'love, but I think that's the boy's view of things. Boys and girls are wired differently. I learned that late, but I learned it. Boys do so love to get on with it. With one girl. Then the next. And the next.'

'Not like that with Simon.'

'No. I see that.' Rosa looks thoughtfully at her granddaughter. As they have been talking, the ghost of the young Bronwen has been shimmering between them.

'I'm glad, though,' she says now, putting a hand out to touch Lily's shoulder, 'that Bronwen followed *her* intuition. How else would we be here, having this strange conversation about the mystery of sex?'

Lily stands up and stretches her arms above her head. 'Well, then. Duly noted. Thanks, Rosa.' And she slips out of the room and along the corridor to her own room.

She stretches out on the bed, pulls over her writing cushion, opens her notebook and continues her letter to the Church Commissioners about a young man who was a curate in this parish in 1974: Matthew Pomeroy.

Autumn Notes

Rosa

It's a dreary half-autumn day. I've been mulling over this fascinating conversation I had with Lily yesterday and I can't settle to work, so I thought I'd write something here.

I took my mother her lunch today. A true Red Riding Hood, you might say. The usual messengers are unavailable. Lily is off with Simon, climbing crags near Coniston. Bronwen is off to Durham to collect her dissertation from the printers and submit it at the University Office. She asked me to do an edit-run on the last draft. All very esoteric but it's very well written and quite compelling to read. Fascinating to see all those perspectives on an event that you think you know inside out. I learned things I hadn't known.

I was relieved to see that elements of the tick book are there only by allusion. No embarrassing quotations. It is clear from where Bronwen placed some of these allusions that she has a suspicion Brock might be Kate's illegitimate son. (They use the terms 'by-blow' and 'love-begot' around here – rather charming . . .) Well, I'm certain that Brock is neither Kate's by-blow nor her love-begot. Bronwen's instinct is wrong there. She seemed quite anxious when I handed her dissertation back to her. She needn't have worried. It's not my field really. I thought it interesting but had very little to say. A bit of syntax here and there to disentangle, but that *is* my thing.

Anyway, I knocked on Kate's door and waited a few minutes before I used my key. Nothing gained by charging in. The mumble of *Woman's Hour* seeped through the living-room door. Kate likes her Radio 4.

She was sitting tucked in her chair by the gas fire, which was barely turned on. On her knee was the *Northern Echo*, turned to today's crossword. The room was chilly. Just like Butler Street always used to be. Chilly.

She looked up at me. 'Rosa. You!' So, not delighted to see me then. I plonked my Red Riding Hood basket on the sideboard and kneeled down to turn the fire up, saying that she should keep the room warmer, at least keep the central heating on so the fire's not heating the room up from clay-cold. I felt quite angry. It's not as though she has to worry about the bill. I pay that. Somehow her keeping the house cold even though I pay the bill is another small victory for her.

She pushed away her paper and took off her glasses and told me that she wouldn't dream of wasting my money that way. 'This fire does me. You know that.'

'That's the point, Kate. It doesn't do you. One day we'll come in and find you hypothermic.'

She was dismissive. 'Be that as it may . . .' (One of her favourite dismissive comments that reduces you to a child again.) Then: 'So, to what do I owe this pleasure? No stories to write or crippled children to teach?' She is so rude. Getting worse. The last layers of restraint are finally peeling off. God save me from being laid bare like that and still alive.

'I've brought your lunch.' I make my usual effort not to sound defensive. 'Chicken pie. Your favourite. It's just ready to bake. I thought we could have a cup of tea while it's cooking.' I escape to the kitchen and unpack my basket. My mother's voice comes to me from the other room. 'Pies! Not so keen on those things these days. You never know what goes into them.'

I tell her that I *do* know, as I put it in and what is in it is free-range chicken, in white sauce with spring onions. Then she says darkly that these days, you never know what goes in the chickens. Have I not read the papers?

I put the pie in the oven and the peeled carrots and the peas in small pans.

Now she's behind me, leaning on the kitchen door and asks me again why I'm here. 'Why here and not on all those important missions of yours to the post office or to that crippled girl?'

'Kate, you can be so rude!' The words burst from me.

'Too tender, Rosa. Always were.' Now she's at my shoulder, edging me out of her kitchen. 'Now is it tea or coffee? I'm afraid I only have instant coffee and none of that smelly tea you like.'

So, I retreated to the sitting room, sat down and allowed myself to be served with coffee in a blue mug that had 'GRANDMA' etched on in gold lettering, and she settled down with a much prettier cup so full of tea that some had spilled into the saucer. Of course neither of us mentioned that.

I brought up the subject of The Party, no longer a secret, of course. No surprises allowed to wrong-foot Kate.

'What I don't want there,' she announced, 'is no Old Folks. I don't want them slavering all over the place and rushing to the toilet. It always reminds me of working at hospital, when you get Old Folks together in any numbers.'

I mentioned Mrs Novelli and Aunties Madge and Laura, the only aunties still with us. 'They'll be all right. I have to say that they don't slaver and are both still continent.' Kate maintains a fairly consistent relationship with her sisters, mostly expressed in a fortnightly game of whist played for real money, alternating with a night dancing at the local working men's club where Auntie Laura's late husband had been on the committee.

I haven't spent any time with the aunts for years. I have a child's memory of their being patronising, even unkind to Kate and all of us when we first arrived here. I suppose they did what they felt able to. God save us all from judgemental children! I sometimes wonder what Lily is storing up about us, in that great brain of hers.

My mother was slurping her tea slightly, her eye straying longingly towards her unfinished crossword. I almost apologised then for interrupting her in her more important pastime. Why is it when I am with her, even her frail and fading present self, this troubled child surfaces, anxious about offending her, disturbing her, worried about her dark thoughts, and having dark thoughts of her own?

Suddenly she speaks. 'I've never understood why you stay here,' she says.

My nerves jump in my body. 'What?' I say, jolted out of my manners. 'Here?'

'Why on earth you've clung on, stayed round here all these years, I can't think. You've got your trade, if that's what teaching is. And you've got your little books.'

Little books! Ye gods!

She goes on. 'You could have got away from here years ago. Right away from the North. Nothing for any sensible person round here. Nothing.'

'The Bloody North!' The phrase comes out of the past and pushes itself through my mouth.

'Precisely. The Bloody North,' she says. 'The last place God made and left his pick and shovel in.'

I move very carefully, putting my half-empty mug on the floor beside me and leaning forward to pull her wandering eyes on to me. 'How can you still say that, Kate?'

She sniffs and says, 'Now don't you start on saying you stayed around for me. I'll not have that. Not enough gumption, that's the problem. Even if you *do* think yourself so clever.'

That's enough. 'Not like Brock, you mean? Brock travels the world and never comes home. Should I have been like him, gone off and never come back?'

'At least he had gumption. Got out of this place. Made sommat of himself.'

Kate normally speaks quite correctly: a kind of sanitised Durham accent. But she's returning then to the world of her own childhood. A dingy place where the most powerful word was escape. I'm so mad at her that suddenly I'm raging on at her about how wonderful it is here in Durham, about the green valleys and the low woodland and the tumbling becks that meander through the fields. And, only minutes away, haven't we the cosy dales and the wide open spaces of the moors? The lovely stone houses, our own exquisite cathedral admired throughout the world?

Kate shakes her head violently, her lip curling. 'Typical! You're doing it again! Making a story of it all. It's all in your head, Rosa.

261

This is a dirty old place. All those collieries spitting out their black, the miserable people. No work . . .'

I am steamed up then. 'Haven't you noticed, Kate? It's all changed. No collieries. Charlie and Brock don't work down any pit.'

'Charlie! Don't get me on about him. No ambition And anyway, our Brock would never have gone down the pit. Far too good for it.'

Leave it, leave it, Rosa. I take several deep breaths. 'The party.' I say. 'You know our Brock's coming to your party?'

'Course I know. I told you. I wrote to him and told him to come. Anyway,' she says, 'what's all this about our Brock? Can't leave him alone? Going on about him.'

I take a breath and ask her, 'Who is Brock, Mother? Where's he from?'

'He's from Lancaster, like you and Charlie. Like I'm from here, for my sins.'

'I mean, *who* is he? You brought him into our family. I remember it. It's there in my journal. The one you gave to Bronwen. I've been thinking again about how Brock came into the house. You brought him in that day after work. You laid him in a drawer. You brought him in . . .'

I stopped. Kate was shaking her head violently and drumming her hands on the arms of her chair. 'No. No! You've made that up, Rosa. You started making things up when you were very young and you are making it up now.'

I went to pick up the photo off the sideboard, the one with the three of us at the Gala in the park. I am sixteen and am wearing a full skirt Kate had made for me, and a deep waspie belt. I'd just had the letter saying I'd got nine O levels and there is the rare glimmer of a smile on my face. Charlie is there, with his hair slicked back, looking as mischievous as ever. And there is Brock, too tall for his age, blond and so good-looking, gazing straight into the camera – and through that lens to the world, which he was going to make his own.

'Look! Look!' I thrust the photo under her nose. 'He's nothing like us. Nothing like you, or my dad . . .'

Kate put her cup in its saucer on top of her folded newspaper. 'Our Rosa, you are talking claptrap. They say that happens when you're coming to the Change. I read it in the paper. Time you went home, love. Back to your stories of children in that fairy-tale, beautiful North of yours. All your fancy. You go, and take that ridiculous tale about our Brock with you.'

I could kill her. I could take her by that scrawny neck and shake her like a chicken. I had to take some deep breaths. 'Mother . . .'

She put her hands on the arms of her chair and hauled herself to her feet. 'I said go! I knew it would be trouble this morning when I saw it wasn't our Bronwen or our Lily bringing my dinner. Send one of them another time, will you? Surrogates. Isn't that what you call them?'

And I was out of the door. I can't remember moving my feet. But standing there on the patch of shorn grass in front of her bungalow I realised that Kate had become as worked up as me as we talked. Her voice was shaking and her body was trembling.

I got into the car and sat there for five minutes before I stopped shaking myself. What is it when we're together that makes us so unhappy? How is it that I, who love her and have never hurt a living thing, could harbour murderous thoughts towards her? I know Kate doesn't act like this when she's with Bronwen or Lily. With them she is funny, clever, the doting grandmother. I suppose sharing those dark days with her, in the war and after, has not really brought us closer together. Rather, those days of her obvious deep depression, and me mirroring it in some pale reflection, have created some kind of black space inside us both, between us; it has effectively drained all the light of our relationship.

This is so even now, forty years later.

But with Charlie, Bronwen and Lily – and some ghost of a remembered, idealised Brock – there is a different and equally true Kate – now benevolent, dry, self-deprecating: one who can evoke warm feeling and affection.

None of which I feel.

After sitting there letting all this stuff drench through me, I finally put the car back into gear and went across town to see young Cherie, waiting eagerly for me in her wheelchair, keen to show off her new reading and to get me up to date on the latest goings-on in *Coronation Street*. The simplicity and directness of Cherie's world is a safety valve in my life. She takes my full concentration. So, for two hours I didn't need to think of my mother, or Brock, and whether I would be able to handle his presence at Kate's birthday party.

But then, here I am writing about it; it's all back again to haunt me. Old habits die hard. And despite everything I am looking forward to seeing Brock.

A Stranger in All These Places

Two days after her battle with Kate, Rosa was standing in her bedroom in front of her wardrobe mirror, adjusting her scarf. It was silvery grey silk scattered with small violets and went very nicely with her dove-grey wool trouser suit.

Young Cherie would comment on the scarf today, just as she always commented on the smallest change in Rosa's appearance: a shade of lipstick, a pretty blouse, new shoes, a new hairstyle. Cherie used her acute magnifying glass of a brain to enlarge and expand the enclosed world of her small terraced house with its tight landscape of mother, stepfather, small brother, television, meals, medicine and toilet.

Now the shrill tones of the doorbell made Rosa jump and she ran down to open the door to Richard Stephens, who stood there looking like the spirit of autumn with his red-gold hair. His face was sharp and finely cut. His grey eyes gleamed. Behind him, her garden, drenched in faint mist shredding itself into the trees, seemed dull and lifeless.

'Miss Carmichael?' He had this nice voice. Attractive.

She must have been staring. 'Of course, Dr Stephens. Come in.' She held the door wide, allowing him past her, then shut it behind him.

'Call me Richard, please. Dr Stephens is what my sister-in-law calls my Sunday name.'

'Richard. And it's Rosa.' She led the way through to the small back sitting room. 'Bronwen's due back but I'm afraid she's not here. She's in Durham on some errand. But she should be back by one. She did say one o'clock, I think. Do make yourself at home here. I'm afraid I have to—'

'I'm interrupting your work. Sorry, ma-am . . .'

She smiled. 'It's rather urgent. Something for the post and then I'm off to see this pupil of mine.'

'Bronwen told me. The one with spina bifida?'

She smiled quickly, as usual faintly irritated at this common habit of making the condition the person. 'She's just Cherie. A marvellous child.'

He flushed, obviously sensitive to the rebuke. 'I'm sorry, crass of me . . .'

She kept looking at him.

'Mrs Carmichael?' he said. 'Rosa?'

'Oh dear. I'm staring again. There's something about . . . well, no matter.' She paused. 'Where did Bronwen say you came from – apart from America, that is?'

He thought she was very direct for such a quiet, almost nervous creature. 'All over the Northwest of England when I was young, then Oxford, then London, then Manchester, then Boston in the US of A. I've been a stranger in all these places.'

'My brother was at Oxford,' she frowned. 'In 1967, I think.'

'After my time, I'm afraid.'

'He was there as a post-graduate. After St Andrews.'

He nodded. 'A scholar, then.'

'He was clever, gifted, much like Lily. But not a scholar. More interested in money, politics. All that.'

'How interesting.'

She sniffed the air. 'Oh Lord, that's my mother's dinner! Excuse me.'

He followed her to the kitchen and watched as she turned off the ring and lifted out the leek pudding on to a plate, working with arms stretched to protect her pale suit. She glanced across at him. 'If you leave it in too long it dries out and it's ruined. With leek puddings there's a moment between soggy and dry when it reaches perfection.'

'Leek pudding? Is this a traditional recipe? I'm impressed.'

'Don't be too impressed. This is no old family tradition. No soul food handed down through generations of horny-handed peasants. My mother's cuisine ranged from egg and chips to the fish and chip shop. But I once did this Women's Institute course in local cooking. Easy food. That's when I learned that you could eat well for next to nothing if you could cook. I realised that if my mother had been a cook when we were young it would have saved us from starving.'

He raised his sandy brows. 'You're telling me you starved when you were young?'

She surveyed him coolly. 'Only now and then.'

She had wrong-footed him again. He flushed again and then came back to return her in kind. 'Well, I wouldn't say my brother and I starved but have you ever existed on institutional food?' He described a meal in one of the care homes 'Even at college it was food at long benches. To be honest, that was pretty sound but my greatest delight even then was my own two-ring burner that I had on a windowsill in my rooms. Culinary independence! Freedom. That was my sixties break-out!' he said ruefully. 'Taking care of myself.'

She laughed heartily and he thought how young she looked. 'So here we are! Just like that *Monty Python* thing on poverty-envy. "I was born in a paper bag in a puddle in the middle of the road." Wasn't that it?'

'You got it, ma'am!' he said. 'Or perhaps it was a hole in the middle of the road?' And they both laughed.

She sobered down. 'All right of course for those smug public schoolboys to make that joke. Me, I'd win any competition based on that. Disadvantaged? I never taught a child more disadvantaged than I was.' She stared at him. 'Really I have to finish getting ready. Just make free with the kitchen. But don't be tempted by the leek pudding. You wouldn't like my mother when she's thwarted.'

Left alone in the kitchen he lifted the lid of the leek pudding and wondered how a pie packed with root vegetables could smell so appetising. Then he made himself some instant coffee and settled down to wait for Bronwen.

Hash

Charlie's wife, May, sent me out to the Starship *Enterprise* to find Cali. 'Always tucked away, them two, Bronwen. That lass is as bad as Theo.' She spoke the words evenly, without rancour. Cali was wrong. May wasn't that bothered about her. 'Good job that lass is going away or the old boy'd get his head turned for sure. Bit of a romantic, your uncle. That's why I liked him in the first place. But there can be too much dreaming, you know.'

I lifted the dragon knocker and dropped it hard on the peeled surface of the door. I smiled to myself, thinking how this might mirror me and Richard being surprised by the Crossfields. I knocked harder.

Charlie opened the door, letting out a gale of heavy metal sound. He blinked at the light like a dormouse. 'Why, hello, pet!' He turned his head and called behind him. 'It's my niece and your mate, Cali. Come visiting.'

Cali was sitting on a chair, booted feet up on another, smoking a joint. She leaned across and turned down the music until it was just a low background wail, then stood up, hugged me and offered me a smoke.

'No, thanks, Cal.' I scrabbled in my bag and pulled out the Jiffy bag holding her dissertation.

'You read it then?' yawned Cali. 'Didn't rush, did you?'

'I've been busy.'

'Well?'

'Yes. It's very good.' It was. The minimum length, exhaustively researched, pithily expressed and beautifully presented. No risks taken there. Cali was full of contradictions.

'Pleased that you think so,' grinned Cali, without an ounce of complacency. 'Although I have to tell you it was the single most boring thing I've ever done in my life.'

'I thought it was good,' murmured Charlie from the long side table where he was sorting and labelling tapes, his spectacles at the end of his nose.

'You read it?' I instantly regretted the surprise in my voice.

He took off his glasses. 'I can read, you know, pet,' he said softly.

'Sorry, Uncle Charlie. That was really, really tactless.'

'It was, pet.' And he went on sorting.

Cali came to drag me across to sit beside her and asked me about my own work, sharing my relief that at last it was done, and bound. She told me it was my own fault that it had taken so long. It was far, far too complicated. Then she asked me about Richard, but I was non-committal, segueing into a highly decorated version of my experience as a tour guide for the Americans.

After that – uniquely in our relationship – there seemed little to say. The shed seemed so very full of Cali and Charlie, music and the whoozy scent of hash, and there was no room, no room at all, for me. I was glad to leave them to it.

Later, having seen Richard's car on the drive, I wasn't surprised to see him at the door of the kitchen.

'Hi, Bron,' he said. He reached out to hug me, then recoiled a little. 'You been smoking hash, honey?' he said, surprised.

I shook my head. 'No, but I've been in the company of those who were. I called on Cali and Charlie and they were in their den being creative. Cali was smoking.'

He pulled me into the kitchen, closed the door behind us, then as I turned my head away he missed my mouth and managed to kiss my cheek. 'Honey, sweet Bronwen,' he said. 'I was wretched when we parted after that disaster with the Crossfields. Curse them.'

I pulled away. 'Don't blame the Crossfields. They were fine. Sweet. Grateful. I couldn't fault them.'

He clasped my hands, stopping me from moving further away.

'Look, Bron, I've rowed up and down the river, done all my tutorials, marked all my papers, been to the faculty meetings and all I want to do is to be with you. I am raging inside. I can't recognise myself.'

I tried to wrestle myself free. 'Is that what I'm about? Love in the afternoon? Well, thank you!'

'No, no. It's not just about making love. I just can't get you out of my mind. And the closest I can get to you is to be with you and to make love to you. Without you I feel lost.'

I looked at him carefully. 'I'm trying, really trying . . . in these months I've *really* tried, to live just in the present with this. Not to think of America and your life with Maria. In some ways I've enjoyed living in the here and now. No future, no past, et cetera. In some ways it's been so simple – such a joy – to be with you. But there in Durham, with those people who are your friends, your compatriots, I really, really felt I didn't know you. It was a shock. There was Leonie talking about your wife as a living being. And here am I, having pushed thoughts of her to the back of my mind. It was as though Maria were there, sitting at the table with us in the cathedral café. I felt a fool. And I wondered just why you let me go with the Crossfields. With her. Bringing Maria into my life. How could you? What was that about?'

He pulled me closer. 'Bronwen . . .'

There was a knock on the door. We leaped apart.

Rosa put her head round the door. She had pushed her spectacles on to her head and her usually immaculate hair was all awry, 'Bronwen, m'darling, sorry to interrupt, but could you possibly take Kate her dinner? That leek pie? She made it perfectly clear to me the other day that I'm *persona non grata* as far as dinner-carrying goes. Anyway, I have to get off to see young Cherie. She gets very upset if I am late.' She looked across at Richard. 'I'm sorry . . .'

'That's perfectly OK,' I said hurriedly. 'We'll drop it off on our way out.' I did not want to stay in the house with Richard. Not today. I improvised. 'I thought I'd show Richard Tudhoe Woods and tell him all about Pitch and Toss. A unique bit of history for the cultural historian.'

270

We decided to go to Tudhoe in Richard's car.

'Pitch and Toss? Fascinating,' he said as he put the car into gear.

As we ground out of the double gates of Arran Lea and on to the road, he turned to me. 'D'you know, honey, I think I could fall in love with your mama?'

I had to laugh at this and shook my head. 'That is fairly ridiculous, Richard. But I have to say I admire your taste. If you were angling for a second chance, you've got one.'

It came upon me very suddenly that the answer to my dilemma was to enjoy myself, and not take him or myself too seriously. I had finished that dratted dissertation. I was with a man I was fascinated by and might even be in love with. So I might as well enjoy myself.

Part Four

The Mirror

Driving North

Callum Carmichael, known to his family, friends and colleagues as Brock, checked his watch – the Sekonda rather than the Cartier – and got into his car, the Ford rather than the BMW. If he drove some stretches over the limit he could do the journey from London in four and a half hours, road works permitting. As he put the car in gear he breathed slowly in and out, telling himself he must treat this as any other journey. It was a trip that had aborted itself more than once in his life. There had been many other trips to London and Oxford on financial, diplomatic and academic business when he could have nipped up north to see them, no bother. But he hadn't.

He was in England this time for a visit to the Department of Trade and Industry in London, with a side trip to Oxford for the funeral of his old post-graduate tutor at St Antony's. The old boy's funeral swilled with the great and the good, many of them front-line Cold War veterans from all over the world. The College had been instrumental in supplying a generation of students whose talents and proclivities conveniently blurred the line between diplomacy, journalism, business and the esoteric patriotism of espionage. Even Brock, who had dipped his professional toe into all these fields, did not really know who among his peers had stepped over that blurry line.

One thing was sure. The man they had honoured today in death had inducted him into the gorgeous elaborate maze that was Russian Culture and Soviet politics. When Brock had first gone up to Oxford the old boy had just been in his forties, fizzing with wry optimism, still boxing with the shadow of Lenin. Since then the old boy grew older, more learned, more guru-esque and essentially less interesting. At the funeral they were saying the creaking destruction of the Soviet Union had tolled his death knell. 'The old boy just turned his face to the wall.'

Brock came off the roundabout on to the A1. All he had to do now was point the nose of the Ford north and keep driving. Ditch the Cartier watch, no BMW. Discretion had always proved to be the better part of valour. He had learned to be discreet out of courtesy when he visited far-flung parts of the Soviet Union, or areas of the developing world where flaunting your wealth was dangerous as well as impolite. York and Durham weren't the Third World but even there it didn't do to stick your head too far above the parapet.

He put the car on cruise control and let his mind float back to that time when he was seventeen, when he won his university scholarship. He'd been dashing for the bus to Durham and had picked up his post on his way out of the house on Butler Street. He didn't open the letters until he was on the bus. One letter was from the Chamber of Commerce. Something about sponsorship. Then he opened another, more modest envelope that turned out to be the key to the rest of his life. A place at St Andrews with a bursary attached. He had burned with satisfaction and blurted out his pleasure to the man next to him on the bus. The man had shifted a little, putting more distance between himself and this boastful young man who talked to strangers.

The man took out a cigarette. 'Not up to me, son, but I haven't got a lot of time for all that.' He took a deep drag and let the smoke float from his mouth. 'Where d'you get the right to privilege like that? Silver-spooners, I call them, people who got to those places. Bought privilege. Ivory towers, all right.'

Gulping back the desire to punch the man on his fat splayed nose, Brock changed seats so he could pore over his letter in peace. His teachers had said he had a chance. His mother had told him to grab that chance with both hands. One teacher had doubts, saying he was only young. He could afford to wait a year, cram a little more into that head of his. But here he was. A firm offer. His exams were a mere detail. He knew he would get them.

At the next stop he jumped off the bus and returned home. The first person he saw was Charlie, who whooped his delight and dragged him off to the Thorn's Club to celebrate. Charlie's glowing pride cut through the nay-sayers. 'This is me brother. Bit of a clever sod. He's going to St Andrews University. He'll show that lot sommat, I'm tellen yer.'

Charlie's friend, Theo, who cultivated his black locks in the style of the great Elvis Presley, shook Brock heartily by the hand. 'Well done, kidder. Like Charlie says, you go up there and show the clever buggers.'

When Brock got back home the house was empty and he prowled around like a caged tiger until Rosa and Kate erupted into the house together: Kate from her late shift at the hospital, Rosa from some teacher In-Service thing, pushing Bronwen in her pushchair. It was hard to tell who was the more excited. Kate bustled about finding some soured Christmas sherry. Rosa gripped his arms, her eyes shining into his. 'I knew! I knew!'

'Well, I've gotta admit it's down to you two,' he said, scrupulously fair. 'All those nights hammering through those stupid papers.' His teacher had got him some papers and, once Brock, Kate and Rosa had stopped laughing at the ludicrous broadness and occasional eccentricity of the questions, they got down to tearing them apart, discussing just what the right responses might be. Rosa, just out of a very basic teacher-training course, listened to his arguments and asked artless questions, making him build shrewd explanations and speculations about the depth and ambiguity of the questions. Kate's tough common sense and hard insights brought experience to bear on the arguments.

In those days Rosa was right alongside him, entirely his equal. But when he got to St Andrews he plunged into the intoxication of college life, the esoteric charms of politics and economics and the increasing compulsion of all things French and Russian, and he seemed to leave Rosa behind. His new life was so utterly compelling and he only came home for flying visits. When he did get home they would comment that he was less earnest, on his bossy, confident manner, on his beard, thicker and tougher with the years. Now he seemed to be treated with almost too much respect. He became a stranger. More so when he went up to Oxford to do his doctorate.

There were odd things. Sometimes, when he was so entrenched in his studies he was 'thinking Russian' he would hear an English voice whisper in his ear and for a moment would not understand a word. Then his mind would flash back to times when he was very young, when Rosa used to lay an extra place at table for his imaginary friend. This flashback visited him at every stage in his life when he was feeling most the stranger. And he was the stranger many times.

All he ever did then were lightning visits. He supposed such lightning visits would have set the pattern for the rest of his life, if it hadn't been for that time just after he had got his doctorate. On that visit, Rosa, who had been a comfortable taken-for-granted player in his life, was glowing with some kind of secret. She was different. At first he put it down to the fact that she'd been married. And she had this kid. Pretty little thing. Rosa was bound to be different. Of course there was that dull stick Duncan Carmedy. Old even when he was young. Hardly on the horizon. It was always Kate and Rosa. And sometimes Bronwen in a push-chair, or clinging to Rosa's hand.

It was only when they went out to eat and she told him about the success of her stories that what he really wanted to do was kiss her. He kissed her. And they made love all night. He fled the next morning and had never been back north. Oh, Charlie and his step-brood had visited him and Louise in France. Even Kate had made the trip to France with Charlie once. But never Rosa. It had taken him a long time to get over Rosa. He was forty before he met Louise and decided that his life should really move on. Even now, living half his time in Moscow and half in Normandy, he was happy to keep the English Channel and often Europe, between himself and his sister, his love.

But now there had been this card from Kate and hints from Charlie about this party. He thought perhaps a twenty-year stretch was long enough penalty for his misdemeanour. The birthday was a good excuse. He hadn't asked Louise if she wanted to come. She might have said yes.

Now he turned on the car radio. Stop thinking, Brock. Concentrate on the driving. First this conference in York, then on further north. Home to Durham.

Pitch and Toss

'Pitch and Toss?' said Richard. 'Are we at sea? "All night the boat pitched and tossed until the new day dawned".'

'We might be all at sea,' I said, 'but this story's on dry land, not out on the ocean wave.'

We were plodging through Tudhoe Woods. The trees, still drenched with the recent rain, radiated rustling yellow from their tops and edges, although at their core they still retained their summer green. The ancient edges of the woods were now infected by the spread of new housing and neat gardens. Even so, the stream, round here called 'The Beck', still ran through the shallow valley attended by old trees and ancient undergrowth. Here and there were the clearings where people had used the woods, in ones and twos to gather bluebells and mushrooms, to make love protected by the dense undergrowth, and in larger groups for picnics and other kinds of horseplay.

The two of us clumped along a narrow pathway still sticky with rain. At one point I slipped and clutched at Richard, and we held hands: a comfortable, natural gesture. We were unusually silent, not filling the air with teasing words, not fencing with ideas, peering into each other's minds; not rushing to talk as usual.

I was thinking that we had known each other for nine months, the time it took to make another human being. Of course I might be being entirely selfish, using Richard to explore my new self separate from Rosa and Lily. Using him for my personal adventure. After all, this had been the time to do this: out of school, in a strange new environment with all these turn-on ideas and people like Cali to shake me out of my quiet self; wrestling with intoxicating, unwieldy ideas at college, then at home forging them with my own ideas to make my dissertation. Taking nine months to do it. A kind of birth, when you thought of it.

Extraordinary that the centre of all this was making love in secret places in a way that reminded me of that single sweet time with Matthew Pomeroy, even though Richard was not in the least like him.

No. It was not just about Richard. He was part of all this benevolent turmoil that was hauling me out of the hard chrysalis shell that had wound itself around me as I endured those nine months waiting for Lily to be born, when I put myself 'on hold' until Lily was grown. And in all this time, my only real life was as my daughter's mother, my mother's daughter.

Now at last I was out on the branch, spreading out my butterfly wings, waiting for them to dry in the sun. It occurred to me now that perhaps I would have had this adventure with anyone. Not even just Richard. Cometh the hour, cometh the man. No, that was Napoleon. An entirely different kettle of fish.

The thought made me smile.

Richard stopped in a small clearing and turned me towards him. 'A penny for them?' he said. 'You're smiling that secret smile again.'

I glanced around the green space lit with grey October light. 'Pennies were the things here. Those heavy old-fashioned ones. Old currency,' I said. 'Years ago they used to come down here and flick pennies. You know? Heads or tails? Even in the Depression, really hard times, they used to come down here and gamble on the turn of a coin. Sometimes they bet hundreds of pounds. It was against the law, of course. Posted lookouts for the policemen. They risked a lot, all on the turn of a penny.'

He laughed. 'Like life, honey. All a toss-up.'

'D'you think so?'

'Take the chance that I turned up here in Durham? Not Manchester or York, which were on the cards.'

I joined in the fun. 'Like the chance that I dragged myself out of school to do this degree?'

'Like the chance that I so loved the river I started to row every morning and I saw you there like some woodland elf in a woollen scarf?'

I blinked away a raindrop. 'Like the chance that . . .' I stopped. I could hardly say, '. . . *the chance that at this point in my life it had to be someone and you were there. You just happened to be there.*'

Then it started to rain in earnest, the drops gathered by leaves and sploshing down on to us. He pulled me under the tree and stood before me, his back to the rain, a hand resting on the bark on each side of my shoulders. This close, his cheeks were ruddy, his hair, flattened with rain, was clinging to his head. He suddenly looked his age. 'So, honey, what about this chance of us? Our own particular Pitch and Toss?'

'What about *us*?'

'How do you see *us*?'

'I see us having an . . . intriguing time. I see us getting to know each other. I see us becoming comfortable with each other. Holding hands. I see us *today*.'

'But what if I said I'd stay here? Stay in England? What if you and I find a little house here? Peter's here. Sophie's here.'

My heart sank, then lightened again. 'You don't mean that, Richard. You're mixing me up with Peter. You and I have met almost by chance. And it's great. Perfect. But it's not your life. Your life is across there. Across the ocean. With Maria and the boys. And it's not my life. Not my future.'

He stared at me, frowning.

I tried harder. 'Look! You've got to see this as a holiday romance. A shipboard affair. This year has been just that for me. A year that will change my life, but somehow a year out of time, on another planet. And you, that is, my knowing you, are part of that extraterrestrial experience. But . . .' I hesitated, 'this change comes from inside me. You're part of that change, not its cause.'

His hands dropped to his sides. 'So now I'm told. Put in my place.' He sounded wretched, embarrassed. 'Now you tell me all this. You've left it till now.'

'I've only just worked it out, Richard, as we walked here in the rain. Here, now.' I put my hands on his shoulders and drew my damp face close to his. 'This doesn't mean I don't love you. I probably do. I love to be with you. I'm more myself with you than when I am with anybody, even Lily or Rosa. I identify with you, I love to talk with you. And I love, *love* to make love with you. It's like giving birth to this new me. That above all. I've loved this living-in-the-present with you. It's brought me alive again.' I laughed. 'My mother would say that I am the princess in the briar patch and your kiss has brought me back to life. Here, now I've suddenly become who I am, who I will be. On this ship which is tending now to pitch and toss.'

'Well . . .'

'Even so, I've no desire to break into your life like a Viking with an axe.'

'If that's how you feel . . .' He removed my hands from his shoulders. 'I wonder now if any of this is worthwhile. Any of it.'

'Don't you dare to sulk on me!' I said. 'Do you really mean that you embarked on this . . . affair – because that's how the world will see it – thinking you'd come back here for good? That you'd leave America and everything it holds for you?'

'Well no, I . . .'

'Neither did I. All of this for me has been one delightful, exquisite moment. I have been in this glorious place where I have escaped from the past and not thought about the future. I have loved it.'

'*Have* loved it?' He stared at me, then turned and peered under the tree canopy. 'I suppose we should get back,' he said, his voice distant. 'It's lightening up again.'

We made our way back to the car in silence, a foot of clear air between us. He opened the car door for me. 'I don't really understand this, Bronwen.'

'To be honest neither do I. I just kind of *feel* it. Maybe the Pitch and Toss kind of made me think of the chance – the chanciness – of our meeting. A kind of illusion. Maybe it's made me wonder if I'd have felt this epiphany of change without you.'

He raised his brows. 'An illusion? Well, thank you very much.'

He got into the car and set it into gear. We sat in strained silence all the way home.

Outside Arran Lea he leaned across and opened the door for me to get out. 'I'll call you,' he said.

I clutched his arm. 'Listen,' I said, 'I haven't said this to hurt you. I am trying to be truthful. True to you and true to me. The best truth between us. I've tried to be honest. I didn't know what I really thought until we were out there in the Pitch and Toss clearing. Before that, all these things were just buzzing round and round in my head without any direction.'

'I get it, honey,' he said, pushing the door wide open. 'I get it. Like I say, I'll call you.'

I stood on the gravel watching him drive away too fast, wondering what I'd done. I liked . . . loved . . . Richard. I was smitten by him, engaged by him. But all his talk of the future did not seem right. My arms longed to hold him, my lips longed to touch his again and again. But the upheaval he proposed was not what I wanted. Not at all what I wanted.

I turned and walked slowly into the house and telephoned Cali to say I was popping down to see her and Charlie at the B & B about the music for Kate's party. There was not long to go now. Even without Richard it would be quite an event.

Living on Air

'I've found him!' announced Lily, perching herself on the small chair in Rosa's study.

'Him? Who?' Rosa looked up from her computer. 'Who have you found?'

'You know, the man who, ever so briefly, was my father.'

Rosa folded her arms. 'You can't have. No one knows who he is. Except for Bronwen, that is.'

'Bronwen told me his name. I forced her to.'

Rosa felt a rare surge of resentment. 'She never told me his name. Never. The mother is always the last to know,' she said gloomily. 'Come on then, who is it?'

'Don't blame Bronwen. I have to admit I had to twist her arm. In my own special way, that is.'

'She has my sympathy in that case. I know about your way of twisting arms. No pain. Just give in straight away.' Rosa turned off her screen and turned the full beam of her attention on to Lily. 'So,' she said quietly. 'Who was . . . who *is* it?'

'You have to promise me on God's honour not to say anything? Especially not to Bronwen.'

Rosa stared at her coldly.

'You have to promise!'

'I could ask Bronwen herself.'

'Then she'll know I'll have broken her confidence, and I'll never speak to you again.'

Rosa drew a long, deep breath. 'Very well. I promise.'

'You'll keep it a secret until I want people to know?'

'Yes, yes! Get on with it, will you?'

Lily told her about the man she'd tracked down. 'He was a curate here once, then a missionary of sorts. But he isn't now. He's a teacher in a school in deepest Hackney.'

Rosa blushed to the roots of her hair. 'Matthew Pomeroy! *Matthew?*' She peered at Lily as though she was seeing her for the first time. 'My God! I see it! Matthew. Why didn't I see it before? That face. See him in you.' Tears welled up in her eyes and she grabbed a tissue from a box on the desk to blot them away. 'How could he?' she sniffed. 'How could she?'

'Well,' said Lily, 'I for one am very glad about it. That I know about him, I mean. He knows nothing about me, you can be sure. Bronwen told me. Nothing at all. He went off – or was swept away – by some family thing in India. He wrote to her but she didn't answer. Never, she said.'

'I saw no letters,' Rosa frowned.

'She made sure you didn't. She burned them. Didn't even read them.'

'I did try to find who he was, you know,' said Rosa, 'even though she was no help. But in the end I just never knew where to look. Matthew Pomeroy! I just can't believe it.'

They sat in silence for a moment, both uneasy.

Finally Rosa said. 'So where is he? Where did you say he is? Does he know about you?'

Lily shook her head. 'This woman in the library told me where they keep the records. Then I rang the Church of England place in London. The lady at the other end was very helpful. I told her I was from the *Echo* and was writing something of the history of this church. Community history and all that. *Where are they now?* kind of thing. She was very helpful.'

'So,' Rosa paused. 'Now you have this knowledge what devastating thing d'you propose to do with it?'

'Well, once we get Kate's birthday over and done with, me and Simon are lighting down to London to hunt him down. Maybe take in some real music in one of those clubs. You can get down on the bus, ten pounds return. Did you know that?'

'What will you *do*, when you see him?'

'Well, I'll say hello and tell him who I am. But then, nothing. Me and Simon will go to the club and come back at the crack of dawn.'

'It could be like stepping on a landmine, Lily.'

'He's the grown-up. It's worse for me than it is for him. Anyway, he's got God on his side. He'll be OK.' Lily grinned, the picture of calm.

Rosa stood up and hugged her granddaughter, very hard. 'Lily, m'darling, I could bottle you and sell you!' She stood away from her. 'Now! Will you go away while I finish this? I have two letters to write in twenty minutes before I have to go down and tell Cherie Bostock about Rumpelstiltskin.'

As it turned out, when Rosa got to the Bostocks, having battled her way through wind and flying leaves, there was no opportunity to tell Cherie the story of Rumpelstiltskin. Mrs Bostock met her at the door, her face gloomy, last night's mascara still clinging to her eyelashes.

'Our Cherie's bad,' she said. She led the way to the front room where Cherie was curled up on a Z-bed, her small body no larger than a five-year-old's under the blanket. 'Got the sniffles bad, an't you, pet?'

Cherie's face was grey-white. She opened her weary eyes to Rosa, gave her a watery smile, and closed them again.

'We're having the doctor. Aren't we, pet?' Mrs Bostock's shoulders slumped. 'That'll be more antibiotics, of course. They wreak havoc on her teeth and do nothing for her belly. We've told the doctor that, haven't we, pet? But he says there's nothing else for it. She's that vulnerable when she catches owt, aren't you, pet?'

The small head on the pillow moved in an Herculean attempt at agreement.

Mrs Bostock slumped on the chair by the door as though her muscles had just given up the ghost. 'Our Cherie!' she muttered in a voice too low for her daughter on the bed to hear.

'I'll make some coffee, shall I?' said Rosa, taking off her coat. 'Let Cherie have a little rest.' She went through to the cluttered kitchen and clicked on the half-full kettle.

Mrs Bostock followed her and sat at the kitchen table, still scattered with the remains of a hurried breakfast: toast with a single mouthful bitten out, a half-eaten bowl of Shreddies. The tray on the high chair was streaked with solidified egg yolk. '*He's* taken the bairn to me mother's; says the bairn wants nothing here when Cherie's bad like this,' she said.

Rosa spooned Nescafé into beakers and poured on boiling water.

'He can't do with it, you know, when our Cherie's bad like this,' announced Mrs Bostock. 'Can't stand it. Turns the whole house upside down. She's like the spoke of a wheel. When she's not right the van goes off the road.'

Rosa put her coffee in front of her. 'Drink this. She'll pull round. She has the steel heart of a fighter, your Cherie, the spirit of a saint. We've been through this before.'

Mrs Bostock managed a watery smile. 'Daughters, eh? Teenagers! You can't live with them, you can't live without them, can you?'

As she walked home Rosa found herself in tears for the second time that day. As she came away she'd met the doctor on Cherie's doorstep and he'd taken a minute to talk about Cherie. Everyone loved Cherie, he said, but it was a marvel the child was still here. She'd survived three years past the prognosis. She seemed to live on air, like those plants one read about.

Rosa wiped away her tears and thought of Lily, only a few years older than Cherie, sitting on the chair, her long legs tucked underneath her, talking airily of discovering her father and taking a ten-pound trip to London to root him out. Then afterwards to some club, where she would dance the night away with her friend Simon.

As quickly as Rosa wiped away the tears they kept on coming, so she tucked her handkerchief away and let them fall, blind to the glance of passers-by who were wondering what a grown woman was doing, walking down the main street crying her eyes out.

Glasnost Days

Brock Carmichael nearly turned back at Scotch Corner, that gateway to the North that was nowhere near Scotland. The conference at York had been just about tolerable. The sessions were the usual piffle: a reiteration of well-trodden opinion with a thin knowledge base followed by a rather nasty vulturesque delivery by an ex-Stalinist, now a born-again Capitalist, preaching about the opportunities delivered by the break-up of the Soviet Union.

Brock had made a couple of mildly useful contacts. Two men and a formidably personable woman made sure they 'hit base' with him. He was a useful contact himself. Same-old, same-old . . .

Once he got past Scotch Corner he told himself there really was no turning back and began to relax. Today, he thought, he felt even sharper, more nervous, than that first time he'd set out for Moscow: and that was a darker, more closed and threatening place than it was now in these flaky Glasnost days. But he wouldn't turn back. The thoughts drilled themselves into his head with the swish of the windscreen wipers. It *would* be all right. It *would* be all right.

He'd felt fear before this but then he'd always had some control over it. Preparation, knowledge, cleverness, his quick wit had always come to his rescue. He'd mentioned this fear to Louise when he spoke to her after breakfast.

Her laughter had tinkled down the phone. 'Fear? *Mon cher* Callum, always you over-dramatise. This is your family! You will visit this family of yours today. It is no strange thing to do.

Everyone visits their family. Every Sunday I visit my dear papa. Is that not so? This is not strange. It is what families do.'

Louise was measured about life. At twenty-five, in her *bourgeoise* fashion, she thought Brock rich enough and mysterious enough to make a decent marriage. A few years later they had Anthony and had acquired comfortable bourgeois homes in Normandy and Paris, a boat and three cars, all Swedish. Louise would never have a German car. At their home in Normandy she welcomed those fragments of his English family who chose to come but apart from that, got on with her own life where she did very little but appeared very busy. She steadfastly refused to join Brock in the rigours of Soviet Moscow. Occasionally she would accompany him to London to acquire household objects as she was rather fond of *le style Anglais* in her domestic interiors.

These days his marriage to Louise was signified more by the regular, comradely conversations they had on the phone than the fact of their being together. She had her *petit ami*, he had his succession of exquisite, polished women in Moscow and the boy was ensconced in school in Engand. The telephone calls sufficed for both of them.

He pulled into the car park at the George Hotel at Piercebridge for a strong coffee to settle his nerves. Ten miles to go. No going back. He surprised the waiter by laughing out loud at his own heroic thoughts. *Over the top*. All those post-war movies. All that wartime heroism. A generation deeply wired with the need for an enemy, supplied by the Germans in the wake of two world wars, then the Russians in the long terrifying chill of the Cold War.

His mother, Kate, had always admired the Russians. Talked of their courage in the siege of Leningrad. How Hitler concentrated on the East so the Allies could attack from the West. All half-baked stuff from the papers and the wireless, of course. But enough for him as a boy to make him question and read, and start on this long peculiar road that had been his life so far. And put him so much on the outside of his family that he was thinking of a simple visit home as though it were the Battle of El Alamein. He laughed again and beckoned the waiter to fill his cup a second time.

In the town at last, he drove past Rosa's house with its gravel drive and untidy hedge and 'Arran Lea' in worn green paint on the gate. Then, checking his map, he drove past his mother's bungalow set in its neat plantation of other council bungalows. How safe and rooted they all were in their snug houses; how small this all seemed after the gross urbanities of Moscow and the historical tangle of streets and buildings that was London.

But where were the great spoil heaps where Charlie used to drag him to play cowboys and Indians? Ah yes, the wide road he was travelling cut right through it. Now it was a green hill, planted with trees and shrubs. A football pitch! Christ! On the old summit they'd actually built some kind of wooden play-fort, a play-place for children. He wondered whether that was deliberate, a kind of gesture towards all the games of cowboys and Indians, Germans and English, Japs and English that generations of boys had played on that great heap.

Too elaborate a thought, perhaps.

And there alongside the road he could see the dog-track where his mother had worked at night for extra college money for him. What a trooper she was. How lucky he'd been in her. How neglectful to wait till now to return. But Brock knew that 'not returning' was nothing to do with his mother. It was all to do with Rosa.

He turned the car and drove again slowly past Arran Lea before driving on. Too soon for that. Far too soon. So he drove on the Durham Road to the B & B. He'd never been there before but he knew it well enough from Charlie's letters. Charlie first.

May, who knew him quite well from her two visits to Normandy, welcomed him with open arms.

'Charlie said you were coming but didn't say when.'

Brock kissed her on both cheeks, French fashion. 'Blooming, as ever, May,' he said easily.

She grinned. 'Well, I might be, all this work and your brother to run after too!'

Brock glanced around the over-furnished sitting room.

'Aye, he's in,' she said. 'But he's out the back in his old Starship *Enterprise*, playing with his music as *per*. Putting together backing tapes for your mother's party.' She led the way through the house.

'There's a lass in there helping him. Mate of your Bronwen's. A queer'n but Charlie seems to like her. No accounting for tastes. Takes one to know one.'

Charlie leaped up at the sight of him and hugged him with uncharacteristic fervour. 'Ye're early, old lad. Didn't expect you till tomorrow.'

May, standing in the doorway of the shed, glanced at Cali, who was swinging her booted feet down from the arm of the old couch. May said, 'Well, I'll leave you to it.' The men didn't look at her and she left them to it.

At last Charlie turned to Cali and said, 'Here we are, Cali, this here's . . .'

Cali was on her feet, frowning. '. . . another brother. I see.'

Brock moved forward under the fluorescent light and shook Cali firmly by the hand. 'I hear you're another musician. Bronwen's friend. I'm Brock, brother to this reprobate.'

She frowned but she shook his hand warmly enough. She said, 'There's something odd here, Charlie.'

Brock turned back towards Charlie.

'When I said another brother I meant . . .' her voice trailed off. The two men were taking little notice of her, just gazing at each other with quiet satisfaction. She picked up her leather jacket. 'I'll be off, then,' she said.

The Visitor

I was helping my mother in the kitchen when Cali came striding in, in her leathers. We were putting the last touches to a tray of corned beef slices. I know I had flour on my nose. Rosa had a capacious apron over her neat grey trousers and crisp shirt.

'I need to see you, Bronwen,' said Cali urgently.

I pulled down my sleeves, nodded to my mother and led the way to the back sitting room. I'd barely shut the door when Cali burst out, 'You've gotta believe me, hon, this really surreal thing has happened.'

'I believe you,' I said. 'Now sit down before you burst. Now what is it? Have you been hurt?'

Cali stood still, staring at me. 'I don't know how to say this.' She paused.

'Just say it!'

'I can't. Just put your coat on and get your keys. Come down to Charlie's with me. Come on!' She fled.

I popped my head round the kitchen door and told my mother that Cali was having a brainstorm and I wouldn't be long. I grabbed my keys and followed Cali's motorbike. At the B & B Cali marched me straight round the back to the shed, which was now deserted. We went in search of Charlie and Brock, who were in the front room, drinking single malt whisky.

Charlie grinned at me and clapped his hands with delight when he saw me. 'Bronwen! Great. Look who we've got here. Your Uncle Brock. The prodigal returns!'

This fair, chunky man lifted his hand. I didn't know whether he wanted to shake me by the hand or hug me. I eluded him. I sat down on the nearest chair. My face felt icy.

'D'you see, Bronwen?' said Cali, her voice threaded with awe. 'See what I mean?'

Charlie frowned. 'What's up? What's up with you two? Bronwen, this is—'

'My Uncle Brock. Like you said.' I stood up and put out both my hands towards him.

He drew me gently to him and kissed me on both cheeks, then held me away from him. 'I'd have known you anywhere. You are your mother's daughter,' he said softly. Then he frowned. 'You don't seem so pleased to see me?'

'I am. I am.' I exchanged glances with Cali, whose eyebrows were into her hair. 'It's hard to explain.' I turned to Charlie. 'Can I use your phone?'

'In the hall, you know where it is.'

At the other end Richard's voice was guarded, cool. 'I'm a bit tied up here, Bronwen.'

'I'm at my Uncle Charlie's on the Durham road. On the way to my house. I pointed it out to you. Come here! Come here now. I can't tell you how important this is. It is the most extraordinary thing. Come now. You must come.' I crashed the phone back on its hook.

They all looked up at me as I came back into the room.

'What is it, Bronwen?' My Uncle Charlie turned to Cali and said more urgently, 'What the hell is this?'

'There's this person I want my Uncle Brock to meet,' I said. 'He needs to meet him before I say anything.'

Then May broke the tension by bustling in with a tray of tea and carrot cake, chattering on how unfortunately she had to get away now to baby-sit her granddaughter as her daughter Anne Marie had a job interview but she would be back to see Brock . . .

I stood up again. 'My mother, I need to ring my mother. She needs to be here.'

'No,' protested Brock. 'I'll see her later.'

His words fell on deaf ears. He sat back in the chair. He must have known that he could not expect a great welcome, but this must have seemed bizarre to him. But I had to get her here. Her and Richard. They needed to be here.

The Mirror

They drew up at the B & B from opposite directions at the same time.

'Are you all right?' said Rosa. 'What's this about?'

Richard shook his head.

I ushered them through the house. 'Now then,' I said. 'Prepare yourselves for a shock.'

In the sitting room Brock was standing in front of the fire, staring hard into the over-mantel mirror. So he caught sight of the visitors framed in the doorway.

'Christ!' he said, turning to face Richard.

Richard frowned. 'Pete?' he said slowly.

With my hand on his arm I led him across the room. I turned them both to face the mirror again. 'Look!' I said.

All of us, everyone in the room stared at Brock and Richard looking at their reflections in the mirror.

Rosa let out a small gasp. 'I saw it! I saw it when I went to see your band, Charlie, when Richard and Peter were there. But . . . I didn't know what I was seeing. And I saw it yesterday in your Richard.'

The two men in the mirror were almost exactly alike. Brock was heavier and much paler, his hair bristle cut, his light-sensitive glasses shading his eyes. Richard was much leaner, brown and weather-beaten, his golden hair left to curl. But they were almost exactly alike.

'You're the same,' said Charlie in wonderment. 'Like brothers. More . . .'

'I *have* a brother,' Richard said slowly to the other reflection in the mirror. 'My brother, Pete. He's more your build, I suppose. Heavier.'

Brock blinked behind his glasses, then took them off. 'Are you telling me there's another one of you?'

Keeping his face to the mirror, Richard extracted a picture from his wallet of himself and Peter in their early twenties, before he went to America. He put it on the mantelpiece. Rosa took from her wallet bag the photograph she always carried, of Brock on the day he was awarded his doctorate, in his fancy gown, without his strange cap. She put that beside Richard's photograph.

Cali whistled. 'Jesus Christ!'

'Peas in a pod,' said Charlie.

Brock turned to him. 'Have you a drop more of that excellent malt, old boy?' He took Richard by the hand and they were finally face to face without the intervening protection of the mirror. 'Whoever you are, mate, it's the strangest of pleasures to meet you.' And he held his other hand out to Rosa. 'And dear Rosa. It's been far too long.'

There was so much tension, so much feeling in the room, I could hardly breathe.

Rosa took Brock's hand and her other hand closed on Richard's. She looked again from one to the other and let out a snort. 'That bloody Kate!' she said. 'That bloody, bloody Kate. What the hell has she done?'

Then they were all hugging each other. I joined the hug, then Charlie and Cali, and we all began to laugh in hysterical incomprehension. 'That bloody Kate,' gasped Rosa. 'That bloody Kate.'

Bloody Kate

They decided that just Rosa and Brock would go to see Kate first. They would see how she was and then try to get something out of her. At the last minute Rosa asked me to go with them.

'You are the key after all. Get hold of the tick book and bring it with you. Kate talks to you. Leave Richard and the others at Arran Lea and we'll bring her round there when she's spilled the beans.'

I had to smile. 'You make it sound like an interrogation.'

'Believe me,' said Rosa, 'that's exactly what it will be.'

Kate's face lit up when she saw Brock at the door. She clasped his hand and drew him into the sitting room, ignoring Rosa and me.

'How've you been, son? Have you been taking care of yourself? Just look at those shadows under those eyes. And you've got not a scrap of colour. Pale as a sheet . . .' I'd never seen Kate in such a state: unadulterated joy laced with sheer excitement.

Kate pulled Brock on to the couch beside her and left us to sit where we might. 'And how is Louise? And the boy? Are they here? No? Well, no matter. No doubt they have better things to do than see some old woman on her eightieth birthday.' She looked at him sharply. 'Is it all right with you two?' She shook her head. 'Of course it isn't. I could tell that, out there, those years ago – 1986, wasn't it? So, will you get a divorce? And—'

'Mother,' interrupted Rosa, 'will you shut up?'

Kate shot her a startled glance. 'What's the matter?' she said sulkily. 'Can't a mother talk to her own son?' She shrank into Brock's side, there on the sofa.

Rosa took the tick book from me. 'You remember this, don't you? You gave it to Bronwen. I think you wanted to remind us of something.' She opened it at a place she had marked with a yellow Post-it and handed it back to me. 'I wrote something in there when I was fourteen, Mother. A very unhappy little girl. I wrote on those pages about something that happened when I was much smaller, the night when Brock came to join us.' She nodded at me. 'At the marked place.'

I cleared my throat.

'At last the door burst open and here she was . . . out of her nurse's uniform, dressed in her soft purple frock that stretched a bit across her full chest. "Now then, you two," she said, eyeing us closely. "Tea finished?"

'Mrs Cator glanced at the clock. "Kate, I don't think . . ." Then my mother was hustling her out of the door, thrusting a shilling in her hand. Mrs Cator looked sour. Usually she stayed on a few minutes and talked to my mother about the hospital and the mad people. And the war.

'My mother closed the door behind her and then, without looking at us, clashed the cups and plates on to the tray and carried it through to the kitchen. I knew something was up. You always did, with her. You could even tell from behind when you couldn't see her face.

'We watched her, wide-eyed. She made these big movements with the tea cloth as she dried the dishes, then shook it out with a crack like a cowboy whip before hanging it on the rail on the back of the door. Then she turned to us. "Now then, you two! Come here!" . . .'

It took quite a time for me to get to the point where the children saw the baby and Charlie, rejecting the name Callum, called him Brock. As I read on, Brock moved about restlessly, at one time leaning right back on the couch to stare at the ceiling.

When I'd finished Brock took Kate's hand and held it tight.

'Right. So I'm not your son, Mum. Seems like you got me from somewhere else.' Kate scowled and tried to rescue her hand but he held on tight. 'You must tell us, Mum. This day of all days you've got to tell us. Just tell us what happened. For God's sake. You have to tell us and we have to know.'

Kate breathed in deeply twice, almost a sob, then let all the air come out on a single breath. She glanced across at Rosa and me, then back up to the impassive Brock.

'We-ell. It's an old story, son. I thought I was gonna get away with it, you know? All these years and it seemed all right. You being away so long was hard, Brock. But I suppose I saw that as a kind of penance. A punishment for what I did. So it was tolerable. Then the tick book surfaced again in the clear-out and I gave it to Bronwen here to see what she made of it. But after that, Brock, I seemed to be seeing you all over the place. A living ghost. Losing my marbles. That would be the greatest punishment of all.'

'What happened, Kate?' said Rosa sharply. 'Tell us.'

Suddenly the tension went out of Kate. She sat back and half closed her eyes. 'Well, then, let me see! Rob was away in Coventry and I was at the hospital working for a bit extra money. I'd laid the tea for Charlie and Rosa as usual and that nosy old Mrs Cator was coming in to watch you. I was just coming down the street and old Mrs Ballantyne caught me. You remember her? A proper old crone but the best of those ne'er-do-wells. Well, she said their Sarah was in a bad way, just on the point of bringing forth. They'd sent for the midwife but she was busy. The war, you know. So many babies. So I went with her. I knew you and our Charlie would be all right with old Cator. She wouldn't leave you in case she missed out on something. So I went with old Ma Ballantyne. I'd been called out in that street more than once to lay out the dead or bring some poor mite into the world.' She paused.

'Go on, Mum,' said Rosa softly.

I closed the ledger and put it carefully on the table.

'Well, it was all very quick. That Sarah might have been a Ballantyne but she was a brave girl. One baby, then another. Boys. Then the father came in worse for drink, and started cursing her for a whore and bringing twins on top of the others, and there being a war on. Not his anyway. Ridiculous. He left soon after that time, with the police after him, you remember?' Suddenly anxious, she darted a glance at Rosa, her head turned away from Brock.

'No. I don't remember that, Mum.'

'Anyway, the old woman had hold of those two babies busting their lungs, they yelled so loud. Sarah was moaning, felt sick, not showing the relief they usually do when the baby gets out. She was shouting.' She finally turned to look at Brock. 'Well, I touched her stomach to help her with the last heave for the afterbirth and it plopped forward. I had newspapers ready by then and I bundled it up and took it out the back and put it on the draining board ready to burn, like you do. Then I went back to see to Sarah, tidied her up, changed the bed, set the babies to her and left her with the grandmother and the raging husband.'

She tugged at Brock's arm and looked into his eyes. 'I'd lost twins myself before, before the war, before our Rosa was born. They didn't get to full term.'

'We know that,' said Rosa. 'And . . . ?'

'And I went back to the kitchen to parcel up the afterbirth properly to put it on the kitchen fire. They did that then, you know. But some people, they ate the afterbirth. I was told that.'

'Oh, Kate!' said Bronwen.

'Go on, Mum,' urged Rosa.

'Well, just as I was rewrapping it something moved under my hand. I looked again and there in the middle of all that blood and mess were hands, legs, a little round head.' She turned to Brock. 'I dragged you out of that and held you up, and you whimpered. You were tiny, so tiny, but perfect.'

We all spoke together. 'My God!' I gulped. 'Oh, Mother,' said Rosa. 'Bloody hell,' said Brock.

'It would never have happened but for the war, you know,' said Kate calmly. 'Strange things happened then.'

Rosa went to perch on the arm of the couch and put an arm round Brock's shoulders, squeezing him tight.

'What did you do then, Kate?' I asked urgently.

'Well, pet, while the afterbirth was burning I cleaned his little face with my nurse's apron and wrapped him in a towel that was lying there. I put him in my work-bag, shouted goodbye to those wretched Ballantynes, and made off. The rest is what you just read out of Rosa's book there. Rosa had it to the letter, young as she was. I brought him home, got rid of Mrs Cator and showed you and Charlie your new little brother.'

'Did my father know?' said Rosa.

'Rob? Oh yes. Eventually. A bit of a shock for him, like. Very cross at first. But he saw we could do nothing about it. I wouldn't have let him, anyway. He understood about Brock and was always kind. That was his way. But like you wrote there in your book, Rosa, he always preferred you and our Charlie. Hardly surprising, that.'

'And *you* always preferred Brock,' said Rosa.

Kate smiled up at the burly man beside her. 'I'm afraid so. How could you not? He was my little lost lamb. And now he's my prodigal.' She was amazingly calm, relaxed, resolved.

As for me, half mesmerised by the uncomfortable familiarity of my unknown uncle who was so like Richard, I saw him cast a very intense look up at Rosa. 'You know this?' he said sharply. 'You knew we weren't really brother and sister?'

Rosa nodded, the faintest smile on her face.

'Then why the hell didn't you say? Why did you let me go on all these years thinking . . . ?'

I know now that there was something between them, or had been, you could tell that.

She kissed him on the side of his face. 'I'm sorry, Brock, but it wasn't my secret to tell. It was Kate's. And now it's told.'

We sat on in silence, listening to the ticking of the clock.

Then I said, 'One of the others is here, Kate. One of those little Ballantynes. Called Stephens, a different name now. He's just met Uncle Brock. I can tell you they both had quite a shock.'

'I bet. You met him?' said Kate, interested. 'How was that?'

Brock coughed to clear his throat of tears. 'Weird.' He shook his head. 'How am I supposed to get hold of this? Meeting him . . . Richard, and now listening to this strange, terrible story.'

'They look nearly exactly alike, Kate,' I said. 'And Richard has this other brother who's just like him. There's three of them.'

Brock cleared his throat again. 'This Richard, he told me that it is a chance in two million that three of you would be alike. Identical, that is. Knows about these things.'

'You used to talk to people when you were little,' Rosa said suddenly. 'You used to make Kate set an extra place at the table.'

He freed himself from Kate, stood up and put an arm round Rosa. 'I wish I'd known this, Rosa,' he said. 'How I wish that.'

She smiled. 'Well, now we do know. Things can get back into balance. Now then,' she looked round. 'We should go round to Arran Lea and Kate can tell her story again to poor Richard, who's still in shock. And Charlie too. Time for the truth.'

Kate stood up. 'Get my coat, will you, Brock? It's on that wooden hanger behind the door. I do like wooden hangers. Our Rosa has wire ones and they're no use at all.'

The Third Twin

When we got back to Arran Lea, Kate went through the story again to Charlie and Richard, a wide-eyed Lily and an even wider-eyed Cali. Brock and Richard listened to the whole story again, sitting side by side on dining chairs, looking so very alike and radiating a peculiar certainty, a complacent warmth. Rosa could not keep her eyes off Brock.

When Kate finished telling her tale she looked Richard up and down. 'You're not *so* alike,' she said rebelliously. 'But I can see you're *it*. I have to tell you I thought it was our Brock haunting me when I saw you in your car. I thought I was losing my marbles, I'm telling you. But you do look different.'

'Lifetimes weathering in different climates, ma'am. Different trials and tribulations. It can make a superficial difference. But I know what I saw in Charlie's mirror, and I can see that we are very *alike*, as you call it. The technical name is monozygotic. Out of one egg.'

'He knows about these things,' said Brock. 'He has studied them.'

'Our Bronwen told me your name was Stephens, not Ballantyne,' Kate said accusingly.

'Name of our first foster parents, ma'am. We didn't bother to change it back. Quite liked it. The Ballantynes had done us no favours.' He turned, then, to talk to Brock directly about his time with Peter being buffeted around in the care system. Then he looked around the company. 'We're all buzzing with shock but

304

from what I can see, buddy, I think you were more fortunate here in this family, than I was, even if I had Pete.'

Lily started to ask more questions about the afterbirth and the angry Mr Ballantyne. 'The Ballantynes never knew, Kate? Never suspected?'

'No,' said Kate. 'It was the war, you see, pet. The old woman used to walk the twins up and down the street in an old pram. She used to show them to me, thanking me for delivering them safely.'

'And Uncle Brock's the third twin?'

'The third twin?' A small smile etched itself on Kate's depleted mouth. 'Looks like he is.'

I looked from Brock to Richard and back again. 'So what do you think now, Uncle Brock? What do you feel about all this?'

Brock looked at his mother. 'I suppose,' he said slowly, 'I suppose I feel angry about what I've missed out on. I felt really angry with you, Mother, when I first heard you tell the story. All those voices in my ear, just beyond reach. Maybe I learned all my languages to try to understand those voices. Look at me! I've made a career of being the outsider . . .' He turned back to me. 'Even so, I have to say Kate was the perfect mother for me. A heroine in hard circumstances. How can I be really angry with her now? The time's past for that. Anyway, how could one wish for a better family than Charlie and Rosa, then you and now young Lily, who is sitting there so demurely, watching us all with those bright eyes? Of course I don't know about how Richard here feels . . .'

Richard had been listening intently, nodding slightly. He looked across at me. 'If anyone was injured here it was Brock, not me or Peter. I've had hard times but I've never been alone. I always had Pete. But family? I can't remember the old woman you mentioned, ma'am, not any Sarah, nor any angry father. Once, when I was old enough to find them, I did peer into a dirty, angry, crowded Ballantyne house and fled. All I remember at the beginning was chaos, then Care. Some bad times there. Some decent enough times. Brock had a better time here with you and I'm pleased for him. Like I said before, Brock, you drew the long straw with this family. I think I drew the long straw with having Pete.'

'So what now?' I said.

'Well, honey, maybe you and me and Brock can go across to the Lakes tonight and acquaint Pete with all this. Then we'll bring him back for your grandmother's party tomorrow. Old Pete needs to meet the lady who brought him into this world, even if she did purloin our brother in the process.'

Seeing Kate's sudden scowl I rushed to speak. 'Bring Sophie too, Richard. Oh, how you'll love Sophie, Uncle Brock! You'll all love Sophie. But I won't come with you Richard. You two have lifetimes to fill in. You don't need me. I've an appointment with Dr Devine tomorrow and, of course, there's the party on Saturday.'

Later, before he got into the car, Richard took me to one side. 'So much to take in here, honey. This old head of mine is spinning. But you and me need to sort ourselves out, see where all this leaves us. Suddenly I'm a kinda uncle to you and that ain't very comfortable, to be honest.'

I'd been thinking furiously about this. 'We're where we were when we came away from the Pitch and Toss. And now we'll know each other for the rest of our lives, one way or another. That seems meant. This year, this time for you and me, has been some bright bonus, a shining platform for whatever we're doing next.'

'But not together?'

I was already shaking my head. He stood still for a moment, then he laughed. 'Well, honey, lose a lover, gain a brother. Life audit!' Then he kissed me soundly on the lips, a long kiss, only stopped by Cali's piercing whistle from where she stood by Charlie's car.

'Get on with it!' she called.

On the other side of Richard's car, Brock was standing holding Rosa tightly by the hand. 'How about this, Rosa?' he said. 'You and me? A lot of making-up to do.' Then he kissed her lightly on the lips before jumping in beside Richard.

I stood beside her. 'You love him,' I said.

'Oh, yes, Bron,' she said calmly. 'Always. Now then, I'd better get Kate home.'

We waved the cars off, with Kate watching from the window. When we trooped back inside Kate had already put on her hat and coat. 'You can take me home,' she said to Rosa. 'And you can tell me about this thing you have with our Brock. I could see. It's not right. Not right at all.'

Lily and I, finally alone together, sat at the kitchen table. Lily looked at me, eyes bright. 'Uncle or not, Bronwen, the American's very smitten.'

'It's over. Anyway, he's not American,' I said automatically. 'And anyway, you should mind your own business.'

'Talking of my business,' said Lily, 'Simon and me are off to London on Monday.'

'London? Nice. Any special reason?' I said absently.

'I'm going to see Matthew Pomeroy.'

I blinked, reddened. 'Him? Why? How?'

'You started it, told me who he was.'

'I didn't tell you his name.'

'Not hard to find.'

'It's not for you to hunt him down. How did you manage that?' I said.

'Not hard. Lists, libraries, phones, helpful people.'

'Does he know you're going down?'

'Yes. I talked to him. He was cautious, then very amazed. More amazed, even, than Uncle Brock and your American. Well, maybe not quite.'

'He's not American. And he's not mine. Matthew – you spoke to him?'

'Yes. He sounds OK. Nice. Amazed, though, like I said.'

'Is he a vicar now?'

'No. Teaching in some East London school. One of those hard places.'

'How . . . has he any . . . ?'

'Yep. Wife and three children. Wife works in the community. She's from Lahore.'

'You got all this from the phone?'

'I couldn't let him go once I'd got him, could I? And I ask good questions.'

'I can see that.'

'He asked straight away about you. And I told him *all* about you. How you're breaking out at last and not before time.'

307

I felt myself blushing. 'You really are going down there? You'll really see him?'

'Yeah. Him and his wife and my little half-brothers.'

'That doesn't worry you?'

Lily shrugged. 'I'm taking Simon for moral support.'

'That's all right then.'

'We've talked a few times on the phone. He was telling me about Lahore. He has some family still there. I thought I might check that out. Could do for my time out before university . . .'

I wondered for a moment where Lily got all this: this self-confidence, this certainty that the way she saw things was the right way. Not from me, I thought, not from Rosa, although in her short life she'd learned so much from Rosa. Of course. She'd got it from Kate. Kate has that same certainty, that incorruptible self-esteem. Uncomfortable to live with but what a skill for survival.

The phone rang but when I went out into the hall Rosa was already answering it.

'Hello? Oh, no! No . . .' The colour drained from her face.

I thought of the car making its way towards the Pennines. 'Rosa!' I said. 'What is it?'

Rosa put down the phone and sat down on the chair by the phone table. 'It's Cherie's mother. Poor Cherie has gone.'

'Where?'

'Gone. Passed away. Poor little Cherie. What a life. What a way to go.' She smiled thinly. 'But she lived every minute to the full, like we all should do.'

I hugged her tight. 'Lily and me are in the kitchen. Come and sit for a minute. We need to talk . . .'

She looked at me. 'I've got to go and see Cherie's mother. Then afterwards we can sit and talk. I promise.'

308

Rosa: End Notes

Heathrow Airport, January 1992

I thought I'd take time to finish off this notebook to while away the time as I wait for the Moscow Flight. Brock's waiting for me at the other end with, he just said on the phone, bated breath and fur coat and hat so I don't freeze to death on the Moscow streets. Kate thinks I'm insane to travel at this time of year but I can't wait to see him. To make this new beginning of ours.

I'll post this to Bronwen and ask her not to read it but to put it in the bag alongside the tick book to complete the record. This is important to me in this year, when again my world has been turned on its head and has miraculously righted itself. Such a volcanic change. And in a lifetime of writing stories, I recognise the need for an ending of some kind, even if it is, like this, a pattern of new beginnings.

My mother's eightieth birthday party turned out to be sedate and extraordinarily celebratory at the same time. The aunts and Mrs Novelli were there, but this new drama in our family history was not mentioned. They must all have wondered with those three men there, looking so much the same and so very different. Brock looked very elegant in his Armani suit with his Cartier watch. Richard and Peter were more casual but eerily, equally elegant. Bronwen had her hair out, round her shoulders, and suddenly looked sturdily ethereal, quite Pre-Raphaelite. Peter's wife wore this wonderful velvet gown. I do so like her. She's like some benevolent giantess from a fairy tale.

As for myself, I nearly didn't make the party. The news of poor

Cherie Bostock's death the day before hit me like a bomb. By the time I got to the house Cherie had been taken away to the hospital. Her peculiar scent, of air freshener and baby powder, impregnated the cluttered front room. Mrs Bostock was prostrate on the crumpled Z-bed. Her young husband was sitting on the chair opposite, clutching the red-faced baby, looking distraught but somehow angry, perhaps because even in death Cherie still had her mother – his wife – in her clasp. He was right, I think.

I sent him off to the supermarket with a shopping list, hauled Mrs B off the Z-bed and persuaded her to help me strip it and fold it back. Then we sorted the room, clearing all Cherie's paraphernalia into one corner, creating a juggled jigsaw of her short life. I hoovered the room, raked down and cleared the fire. Then I stood over Mrs B while she washed her face and hands and combed back her wild hair.

I talked about Cherie, and how she always liked things to be nice. How she liked her mother in a particular red dress with shoe-string straps and the matching bolero. So, obeying Cherie's words from the grave, Mrs B vanished and returned wearing the red dress.

I stayed all evening as she sat and talked on about Cherie and how she was more than any daughter to her, how she was her friend and how Cherie had helped her get through the hard times.

'Ralph doesn't get that, you know. About me and our Cherie. He thinks Cherie caused the hard times we've had, but it wasn't like that. She and me were one. You'd know about that, Miss Carmichael, having a daughter.'

But Mrs Bostock's experience isn't mine. In my family – mother-daughter-mother-daughter – we've each made our own separate circle, complete in itself. These circles sometimes happen to overlap and communicate. They sometimes collide – as in the case of me and Kate – or they sometimes overlap quite elegantly, as in the case of Kate and Lily, or Kate and Bronwen. And Lily and Bronwen and me.

Even so we are *not* 'part one of another'. Not in the way Cherie was with *her* mother. And I suppose I must conclude this is not a bad thing. I could not love Bronwen or Lily more than I do. I could not be more perversely fascinated – even admiring – than I am of Kate. But I've always known I am on my own, circling away in my own world, ever since I wrote in that first tick book. All down the years.

I've tried to explain this to Brock but he doesn't get it. He tells me now I'll never be on my own; he'll be there. He says being with someone properly – that is, *making love* – is the rehearsal that teaches us about being 'part of one another'. I asked him if he'd learned that from Louise, or even his glamorous fixers! He says no, he learned it one night in an unglamorous motel in County Durham over twenty years ago.

Brock and his new-found brothers have spent the last month glued to each other's side. He's been in the forests with Peter and has dined in Hall at the university with Richard. Those three men are zinging with delight, gloating like boys over this newly discovered mutual identity. Kate looks on quite smugly, as though they were all her sons. Bronwen stands back quietly, enjoying it all.

Perhaps those three delightful men are the best paradigm for being 'part of one another' – so in tune after being apart for nearly fifty years. At last Brock is resolved, no longer the outsider, having now faces to put to those voices of his childhood. 'I have my brothers, and I have you who are not my sister, but my own true love. What more could I want?'

There are losses, of course. Although they appear warm friends still, Bronwen and Richard seem less close now. I don't know whether that's to do with Kate's revelation or not. The thing is, none of this, none of these reversals could have happened if those two had not met. That meeting was the beginning. Without that, Kate would have taken the secret to her grave.

Still Bronwen flourishes. That woman professor of hers seemed quite carried away about her dissertation (contrary to what Bronwen had thought). Apparently the woman congratulated her on NOT being too influenced by Dr Stephens. She even offered to support her towards a doctorate. But Bronwen turned that down flat. With Lily in India she has nothing to keep her so she's gone off to London with her friend Cali for whatever adventures may await them. Then, I think, she will make her way back home. Of us all she loves the North most. It is her heart's home.

And Kate? Well she's finally on her own. She has told me quite clearly to get myself away, and not imagine I – or anyone else – was indispensable. She could manage on her own, thank you very much! Hadn't she been on her own since Rob died, and nothing changed, did it? And hadn't she always told me to get away from the Bloody North? It was my own fault that I had stayed, like some little mouse hiding in a hole.

Sometimes I could kill her but there is no denying that she is the beginning, the first line in all our stories.